Praise for *A Theater for*

"Sublime and immersive . . . If you wish y̶   ̶p̶p̶e̶a̶r̶ ̶t̶o̶ ̶a̶
Greek island right now, I highly recommend."
                    —Jojo Moyes, #1 bestselling author of *Me Before You*

"An alluring historical novel . . . [and] a delectable work of escapism . . . Seductive time travel, with an edge."
                    —*Kirkus Reviews*, starred review

"This gorgeous, glimmering summer read is itself perfect summer: irresistible and deep, Samson's lyric sentences pulling you into unforgettable sunlight and shadow."
                    —Amy Bloom, *New York Times*
                    bestselling author of *White Houses*

"[Part of] a growing tradition of fine British novels that have emerged in the wake of Brexit."
                    —*The New York Times Book Review*

"Longing for a trip to Greece this summer? Just pick up *A Theater for Dreamers* . . . Reading the evocative novel, you'll ache for your own bygone summers, and worlds that can only be recovered through stories (or, in this case, songs)."   —*Oprah Daily*

"Spellbinding . . . An immersive read, steeped in nostalgia. Samson's poetic prose is so evocative that, by the end, you find yourself googling those entrancing images of Hydra, 1960, just to wallow further in the poignancy of it all."   —*Vanity Fair* (UK)

"Beautiful . . . Perfect if you want to escape the drudgery of another lentil dinner and dream of 1960s Hydra with Leonard Cohen."

—Dolly Alderton, author of *Everything I Know about Love*

"Delicious."

—Nigella Lawson

"Samson's achingly beautiful depictions of the sun-soaked Greek paradise contrast strongly with the dark inner lives of its inhabitants. Tantalizing summer reading."

—*Booklist*

"Samson summons the vision and the reality in a beguiling, deeply evocative portrait of a vanished era."

—*The Guardian*

"The novel's meandering, dreamlike writing style is delightful . . . *A Theater for Dreamers* embodies a summer vacation, capturing the essence of Hydra in vibrant, saltwater-scented impressions."

—*Foreword Reviews*

"A surefire summer hit . . . Feels at once like a gift and an escape route. At once a blissful piece of escapism and a powerful meditation on art and sexuality—just the book to bring light into these dark days."

—*The Observer*

"A great beach read, but this novel does more, exploring the moral codes and unfulfilled promise of the era."

—Minnesota Public Radio's *MPR News*

"Heady armchair escapism . . . An impressionistic, intoxicating rush of sensory experience."

—*The Sunday Times*

"One of the year's most lushly enjoyable novels . . . It transports us straight to a Greek island and leaves us yearning for the sight of a lemon tree against a turquoise sea."   —*The Daily Telegraph*

"So well written, immersive and fascinating."
                                        —*The Seattle Times*

"Samson draws a vivid picture of this time and place: a Mediterranean paradise shot through with poverty, friendship, abuse, genius, betrayal, love, and tragedy. Samson's writing is in places poetic and brilliant. I experienced the heat on my shoulders, the salt in the wind, the wine on my lips . . . This story reminded me of *The Great Gatsby*, with its outsider narrator full of nostalgia for a long-gone time and place."   —*Historical Novels Review*

"Samson is an intensely sensual writer, conjuring up blue skies, the tang of wild herbs, the vivid splash of bougainvillea . . . As good as a Greek holiday."   —*Financial Times*

"Samson takes readers on an engaging tour of 1960s Hydra . . . deliver[ing] a feast for the senses with the sights, smells and tastes of this Greek island . . . Intoxicatingly atmospheric. Jump into all of its saltiness and enjoy the ride."
                                        —*The San Diego Union-Tribune*

"Samson's sun-saturated novel set on the Greek island of Hydra might be just the escapism you need right now. Samson captures the darkness, emerging fractures and the beauty of their lives in a sharply feminist novel."   —*Daily Mail*

ALSO BY POLLY SAMSON

The Kindness

Perfect Lives

Out of the Picture

Lying in Bed

A Theater for Dreamers

A NOVEL BY

POLLY SAMSON

ALGONQUIN BOOKS
OF CHAPEL HILL
2022

Published by
Algonquin Books of Chapel Hill
Post Office Box 2225
Chapel Hill, North Carolina 27515-2225

a division of
Workman Publishing
225 Varick Street
New York, New York 10014

First US paperback edition, Algonquin Books of Chapel Hill, May 2022.
Originally published in the US in hardcover by
Algonquin Books of Chapel Hill in May 2021.
First published in Great Britain by Bloomsbury Circus in 2020.
Printed in the United States of America.
Design by Steve Godwin.

This is a work of fiction. While, as in all fiction, the literary perceptions and insights are based on experience, all names, characters, places, and incidents either are products of the author's imagination or are used fictitiously.

LIBRARY OF CONGRESS CATALOGING-IN-PUBLICATION DATA

Names: Samson, Polly, author.
Title: A theater for dreamers / a novel by Polly Samson.
Description: First edition. | Chapel Hill, North Carolina :
Algonquin Books of Chapel Hill, 2021. |
Summary: "In this novel based on real events and people, a young
woman arrives on the Greek island of Hydra in 1960 and falls in with
a bohemian group of poets, painters, and musicians, including the young
Leonard Cohen and his beloved Marianne"— Provided by publisher.
Identifiers: LCCN 2020046436 | ISBN 9781643751498 (hardcover) |
ISBN 9781643751504 (ebook)
Classification: LCC PR6069.A492 T47 2021 | DDC 823/.914—dc23
LC record available at https://lccn.loc.gov/2020046436

ISBN 978-1-64375-259-4 (PB)

10 9 8 7 6 5 4 3 2 1
First Paperback Edition

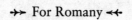 For Romany

We are all embarked on our journeys . . . shooting out on the current, out and away into the wide blue frightening loneliness of freedom, where every man must navigate for himself. Still—the thought is consoling—there are islands.

—Charmian Clift

I'm living. Life is my art.

—Marianne Ihlen

A Theater for Dreamers

It's a climb from the port and I take the steps of Donkey Shit Lane at a steady pace, a heart-shaped stone in my pocket. I walk alone and, though there's no one to witness, I resist the urge to stop and rest at the standing posts after the steepest part. I watch my step, a stumble can so easily become a fall, a thought that disgusts the gazelle still living within my stiffening body.

The marble slabs shine from centuries of use; the light is pure. Even on a morning gloomy as this, with the sky low enough to blot out the mainland and clouds crowding in on the harbor, these whitewashed streets dazzle.

Two young lads skip, arm in arm, down the steps towards me. I'm as anonymous as a shepherd or a muleteer in Dinos's ancient tweed jacket, my hands bulging its pockets, my boots comfortably laced. The lines on my face have been deepened by these years in the sun and my hair hasn't seen dye, or even the hairdresser's scissors, for who knows how long, but so what? It's off my face, in a loose tail, the way I've always done it. I'm still here, a little bruised, a little dented, but remarkably the girl who first set foot on this island almost sixty years ago remains. I suspect only those who knew me then can see through the thickening patina and it breaks my heart how rapidly the crowd of seers is diminishing.

The call about Leonard came last night. I sat quietly for a while, listened to the owls. I took out my old notebooks, the threepenny jotters that came with me to the island in 1960, found him in my hopeful, curly scrawls. My neck got cricked. The cocks crowed all through the night. I slept badly and woke to a morning crowded by dreams.

The summer visitors are long gone; there's unrest in Athens as austerity bites, refugees, lost children, fires in the streets. Boats are going out, pulling people from the water. There's plenty for us to chew over so you might think we'd let the American election slide by. But at the port this morning, as I idled with my one good bitter espresso of the day, watching the mules being led away from the boats with their cargoes, the news of the new President found me. It slithered from the water with the morning pages and spread rapidly like a stench along the agora. There were horrified groans, even from the donkeys, disbelieving splutters from every table, passerby and boat. For a moment it was a comfort to think that at least Leonard has been spared this.

I stop outside Maria's shop at Four Corners and listen for voices. I would feel a fool if anyone saw me approaching his front door with my heart-shaped stone and I prepare to walk straight past as I turn the corner from Crazy Street. The street isn't actually named Crazy but something that sounds similar and that's what we heard when Leonard came fresh from the notary, pulled off his sixpenny cap and landed the deeds to his house beside it on the table, his grin a little bashful at first, self-conscious, like we might all think he was showing off.

Later that day we came armed with borrowed pails and long-handled brushes for whitewash and Leonard had new batteries for the gramophone that he'd placed in the center of the stone floor. Some of his records had warped like Dali's clocks and become unplayable but there was Ray Charles and Muddy Waters and a woman singer I liked but whose name I don't remember. Later still, a fire of lumber among the lemon trees on the terrace, jugs of retsina, a little hashish, dancing. Paint-spattered shorts, brown limbs, bare feet. War babies, most of us even younger than him and him just a cub, really. We lapped up the freedom our elders had fought for and our appetites reached well beyond their narrow, war-shattered shadows.

Was it drugs and contraception that made change seem possible? Was it a conscious revolution? Or were we simply children who craved languor and sex and mind alteration to ease the anxiety that was etched into our DNA, detonating in each of our young brains its own private Hiroshima?

Ha! To my dad I was a bloody beatnik.

We asked little of this island except days sunny and long enough to keep the Cold War from biting, a *galloni* of wine for six drachmas, and a solid white house for two pounds and ten shillings a month. We paid only lip service to its name: Hydra. A name that means "water" though an ancient earthquake buried its springs and turned it dry but for a few sweet wells.

In Greek myth, the monstrous Hydra is doorman to the Underworld.

"A many-headed serpent with halitosis so bad it kills with one breath," I say when it's my turn to set a riddle.

Leonard laughs. Someone has a bouzouki, someone else a guitar. There's ouzo, stars, a slice of moon as thin as the edge of a spoon. Some old brushwood burns with a resinous crackle; our eyes brighten in an explosion of sparks. We grow wilder, smash our glasses to the wall of Leonard's new house. For luck!

But Marianne, fetching a broom, asks: "What is this crazy custom?" And not one of us—not American or Canadian, not Greek, English, French, Swedish or Czech, not even the Australian brain on stilts that is George Johnston—can come up with an excuse for this rain of broken glass, except that Marianne threw hers first.

I give the stone heart in my pocket a squeeze. I'm trying to remember why they left so soon after he bought his house. Little more than a month, and Marianne's skipping through my memory and slipping the stone from her hand to mine. I'm guessing November.

A Russian wind with icy breath, waves scattering across the stones of the port, octopus strung like old tights along a boat rope at the jetty. Leonard in his raincoat (yes—blue, though not remotely famous yet), passing his leather case to the boatman, and here comes Marianne, in rain-splotched and rumpled shirt and sailor pants, hefting several large bundles, lithe and quick as a boy. She turns and calls my name; the wind streaks hair across her face.

It's the first time she's even looked at me for weeks. "No, no. I can't bear it if you cry." She dumps the luggage, comes running back, the rain pretty on her skin. I can't stop hugging her, I'm so relieved that she doesn't want to leave on bad terms.

"Please don't look so lonely," she says, pulling away and closing my fingers around the stone. She tells me it was the first thing Leonard ever gave her. The stone fits in my palm, meat-colored and marbled with white and mauve. It truly is a heart, and by the way she's looking at me I know that now she and Leonard are leaving together, I have been forgiven.

Her smile is so sweet, so full of hope. "Just when the one in my chest had been pounded to pieces by Axel. He said I could probably use a replacement."

Marianne's eyes are blue as summer skies; her hair is the startling sort of blonde. It's hard to believe she'd ever think of me as a rival.

"So much has changed, be happy for me, please. My baby boy waits in Oslo but my heart stays here on the island with you until our return . . . Oh, sweet Erica, you mustn't cry."

Leonard offers me his handkerchief and directs my gaze from the wet port and up to the streaming grey and purple mountains. This place has been kind to him. This island. This woman. He's pointing back the way they came. "There is my beautiful house, and sun to tan my maggot-colored mind . . ." He ruffles my hair like you might a little girl's and tells me he isn't planning on staying away long.

Leonard doesn't look back, not even once, but Marianne's waving and waving until the boat is lost in churning foam. It's simultaneously yesterday and ancient history, thinking about this. I'm swept by a surge of loneliness. Too many goodbyes.

A lemon tree grown taller than the wall is hung with strips of insecticide. I pretend to myself that she's still here, just the other side, picking tomatoes on the terrace. Leonard and that tragic boy of hers too. Marianne was happiest making a home, bringing flowers to his table and calm to his storm, sewing curtains, pouring wine, baby Axel lulled to sleep by the strings of his guitar . . . I think of Axel Joachim, or Barnet as Leonard took to calling him, sleepily sucking his thumb, his sun-bleached hair as white as his pillow.

Leonard brings his guitar out to the terrace, watches us dancing. The embers glow beneath the lemon trees, just the other side of this wall, but the bellowing of a workman snaps me back to earth and it might as well be Mars. We were heady with ideals, drunk with hopes of our languorous lope into a future that had learned from its past. I reach the door of Leonard's house feeling quite giddy and a groan escapes me at the thought of that man in the White House, of a world turning backwards.

The nightmares will always find you even if you do live on a rock.

There's nobody about to hear my muttering, though flowers have already been left on the step. The white walls of Leonard's house rise blankly, grey shutters shut. By the look of it, Fatima's brass hand has recently been polished. I hope someone has been in to cover the mirrors. I bend to the step and place the stone among other offerings: drying carnations, tea bags, oranges, a single gypsy rose. I think about snatching it back but it was his and Marianne's, and not mine at all.

"A talisman," Marianne said, and added with a giggle, "maybe it's the petrified heart of Orpheus."

I kneel at the step. The other side of this door, in the hall, the mirror keeps its secrets above a polished table with a lace cloth where they laid out their treasures.

Marianne and Leonard made up stories; along with Orpheus's heart, they had a fossilized goat's horn Dionysus had drunk from, gold and blue fragments from Epidaurus, an iron monastery bell that Marianne once found buried in a pine forest in Santorini, a large rusting tin box with a relief of a blindfolded woman playing a harp without strings. The carved mirror was their oracle. Leonard painted in gold ink: *I change. I am the same. I change. I am the same. I change. I am the same.* He once made me stop and look into it. He lit candles and said some sort of prayer, bid me to keep looking until I knew who I was.

I change. I am the same. I guess he meant well even though he got carried away and Marianne hated me for a while. Ah well, that's how it was in those days.

That was the last year without electricity up here. Sometimes it seems a shame. An hour or two after sundown the town generators fell silent and we were lit only by moon and flame. Lanterns, charcoal braziers, icons flickering above bowls of oil with little flames floating on corks. Everyone is beautiful by candlelight. I take my cooker and fridge for granted these days but my memories are golden. I change. I am the same.

I was here one Shabbat. The lighting of the candles, the little dishes of salt and oil, olives, fresh anchovies. Marianne had somehow managed a challah loaf from his temperamental oven. Leonard's benedictions were not misplaced. The hand-embroidered tablecloth, sweet water from the wells, the glass of the kerosene lamps sparkling, white anemones gracefully dipping their heads from an earthenware jug; even the air around her was luminous.

I think of those nights lit by lamps, music and dancing, of Magda's mournful Russian songs, shadows leaping on the walls, of guitars and bouzouki and accordion, Mikhailis with his fiddle, Jewish songs known to both Magda and Leonard, and sometimes, strumming his guitar, a few hesitant lines or verses of his own that seemed to stalk him like cats to the creamery.

I don't think he's been here for almost twenty years so I'm surprised to find myself weeping like this. I haven't even brought a tissue. But then, unlike Leonard, who leapt right in with this house and another man's wife and child, I didn't expect this place to become home.

ONE

Many dine out on well-worn yarns of backpacking along the winding dusty roads east that became known as the hippy trail. The man across the table will tell you of his summer of love almost before you've caught his name, and as he pours the wine your mind replaces that grey suit with patched shorts and tanned shoeless feet, a guitar on a knotted string. But we didn't hitchhike to Greece and hadn't thought of India, or even Istanbul or Beirut. And we weren't hippies, at least not when we set off. I'm not sure that hippies had even been invented as early as 1960.

My journey that Easter was mapped by a mind that dreamt only of a boy. Specifically, Jimmy Jones, who combined a face for poetry with a naturally graceful and muscular body that leapt and ran and balanced and twirled and invariably triumphed in press-up contests with my brother. First love arrived in a flare of flaming lust, a genie sprung from a grubby lamp that brightened my life and opened the world.

Jimmy Jones was twenty-one, four years older than me, and his wishes extended beyond simply granting mine. He had plans to travel that summer and his backpack shook with impatience at the foot of his rickety bed. I was needy and adrift since caring for my dying mother had so abruptly reached its conclusion and wanted nothing but Jimmy Jones's warm skin and soft kisses and a backpack of my own.

Mum left me the means to escape by way of an enigma. There wasn't much to go on, just the surprise of one thousand unexplained pounds in a Post Office Savings Account and, in its wake, the serendipitous arrival of a book. The author of the book was Charmian Clift, an Australian writer who lived here on Hydra and who, for several years in London, had been my mother's closest friend. I was looking for any sort of road and thought Charmian might shed some light on the secrets my mother had taken to her grave.

The typing pool where I worked was a torture chamber in triplicate of clattering keys, pinging bells and bottom pinchers. The most exciting thing to happen was a cream cake on a birthday. This was not the stuff of dreams that my dying mother had wished for me. I dreamt of the sun and a glittering sea, of a beautiful manboy diving from high rocks, surfacing, surviving. I dreamt of light through shutters falling across a bed, though I'm sure I had plenty to say at the time about freedom and escaping the rat race. Mainly I dreamt of dreaming.

My education petered out when my mother became ill and my future remained an unimagined thing. There was little to tie me to London. My father, had this been the Middle Ages, would most certainly have had me fitted with a cast-iron chastity belt. During the dreary London winter that trailed my mother's death he knew that something was making me cheerful and decided that that something had to be stopped. That boy—that dropout—was not allowed over the threshold.

The days stretched into weeks of half-hatched plans to run away. It was unrelentingly cold and rainy; al fresco activities in the secret dips and wooded corners of London's royal parks became soggy affairs. Most days, since my father rarely allowed me out, Jimmy waited in the greasy spoon across from my office to walk me back to Bayswater through the dripping trees and sodden grass. We snatched moments in the pavilion of the Italian Gardens, or in the shamefully familiar hollows in certain trees of St. James's. I'm amazed we were never arrested! I clung to him while we plotted our escape with his raincoat a canopy above our heads.

Mum's death had been as ordered as her life. She left no loose ends for us to tie. At home we were suffering strange and constant tensions, a sort of thrumming at barely audible frequencies, just beneath those of grief. It was as well that Bobby had moved out.

Mum's was a life scented by the fresh, good smells of hot ironing and baking cakes, a dab of Ma Griffe when Father got home, though sometimes there was also a breath of sherry and tears. Generally, the shedding of tears was forbidden by our father. When she lay dying, Bobby only cried in the chair beside her bed when he wasn't home.

In the final stages of her illness, I stayed by her side. A teacher came down on the train from Ascot to talk to me but left without my promise to return. Mum's nurses counseled me too, said I'd get stuck if I didn't go back to school and sit my O levels. Everyone assumed that I was scared she'd die if I left the room but I was more terrified of leaving her weakened and alone at the mercy of my father than of her dying.

Bed linen, nighties, clean, freshly ironed. Reading and snoozing and later doing all the community nurse's jobs too. Mum slept

more and more as the months drifted by, smiled to find me when
she woke. I sat writing stories in her threepenny jotters, savage
tales of girls and wolves and houses with hidden rooms. When she
was bright we made lists in the jotters and she instructed me in
keeping the home the way Father liked it. Home was two floors of
Palace Court, eight tall rooms to keep army-shape and spotlessly
clean. His castle, her prison. It was unbearable really, what she put
into a life that wouldn't contain her.

Soon no one seemed to care that I was no longer going to school,
least of all me. My brother was at Hornsey Art School and worried about missing classes while gnawing at his fingers in the chair
beside her bed.

"I don't mind if you draw me while I die," she told him when
she was still strong enough to comfort us like babies while we
bawled.

Her last day flickers behind my eyelids like something on film.
The tints are off, light flares, the frames jump and stall. She woke as
Bobby came into the room. He hadn't made it for ages and sailed in
on a sea of excuses. I buttoned my lip, plumped and rearranged pillows, helped her to a more upright position, tidied what remained
of her hair. Her voice was effortful because of the medication and
her arm tremored as she pointed to her rolltop desk: "Today I need
you two to help me straighten out my things."

In a locked drawer were two small rectangular packages,
addressed one to me and one to my brother.

"They're for later. Please don't look now," she said. She pressed
my package into my hands. "Have some adventures," she said.
"Dare to dream."

It happened that night. A sleeping angel, her hands crossed at
her chest. Somehow an inquest was avoided though I'll never not
suspect that she and her good doctor hastened the end.

In Bobby's package were the keys to a car, porcelain green, a convertible, parked in the square behind Palace Court. And here's the thing: no one had known she owned a car until she died, though we knew she could drive because Father would occasionally allow her to take control of his Austin while he sat in the passenger seat not once allowing her to decide for herself when to change gear or indicate.

It was always better if Father wasn't reminded of the car. Bobby was careful never to enter the flat jangling his keys or mentioning the price of petrol.

There was a biblical downpour the day that Charmian Clift's book arrived—as I've said, it was always raining in the London I remember from that time. Bobby came in shaking water from his hair. He looked almost indecently healthy, more front of scrum than starving artist, his cheeks reddened from running through the rain and his hair a wet haystack. He started sorting through the post on the hall table, pocketing a letter that had come for him and leaving to one side a package addressed to Mum.

"We should've sent out something to let people know . . ." He tailed off with a heavy sigh. "Oh, well."

Since my dad couldn't cope with even the mention of her name, Mum's post stayed in the hall until I took it away and wrote the sad tidings again and again.

"You know he never deals with any of it," I said and Bobby shot me a look to be quiet because at that moment Father emerged from the bathroom, drying his hands and handing me the towel, as he might to a cloakroom attendant. "This hasn't been changed in weeks," he said and shooed us. "What are you two up to loitering by the front door anyway?"

He made a grab for Bobby's chin and forcibly turned his face to the light.

"For pity's sake, Robert. Did I not teach you to shave properly? What's this with the bum-fluff? Are they supposed to be sideburns?"

"Leave off," Bobby said, but Father only tightened his grip.

"I hope young Robert is not thinking of becoming a Teddy boy next," he said while half slapping, half patting Bobby's cheek.

Please, please, not a row. I put my hands to my ears. Father might make me stay home on a whim. Jimmy Jones, who I knew to be waiting back at Bobby's digs, was very much on my mind. My new primrose-yellow jumper had a zip.

At last he let us be and it always felt like we were escaping even if it was only to go to the pub. Sprinting through the mizzle, we couldn't help but hold hands, and whoop as we reached Mum's little green car.

"Has it been bad all week?" Bobby asked as we settled into our seats and, not waiting for my answer, "We'll get away soon, doll, I promise." The doggy smell of his wet reefer jacket filled the car. It no longer smelled of Mum's perfume. Still, I liked that he called me "doll."

I came tiptoeing back at dawn, sneaky as a cat. I was what my father, had he ever caught me, would've referred to as a "dirty stopout," "a trollop." Mum's brown-paper parcel still waited in the hall. It was tied with tarry string and the stamps were beautiful: a large olive tree, an owl, a primitive saint. I wondered who was writing to her from Greece, and snuck to my room taking it with me. It was a risky routine, this five a.m. return, with a father like mine. My heart was pumping as I sponged myself down at the basin. Still damp, I sat at my dressing table and cut the string of the parcel that had been addressed in firmly inked capitals to Constance Hart, and not, as would have been correct in those patrician days, to Mrs. Ronald Hart.

A book with a scene of white houses around a little harbor on the cover, *Peel Me a Lotus* its title and its author Charmian Clift. I looked at her picture and saw nothing of the chic upstairs neighbor I'd once known to be my mother's friend. I summoned her up, this other Charmian Clift: elegant, tall in a tightly belted camel coat, crocodile handbag hanging from the crook of her arm, bright lipstick, an enormous smile. I'd encountered her only occasionally, and years ago, though I often thought about the first time we met, wondering what it was that had made her cry. She'd come across me outside in the entrance hall, where Mum had put me for safety while our father gave Bobby a hiding. I was cowering, tears and snot streaming, when I heard the rattle of the street door, felt a gust of air. I shrank into the shadows, ashamed at the sounds that were coming from inside our flat. Charmian led me upstairs by the hand, asking my name and what school I went to, what books I liked to read. We ended up sitting together on the top step. Her arms were around me, and though I was usually cautious of strangers, with Charmian it felt perfectly natural. She asked me my age: eight, I said and was surprised by her sudden silence and a tear that slid down her cheek. She got my name wrong after that, called me Jennifer, but I didn't mind because I thought it prettier than my own.

The picture on the book showed her beauty grown wilder, almost in disarray. Between jutting cheekbone and brow, her eyes deep and soulful, bruised almost.

The blurb spoke of an island in Greece, the expatriate life, but now here was my father throwing his shadow across any possibility of sunshine. He was thumbing his braces and, since I was in my dressing gown, completely incapable of looking at me.

"You're up early," he said, as he stretched his braces back and forth. "I thought I'd better check as I didn't hear you come in last night."

"I'll have your shirt ironed in a jiff. That's why I set the alarm," I lied, yawning and indicating my artfully rumpled bed. He cleared his throat but I got in first. "Oh, by the way, I opened this. It came for Mum. It's from Greece. Do you remember Charmian Clift with the two little children from upstairs? She sent it. It's her book . . ." I prattled on, successfully changing the subject. As devious, it would appear, as my mother.

He gave a sour sniff. "Oh, she's written another book, has she, Lady Airs and Graces, *and oh, do have another cocktail.* They were Australian, you know, the pair of them . . ." The word "Australian" might have been gristle the way he spat it out, and with a final snap of his braces he stalked from my room so that I might finish getting myself "decent for work."

I read Charmian's book on the bus. I read it in my booth while the yards of punched tapes clicked and clattered through the telex machine. I read of a life of risk and adventure, of a family swimming from rocks in crystal waters, of mountain flowers, of artists admired and poseurs quietly ridiculed, of her husband George (who sounded very witty and clever though I had no memory of ever meeting him at all), of poverty and making do and local oddballs and saints and the race to prepare a house for the birth of her third child, of an invasion of tourists and jellyfish, an earthquake, of lives spent flying close to the sun. It was little wonder I found myself still lost in its pages well beyond lunchtime and had to be ticked off by Betty, the typing-pool queen. Slipped inside the book was Charmian's folded card, quite plain.

"Darling Connie, I wrote this book about our family's first year here on the island and it's at last being published in Great Britain. Spread the word in any way you can and most importantly don't let what I've written put you off coming. There's always a warm welcome for you here from one who firmly believes you still have a chance, Charmian."

I felt a fluttering of desire as I read her words and an intense craving for that warm welcome and a chance for myself. I couldn't wait to press Charmian's book on Jimmy.

Jimmy Jones had long broken his family's bindings by dropping out of law school and emerging as something brighter and more colorful, more drawn to Jack Kerouac, Sartre and Rilke than to the laws of tort. Jimmy's wings carried him to a wooden studio at the bottom of Mrs. Singh's garden where a few odd jobs freed him to paint and write poetry and stay in bed until lunchtime.

My thoughts of the island were too exciting for the telephone and Father's acutely tuned ear. He remained in a foul mood and came up with plenty for me to do around the flat. I wasn't even allowed to throw out a pair of socks of his where the entire heel had gone. It's one of my abiding memories of those grey months after Mum died. Being bid to sit in what had been her chair, a pretty one, button-backed and covered in pea-green velvet, her sewing box at my feet, while he sat slurping tea, slumped in his wing chair watching *Dixon of Dock Green*.

I returned to the subject of Charmian Clift and her book. It was a Tuesday, toad-in-the-hole, his favorite. I'd made gravy and mash so there was a chance he'd be in a better mood.

I was wrong; by the look on his face you'd think something was rancid: "Erica, do we really have to talk about your mother's friends while we're eating."

It was hard to believe Mum's stories of Dad before the war, his handsome smile and dancing feet. His famed quick wit had taken a direct hit at Dunkirk; his get-up-and-go had departed. He used to climb mountains for fun, proposed to her up in the clouds on the peak of the Brecon Beacons. When he was stationed in Cairo he arranged for flowers to be delivered to her every week he was gone. He didn't stint on paying her dressmaker's bills, nor for her shampoos and sets. She still dressed every night for his return from the office, though I have no memory of him ever sweeping her out the door to a restaurant or the theater. Routine was the only thing that kept him sane: his whiskey on the tray, ice and silver tongs and the folded newspaper, dinner, then his chair and television while she fluttered in and out with tea and mending.

When we were old enough to be left, she'd escape for the occasional weekend—Great-Aunt Vera's in Hampshire, Cousin Penny with "the problem" in Wales—but not without punishment on her return. One time he threw a casserole across the kitchen floor and made us leave it until she got back two nights later. He stood over her, soundlessly watching, while she was down on her knees scrubbing the congealed mess with brush and pail. I preferred not to think of her on the floor, flinching at his feet. I decided to punish him, persevered with talking about Charmian.

"They'd had enough of the rat race. Apparently they went to a different Greek island for a year and Charmian wrote a book about that too. I wonder if Mum ever read it . . . ?" but now he was pulling off his napkin and scraping back his chair.

"Don't bother checking the bookcase, you won't find it here. No shame at all, these decadents, dragging their children from pillar to post, despising ordinary people, staying up drinking all night with their lah-di-dah artists and poofter friends." He wiped his mouth savagely and threw the napkin beside his empty plate.

I went to my room and added a PS to my letter to Charmian Clift. Could she find me a house to rent? And how much would it cost?

And here, at last, is Jimmy, in a slice of light as though straight off the screen, and to my mind more handsome than any film star. He's opening the door to me with a sly grin. To this day I've never known a face so transformed by its smile. Jimmy in repose was rather haunted. But when he smiled it was like the sun coming out and, just as I'd imagined, he was reaching for the zip of my fluffy new primrose jumper.

"Will you come with me to an island in Greece?" He was behind me as I climbed the ladder to his bed and answered by sinking his teeth into my bottom.

We did the math. By the time we joined Bobby and the others at the Gatehouse, we'd given ourselves a year. The band was winding down. I was pleased to see the old sax player was there, a lugubrious veteran in his worn mackintosh with the most soul-rending tone to his playing. Paper moon. A cardboard sea. I thought of Jimmy Jones and me on Charmian's island, of the seasons turning, extra blankets for our bed, charcoal burning in a brazier. The double bass plinked; the saxophone's song dwindled to a horizon borne on a few mournful breaths. I took a cigarette from a friend of Bobby's and perched at the edge of their table, pregnant with plans. Jimmy went to queue at the bar.

Bobby's new girl was from the art school: his usual type, lean and bird-boned, dressed like an off-duty ballet dancer in cable-knit sweater and tight black Capri pants. She was studiedly monochrome, her face too small for such extravagantly black-fringed eyes, raven hair cut to a delicate nape, the neck of a swan. She sat on a stool in the middle of the group twining and untwining her long legs, saying "cool" and "super hep" without appearing self-conscious.

"Edie Carson, this is my sister Erica, prisoner of Palace Court, Bayswater; Erica, this is Edie, Queen of Wood Green." Bobby was gesturing with a pint mug brimming with beer. It slopped on the table between Edie and me and, as we both reached to mop it, our heads met with a bump and Bobby said, "Glad to see you two hitting it off," and we both groaned.

Soon we were back to Jimmy's studio and, though it was cold enough to see your own breath, we kept each other warm. Jimmy's bed was on a ledge high up inside the skylight, Bobby's a divan behind stacked easels and a curtain of purple velvet. Edie was not shy about crying out.

A few nights later Bobby told Edie Carson about our plans to travel, because as soon as Jimmy and me got serious Bobby knew he didn't want to get left behind. Edie had plans of her own; she and her best friend Janey weren't hanging around waiting for spring. We made a date to meet Edie and Janey at the port of Piraeus the week before Easter.

TWO

Mum's money kept us in fuel and food so the trip from London and on through France and Italy went without danger or hunger. The boys recovered quite quickly from the putrid horrors of our first squatting lavatories. I'm not sure I ever have.

We made it almost as far as Paris by night one, stopping only for fuel and baguettes, pâté and fizzy orange. At a hostel in Chantilly we fell exhausted into an enormous and very creaky bed with surprisingly crisp linen sheets. Breakfast was a memorable highlight: yellow sunshine at a window, a checkered cloth, a large bowl of milky coffee and my first croissant, which was flakier and more buttery than any croissant since. Mum's car was beautifully behaved and didn't break down once. I wish the same could be said of Bobby.

We'd left London a whole three weeks late—my fault entirely as Bobby never tired of telling me. There hadn't been a right time to broach the subject with Father, who had reached a stage of grief that involved tearing Mum's books from the shelves and making me clear her wardrobe. Her smell wafted from the folds of her clothes. He caught me with her rose silk petticoat to my face. "No use for you, any of this stuff," he said. "You don't have her figure."

As we drove from the hostel and skirted Paris, Bobby's irritation cast a black spell. "Might have been nice to visit the Louvre, but no . . ." he said, turning to Jimmy, who was still holding out some hope that he would relent on this mad dash to meet Edie in Piraeus. "And you can forget the Crazy Horse, mate. I hope you think waiting for the kid was worth it. Don't say I didn't warn you: we've got nothing ahead of us but the N7."

I hated being called "the kid" but ached to hug my brother all the same. When one of us needed to cry about our mother we did it in the arms of the other. Maybe I was a cowardly little girl, as he said, but was there to be no letup in my punishment, no forgiveness? Bobby had been schooled in the seething house of our father, so it seemed not.

All his life Bobby had been scared of Father. We all were. I'll never forget Mum's face the first time she saw the marks his belt left on him. Boiled eggs for tea and me in the high chair so Bobby could only have been about five or six. "Why won't you sit down?" Mum was exasperated with the pair of us grizzling, until finally, he gingerly lowered himself to the seat and winced. Bobby was twisting and screaming as she pulled down his shorts to find his bum, which was normally as white as her pinny, lividly striped and shocking as a burn.

Father had no shame, the way he came striding in, swirling ice in his drink. "Now, young fellow, you'll know in future to do as you're told."

I saw Bobby cowering, then and other times too, until he learned to stay in his room. And Mum curled over sobbing into a tea towel and me trying not to flinch as Father's big face comes towards me.

I'd like to get away and hide but I'm strapped in my chair. To this day it makes me panicky to think of it. The mess of crushed egg and shell as Mum opened her fist.

Bobby was tense the whole trip but I didn't expect so quickly to fill the space of the common enemy we'd left behind. Nothing I said could raise a smile and then, in Grenoble, I drank the local water and was so doubled up by the morning that Jimmy insisted we pull over and pitch the tent long before we reached Bobby's goal of the coast. We lost another day because of my guts and, as I sat shivering and unwell, I thought I'd lost my brother's love forever.

I came across him outside the service station near San Remo. I thought he was crying. He scowled, said it was exhausting driving for fourteen hours to the border without stopping.

His tears had left tracks, his face dusty from the road. I persevered, trying to talk to him about Mum, about Dad, but Bobby shoved me, hard, said he was through with even thinking about the pair of them.

"Believe me, family's an overrated concept; the sooner you realize, the better," he said.

We drove on, ignoring Pisa and a distant view of the Leaning Tower as we turned inland. I sounded whiny to my own ears each time I begged that we stop somewhere to take in the sights, or even to stretch. My first trip abroad was not turning out to be a dream. Domes and towers whizzed by, cypress trees lengthened their shadows, Roman ruins beckoned and proffered the shade of umbrella pines, but not for us. I was beginning to hate Edie Carson. Not for Edie Carson this ever-unwinding road of resentment. Bobby said he should've sold the car in England and gone on the train instead of waiting for Jimmy and me. I said I wished he had. Edie had a Spanish friend in a French circus, some dodgy-sounding gig with a sculptor in Rome, Janey's aunt had invited

them to her *castello* near Siena. I wondered aloud if a Greek island
and Bobby would prove such a vital part of her itinerary.

He thumped the steering wheel. "Everything's your fault," he said.

Jimmy sat jackknifed and silent beside him with the map. I was
stowed like the sulky child I'd become between our camping equip-
ment and the luggage. Occasionally Jimmy's hand would find me
there but then so would Bobby's eyes in the rearview mirror.

I was supposed to have sorted it out; I'd kept them hanging
around promising I would. In the end we'd had to wait until my
eighteenth birthday before Bobby came over to wrestle my passport from Father's hands. It was an ugly scene, the ugliest really.
Again it passes behind my eyes, a juddering reel of a home movie
or the onset of a migraine: accusations of Bobby's corrupting influ-
ence, Father's face boiling, Bobby throwing back at him that he
only wanted to keep me as a skivvy now Mum was gone.

Father, his crazy, twisted mouth bellowing: "Better than you
turning her into a tart for your friends?"

Bobby, suddenly very tall and cold: "Thank God Mum's not
here to hear you, old man."

And Father, a chair toppling as he roared: "Damn you, Robert,
you're no better than a pimp. Your mother is turning in her grave."

Bobby surprisingly fearless. "She had to die to get away from
you . . . she hid everything from you because she was frightened . . .
she was too scared to even let you know about the car, no wonder
she . . ." and our father came at him with the scissors I'd been
using to cut coupons from a magazine, my hands too shaky to keep
going. Bobby's kick threw him off balance. Father was floored,
heaving for breath, and Bobby with planted feet panting above
him, the neighbours banging on the door. Father's portrait had
been knocked from the wall, the glass shattered. From behind the

cracked glass, a young soldier with a trim black mustache and a pair of stripes newly fixed to his sleeve. The broken man coming roaring towards us bore little resemblance to this proud defender of the realm. He came at us with my passport in his hands, shoved it at Bobby, went to make a fist then let it drop. "Take it. Take her. Don't either of you darken my door again."

"If it wasn't for Erica we could have enjoyed all of this," Bobby was saying, gesturing at the medieval town that we were leaving in our wake.

By the time we reached the overnight ferry at Brindisi he had stopped talking to me altogether. He was morose, hunched over the steering wheel, certain that Edie would be lost. We drove straight off the ferry, queasy after the sixteen-hour crossing, and on along the coast towards Corinth, through domed villages and past tavernas, olive trees, pine forests, the constant invitations of a milky blue sea. No, there would be nothing, not even a Greek coffee.

The first time our feet touched Greek soil was close to sundown that day. Bobby pulled over for clarification on the map. The village was deserted, bathed in dusty golden light. There was only a man who looked like he'd stepped straight out of the Bible: bearded and robed and using a staff to herd a few stringy goats up a path. Jimmy sprang from the car, stretched and leapt in one bound to the top of a wall, looked around and pulled me scrambling up after him. I followed him through the silver shimmer of an olive orchard, sniveling and crying. Eventually Jimmy noticed and stopped monkeying around, blotted my tears with his thumbs.

"He's been treating me this way since his fight with Dad,"

I sniffed as a volley of furious Greek broke out behind us. The bearded man was waving his staff. Had he really just spat straight at Bobby?

Jimmy turned to me. "What the hell . . . ?"

Bobby had his hands to his face; the man was retreating, goat bells clanging.

"I'm not a bloody Hun," Bobby shouted after him.

"*Germanos, Germanos* was all I understood," Bobby said. "That and 'bastard,'" and then, without warning, when I started to laugh, he launched himself at my arm and gave me a Chinese burn.

———

We arrived in Piraeus just one day later than planned. Edie wasn't there and Bobby didn't track her down for a further two hellish days. He had been tearing around looking for her; his T-shirt was stained with sweat. She and Janey were perched at a pavement table near the youth hostel, laughing with others they'd gathered along the way: a pretty girl with orange hair and a pair of muscular Scandinavians who looked like twins. Edie and Janey both wore French berets.

I saw my brother grinning for the first time since we left London as he crept up behind her and stooped to kiss, or maybe even lick, the innocent length of her neck. One of her companions leapt to his feet, "Hey, hey!" but Edie was laughing and grabbed Bobby's hand before even turning around. "I knew you'd show up eventually," she said.

THREE

The port of Hydra sweeps into view suddenly, dramatically, like a curtain has been raised between mountains. The symmetry of stone walls and mansions imposes a perfect horseshoe around the water where tiers of white houses rise like the seats of an ampitheater.

It's a magic trick from barren rock, a theater for dreamers. The stage is lit by sun and sea and I'm gripping the rail on deck and Jimmy's got me by the waist as though he thinks I might leap as the port and its toy town come at us out of the blue. I look from the mountains to the ziggurats of houses and back to the colorful boats in the harbor and for the first time since we left London I'm happy. I imagine myself unfolding against the island's backdrop of green-smudged hills, finding my way among the terraces and clustered pine. There's salt spray on my face and my mum's words in my ears; if I had wings I'd be soaring. Spice-colored rocks, scrub, brush, acid yellow, herb. Pitched orange roofs and salt-white houses that rise to the gods, all eyes to the port.

People pour on deck for arrival, pointing out windmills and likely swimming spots, black cannons lined up along the fortress walls. Jimmy's been reading Henry Miller and whispers in my ear, "Here it is. The wild and naked perfection." I shake myself free of Jimmy and hug myself at the prow as Hydra draws closer.

The fumes make you cough but I've been up here since Bobby announced, in front of everyone, that he wished he'd simply sold Mum's car rather than saddling himself with me. I think my crime was losing sight of Mum's old suede bag with the traveler's checks inside. I found it soon enough and mended the strap and came up here with thoughts of giving up and going home. Jimmy made a lame attempt to follow me but backed away when I said I was sick that he never bothered to stand up for me.

I immediately regretted it but was glad to escape Bobby spoiling everything; to be free of the scrutiny of the black-shawled women down below with their missing teeth and trussed-up chickens. But left alone, my thoughts swelled from my problems with Bobby to an overwhelming homesickness for my mum, and I allowed myself a good Aegean-sized cry. Mum would've got to the root of what was bothering Bobby and I ached for the steadying grip of her hand. I even allowed myself to think my brother deserved a good beating by our dad.

The ferry lets out two long bellows on her horns. People and donkeys are gathering at the landing stage; in the orchestra pit the painted caiques have been set swaying by our arrival. In a burst of superstition and excitement I push myself past the other passengers to be first to set foot on the island.

I step from the gangplank. Stand for a breath. The polished

flagstones are pink marble. Men with wooden handcarts are unloading sacks; livestock skitters; earthenware jars are passing from shoulder to shoulder; crates of loquats and tangerines; people shouting. The port is festive with flags and bunting, blue and white like the sea and the sky. I scan the waiting people for a face that might be Charmian's. There are women with market baskets and priests in black robes and dark glasses; shops and cafés and bars; striped awnings; donkeys decorated with beads and strung with improbable loads; drums of kerosene being rolled along the waterfront; the thump of barrels of wine being stacked.

I leave Jimmy to struggle from the boat with our luggage and run off to find her. Was I supposed to meet her beneath the clock? The chip-chip-chip of workmen's tools rings and echoes. I can smell donkey shit and diesel and fish as I race along the waterfront to the white marble tower that rises at the center of the port. I'm ignoring Bobby, who doesn't have an iota of faith in any arrangements his teenage sister might make. He's yelling at me and I turn to flick him the V and catch Edie and Janey checking out a group of young seamen, dazzling in white with peaked caps.

Stonemasons are strapped to a wooden platform at the top of the campanile and, facing me, the white marble statue of the hero with his lion mounted on its pedestal, Greek flag proudly flying, and Katsikas the grocery store on the corner, Van Gogh chairs and tables on the cobbles just like she said.

I head for the entrance; she's not out here where only one of the tables is occupied and that by two men. My eyes adjust through the doorway: oilcans, tin baths and shovels hang from the walls, bales of cotton waste. Click, click, click. Dice, tile, chessman, *komboloi*. A strong smell of aniseed and frying fish. Only men at the marble-topped tables and a sick feeling is dawning that Charmian

Clift isn't here and I'll have to go back to Bobby through the Easter swarms all looking for rooms and tell him we have nowhere to stay.

At the table outside, one of the men is pushing back his chair. He unfolds like a razor, tall and raw-boned with scruffy brown hair, a jacket hanging at least three sizes too big for him.

"You looking for Charm?" The skin of his face appears three sizes too big for him too. "I'm guessing you're little Erica from the Bayswater Road?" He clears a throat gruff with tobacco: "So, big enough now to go walkabout, eh?" and rests his cigarette on a saucer, extends a leathered hand with a strong grip.

"George Johnston," he says. "Her hubby."

I flood with relief as well as shyness. His is a strange sort of gaze that flicks like elastic between mischief, scorn and anxiety. "I don't think we ever had the pleasure in Palace Court." It's a face of contradictions. His eyes beg for a crumb but his under-hung lip is set for cruel mockery. He might bite any hand that feeds him.

"Yes, I'm Erica . . ."

He inclines his head towards his drinking companion, a doleful man with a long stooping back and straggly beard. "And this is Pat Greer." The man flings George a tired grimace. "I mean Patrick, never Pat," says George with a smirk.

"No, and by Jesus, not Paddy either," Patrick says, broadening his Irish accent to make his point.

I smile quickly at Patrick and turn back to George.

"I was supposed to be meeting your wife when I got here. She wrote to me about a house we could rent?"

I shoot a glance up the port to the ragged group weaving towards us. "The others are on their way," I say, attempting to keep the panic from my voice.

A right mixed bunch we've managed to gather at Piraeus and

on the boat, all struggling with bedrolls and guitars and easels and backpacks, Bobby shamefully red in the face from shouting my name and Jimmy hauling my luggage as well as his own.

"Pull up a pew, Ricky," George says, "she's not here," and before I can decide if I like this novel shortening of my name calls inside, "Hey, Nikos, get this weary girl a drink, and while you're at it I'll have another Metaxa."

He taps his empty glass, "I take to drinking when Charm's not around," and introduces the laughing proprietor as Nikos Katsikas, "the only man you'll need to chat up on this island . . . if you don't want to starve. And luckily for us all, one of the few who speaks English."

"But where is she? Where's Charmian?" My voice comes out squeaky. Bobby has spotted me; he's leading the pack across the port.

George follows my gaze, turns a drawl on Patrick: "Here they come, more and more of these bludgers, lured by our fantastically blue water and cheap rent to live out their carefree immorality away from prying city eyes. God help us all."

I squeak a bit more while George weighs me up from the rim of his empty glass. I sound about six, I can't help crushing my r's when I'm flustered, and I'm certain I'm blushing.

Patrick breaks the tension. "Charmian's on Poros. She's gone to see the bank there."

George gnaws morosely at a fingernail. "She was supposed to get back this morning." It's unusual to see a grown man with nails bitten to the quick like this. "But where Charm is and where she says she is are not always the same thing," he's saying as Bobby and the others come crashing over.

"Strewth." George throws himself backwards, raises his hands in exaggerated horror. "Ricky . . . how many of you are there?"

Bobby stands panting. "So stupid to just run off like that, Erica."
An untidy pile of people and baggage spreads around the tables; there's a clamor for drinks and the loo.

"Christ on a bloody bike," George mutters to me. "Is Charmian supposed to be responsible for this whole mob?"

"There's just five of us for the house," I reassure him as he tears again at his nail. "The Swedes have somewhere. And I think most of the Americans have rooms at the art school."

I motion the others closer. "Last thing this island needs is a load more pissant painters and pansy poets," George grumbles.

"Bobby's here to paint, as are Edie and Janey," I say, trying not to giggle. "And this is Jimmy; he's a poet but not a pansy one. He's been published in *Ambit*." I haven't been able to stop myself boasting about my boyfriend's poem but as usual Jimmy makes light of it. George pulls on a cigarette, screws up his face.

"It's never the poor kids turning up here, is it? Now, why the bloody hell might that be?" he says, eyeing us through the smoke. "All these young Orphics with things to paint and write and sing about. It's only ever the ones with a nice bouncy safety net back home."

I start to protest but now George remembers Bobby from London and launches himself at him.

At the same time, the Swedes, Albin and Ivar, are deep in conversation about the number of rooms in the house they've been lent and Edie and Janey are pulling chairs to their table. George is guffawing while he regales Bobby with an unlikely tale involving the staircase at Palace Court.

"You slid straight off the banister and knocked my mate Peter Finch flying, then had the bloody cheek to run back and ask for his autograph."

Bobby is torn between defending his younger self to George, and Edie who, judging by her body language, seems to be veering towards a room with the Swedes. He excuses himself to reclaim her.

"Of course, Mr. Finch didn't object to my wife's consequential laying on of ice packs," George says. "He has quite a thing for her."

"Haven't we all," Patrick agrees, and his eyes turn to a man who saunters in from a side street in a red shirt and frayed shorts. The man is small and muscular with the looks of an aging cherub. His hair is thick and blond and a mat of golden curls escapes his mostly unbuttoned rag of a shirt. He pulls up a chair beside the girls, twirling a single white flower between his teeth.

"Bloody hell. The day only gets better. Why does he keep coming back?" George says, crashing his glass to the table. "He's like a dog that has to keep turning around to sniff his own shit."

The man is introducing himself to Edie and Janey, his French accent strong, his smile slow and bright.

Patrick is gathering his papers. "A boat that brings Jean-Claude Maurice brings a boatload of trouble," he groans from beneath the weight of the world. "Anyway, my typewriter awaits. Nancy says she's got enough eggs for an omelette if Charm isn't back and you and the kids need fodder later . . ."

The American students hover, seeking directions to the art school, and George points up the cliff and sends them sloping off towards the Tombazi Mansion with their luggage rolls and easels, the girls with horsetails swinging, the boys in blue jeans, one with a guitar strapped to his back.

"I hope they realize how lucky they are," George says, watching them go. "You know, sometimes I imagine good old Admiral Tombazi coming spinning from his grave at what goes on beneath

his classical porticos. And the monkey splat that passes for art . . ."
George is coughing into his handkerchief. "A right load of Pollocks
and Twomblys."

Drinks have arrived; my first retsina almost makes me gag.

"I don't suppose any of you have any of the rags from London?"
George looks from face to face without satisfaction. "Charm might
have asked you to bring the *TLS* if she knew you were coming?"

Jimmy springs to life, dives into his rucksack, certain he's hung
on to the new issue of *London Magazine*. George's glass is empty
again. He has taken to shredding a matchstick while Jimmy rum-
mages for the prize.

"It's got some unpublished Wyatt poems," Jimmy is saying,
emerging triumphant, but now George has the seedy French cherub
in his sights. He taps another cigarette from his pack.

"So, about the house . . ." I try again, but I've lost him as the
Frenchman stares straight back at him, white stem twirling.

"I imagined you'd be on Poros," George says.

"Why would I want to be on Poros, when I could be on Hydra
being slandered and picked on by the likes of you?" Jean-Claude
replies. Everyone is listening and watching, glasses raised halfway
to lips, spoons stalled in coffee cups.

"I'm surprised you'd show your flyblown face here after what
happened last time," George says, but is overcome by another bout
of coughing and can't go on.

He snatches a look inside his handkerchief before stuffing it
away and, with an exaggerated shrug and a curl of his lip, Jean-
Claude returns his attention to the girls.

Men are sorting nets; a black cat snakes around Jimmy's legs;
boxes of fish are unloaded from boats; the chip-chip-chip of the
stonemasons continues above our heads. George shakes his fist to
the heavens.

"They've been perfecting that clock tower for bloody years. I wish they'd stop now, most of us don't need a constant reminder of the bloody earthquake."

"I read about that in Charmian's book. I'd be petrified if the quayside started turning to jelly beneath my feet," I say. "You don't think there'll be another, do you, George?"

George drags deeply on his cigarette and twists me a grin. "Ah, don't you worry your pretty head about that, Ricky; she exaggerated to discourage tourists. Our Charm has never been averse to turning a little tremor into a full-blown bloody earthquake." He turns to the others: "So you're all here for painting in the beautiful light?" and they nod.

"I'm not," I say.

George cocks an eyebrow. "Well, what are you here for then, little Ricky of Bayswater?" I feel the blood rush to my face while he waits with his cigarette stuck to his lip. Mum used to say that I was a pearl and the world my oyster.

"Oh, Erica's a striptease artiste." The drink seems to have gone straight to Jimmy's head. George ignores him, continues his discomfiting stare.

When Mum handed me the money she told me she wanted me to follow my dreams. Out of nowhere I blurt it, the thing I've never said out loud, "I want to write books—"

George snorts. "You'd earn more as a stripper. I work fifteen hours a day, seven days a week and still my food's on tick from the great Saint Nikos. He's the same . . ." He gestures at Patrick's retreating back. "And Paddy is bloody good but the poor bastard can't get a whiff of publishers' ink. Go buy yourself an ostrich fan before it's too late."

I mock putting my hands over my ears and see that Edie is wearing her sulky face, telling Bobby: "Hey Daddy-o, I'm not planning on sleeping on the beach tonight." Bobby blames me with a look. Jimmy's eyes have wandered to a slim woman in red shorts who is clambering aboard a caique, his hand absentmindedly stroking the black cat.

I try again with George. "Did Charmian actually say if there was a house for us? I mean, that's what she told me in her letter . . ."

But I've lost him. He's ready for another bout with Jean-Claude, this time swiveling around and addressing himself to Janey and Edie: "Has Frenchie here told you yet about his mate Jean-Paul Sartre? Doesn't usually take more than a minute . . ."

Janey and Edie look up at him like startled does as he warms to it, cigarette waving in his hand.

"There was poor old Sartre just wanting a quiet café au lait while he chowed down on important questions of existentialism and phenomenology but, no, along comes Goldilocks here . . ." George is now playing to the entire agora. He stands to make himself heard.

"When will you ever stop this?" Jean-Claude spins around and hisses to silence him. It's then I notice his gold earring and have to stifle a giggle. Turns out I know this little Frenchman from the pages of Charmian's book. He's a figure of fun in a G-string of knotted paisley handkerchiefs, a scandalous seducer who eats raw eggs and sleeps on a goatskin rug. "A little curly dog on heat" was how she described him. If I'm not mistaken, his flashy white teeth will turn out to be screw-ins. I long for him to smile.

But Jean-Claude's eyes are leveled on his aggressor and he isn't smiling. There is a long silence. The audience holds its breath. It seems even the stonemasons have put down their tools.

"*Ferme ta gueule*, George; it's you who is always boring everyone with your war reporting like you is some 'emingway. *Pooft!*

For the 'undredth time. How many countries was it? How many stamps in your passport? Sixty-three, wasn't it? But when was the last time you got further than Athens, eh? *Alors!*" And with a contemptuous whistle he turns his back. Edie and Janey lean in as he audibly whispers: "So what if I fucked his wife . . ."

FOUR

Charmian Clift squints into the darkened room from a sunlit hatch in the ceiling, her face framed in a furious cloud of cigarette smoke.

"Not now! Go away, go away, whoever you are . . ." At the foot of the ladder a large brown-and-white dog is barking at me and simultaneously wagging its tail. "Max, stop that," she yells.

I step out from the shadows of the long, shuttered room. She gives a yelp and throws a hand to her mouth as I proffer my ratty old textbooks and a jar of peanut butter like they're religious offerings.

"Oh crikey, yes, of course. It's Erica, isn't it?" she says as the dog slumps beside me to the floor, watching her with hungry eyes. "I'm ashamed to say I forgot you were coming and only got back myself this morning." Her voice is clear and bright but her skin has that over-scrubbed look like it's been rinsed with tears.

"I'm sorry, it's all tremendously stressful here at the moment," she says. "Please forgive me for not meeting you."

She swings herself through the hatch and perches on the top step
to study me. A faded blue-and-white cotton skirt bunches around
her legs and her feet are bare.

"The bank manager in Poros was delayed by a funeral and
made me miss my boat . . ." she casts her eyes theatrically to the
room behind her ". . . and now there's hell to pay."

She hugs her knees through the skirt. Her feet and ankles are
long and slim, her hands as large as a man's but graceful. Her
mouth is as generous as I remember it, "Look at you all grown
up! Oh my goodness, how fast time flies," but a missing or brown
tooth spoils the glamour of her smile. She sees me notice and pulls
her hair to conceal it.

Her face is free of makeup; sunlight stripes her strong bones,
giving her the air of a warrior queen as she comes bounding down
the wooden steps, "Here, let me get a good squiz at you," and
grasps me at arm's length.

"Connie's girl. I remember you as a shy little thing with a lisp.
Do you still have one? Oh, sweetie, I can't tell you how sad I am
about your darling mum." Her eyes are green as bottle glass and
swimming with tears.

She smells of warm things: cinnamon and toast, campfires, polished oak, Nivea, tobacco. She rocks me as she did the first time
we met and for a moment I'm back on the staircase in Bayswater,
a frightened little girl finding comfort in the arms of a stranger.
Then, just as now, I want to stay in the warmth of her embrace,
simply breathing, but all too soon she releases me.

"Crikey, Erica! Look at you! You're the image of her."

Her skirt is nipped in by a wide leather belt; it swirls from her
waist as she moves. She throws open some shutters. Rafters are
festooned with bunches of herbs and plaited strings of alliums;
a dresser is stacked with blue-and-white china. The light comes

dappled by the courtyard's leafy trees and vines, and falls on unwashed pans at the sink and a family table with tales to tell of a clumsy breakfast. A three-legged cat eats from a frying pan. Flies swoon in spilled jam.

Charmian flaps her hands at the cat. "Tripodi, get down!" She pulls her dark hair free of its shoelace.

She looks nervy, and so altered from the Charmian of Palace Court that I start to doubt my memories. She gives her hair a quick comb-through with her fingers.

"Everyone got going early this morning. Zoe's taken them for a hike to the beach at Limnioniza so George and I can make some sort of progress on this nightmare book of his," she tells me while Tripodi snakes around her bare legs.

"Look, I brought everything I could find," I say, untying the string from the books and bathing in her smile. It had taken up most of her letter to me, her worries about the shortcomings of Shane and Martin's school. Apparently Martin was wretched with the science teaching and, though they had Homer backwards and forwards, she felt they really ought to know their Shakespeare.

At the sight of the books she forgets her haste. She clears a space for them among the mess.

"You darling, darling girl," she says as she swoops on my Latin primer.

She puts me in mind of a panther, the way she prowls and purrs, all proud posture and wide, high bones, her eyes slanting and well defined. I've brought meat to her cubs.

"I found some of Bobby's too. Here's some of his O-level science ones and I apologize now for all my hopeless scribbles in the margins of *The Tempest*."

Charmian wipes her eyes on her sleeve. It gives me an ache that her children's education can reduce her to tears. Her children haven't even cleared away their own breakfast things.

"Oh, I am such a terrible sook!" she says. "Anything can set me off."

"Charmian," I say. "Did you manage to find a house for us to rent?"

She appears not to have heard me as she springs on another book. "Oh, and Hoetzinger. Martin loves reading about the Middle Ages. It's not so very different from the life we lead here, though I'm yet to see anyone's head on a pike . . . and Bradley on Shakespearean tragedy; you have brought an oasis to a desert, Erica!"

Upstairs George is coughing and stomping.

"Oh, but I can't even offer you a coffee. I really must get back to the work. George has been finding this book so terribly impossible and now you've come across us in the middle of a breakthrough." She plants the briskest of kisses on my cheeks.

"About the house," I try to insist, panic rising.

"It's tough on him that to write this book well means revisiting the trauma of his first nervous breakdown, so I'm sorry but we are rather governed by his flow."

"But the house?" Is it rude to keep interrupting while she's telling me about George's book? Probably.

"It's set against a nightmare of a journey George made as a war correspondent in China. Now he's stuck and I have to make him relive it, every heartbreaking mile of the famine road to Liuchow, and force him back among the hundreds of thousands of refugees who were all starving or dead and rotting where they'd fallen. Can you imagine dredging that up?"

"It must be very depressing for you too."

She frowns distractedly towards the hatch and shakes her head. "You've no idea. Sometimes I'm stamping my foot while he suffers, because I'm not getting on with my own work at all and my words will insist on bubbling up. But on a day like today my own book seems so trifling by comparison. If there's a good novel from George it may save us. So every day I sit on a step beside him and painfully squeeze what he needs me to squeeze out of him until it's down on paper. It's better done before he hits the grog so please forgive me if I fly now."

That smile, the house, the dog, the creative disarray; it all makes me swoon. There are pictures, icons, a bone-handled knife mounted above the door. Icarus flies; admirals line up along the wall.

I notice a familiar etching hanging from a nail above the piled-up sink. "That's Rembrandt," I say. "Mum has the same one. The fat oriental merchant. Once she made me a hat like his, with a feather and a jewel . . ."

Charmian stops in her tracks. "Oh yes, it's lovely, isn't it? I'm glad Connie got to keep hers. Joel sweetly bought one for me when he bought hers—"

Her hand flies to her mouth. The space between us vibrates. I reach for the back of a chair. "Who is Joel?"

She wags a finger at the fat merchant.

"I'm getting carried away because half my mind is upstairs with George's book. I mean, of course, I bought it for her; it was from a place near the British Museum. I bought one for each of my women friends; this edition had somehow been nicked on the platemark so they're worthless to a collector." Color has rushed to her cheeks. "But, you know what? If a woman has to be stuck in the kitchen, it might as well be with a Rembrandt on the wall."

She turns away and I follow her across the flagstones, across bright woven rugs. She throws open another set of shutters. In one corner a gilded birdcage spins from the ceiling, beneath it a covered well. Charmian perches on the lid. The birdcage is studded with glass jewels.

"No birds, just the cage," she says, and I can see her thoughts gather as she fiddles with her rolled-up sleeves. The shirt is washed thin, white cotton, possibly one of his. Her shoulders are formed from noble bones and maybe that's what makes her one of those women your eyes can't help but drink in. Like Mum.

"Was Joel her lover?" I try to make it sound light but she's not fooled, only shakes her head. Upstairs George is pacing up and down. I tell her about the money Mum left me, about the car, but Charmian simply raises an arched brow, says: "How very intriguing."

"George tells me he found you rooms at the Poseidon Hotel last night," she says.

I nod, blinking back tears, appalled at how powerfully I want her to hold me.

The birdcage throws colorful patterns to the wall, plants reach towards her from their pots, her skirt swishes as I trail her back to the kitchen.

"It's Easter Friday now, which is, you know, quite a thing here . . . so I'm sorry but I probably won't get your keys until Christ has arisen. But it's a nice house and not too many steps up from the port."

I tell her it's OK to wait though really I'm dreading Bobby. He's already threatened to make me pay for everyone's rooms at the Poseidon.

Charmian is saying, "You'll have fun with the festival," but

George is hollering, and she bolts again for the ladder. "I'm sorry. Inspiration is a flighty mistress."

She turns with her foot on the first step, a hand to her heart. "And really, Erica, thank you for the books."

I shrug, helplessly overcome with an impulse to do the washing up. Something cracks. She swoops and throws her arms around me, pats my shoulder while I sniff back tears. Says: "Hell, you're only a girl. Connie's little pearl. You know that's what she wanted to call you? She told me that your dad insisted on Erica . . ."

I am failing with words, failing not to cry; I manage only to wail about how beastly Bobby is being to me. I've made her shirt wet with my tears. She fetches me a soft cloth and a glass of water from an earthenware jug but as I blot my face and gulp at the water George again roars her name.

"We've only got daylight to work in before Zoe gets back with the kids, but it's Epitaphios tonight so we'll see you at Kamini. It's a lovely bay and you can walk with the procession from the village. It'll be magical, I promise you, bring candles. Come here for dinner later," she says, her foot to the step. "But right now I have to wring some more words out of the poor blighter up there."

I hear them talking as I turn to leave and she calls down, "Look, George says there's no need for you to waste money on the hotel, you can doss up here for a couple of nights."

"There's five of us," I call back.

"That's OK. It's only beans and greens, it'll stretch, and if you've got sleeping bags you can line up on the terrace in your cocoons like cozy pupae. It won't be the first time."

"No, nor the last," George barks. "It's like a bloody youth hostel round here."

"If you need anything before then, help yourself in the kitchen," she says.

Something crashes to the floor and she yelps. I roll up my sleeves and look around for soap to wash the dishes.

FIVE

George and Charmian's children are pretty free-range, tumbling in and out with bread they've stolen from taverna tables. I was away at school and barely ever met them as tots in London and now Martin is a gangling twelve-year-old with a nervous habit of squinting his eyes when he speaks and Shane's natural expression makes her look like she's thinking bad thoughts about you from behind her flaxen fringe. She's only ten but already she dresses like her mother, with her waist cinched in and a swing to her hips. She and Charmian row because she refuses to speak anything but Greek while they are struggling to encourage their youngest, four-year-old Jason, or "Booli" as he's known, to learn English. Shane boils with mischief while Charmian cooks and breaks up fights between the older two that turn swiftly physical, the angelic Booli wiping his face in her skirts, babbling in Greek. Pans boil over, gas bottles run out, Tripodi the three-legged cat comes in dragging a rat that isn't quite dead, and we all heap our bowls from dishes that Charmian brings to the table.

Very few islanders speak anything but their own language, which comes as a shock, as does wine from the barrel cheaper than lemonade, and the three warning flicks of the lights at the port each night before the island is plunged into darkness. There are no cars, not even bicycles; the streets are too precipitous for wheels.

"On this island the sea stands in for the grave during Epitaphios, because that is where their men have been buried," Charmian explains as we gather at the harbor of Kamini among the candled masses on Good Friday. The priests come intoning from the mountains and the catafalque, glittering with icons, is carried into the water on the shoulders of six handsome pallbearers. Women and children step forward, set lone candles for their drowned loved ones into the sand at the water's edge. There are shiny red eggs in the shop, displays of palm leaves and lilies from Athens. The following night there is so much incense at the Easter Mass that the priests keep coughing, which gives Edie and Janey the giggles. I step away from them, find myself at Charmian's side. She reaches for my hand and squeezes it. The heat from the candles and incense burners is immense, the priests chanting, the congregation swaying as though in a trance. I'm so swept up by it all I almost kiss the icon.

"*Christos Anesti, Christos Anesti.*" George is so roaring drunk by the time Christ has arisen that Jimmy and Bobby have to carry him up the stairs to his bed.

The smell of the feast is in the air as we leave George sleeping off his hangover. We pass lambs and goats turning on spits in the streets, and through the clanging bells take possession of a house up the hill with neither electricity nor running water. The freedom to do as we please is going to be harder work than we anticipated. Charmian has kept the Easter candle burning all the way up from her house and uses it to mark a sooty cross beneath our front door.

"You will need every blessing if you're planning to live like peasants," she says as we crowd around her in a kitchen with white walls so thick it is cool as a cave. The floor is local Dokos stone, shiny red and marbled like raw steak. There's a single window, cut deep into the wall above a sink. From a crack between the shutters, dusty light falls to the charcoal range, copper cups, earthenware, wooden shelves. Jimmy's eyes are shining. "It's like stepping into a Brueghel," he says.

A lantern of wood and mesh hangs from the rafters to store food away from flies and vermin. There's an icebox made of zinc, several ribbed stone Qupi jars for well water and a rainwater cistern to pump.

We have rotas—not that the others are any use at sticking to them. I'm the kid with time on my hands while my housemates hide behind their canvases on the terrace. The light is even more miraculous than they imagined and I've become as skinny and fit as a shepherd boy from running up and down our one hundred and ninety-two steps.

I have an order with the ice man and for sweet water at the wells, a place I buy kerosene, and a man with a donkey who'll see about our rubbish as well as another who brings sheep's milk down from the mountain. Our mattresses are less damp now we have charcoal for the braziers and Bobby and I coped with our malfunctioning cesspit without coming to blows. Edie has singed her eyelashes on the unpredictable kerosene stove, Janey has seen a ghost in her room and is sleeping on a mattress with Bobby and Edie, in what is, of course, the best room with a view to the harbor. Jimmy and I are away from it all behind the kitchen in a cool room cut into the rock. We sleep with a sea breeze bringing the heady scent of citrus flowers through a door from the terrace. Much of our time in that rusty-sprung bed isn't spent sleeping.

———

It's Wednesday, my day to cook, and Charmian has already haggled on my behalf at the vegetable boat, picked out every bean and onion with poignant care, putting tomatoes to her face for their scent, accepting quarters of oranges from the boatmen with a child-like pleasure. Nobody speaks English. She teaches me "*Signomi Kyrié*" and "*Poso kani afto?*"—excuse me and how much?

In my basket are eight glossy aubergines, a vegetable I've never met before. Charmian has promised to teach me to make moussaka. I need to pin her down to a time, preferably when I can get her alone to talk about Mum. People keep getting in the way. When she isn't slaving with George, or drinking with this crowd, her children devour her.

It's noon and the foreign community gathers around her and George outside the store awaiting fortune's sunny smile. The mail arrives on the same boat as visitors and today is just the sort of day that a check might choose to sail in on.

The sight of so many writers is not an enticement to join their ranks. Disheveled and miserable are two words that spring to mind. The American novelist Gordon Merrick has come down from the hills sporting a black eye. "He and Chuck have a taste for young sailor boys," Charmian whispers. "Sometimes things go wrong." George has shredded several matchsticks and with nico-tined fingers is building a little pyramid out of them on the table; the Norwegian Axel Jensen has sores on his lips and trousers worn so thin they are indecent at his splayed crotch; Patrick Greer is pointing and wagging his schoolmaster's finger to win some point or other.

"One of these days that finger will go off bang," Charmian mutters and Nancy, Patrick's wife, a bountiful Mrs. Sprat to his Jack, hears her and laughs.

Jean-Claude Maurice sits across the aisle with the sun glinting on his hair, his back to everyone but Trudy, the pretty redhead art student we met in Athens who is ever hopeful of being reunited with her lost luggage.

Axel Jensen nervously bolts a coffee. The girl in the red shorts leans over her sketchbook, one bare foot crossed to her knee. Her hair falls in a sleek shiny curtain; her arms are slim as flutes. She's busy ignoring everyone, shading with a pencil, another between her teeth. Axel Jensen watches her. Jimmy does too.

Cats laze on warm rocks; the harbor is flat as a mirror. The Easter bunting has been spirited away, fishing nets are laid out for mending, donkeys carry bales of dried sponges from the factory to the dock, the butcher walks past in his bloody apron. Though it has only been a fortnight since my arrival, this girl with her basket of shiny aubergines feels like she's part of the island's welcoming committee as the Canadian poet disembarks.

He arrives in the port unhurried in soft soles, looking around and smiling at everything he sees like someone returning home from a long journey. He looks easy in his clothes, wears a cap and sunglasses, carries a green typewriter and a smart leather suitcase, a guitar strapped to his back. Janey and Edie skip beside him, in tight pedal pushers and striped sailor shirts, clearly ecstatic to have met such an interesting new friend on the boat back from Athens.

I narrow my eyes as they dance attendance on the approaching stranger. I've grown possessive of the island, as bad as the oldsters out here on the cobbles, with our judgment as bitter as Nikos Katsikas's coffee beneath its sugar.

George is pretending to take an interest in my plans, ribbing me. "So, what does a little Ricky of blessed Bayswater find to write about? What's your plot?"

"I'm thinking of a mystery story about my mother," I say, making sure Charmian hears.

She flashes a distracted smile my way. "Sounds like a winner," she says.

"I mean, did she ever drive you any place in her open-top car?"

"Shhh," she says, diverting our gaze with a bossy tilt of her head.

Janey and Edie lead the newcomer to our table like sirens overjoyed by a lucky catch.

Leonard is courteous, pulls off his cap. His hair is thick and wavy, his brow dark and serious. His grin is lopsided, there's something charming in the stoop of his shoulders, a carapace of shyness perhaps, but as he says his hellos, his voice is as deep and confident as that of a village elder. Charmian welcomes him with the full force of her smile, sends Patrick scurrying to find him a chair.

Axel Jensen is standing to leave and the dark-haired girl is folding her sketchbook. Jimmy is staring so hard at her I want to kick him.

It isn't only the newcomer's voice that commands attention. Dark stubble and good manners make him seem older than his twenty-five years. He lights a cigarette and hands it to Charmian as you might to a long-acquainted friend, lights another for himself. He leans back and runs his hand back and forth along his chin and jaw, says his last shave had been at his digs in Hampstead. The writers pull their chairs closer when they hear that he's a published poet. They are devils at a feast, tightening the circle as he talks of a little room where he might finish blackening the pages of a novel.

"The materials are very beautiful, everywhere you look. Nothing insults you," he's saying as Edie and Janey snake around.

"Well, we're not short of young writers here. This one's little Ricky all the way from Blighty, not long out of the pram," George says, taking it upon himself to do the introductions, and guffawing until, judging by the look on her face, Charmian wants to kick him just as badly as I do. Leonard holds my hand as I struggle to get my voice to behave.

Edie is twined around one of the awning poles, dramatically beautiful, her singed eyelashes hidden by Jackie Kennedy–style sunglasses she went all the way to Athens to buy. I wonder why Bobby hasn't come down from our house to meet her from the boat. It seems he's getting moodier by the day.

Leonard keeps hold of my hand. When I meet his gaze there's warm humor beneath those serious brows. He tells me I look like a cool kid. Janey tugs his arm.

"Erica's our runaway teenager, the one I was telling you about on the boat. You know, with the mysterious bequest from her mother . . ." she says and Leonard nods at me and gives my hand a squeeze before returning to Charmian.

Janey looks quickly from me to Edie and Edie nods at her in vigorous assent to a question I haven't yet understood.

"There's a bed at ours if you need it," Janey tells him and I see the swell of his Adam's apple as he gulps.

Charmian flies to his rescue, batting Janey away. "It's like a lunatic asylum up there, all those English kids shouting and paint everywhere. No one could possibly get anything written." Her chair is pulled in so close to Leonard's that they touch.

"You're welcome to a very comfy divan at the top of our house," she says. "It's just up from here, beside the Church of Saint Constantinos by the town well. Everyone knows us. Just ask for

Australia House and they'll direct you, and the weather's warm
from now on so you'll be able to write on the terrace until we find
you something of your own."

Janey looks at him through her lashes and pouts. "Or you could,
you know, just bunk with us . . ."

Janey's little mewl is lost on Leonard. Having thanked Charmian
for the lifeline, he's asking George for directions to the house of the
painter Nikos Ghikas, where he has an invitation, his only one
on Hydra. Patrick summons a donkey and George walks the first
few paces with him along the agora on his way to the hills above
Kamini. Leonard strolls beside the donkey, does a few jaunty
dance steps for those of us watching him go, a man free of a heavy
load.

Charmian sighs. "Well, lucky him if he does get Ghikas's house,
which is quite obviously his intention," she says. "Forty rooms.
The most beautiful house on the island, would you agree, George?"

George has returned to the table deep into a hangnail and
doesn't respond.

"I've been as far as the door." Jimmy is still watching the girl in
the red shorts. "I went up there to check out where Henry Miller
wrote *The Colossus of Maroussi*," he says and I feel piqued that
he's been exploring without me.

"Ah yes, many good writers," Charmian says. "Larry Durrell,
George Seferis, Paddy Leigh Fermor, Cyril Connolly—oh, and so
many painters have produced great work there too. Our good mate
Sidney Nolan stayed a couple of years ago and there were many
memorable gatherings. It's a climb but so tremendously romantic."
She gazes towards the hills. "The land is more fertile on that side
of the island, the barley so very lovely. George and I used to go for
sunset before his breathing got bad."

Patrick pulls miserably at his beard. "Well, Mr. Ghikas has been a little keener on aristocratic English types recently. Our Canadian friend must be well connected," he says.

George takes a break from gnawing at his nails. "We're getting overrun with people writing bloody novels here."

"Yes, well, that includes us, darling." Charmian mimes cracking a whip at him. "Come on, George, back to the workstation."

"About the moussaka . . ." I say, my hand on her arm.

"Maybe Jimmy should learn to cook too," Charmian says, but Jimmy is watching something and frowning. We follow his gaze along the waterfront to the disappearing form of the girl with the red shorts as she catches up with a slow-striding Axel Jensen on the road to Mandraki.

Axel grabs the girl's arm; she shrugs him off, turns and pushes him away. This happens again and again. By the time they round the corner he's worn down her resistance and his hand is stuffed in the back pocket of her shorts. Charmian rolls her eyes at the others. "Axel's obsessed with that girl. He's making no secret of it."

Nancy has her hand to her bosom. "Poor Marianne, I don't know what's going to happen when she gets back here with the baby."

SIX

I'm sure Charmian knows I have a crush on her but she always seems pleased to see me. I make myself useful with her children, set them a good example by clearing my plate or laying the table, encourage little Booli to speak a few words of English. George is occasionally less grumpy now he's used to my face; in fact he seems to relish a new and willing ear for his stories. I have become almost as drawn to him as I am to Charmian and find myself acting a little more sparkly around him in my desperation to make him like me. His outbursts sometimes frighten me and sometimes make me laugh.

He's at his workstation upstairs; he's on a bit of a roll, Charmian says. She cocks her ear to the rattle and ting of his typewriter, gives a thumbs-up as I unload my basket. I'm still a bit lovestruck and woozy in the afterglow of my siesta with Jimmy, my legs shaky from our exertions. I've left him sleeping and naked, tangled in the rags of our sheets.

Charmian takes the greasy package containing the unthinkable scrag end of lamb she chose for me at the butcher's, unwraps it, briskly chops it to pieces and shows me how to mince it in a machine that is bracketed to the worktop.

I turn the red wooden handle while she pours us each a glass of retsina though it isn't much past four o'clock.

"Oh good, I'm glad we're alone," she says, propping herself at the door to the courtyard with her drink. "These last few nights I've been racked with thoughts of your lovely mum—you know when things went badly between George and me in London, Connie was always so kind . . . and I've been thinking about that friendship and her being gone and you turning up here. I mean, she wanted the world for you. There are things I should say . . ." I force myself to keep turning the handle while she pauses and fiddles with her hair, twisting it and retying it with the shoelace. "I have to say, from what I've observed, that big brother of yours isn't taking very good care of you. Do tell me not to stickybeak, if you like . . ."

Come on, I think. Never mind all this, talk to me about Joel.

She shakes a cigarette from her pack, fumbles with matches. The pink worms of meat squiggle to the bowl.

She takes a deep drag and blows out the match. "And what about your Jimmy? Why is it always left to you to cook?"

"Jimmy does his best work while everyone else sleeps. He'll need more than bread and cheese—"

She interrupts me with a furious burst. "All I've seen so far is you doing all the running around while everyone else bludges," she says. "Don't you have better things to do with your life? Look how your mother was bound and constrained. Two children, plus your dad, and that flat was more than a full-time job. And you've seen what it's like for me here; I'm lucky if I make a page of my own in a week with all the things that need to be made clean before getting dirty again . . ."

Max the dog is on his feet, wagging his tail and scratching at the door from the street. Her tone becomes urgent.

"Now, Erica, listen to me. What I'm trying to tell you is that if you've got things to do it's better to get on with them, it's not enough to simply enable some bloke to do his thing. Don't let the buggers clip your wings just as you're learning to fly."

But now Max is leaping full pirouettes and Nancy comes charging towards us like a one-woman harvest festival, floral dress and market baskets overflowing.

Charmian grasps my arm. "You know, that nice young Canadian poet earlier, when he asked me if I knew of a room, a nice simple room, he said, with maybe a bed and a desk and a chair? I was jealous, so jealous that for a moment I actually hated him. Imagine what I would get done, I thought, at a table in that little white room with nothing but my typewriter for company."

"Imagine what you'd get done if you had a nice wife rather than that needy old bugger up there," says Nancy, who is wheezing and out of breath.

"I hope you have safety pins." Nancy is so bursting with news her dress has come apart at the seams. "Oh dear Charm, I have to talk to you. I've just seen them—Axel and that girl. Someone must write to Marianne to stop her coming back to this . . ."

"Idiotic Axel." Charmian is pointing Nancy in the direction of the mending basket while Max rolls on his back, begging a tickle. She turns to finish making her point. "Erica, think. What would Connie want for you?" She touches my cheek, makes me look at her. "You're so very young to be roaming around . . ."

I'm overcome with that feeling again, I can smell her scent, the warmth of it, have to fight not to fall for it. I stick out my chin, point to the Rembrandt etching. "Is there a Joel?"

Charmian puts her palm to her forehead.

"I'm not sure what it is you want me to say, Erica; I mean, I have no idea." She changes the subject. "Though, you know, it would be irresponsible as Connie's friend not to talk to you about birth control." A burn comes to my cheeks as across the room Nancy pulls a lobster from her basket and Charmian grabs a tin bucket and runs to the well.

Nancy follows her, the lobster held before her at arm's length, clacking like a clockwork toy.

"Axel says the baby's over his croup and Marianne will be here in time for her birthday. Oh, that poor lovely girl," Nancy is saying as they plunge the lobster into the bucket.

"Have you been introduced to Axel Jensen yet, Erica? You know which one he is, yes? The young Norwegian writer who lives up beyond the wells?"

I shrug. "I know who he is." If Charmian and Nancy want to gossip, I might as well hurry up with the moussaka and get back to Jimmy.

"Axel can be very charming," Charmian says. "He's doing well . . ."

"Yes, he told me his last novel is being made into a film now," Nancy interrupts. Charmian nods at Nancy and continues.

"He's dangerous with ideas, which can make him thrilling company. But any time over the years that I've found myself warming to him I see these little scars he has on the back of his hand and those scars tell me more about Axel than any of the fine words coming out of his mouth. He's lucky he didn't sever the tendons. Mucking about with a knife like that, you know at a bar, stabberscotching it between his fingers the way tough bastards do. He was drunk and raging at poor Marianne and drove the blade clean through to the table." Charmian plunges an imaginary knife at her own hand. "Appears like he went through more than once," she says.

Nancy looks up with a shudder from pinning her dress back together. "And this thing of him buying a boat as a present to himself to celebrate the birth of his son, that tells you quite a bit about him too. What a cad."

"Not only a boat. I hear a sports car as well. Magda's here helping to set up the Lagoudera bar and she's had a letter from Marianne. Apparently she's nervous about driving all this way from Norway with such a tiny baby. I've no idea why Axel didn't drive his silly car himself."

"Drink-driving, through the streets of Oslo on the night the child was born," Nancy says. "He's had his license taken away. Oh, that poor girl."

Nancy helps herself from the retsina jug, gives Charmian a refill and settles herself more firmly in her chair. "I had an arrangement to meet Christos for the lobsters at the boatyard in Mandraki. I get a very good price from him. Anyway, I got there a bit early and wandered around. And there they were, the pair of them . . ."

"Who?" Charmian looks up from the cheese grater.

"Axel and the American girl—do pay attention, Charm. They were painting the Plimsoll line and the name of his boat in red paint. It's called *Ikarus*, by the way."

"Predictable . . ." Charmian snorts. "Go on."

"You might say I caught them red-handed. He was pressed up behind her, while she was trying to paint the lettering. I didn't know what to do; I couldn't just turn back because I'd arranged to meet Christos. Axel had his hands right up that girl's shirt. He turned and nodded at me when I called, but left his hands where they were, even though the girl was clearly embarrassed and attempting to get away."

Nancy is fanning herself with her hand. "I was furious. 'Axel, what are you doing?' I actually shouted at him, it was quite involuntary."

"Oh, poor Marianne."

Charmian fills me in while I take over with the cheese. "Marianne is Axel's wife, possibly the sweetest young woman who ever lived. She and Axel came here from Norway, oh, more than two years ago now. They're the only foreigners other than us to have bought our houses; he's flush with readers in several languages though a bit Kerouac for my taste—"

Nancy interrupts Charmian's lit crit to hurry things along. "Marianne's been in Oslo to give birth to their baby but she's due back on Hydra any day now . . . Anyway there he was with his boat on the joists and me shouting at him. The girl didn't turn around, she still had the paintbrush in her hand. I stood my ground. I said, 'Axel. Are you getting the boat ready in time for your wife's return with your son?' The girl was flinching. 'Stop mauling me, Axel,' she said. Axel was cold with me. I said something else about Marianne, asked about the baby's cough. He spun the girl around by the shoulders, the front of her shirt was streaked with red paint. She hid her face in her hands while he introduced her. 'This is Patricia,' he said. 'We are in love. What do you suggest, Nancy?'"

Charmian shakes her head. "I don't think the island can cope with any more drama," she says.

After Nancy, in comes the young widow Zoe with Booli at her heels. Zoe is given onions to chop and an old hen to gut while the little boy follows Charmian to the courtyard to pick herbs. Zoe and I manage only a few words but do a lot of smiling at each other. She has about as much English as I do Greek.

"*Kartopoulo*," Booli cries, licking his lips when he sees what's for supper.

"Chicken," I correct him, stooping to collect a fistful of oregano. "Thank you, good boy, Boo," and I get him to repeat "chicken" as Charmian takes her sharpest knife to the shining globes of my aubergines, palest gold beneath their regal skins.

Martin bumbles in from school with a dead grasshopper in his pocket. Martin's legs are ridiculously too long for his shorts, thin and prominently jointed so he looks like an insect himself. He hides his clever eyes behind a mop of streaky hair, stops only long enough to dump his books and tear a hunk from the loaf. He shares his father's habits of sudden bursts of conversation and self-absorbed silences.

While Charmian cooks the meat sauce, she tells the sad story of Costas, who was drowned off the coast of Benghazi while sponge fishing. At her husband's name Zoe crosses her hands at the bib of her apron.

"Ugh, they had to cut his line because they couldn't pull him out of the sludge. He wasn't much older than your brother. And two other crew members crippled with the bends in the same season—that captain won't be setting sail again . . ."

"Bugger, bugger, bugger!" George comes crashing down the ladder, rolling his sleeve to his elbow. "Bugger, missed my shot; why didn't you remind me, Charm?" He takes her pack of cigarettes from the table while she sets a pan of water to boil on a Primus, still talking to me.

"Sponge was the main industry here, a tough one but dying out."

George is scratching at his arms. Charmian takes a glass syringe from a tin, fits it with a needle and drops it into the water. He lights a cigarette.

"Sponge. You can't get away from it. The death of it all," he says, narrowing his eyes at me through the smoke. "You smell it here in the street, from the factory. No bleach can wash away the stench, and I take it you've noticed how many crippled men we have?"

Charmian grasps his arm, grimaces. "Oh George, it's like a pepper pot. I think this one had better be in your arse." I don't know where to look. Surely I shouldn't be here? Is George some sort of addict?

Booli and the dog are racing around with a paper kite Charmian has made from some string and a paper bag.

"Hey, it's like a bloody circus ground," George complains and Zoe claps her hands for Boo to play in the street.

"And here's our lovely Zoe, widowed at twenty-two, childless and without much hope of another match with half the blokes away at sea. A sailor boy sending money home is the way most of these families survive now," George tells me. "You larrikins who come for the sun have no idea how bloody hard it is for the people who live here. That daily grind of finding food and carrying water is not a bloody lifestyle choice for them," he says, helping himself to Charmian's glass and draining it in one gulp.

"Stop it, George," she says, lifting the hypodermic from the battered pan of boiling water with tongs. "Leave the poor girl alone."

He's still going on so it's a relief when Martin comes bounding in. "Hey, what's up, professor?" George says and Charmian hisses, "Will you stop calling him that," as Martin urges us all to his room to view the grasshopper's eye under his microscope.

Charmian is taking a small bottle from the icebox. "When I've done Dad's shot," she says, filling the syringe.

George is still booming at me. "I, for one, thank the yachts and the film people! You'll see if you stay: it gets hellish all summer long. But it's a bloody good job people have started to come because the island will need to do something now synthetic sponges are taking over the entire industry . . ." He's unbuckling his belt. "I say hurrah for Sophia Loren!" he cries as he drops his trousers, and I yelp.

"Oh crikey, Erica! You must be wondering what the hell's going on." I suspect Charmian of enjoying my confusion. "Streptomycin for his TB." She flashes the syringe. "I've become rather expert at doing this since he got back from the hospital in Athens."

George leans over with his hands to the table. His shirt-tails are mercifully long enough to spare my blushes. His legs are gangly as a schoolboy's—exactly like Martin's, in fact. "Yes, better here than in Athens," he growls as Charmian approaches. "I need to be on the island to keep an eye on my wife."

She raises her eyebrows and makes herself wicked in a sexy sort of a way, taps the syringe. "Darling, you may find this hurts."

Martin rolls his eyes at me as she starts to recount Nancy's story about Axel and the American girl. "Come on," he says, tugging my shirt. "It's got compound eyes."

———

By the time I head home the day is dissolving. The black sea is squiggled from mast lights, silvered with stars, spangled green and red from the harbor beacons. A bright gibbous moon rises from the mountains; the cicadas pour their love songs from the trees. The climb up Voulgaris Street from the port no longer makes me out of breath; the moussaka is still hot from Charmian's oven when I arrive home.

No one has lit the kerosene lamps though I can hear voices and people moving about upstairs. I plonk the dish on the table, call out, light a lamp. The room is exactly as I left it. Shadows leap from flowers that Jimmy and I picked on the mountain: yellow daisies and poppies in a green glazed jar. The table is laid with earthenware plates and half a ring of bread on a board, a dish of oil, two jugs of Kokineli and our copper beakers washed and ready to receive it.

Jimmy sneaks up on me while I'm filling a jug with water from the Qupi. He's shirtless, smooth-chested, smelling of bed. The frenetic comings and goings at Charmian's fall into a fold in time as, grabbing my lamp, he leads me back to the still-warm sheets.

SEVEN

The problem of what to do about Marianne rumbles on for days among the foreign community. Fresh sightings of Axel and Patricia are brought to Katsikas to be picked over. Friends come and pour their concern into glasses at Charmian's table, douse their forebodings with ouzo. Nancy wants to write to her in Oslo, Charmian favors staying well away.

The Canadian poet is upstairs on the terrace tapping away at his green Olivetti.

"That housekeeper is very loyal to the first Mrs. Ghikas so Leonard dropping the name of Nikos's new fiancée when he introduced himself was unfortunate to say the least." Charmian is warming to the latest island scandal which concerns the new poet's housing. "Barbara Rothschild had better watch out for Mrs. Danvers when she marries him."

News of Leonard's rejection from the great painter's grand house has ricocheted from wall to well. George is writing Nikos

Ghikas a letter. A door slammed in the young man's face, but worse than rude. "We don't want any more Jews here" was what the housekeeper said. Was the island harboring a Nazi? George is railing; not much of his monologue is making it onto the page.

By the time I run into him Leonard is nicely settled over his typewriter, his shirtsleeves rolled, a Greek cigarette burning between his fingers.

I've been shooed up here to the terrace with an offering of watermelon. He's set himself up facing out to sea and stops typing when he hears me, stands silhouetted against a blazing blue sky.

His back and shoulders remain hunched from the worktable. "Please, I didn't want to interrupt you," I say. It feels awkward, being alone with him. He's removed his sunglasses and I get the sense he's looking at me as though the bowl of cut fruit is suggestive. I'm young enough to find this sort of consideration from a grown man with stubble and hairy arms mortifying. I know I'm blushing as red as the watermelon I'm thrusting towards him. For want of something to say I tell him I'm shocked about what happened to him at Ghikas's house. The sun spikes his eyes with green so they are the same khaki as his shirt.

"Well, you know I put a curse on the place?" and, though he chuckles as he says it, his face darkens.

He has everything he needs. A divan, a chair, his typewriter and a workbench set up with a view to the port. The sun is strong enough to make him squint as he takes the bowl of melon and places it on a low wall within reach of his work.

Pots of rose geranium and basil sweeten the air. Written pages flutter their corners to a breeze. A loop of amber *komboloi* beads and a pottery pomegranate prevent them from flying away. He reaches for his sunglasses, tips me a salute as he returns to his typewriter. He seems to be blackening a significant number of pages, certainly more than either Charmian or George.

———

The days grow longer and the sun stronger, enough that Janey gets badly burned while sunbathing on the terrace. Naked, naturally. Now she's pink all over like strawberry ice cream, a moaning calamine ghost. I buy cartons of sun cream from the pharmacy and become helpless beneath Jimmy's hands as he rubs it in. He's already tanned enough to switch to olive oil. We arrange some foam mattresses and cushions, beyond the painting tables and easels, where our terrace meets bare red and gold rock. A few straggly olive branches are strung with our clothing; flowering thyme and white star-of-Bethlehem spring from fissures in the hillside. Jimmy sketches the rocks and the roots, fills a few pages of his notebook. There is only the most flirtatious of breezes to stir the perfume of spruce and donkey shit and flowering herb. I lie propped on my elbows with the sun on my back while Henry Miller heavies my eyelids. Jimmy reaches across me for wine. The mountain shimmers. Poppies blush. I want to snap my whole being around him, like some sort of carnivorous plant that his fingers brush up against.

———

Jimmy and I make a good team in the beginning. We get everything done before lunch so most days are like this one, languid and free as the water that gently bobs the boats below our nest on the hillside. We've been up and down the steps three times already, from the vegetable boat and the market, the bakery and the butcher. We earn our siesta.

I'm first out of bed every morning, up with the Orthros bells. I'm usually first to sleep at night too because Jimmy and my brother and the girls stay up late drinking and playing poker on the terrace with Trudy and the other American students. The guardian at the art school is, by all accounts, a gorgon so they are regularly locked out for not making her curfew and have to doss here.

There's no electricity to run a fridge. Every second morning I fetch our block of ice from the foot of the steps where it has been deposited by Spiros and his mules. The others sleep right through the bells and the donkeys and the workmen hammering; if left to them our ice would be a puddle so it's as well I'm a lark.

I stretch my eyes across the gulf towards the mountains of Troezen. Beauty rises up to greet me. The sea lies waiting, the port promises drama, the rocks clang with bells from the island's many churches. I stand at the top of the steps and drink it all in. The hills flame with yellow flowers, the mountains are tipped with rose gold, every whitewashed wall shines crystalline with quartz. Leafy vines drape the white tunnel of steps. An arched door is garlanded by ripening apricots; wildflowers sprout from cracks in every tumbledown wall and ruin. A woman shakes a rug from a doorway and even the dust glitters.

I cart our block of ice back up to the house, stopping only to make way for a jingling train of donkeys and to talk to various cats sprawling in familiar patches of sunlight along the twisting steps. My favourite black cat has hidden her kittens among clumps of rosemary in the rubbled terrace of the crumbling house below ours. I push the branches aside and talk to her as they suckle and her semi-precious eyes shine.

The early morning is mine and I'm glad of it. Back home, I bumble about in my vest and shorts, tipping water from the icebox into a bucket to swab the floor, pushing the new block into place. I boil coffee on the Primus and sing to myself as I start clearing away last night's dinner things, carefully observing our systems for the conservation of water.

As I've said, Hydra is dry apart from a handful of wells, but it's not difficult to clean a whole kitchen with one bowl if you do things in the right order of greasiness, and there is a certain satisfaction to it. I start with the glass of the lanterns, bring them to a shine with a lemon wrapped in a wet cloth the way Charmian showed me, trim the wicks while I'm at it. It's Jimmy's turn to cook so I sort through some dry beans and leave them to soak. There will be fresh vegetables if we get down to the market in time, and we can probably all do with a bit of meat of some kind.

The black mother cat comes to the door for scraps. I treat us both to a creamy swirl from a can of evaporated NouNou, mine in my first coffee of the day, hers in a saucer, and lean against the doorjamb to drink it. Across the ridge comes Fotis the shepherd and his donkey, on its back the milk cans glinting in the sun as the donkey's little feet pick a careful path down the mountain. It's a jolly-looking donkey, its bridle decorated with blue beads and a tassel swinging from an evil-eye amulet at its brow. Fotis ambles behind, his usual sack and shovel at the ready, but this morning his waistcoat is unpatched and he sports a nosegay of mountain hyacinths in his buttonhole. It's a feast day of some kind; that's what all the bells of the island have been trying to tell me. Several cats skulk a perfectly measured foot-kicking distance from Fotis as he pours milk into my jug. He has terra-cotta pots of sheep's yogurt in one of his panniers so I am especially glad I waylaid him before he reached the market.

The skin of the yogurt yields slightly to the edge of my spoon, thick and delicious with a dollop of honey from Mikhailis Christopolous's bees, a whole comb in a big jar on our windowsill, shining with the amber light of a local man's approval.

Jimmy's day starts later than mine but no less picturesquely. He comes yawning and stretching from our room. He wears only a small yellow towel, wrapped at his hips. He knows I watch him and pulls a few Mr. Universe poses as he bends to the pump handle. It takes around half an hour to get the day's water from our cistern and up to the tank and it goes with a satisfying slosh and a thump. Jimmy's arms work like pistons, his shoulder blades stand proud of the slender curve of his back. It's this harmony of proportion that gives him the easy tumble and turn of an acrobat, and a surprising strength. He stops for a moment to rake back his hair, catches a drop of sweat on the tip of his tongue. Before he bends once again to the pump he flashes at me with the towel.

Soon enough the smell of frying fills our kitchen. A dozen eggs spit in the iron pan that Bobby tilts over the charcoal. For the moment we've all given up on the kerosene stove that took off Edie's eyelashes. Janey squeals from the privy. Someone has blocked it again. Edie shimmies about in one of Bobby's striped shirts, making a pot of tisane with leaves from the mountain. They're all talking about last night's poker, about the American boys who are either flukes or cheats and, gripping their heads, cursing the mastika they downed while I lay dreaming.

Edie's so slim you could probably fit three of her into Bobby's shirt. In fact, we all appear gamine beside him. Sometimes I think Bobby looks like a different species. On Hydra his great shoulders bring us the sweet water from the wells and he eats a proper breakfast to fuel the climb. He'd manage twelve eggs on his own, I reckon.

Trudy has stayed the night. She perches by the window and

blinks at the day. Her hair is all copper filaments, her face spattered with freckles. She's dressed in the same pale blue shirt and trousers she was wearing when she arrived. She's given up on ever being reunited with her luggage.

"Don't forget about my party," she reminds us. "We're not letting anyone in who doesn't bother about the dress code." Trudy is forever without things. She has no swimsuit, no books, no footwear suitable for hiking. And, she informs us now, she has no Boston grandmother's Dior gown to wear on her twenty-first as intended. As a consequence she has decided that we must all fashion party-wear from items found on the island.

Edie hugs herself through Bobby's shirt as some sort of clever design blossoms. "Come on," says Janey, hands on hips. "Share." Both Edie and Janey studied costume in London, they're at an advantage. "Hey, baby J," Edie says. "Let's make Trudy a fabulous birthday gown," and when Janey agrees Trudy leaps up and hugs them both.

Bobby grumps that he'll buy something from Tzimmy, the crippled sponge diver, who sells dead men's clothes at the port. Janey wrinkles her nose. Jimmy's idea seems the best to me. "We can paint on sacks," he says as Trudy spies a flash of bright blue through the window and the smile is wiped from her face.

"How the hell does he know I'm here?"

Jean-Claude Maurice stands at the open door, in an unbuttoned shirt of cobalt-blue silk. "There is no point in me making a class at Tombazi if you do not come," he tells Trudy with a sullen pout. He twiddles with his earring while he waits. His tan looks deep-grained, like a much-polished old handbag. He *is* old. Thirty-five at the very least. I shudder as he takes Trudy's hand and leads her the back way, every step the satyr with his gold hair and springy brown legs.

We have fresh bread from the bakery, two rings, studded all over with sesame. Bobby slides the fry-up from the pan and we tear at the bread and scoop and dab up the eggs and tomatoes. Trudy and Jean-Claude are framed in the window as across the hill to the art school they go, his tiny shorts and explosive laugh, her Venetian hair flaming.

"So the pervy old French painter has tracked down our Titian maiden," Bobby says. "Of course he wants to paint her naked."

"Yeah, and knowing Jean-Claude she'll succumb . . ." I say and when he shoots me a puzzled frown I remind him about Charmian's book. "It just goes to show what a good writer she is. You know, she pretty well has him pinned to the page, don't you think?"

Bobby still hasn't a clue what I'm talking about. Jimmy has jackknifed himself in the window recess with a well-thumbed Mervyn Peake that's been doing the rounds. He looks across as Bobby cracks our three remaining eggs into the pan.

"It's quite obvious Jean-Claude is the model for Jacques in the book," Jimmy says. "You know, the French existentialist who comes to the island and seduces everyone . . . ?"

Bobby jumps from a burst of spitting fat. "I never read her book," he says, and Jimmy and I exchange astonished looks.

"Well, that seems spectacularly un-nosey of you," I say.

Bobby talks to the frying pan, he's furious with it. "Not everyone is as fascinated by our raddled old neighbor as you seem to be. I don't know how you can stand to spend so much time with those oldsters all bitching away about each other and so drunk they can barely stagger home." Bobby's big jaw is set against me for reasons I can't fathom, his cheeks are reddening. He stabs at the eggs with his spatula, breaks a yolk. Jimmy takes refuge in *Gormenghast*.

"Well, that's gratitude. If it wasn't for our 'raddled old neighbor' we wouldn't be here now," I reply. "And anyway, I like them, I like being around a proper family and . . ." I find I can't go on. The word "family" has done for me and the room has started to swim. I go to the door and gulp at sweet sunshine. I sweep my eyes across folds of pine and tumbledown terraces and up to the bronzed mountains and the sky. I don't want to be crying any more.

This is an island that holds you steady in its lap, its mountains solid as shoulders. I fold myself in, cleave to it, while behind me Bobby carries on ranting. Beneath the school I can make out the corner of Charmian and George's terrace, Hydriot flag flying. "I just don't get the attraction. That George banging on like he's Hemingway. Who the hell are the Kuomintang anyway? As for those know-it-all children—"

I don't want to hear it and spin around to tell him so. "Besides, I want to find out what Charmian knows. Bobby, do you really have no interest in our mother?"

"Oh Erica, stop!" He bats me away with his spatula. "You plague that woman like a mosquito with your questions. I can tell that you irritate the hell out of her. And so what if our mother had a secret admirer? Maybe she was a high-class tart and we just didn't notice. But I'll tell you what. I. don't. care. I keep telling you, family is a terrible construct. We'd all be better off without it."

Jimmy drops his book and springs between us, gives Bobby's arm a tug. "Come on, grumpy old donkey. Get your yoke across those shoulders and once you've got the water you and I should attempt that trek up to Episkopi," he says, patting him on the back.

I race Edie and Janey down the steps, clutching our straw hats to our heads, beach bags bouncing at our hips. That Trudy makes too much of her lost luggage. In reality we're all wearing very little anyway. Edie's dress is a scrap of white cotton, worn thin and torn at the front so it looks in danger of slipping from her shoulders.

We pass old women sitting on their stoops.

"*Yia sou*, Kyria Katerina; *yia sou*, Kyria Maria," we cry.

"Sss, sss," they reply without raising their eyes from their embroidery. The light shines through Edie's dress. She skips down the steps and the fishermen coming towards us will see straight away that she is naked beneath it.

She and Janey veer off at the clock towards the slaughterhouse on their mission for fancy-dress materials, leaving me asking boatmen for sacks, which isn't easy without the Greek words.

"*Efcharistó*, Niko!" Nikos Katsikas takes me to his brother Andonis at the back of the store; there's a pile of old grain sacks he can let me have. Charmian is at her usual table, waving to me with a hand that's already occupied with her glass and a cigarette. Leonard raises his cap. He sits so close to Charmian that occasionally the broad brim of her straw hat throws a shadow across his face. The tables are all full of foreigners now. Every day more and more, the day-trippers from Athens but also people like us who can live for a year in the sun on what it'd cost us for a month in a dingy bedsit at home.

There's a new man in George and Charmian's group, Scandinavian by the look of him, with somber eyes and a soft-lipped smile.

"Meet Göran Tunström," Charmian says, waving a hand towards him. She's in full flow, the others bend to her drift, though she remains erect and so queenly I could almost curtsy. Göran and Leonard are exchanging books with their names on the dust jackets; each tries to outdo the other in self-effacement until Charmian claps her hands at them to stop. Leonard is saying, "Whenever I hear that a guy writes poetry I feel close to him. You know, I understand the folly."

I would join them but Bobby's words are still jangling. Am I really nothing but an annoying mosquito?

EIGHT

Tomorrow is May Day and Axel Jensen will sail *Ikarus* into the port with Marianne and their baby. Leonard will be drinking coffee at George and Charmian's table. The little sloop will cut a dash past the fat-bottomed caiques and Marianne will lower her face to adjust a white shawl and to shield the baby from the sun. Everyone will be watching, but perhaps none so intently as Leonard. "What a beautiful Holy Trinity," he'll say. And Charmian will arch her brows at George and say, "Let us pray."

Tonight the stage is set for a more ancient drama, rooted in Greek tradition. All day the girls and young women of the village have been gathering flowers from the hills. They walk past us in pairs in black skirts with swinging baskets, shoes ringing on the cobbles. The young women's arms are covered, the girls wear black-buttoned smocks, headscarves wound around neat dark faces, their pretty blouses modestly arranged in stark contrast to our casual display of burnt skin and sea-salted hair.

This evening has been born from one of those murmuring

sundowns, our bodies molten as the sea and the sky turned to honey. We've been dipping and diving and drying off in the sun all afternoon. The night-scented jasmine is soporific as a lullaby.

We drape ourselves around a couple of tables outside Katsikas. Edie and Janey are wrapped in Indian print sarongs tied in a knot at the shoulder, the boys all have unbuttoned shirts. I'm wearing shorts, my gingham swimsuit and ponytail crusty with salt. We're all barefoot. We can't even remember whose turn it is to cook, but everyone's here, gathering at tables, and tonight an entire shoal of red *barbounia* has met Sofia's charcoal grill at the back of the store.

There's a couple of bouzouki players seated beneath the wine barrels, already tucking in. Young fishermen wear clean white shirts.

"There'll be dancing later," Charmian says and her eyes shine. "Watch Panayiotis, he has the grace of Nijinsky when he's hit the grog," she adds, pointing out one of the fishermen, and she waves to Ntoylis Skordaras who sits in the window with an accordion folded at his feet. It's a public holiday tomorrow and the local women wait indoors as usual. Only the men of the village will have hangovers by morning.

We're as hungry as toddlers after a good long nap. We eat squid and octopus now like we grew up on it, pick fish from bones, use bread to wipe our plates clean.

Kyria Anastasia from the bakery hurries by with her twin girls. Charmian jumps up, urges me to follow. The girls stare at my salty bare legs. Kyria Anastasia chatters in Greek as she shows Charmian bunches of flowering herbs and branches that they've gathered. One of the girls shyly hands Charmian some blue mountain flowers, the other some stalks of pale green oats.

"You should get on the right side of Kyria Anastasia," Charmian says as we head back to the tables. "I've told her you're my goddaughter. It's a blessing if you can get them to pop your dinner in the bakery oven. A bit of meat, even a stringy old hen, and a few vegetables can be made splendid if it gets the slow-cook, a bit of seasoning, a slosh of wine. Just get it there any morning with your name on the tin and ask nicely." The lump in my throat is almost unbearable. "It's the best way, simple and tasty," she says and I have to swallow hard before thanking her.

George pulls out a chair. She arranges the flowers in the water jug, but looks so sad while she's doing it she might be tending a grave.

"These are to celebrate the victory of the summer against winter," she says. "Tonight's the night the women and girls will be at home making wreaths because it's May Day tomorrow when everyone celebrates the blooming of nature and the birth of summer."

"Meanwhile all the blokes are out in the taverns getting a bootful," George says as he pours the wine. "But these are pre-Christian traditions and there's a day off for the workers." He raises his glass, "I'm all for workers, so here's to them," and downs it in one gulp.

"Maios is the goddess of fertility," Charmian says, arranging the green stems among the spiky blue flowers.

George refills his glass and raises it once more. "And with Maios we celebrate the victory of life over death," he says.

Charmian sloshes wine to her own glass, "Yes, I'll drink to that," and clinks it to his. "And to you, George." She pauses a moment with her glass in the air, and their eyes lock. "To better times ahead." When she turns away her eyes are bright with tears. "This winter we didn't know that he would make it, so I'm all for giving thanks," she says and lays a hand across his. He draws her face to his shoulder and rests his cheek on the top of her head.

Jimmy and the others have pulled their chairs up to Göran's table and I can hear snorts of laughter. "*Skål*," "*Yamas*," "Cheers."

I'm transfixed by Charmian and George, the way her head fits his shoulder, the side of his face her head. I imagine them asleep like this, brain to brain, heart to heart, two souls molded as one in warm clay.

I must've been staring because Charmian returns to our conversation with a blink and a nervous laugh, tells me of the young island girls who will rise before the sun and walk to the wells with their flowers.

"It's a slightly different ceremony in other parts of Greece but here they'll fill the flower vases with the 'water of silence' from the sweet wells and return to their homes without uttering a word," she says.

For reasons I can't fathom, Jimmy and Bobby are now doing handstands on the flagstones while the others clap and call out. "Someone should fill *their* vases with the water of silence," I say. Jimmy's walking on his hands, his body bent like a scorpion coming in for the sting, and they cheer him ever closer to the harbor's edge.

George grimaces. "That poet of yours should join the bloody circus."

Charmian sighs, continues. "Later, they'll wash using the same water and make a wreath from the flowers which they'll keep on the door until Midsummer's Day. It's one of the few remaining festivals that isn't associated with the orthodoxy," she says.

"Gosh, that's lovely . . ." I picture myself as a silent somnambulist, a flowing white gown, my arms laden with virginal blooms. "Maybe I should climb to the wells before dawn," I say, "I like that idea," and Charmian gives me a fond smile that seems to say, "That's my girl," and George calls for more wine.

Charmian is talking about Kalymnos again, with the wistful air of one recalling another lifetime, though it's only been five years since they were there. She speaks softly, dreamily, of villagers climbing through the mist to the peak of the island. Like silent pilgrims they ascend and with their vessels of water they wait for the sun. "Can you imagine, Erica? Shepherds, sponge divers, fishermen all ranged together at the top of the mountain with their fistfuls of asphodel held aloft, all worshipping Apollo . . ."

The lights flicker on and off three times along the port. Fifteen minutes until the generators are cut. Women call for their children from side streets, a flurry of men trundle heaped wooden carts along the waterfront, fish boxes are hurriedly stacked at the mole for the night boats. There's only the faintest sliver of a moon in the west and the art students take off for the Tombazi Mansion before the island is plunged into darkness.

George gazes at her, "Oh darling, yes. It was lovely. If only my lungs weren't bloody buggered I'd climb Eros with you tonight," and again Charmian looks like she might cry.

We move inside for the light and crowd around six tables facing the players in the back room.

Charmian is still in her dream. "And once Apollo has risen from the sea, it's the silent descent and your house blessed for a year by the flowers you bring back from the mountain for a wreath . . . oh, how alive our ancestors were, and even the first few years here we all kept it up." She looks downcast once more, pulls a few strands of hair across her face. "We used to climb Mount Eros, a great gang of us. Now, even my children have given up joining in."

The lamps are lit with small blue flames and one of the bouzouki players starts to strum. I grab my opportunity. "I'll come with you," I say, though the idea of such a long climb is horrific. "Please say yes, I'd really love to."

"Goodness, Erica, what a little pagan you are," Charmian says.

"What a top idea," says George, rubbing his hands.

"I suppose I do have much to thank the gods for, and it's always nice to have company . . ." Charmian looks at George with laughing eyes. "Oh, why not?" she says, making butterflies whirl in my stomach.

I drink more wine. The air is thick with smoke and the smell of aniseed and garlic and cooking fish. Some of us join in as village men rap their knuckles in time to the bouzoukis, the night waiter runs back and forth and Andonis is up and down the ladder refilling jugs from the barrels. Jimmy dances the *tsambikas* with the fishermen; at each end of the line a white handkerchief flutters. As the music grows faster he attempts to keep pace with their nimble feet and the look of concentration on his face makes me scream with laughter.

Edie and Janey haul Bobby to the floor and Charmian calls out, "Hey, any of you lazy toads fancy a hike up Mount Eros tonight?"

"You've got to be kidding. It's miles," Bobby says.

Janey pulls a face at the others. "I've got a splinter in my heel that won't come out."

"Oh, that's a pity," Charmian says with a sudden wicked flare. "Our Canadian friend will be so disappointed."

It's four in the morning; the night has turned moonless. We meet at the wells with our duffels and flasks. Leonard brings bread, some wine in straw caskets. There's music from goat bells above the dark houses. Charmian has a tartan rug thrown over one shoulder. She and Leonard both wear proper walking boots.

Janey appears to have forgotten all about her splinter as she and Edie dance between the mulberry trees. They wear matching white turtlenecks with black scarves wound around faces as innocent as nuns. Jimmy sits on a low wall peeling an orange he's taken from a tree in the square.

"Well done, you lot. I'm glad you've got blankets. It can get chilly in the early hours at the summit," Charmian says.

Leonard pulls up the collar of his jacket and shivers. Smiling, she shows him the spare rug in her knapsack. Leonard winds the well handle and she bends to fill two battered tin canteens with water from the bucket, takes my flask and fills it too, still talking to him over her shoulder.

"I don't suppose your digs has much of anything. I'm sorry it's rather more basic than Kyria Pepika led me to believe," she says, and when she stands I see her face tilt towards him, as it might for a kiss.

His grin strikes me as lupine. His charisma relentless. "You know, I find the simple life voluptuous," he says. "I like a good table and a good chair—"

"And a good bed, obviously," Janey butts in.

Charmian shoots her a look and carries on. "I'm sure I can sort you out a few bits and pieces and you should be able to work on that little balcony when it gets really hot later on," she says and there's a great collective sigh at the thought of days and months that would grow even longer and sunnier and Jimmy pops a sweet segment of orange into my mouth.

The conversation turns to work. Charmian and Leonard agree that the morning is best, though Charmian complains that George's book remains a painful extraction at any time of day or night. "Really, if we didn't need the cash, I'm not sure I'd be making him go on with it," she says. "It feels sadistic to force him to revisit the horrors of famine." Leonard sympathizes, says he's disappointed that George hasn't joined us.

Charmian fiddles with the fringe of the tartan blanket. "That's good of you, considering the last time you saw him we were having that awful brawl." She lowers her eyes and pulls the blanket in front of her mouth, speaks through it. "I'm afraid our marital spats have got quite out of hand. I do especially apologize for the bloody rotten things he said to you."

Leonard chuckles, touches her hair. "It is bewildering to me, quite seriously, the relationship between a man and a woman. It's such a bitch. I mean, nobody can figure it out right. We all have trouble on that one." He pushes the blanket aside and she smiles at him in a way that could be grateful or it could be coquettish, it's hard to tell. The island is silent but for the braying of a distant donkey and those few goat bells; the black sky is spattered with stars.

"This is the water we shall offer to our great god Apollo as he rises from the sea," Charmian says, tearing herself from his gaze and lifting her flask in veneration to the impossibly distant jagged black lines of Mount Eros. "And if we're climbing all that way we must take our rites seriously," she adds. "So, try not to spill it. We don't want the gods to think us stingy."

Leonard stoops to fill his tin pot, stands and makes some sort of incantation—in Hebrew, I think—before inserting the cork stopper. We are solemn, Leonard a bit baggy and stooping beside Charmian who stands tall, her wide leather belt and the tartan rug giving her the air of a Scottish queen.

There's a shout. Her face lights up. But when she turns, around the corner comes a wheezing Patrick Greer. "Oh, bloody hell. Dreary," she says, beneath her breath. "Last thing we need is a Greer-shaped black cloud to obscure the sun."

We wait while panting Patrick draws his water. Jimmy and Leonard lean against a wall smoking and talking about the poetry scene in London. "Whenever I hear that a guy writes poetry I feel close to him. You know, I understand the folly," Leonard says, and though I've heard him use those exact words before, it gives me pleasure to hear Jimmy purr.

Patrick stands so close to Charmian he might be trying to breathe her in. A button hangs from a thread of his jacket, its tweed giving off a scent of old bonfires and disappointment. "George told me you'd be here. I reckon he didn't want you clambering about with only the charming Canadian for company," he says, his voice even more brandied than usual. "But now I see you've already gathered extra disciples of your own."

Charmian tries to ignore his innuendo and checks again that we each have our offering of water, reminds us not to drink it on the way up the mountain. Edie and Janey don't have torches of their own so they skip ahead with Jimmy and Leonard who both have new batteries in theirs while I wait with Charmian and the inconvenient Patrick.

"I'm surprised Jean-Claude Maurice isn't tearing up here in hot pursuit," Patrick says. "I mean," and he gazes pointedly from Charmian to me, "with one notable exception he relishes his *filet* pleasantly *mignon*."

Charmian springs away from him. "Really, that's too spiteful." Patrick is rambling. He sounds neither sober nor sorry.

"Oh Jesus, has Jean-Claude got an inkling of the nasty surprise George has got coming for him in that despicable book of his?" he says and she gives him an exasperated shove.

"Patrick, if you don't mind, I am not in the mood to discuss this." She storms up the winding steps, pulling me behind her.

The path narrows. I keep my grasp on her hand. "What does he mean by George's despicable book?" I say and she calls a halt.

She shines her torch from face to face. "Shhhh, all of you," she says. "Remember, if we are to do this properly, this is a silent pilgrimage."

I stomp as I climb, become careless with my feet. The path zigzags unrelentingly past tumbledown cottages and upwards towards dense-shadowed pine. The only sound is our footfalls on the shale and our breathing, the only light our torches. I hadn't for a moment taken on board the silent nature of Charmian's ceremony. I see again a flicker of laughter passing between her and George.

Charmian leads the way, the silence dark between us. She's always ahead of me, I'm always in pursuit. I know she's keeping secrets from me, I see them jumping behind her eyes whenever I get close. Why won't she tell me what she knows? I've told her I'll only think worse things of my mother than she can possibly reveal. I've told her the mystery of it all is what's killing. And this hill is just getting steeper, there are insects that rise up in the halos of our torches and Edie shrieks at the scaly tail of something that skitters.

And no wonder George was so keen, and the way she gets all flirtatious around Leonard I can't say I blame old George for his jealousy. And what is it about that one that's making everyone go weak at the knees anyway? Leonard's not even tall, but Charmian's like a kitten and it seems every woman, every girl, even surly Kyria Soula at the fish stall in the market, has fallen under his spell.

I am caught in the beam of Charmian's torch. She lifts the tartan blanket, gestures for me to come inside and we walk for a while arm in arm through the velvet night and my bitter thoughts become swamped with the scent of juniper and pine and blanket and longing.

There was a time when we were lost in the woods. I have just the briefest vision of our mother, an ash-white panic on her face as we stand in a clearing. The foliage is thick and the earth beneath our feet is gnarly with roots, the day darkening and scented with danger. It's just the three of us, Bobby and me ready to protect her with our stick guns, and Mum's face is very stark above the fox fur of her collar. I guess it was one of the times when our father was in hospital, there were some woods in the grounds, but I don't know what had happened to make her so frightened, only a sense that something hung on the brink. When we found the path it led to an unknown cobbled street with warm lamplight and we stopped at a tea shop and I started crying and hid in the folds of Mum's coat because I'd sensed that my twig of a gun wouldn't be enough to save us and her hand shook as she poured the tea from the pot.

Charmian pushes me ahead as we start to climb the steeper rock, feeling our way beneath low branches as pine turns to scrub and the scree becomes treacherous with loose footings. We stop to rest and, wetting our mouths, gaze across the starlit gulf.

I'm missing Bobby, though even in the dark I can tell that Edie couldn't care less that he's chosen not to join us. I can see her smile as Leonard so gallantly lends her a hand. Now he's waiting while she rewinds and reties her dramatic black scarf. Edie always seems to dress as though for a part; I'm surprised she hasn't gone the full wimple. I just don't have a gift for it. I've had to put a twist in my belt to stop my trousers falling down. My puppy fat has dropped away, and when I lie flat I'm surprised at the triangular bones at the peaks of my hips and the hard round balls of muscle at my calves. I've become slim enough for Mum's clothes, a thought that brings with it an unpleasant memory of my father, in what feels like another lifetime, and still I flinch. He dismisses my figure with a glance as we pack her fine things for the poor box.

I regret letting go of the rose silk slip. For as long as I can remember I've an image of her wearing it, or at least one very like it, with a frill of darker lace along the straps and where it plunges at the front. She's sitting at her dressing table pressing loose powder along her collarbones and between her breasts with one of those amazingly pink and fluffy powder puffs that bring to mind boudoirs and courtesans. She hasn't noticed me come into the room. The talc glitters in the soft beam of her dressing-table lamp. She sees me in the mirror and swivels in her seat, her mouth a lipsticked "O." Some of the powder has dusted the dark lace, the straps hang in loops over her shoulders. She swoops down and wraps her arms around me, covers my eyes with her hands, sweeps me from her room. At the door she gathers me into her arms and carries me across the hall to my bed, soothing me for a bad dream. I fall asleep, snug as a nut in the sweet-scented folds of her body.

Whenever the path is wide enough Charmian lets me under her blanket. But now we are leaving the scrublands behind us and in some places the path has become tricky. We stop at a plateau, squat on our haunches. Across the familiar gulf the charcoal burners cluster like glowworms. There is nothing but this rock between the stars and the tide and it's in this bath of silence that the picture starts to develop. Mum is at her dressing table, the straps of her petticoat fallen. I smell her perfume, stumble towards her warm skin. For the first time I see him, the man in the room. I make a run for her. He spots me before she does and it's his panic she catches in the mirror. The powder puff flies from her hand. It's the last thing I see before she covers my eyes.

The stars are fading as we reach the peak. Somewhere below us a dog barks. The monastery at Profitis Elias glows sugar-white beyond the rocky silhouettes of land that falls away in ripples and humps and herb-filled ravines. We are as close to the heavens as anyone tonight. There's a small iron bell mounted on rock which we long to ring though daren't before Apollo has made his grand entrance.

My hair is damp to the touch; a fine skein of mist is caught in the nap of the blanket that Jimmy and I share. Charmian has found us a fold of rocks that is carpeted by plants with soft downy leaves and clusters of tiny white and baby-pink flowers. "Dolls' flowers," she calls them. We're in a row facing east, all except Leonard who stands, stretches his arms, finds a rocky perch and stares out alone. Bands of aubergine and plum seep from the horizon, herald the first streaks of amber fire. We've gathered flowers for our benedictions. Charmian brought a knife for the asphodels and, as well as all the ones I don't know the names for, there are poppies and irises and tiny snake's-head fritillaries. We stand along the ridge with our water and flowers until the great ball of the sun emblazons the sea by unfurling its bolt of orange satin.

The cocks are crowing, there's birdsong, more barking dogs. We follow Charmian's lead and splash our faces with well water. Leonard pours his tin jug over his head and, grinning, shakes the drops from his hair like a dog. Edie and Janey sit cross-legged weaving flowers into their hair and Jimmy is limbering up to the morning, leaping from boulder to boulder, his arms gracefully handling an invisible tightrope walker's pole.

Leonard squats on his haunches breaking the bread. We dunk it in sweet Lipsian wine as the island gently steams in the first rays of the sun and Charmian is first to free us from silence by ringing the iron bell.

NINE

Marianne has joined us above the cave at Spilia. Her folded arms rest on modestly arranged knees so that as much of her pale slim body is obscured from prying eyes as possible. Her tan is yet to catch up with her return to Hydra, though the tip of her nose and the apples of her cheeks have already turned pink. She perches neat as a little white bird, from her pearly-painted toenails to her golden hair, which is pinned into a roll at her nape. It's the first time I've had an opportunity to study her and she possesses a curious stillness. She's chosen one of the concrete steps just below Charmian, who holds sway from her usual stony cradle. Charmian looks broad and brown and muscular beside her, and rather shabby. Her once-black swimsuit gapes unflatteringly where the elastic has gone. Her face is animated while she talks but the sploshing of waves against the rocks makes it hard to catch what she's saying. The gist seems to be that Marianne should worry less about Axel and concentrate on simply enjoying her baby. Marianne wears a small smile and listens with her cheek pressed to her shoulder. Her bikini has a halter tie and is blue with white dots which makes me instantly wish for one just like it.

The summer invasion is not yet in full swing so we all lay claim to our favorite sprawling spots on the sunbaked rocks. Ours is a flat platform between two boulders that's been filled with concrete and I think poor Marianne can't help but feel our curious eyes. A broad stripe of light catches the carefully arranged angles of her body, zigzags the origami folds of her limbs. She has the smile of a sphinx and is so strikingly pretty I can't really feel too cross that Jimmy's put down his book and rolled onto his front to study her.

Neither do I think I'm imagining how Göran and Albin and Ivar have started behaving since Marianne's been here. There isn't a moment one of them isn't striding to the edge of the cliff and performing various daring and athletic entries into the sea. Now Göran's crouching down beside her, dripping onto the rocks. He's reminding her that last summer she made him hot cocoa every night. He's been dreaming of it ever since he got back here. You might think there was something between them, the way she's blushing and laughing, but then we're all crowding around at the head of the cave as Jimmy balances with his toes curled over the lip. Jimmy's beauty almost hurts my eyes as he spins and springs high to the sky with cruciate arms and into a backwards arc that seems to hover at its apex before entering the water with barely a splash.

There's a squeal. Charmian is pulling Marianne behind her, "Come, make the most of it while Axel's got the baby," and they race past and leap and without letting go of each other bomb the water around Jimmy with a wild whoop. After that we're all diving and pushing each other back in, treading water, bobbing and chatting in a ring.

Charmian seems almost dangerous with energy; she's always much livelier when George and the children aren't around. In the glitter of the ocean something wild fights to be free. "There's at least an hour until sundown—who wants a race to Avlaki and back?" Charmian is built to win. Her long legs and broad shoulders provide a powerful crawl that even Bobby can't match. Marianne and I can only wave them off.

Marianne stretches out beside me to dry. She has a scar like a small pink centipede running along her bikini line, otherwise she is perfect and smooth as an empty page. Her belly is so flat it is hard to believe it recently contained a baby and she looks at me a little startled when I tell her.

"*Pfft*, in Norway the women are not encouraged to take bed rest. Momo, my grandmother, was rigorous about staying fit. Besides, on an island of steps, there's no other way; if you didn't stay strong you'd starve to death." Her accent is charming and there's something compelling and breathy in her voice that suggests secrets and confessions. We cup our hands across our eyes to check on the progress of the swimmers. Charmian's nothing but a dot, the others ranged like splashy goslings in her wake. "Charm's a strong woman," Marianne says.

She turns onto her front, propping her elbows. She seems to be avoiding eye contact. I agree, tell her I think Charmian is amazing.

"Axel's about the only man on Hydra who can swim as fast as her," Marianne says, though I hadn't meant swimming in particular. She has one of those faces that falls naturally to a pleasant smile. Her teeth sparkle; her eyes do too, in a ready-to-be-amused way. I've never seen skin this flawless. She speaks without looking at me: "Charmian says you've been here since Easter. So I guess you've run across my crazy husband?" The mild smile remains fixed and I feel myself flush, though I have nothing to feel guilty about.

She raises her eyes to meet mine. She is squinting, poised for pain.

"I've seen him come down for his mail but I don't think we've been introduced." My heart races as I change the subject. "Do you know anything about this book George has coming out? I'm dying to know what it is. Patrick Greer was hinting that he's written something indiscreet. He said it was 'despicable' and Charmian seems upset by it."

Marianne shakes her head. "Yes, yes. I think this must be the thing he wrote in a great rage last year when he was in Athens with his TB. He wasn't thrilled about Charm's lover and kind of vented it, I guess . . ." She stops and bites her lip.

"How did he find out that she was having an affair . . . ?"

"George was impotent, that's what she told me. Side effects of his drugs. She always tries to be careful but on an island like this one all the birds have to do is chatter all day."

I glance across the bay. The swimmers are out of sight around the headland. "No wonder she's embarrassed. Who was her lover?"

Marianne reaches into her basket for a bottle of orange juice. "Oh, it doesn't matter who. It was a very bad time but really he drove her to it. There was much breaking of china; everyone here thought they'd split up over it," she says, offering me the bottle.

The juice is sweet and warm. I try not to be greedy. She gestures for me to take more. "This is the problem with these highly strung people," she says. "And when we're all bored and thrown together like this it becomes everybody's business. Now, why don't you tell me about your Jimmy? How did you two come to be here?"

I explain about Jimmy dropping out of law school, about my mum and the savings book and the car, and about how I'm sure Charmian knows more about my mysterious mother than she's letting on.

"Sometimes it's best not to poke the sleeping bear," she says and I tell her that my brother would agree. She's easy to talk to, a good listener, and I find myself unloading my worries about Bobby, his moods and barely restrained violence.

"He hasn't been right in the head since we left London," I say, and immediately regret it because it seems disloyal.

Marianne thinks he may be depressed and promises to take me to see Kyria Stefania in the hills above Vlychos, who gathers medicinal herbs for miraculous teas that she says work wonders whenever Axel is blue.

I don't mention that I want to be a writer because she doesn't ask. It's Jimmy she wants to know about so I tell her he's here to see what he can do with his book idea and I boast about the poem he had published in *Ambit*.

"Oh, bad luck that he's a writer," she says with a small laugh.

"What do you mean?" I start to explain that Jimmy does other things, that he paints, that he's one of those annoying people who excel at everything, but she continues:

"Axel says it comes with the job: the woman always ends up in the book. Look at Charmian about to be exposed by whatever it is George has written. And Axel's last novel is about me; in fact he ends up almost murdering 'me' in a jealous rage. Can you imagine having to read stuff like that?"

There is not a trace of outrage while she tells me this; instead a soft glow has settled on her face.

"And it's so explicit that *Aftenposten* refused to review it, so you can guess what sort of things Axel has written. But that hasn't stopped it being popular and now it's being translated into all the other languages and being made into a film. And the teenage actress who plays me will be the first Norwegian to show her breasts on the movie-house screen so Axel's expecting that to cause a scandal when it's released . . ."

She rolls over and gently removes a large black ant from the juice bottle and sits up. "The director thought I should test for the part but Axel wouldn't hear of it." She pulls a sad-funny face as she crosses her arms over her chest. "Axel says the girl who plays me in the film has much bigger ones than me."

She sees my eyes settle on her scar and prods it with her finger. "This was a gift of our long journey from Oslo. My appendix almost burst. We were on a little dirt road out of Delphi, bump, bump, bump, my God, the pain, but somehow, in the middle of nowhere, Axel manifested two angels. He had a vision, did a detour and *boom*, there in his headlights, all in white, two sisters from a medical center. Axel thinks the surgeon was most likely a horse butcher, he fainted when he cut me, but *pfft*, here I am. Quite honestly, I'm surprised Axel hasn't made himself known to you, Erica. Sexy dark-haired girls with puppy-dog eyes have always been his thing."

This last bit gives me quite a jolt. The American painter in the red shorts certainly fits the bill and it makes me giddy to think Marianne's description might apply to me also. I widen my puppy-dog eyes at her and we both laugh to ease the tension and she asks me to excuse her suspicious mind.

"I'm really not his type, you see. And not clever enough either. One year he drove me so crazy with one of his brainbox brunettes that I went to Athens and had my hair dyed black. And now I will tease him forever because that was when he asked me to marry

him." She touches the wedding ring on her finger, as though checking it's really there, twists it around.

"I hope now we have our little baby I can be enough for him,"
she says and my heart wrenches when she tells me that she was
so sad when Axel left Norway that she was unable to make milk
for the baby. "He had to get out for tax reasons," she attempts to
excuse him. But she knows what he's like and everyone's been a bit
awkward around her since she got back to the island. "Axel's pretty
way out," she tells me with an exasperated sigh.

While she's talking I'm convinced my pulse is racing but keep
my face as immobile as I can manage. "I know how it is," I say. "I
see Jimmy looking at other girls all the time."

She snorts and dismisses me with one of her *pfft*s.

"We're getting married," I tell her, and she shakes her head at
me, makes her eyes merry.

"You're children. You should have fun in the playground while
you're young."

We both stare out to sea for a while and I think about this,
about how sure I am that for as long as I live the only man I'll ever
want is Jimmy Jones. Knowing this makes me sad for my mother
and for Charmian having an affair and I wonder how it will be
when everyone gets to read George's bitter account of it, and if out
of decency I'll be able to resist. Then I look at Marianne sitting
beside me and hope with all my heart that Patricia will soon leave
the island.

We smile at each other and Marianne stands and pulls on a
bright orange dress. It is made from some sort of floaty material
and she can see I'm admiring it. "Silk. Axel bought it for me in
Rome," she says, fastening a row of tiny buttons. "We were young
and in love, on our way here in his little Beetle motorcar. I think

I must look good for him now I'm back with our baby, not all
gameldags and *mamsen*."

The sky is mother-of-pearl. She reaches to refasten a couple of
pins in her glinting hair; the sun behind her turns the orange dress
diaphanous, and I think Axel must need his head examined.

"Tell me, what are they wearing in London. Is it all culottes like
in the magazines?"

It feels like an age since I left. The buttoned-up wool coats,
court shoes, girdles and splashed stockings of wet, grey pavements
seem a lifetime away. "Edie's better at knowing about fashion than
me," I say. "None of my clothes even fit me anymore. I was much
fatter when I left London."

"Get Charmian to take you to meet Archonda, she's a good
seamstress," Marianne advises and, rolling her towel, flatters me
by saying how good it's been talking. She's in a hurry now to get
the baby's milk, tells me she's worried that if he cries Axel won't
be able to work.

"Axel Joachim can nearly sit up all by himself, you know, a
good strong boy just like his papa. Axel thinks he looks like a
Buddha. He calls him 'the little man.'"

She scoops her few bits and pieces into her basket and I realize
that I've learned much about Axel but very little of Marianne herself.

"Tell Charmian I'll come with the baby as soon as I can. Or
maybe one night you will be my babysitter?"

I am alone now. I roll down my swimsuit and spread myself on
the warm ledge, waiting for the others to return from their swim.
The sun sinks low over Dokos island, turning it black as a sleeping
whale. There's the simple thud of the gri-gri boats and behind my
eyelids everything swims as orange as Marianne's dress. Jimmy
spins like a gold coin against the sky and falls to the water, scattering sun-dazzles as he surfaces, and I'm thinking, what does he see

in me? I have no idea who I am. I seem to have hatched while no one was looking. And just for this moment, I am veiled in a golden glow of loveliness bestowed by a Scandinavian goddess who considers me a love rival.

I feel a great surge of affection the following morning when Marianne comes clacking down the hill in her wooden-soled sandals.

Jimmy and I are sitting outside Katsikas with the usual crowd awaiting fortune's blessing. Bales of flattened sponges are being unloaded from wooden carts at the dock, the men sweating in the heat of the noonday sun. Some fishermen are stretching their nets at the water's edge, the usual cats hanging around as we pick over morsels of octopus that Sofia brings to the table from the grill. I watch Marianne as she clops up the steps to the bakery, a large basket in the crook of her arm.

George is drinking brandy. He calls to one of the fishermen and raises his glass in greeting. The fisherman stands from darning his net and George offers him a drink. Panayiotis declines but shakes all the men's hands when George introduces him. I remember that Panayiotis is the dancer. Like Nijinsky in his cups, Charmian once said. The tautness of the body beneath the shirt is at odds with his blackened teeth and the lines on his face. When he smiles the fisherman's brown face creases into a child's drawing of the sun. He's talking enthusiastically in Greek and George nods to show he understands. "*Tha Thume*, we'll see," he says as Panayiotis wanders back to his nets and Charmian reaches across and covers George's hand with her own. He looks sulky. "The next few nights he reckons their lamps will suck up the fish like magnets," he says. "Ah bloody hell, pass me a smoke."

"Time was George used to go out with the night boats," Charmian explains as he taps a cigarette from the packet.

"The sea at night is very cold on the chest," George says, cigarette wagging. "Doctor Spoilsport in Athens advises against it."

"Do you think he'd take me? It's kind of what I'm thinking about in my work," Jimmy asks, while as if to illustrate old Spoilsport's point George succumbs to a bout of coughing.

"You know," Jimmy says. "What lurks beneath the wine-dark sea . . ."

Charmian flicks him an indulgent smile. "I think they leave the more mythical creatures to the deep, but you'd see plenty of squid and octopus."

George is putting away his handkerchief. He swallows his brandy with a grimace, draws again on the cigarette and growls at Jimmy.

"There's a good moon at the moment, if you fancy it. It might even make a man of you. Though a little squab like you might need to ready your guts for the sight of a man biting out an octopus's eye."

I find I can no longer chew the chunk in my mouth.

"They all do it, you know, but give me that over the Turks who turn the poor thing inside out before bludgeoning it to death."

Jimmy turns to me as I spit into my hand, his enthusiasm undampened. "You want to come fishing if they say yes?"

Charmian shakes her head. "Dear Erica and I will never know what it's like beneath the moon in a little fishing boat." She isn't looking her best. There are dark shadows beneath her eyes which, lacking in shine, are the dull green of bladderwrack. She lights a second cigarette from the one she's about to stub out, takes a drag.

"I'm afraid these Greek fishermen are far too superstitious to tolerate a woman's participation; I think they'd rather sink their boats than allow someone aboard without the correct, um, tackle."

Jimmy returns from the mole smiling and doing a thumbs-up. "If I understand the sign language, they're planning on dynamiting the fish on Saturday night," he says and George scowls.

The ferry from Athens is approaching. I live in hope of a letter from my father, if simply to let me know he's still alive. I'm not the only one with my fingers crossed under the table. Jimmy is waiting to hear if a couple of poems he's submitted to *Ambit* have met with the editor's approval. Patrick Greer expects a new rejection slip to add to his growing collection.

Göran and Leonard are both owed letters from their publishers. They try not to let the terminally unpublished Patrick overhear as they talk about how they each came to have a poetry collection in print. Leonard holds his *komboloi* dangling at his side. He flicks the amber beads with the dexterity of one born to it as he confesses that he started writing poetry as part of the courting process. He says he thought it was something all men did for women.

"I must have looked extremely absurd because I wrote all my poems to ladies, thinking that was the way to approach them," he says. "Anyway, for some reason or other, I put them all together in a book and I was suddenly taken seriously as a poet, when all I was really was kind of a stud . . ." Göran snorts as Leonard pauses for a beat. "Not a very successful one either, because successful ones don't have to write poems to make girls like them."

Marianne's wooden sandals clack as she crosses the agora. She wears a pleated skirt of faded indigo cotton and a large wheel of bread protrudes from her basket. She waves at us as she enters the store.

"Good. I guess this means Axel's spending some time with his family," Charmian says. "Really, it's too bloody cruel the way he carries on, especially now there's a baby."

Göran agrees, and departs for the post office with Patrick and George, all three convinced that standing there waiting will encourage Giorgios, the sadistic postmaster, to sort the mailbags less slowly. Charmian keeps her voice hushed though there's little chance of Marianne overhearing what she's saying from inside the shop.

Leonard pulls his chair closer as Charmian gossips. "A couple of years ago Axel came back from Norway, having been thoroughly lionized over some book or other, and he sent Marianne away from Hydra to make way for an intoxicating brunette he'd met at his publication party.

"None of us could talk any sense into him, not even George. I tried to make him see that his star was only hanging that high because Marianne had put it there, creating a perfect universe for him to write the damn book without once having to worry about food or water or kerosene, or even carbons or typewriter ribbons. It made no difference to the crazy bastard that Marianne was distraught. He'd sent this new woman the train tickets and all he could do was count the days until her arrival."

Charmian grins and takes another slug of beer, keeps the good bit to herself for a moment. "Actually, it was all rather delicious," she says, smiling, and it's good to see a spark of light return to her eyes. "Axel's new woman cashed in the tickets and was never heard of again. Meanwhile Marianne was getting over it all crewing for nice, handsome Sam Barclay on his pleasure yacht *Stormie Seas*. How could they not fall in love? Axel was stuck here convinced Sam would steal her forever. So, then it was the big gesture, down on bended knee and she, despite all wise counsel to the contrary, accepted. But all Axel cares about is Axel and, brilliant though he may be, he certainly doesn't deserve to have that young woman tending to his every need in the way she does . . ." Charmian downs the remains of her beer in one indignant gulp. Leonard swivels around to face the entrance to the grocery store as she goes on.

"You know, she makes their little house so tremendously pretty. She finds these bits of lace and embroidery in the old market at Piraeus. There's always dry wood neatly stacked for the fire, something yummy in the pot, ice for his drinks. And every morning, before he starts work, on his desk there's a little sandwich and a fresh gardenia."

Leonard scrapes back his chair and strides to the open door of the grocery. He sweeps his sixpenny cap from his head as Marianne moves into the light.

"Would you like to join us?" he says. "We're sitting outside."

TEN

I scribble a few words in my notebook. There's still ink in my mother's fountain pen. "I'm in such a good mood. Last night in bed Jimmy told me we should find a way to stay on Hydra forever and we talked about how our children will walk up the hill to the school by the well from a white-painted house all of our own and how Jimmy will learn to sail and have a little boat like Axel's."

Jimmy's very brown and his hair has grown long and curls like a gypsy boy. I look at him and chew the pen more than I write with it. His own notebook is filling up with sea creatures; allegorical tales of love and war, he says. I can't wait for him to read something to me. In his corner of the terrace Bobby breaks a yolk on a saucer and on a sheet of glass he arranges tiny pyramids of pigments and paints in egg tempera. Beasts with twining tentacles and slippery skin look out at the world with the sorrowful eyes of human saints.

It seems everyone but me is in the grip of creative fervor. Edie and

Janey spend hours cloistered upstairs, sewing costumes for Trudy's party, secretive as brides, an old boat awning, once red, now a sun-bleached chalky pink, falling from the ledge between them. Out on the terrace Jimmy decorates our linen sacks in flesh tones which he plans to fix with real fig leaves at the front, while behind he's painted us realistic and rather shapely bare bottoms. Later on he wants us to gather vines and flowers for our headdresses.

Bobby takes a break from the easel. I join him to help sort through some stones that he's been collecting from the beach. They are mostly no bigger than marbles. The greens are like jade and malachite and cheese mold and lichen. There are reds in all shades of the butcher's; sienna and bronze and grey with white marbling and bone-white and pure-black obsidian. The sea here is so clear that you can swim well out of your depth and still all these colors shine up at you like jewels through the water. Out here on the terrace they look dusty and incongruous, heaped up among the flaming geraniums. Bobby empties another pocketful at our feet. I'm willing to do anything to be close to him. This has always been our way.

Bobby and his ideas: it's easy to get drawn in when you have none of your own. For as long as I can remember I've been his willing assistant, my pockets crammed with snail shells collected in the park, painting macaroni or cutting shapes from maga-zines, grinding pigments, boiling glue with zinc to prime his canvases.

We're companionable, children once more. Jimmy's moved across the terrace to the table to play poker with Marty, a six-foot-five Texan with an impressive drawl. We have batteries for the radio, which we keep tuned to the Armed Forces radio station from Athens. It's mainly country and western but this pop song comes on that's been in the charts and we know the words and sing along. At each chorus, Jimmy swings around to sing at me: "There will never be anyone else but you for me. Never ever be, just couldn't be, anyone else but you." And I look at him there in the luminous air with his cards fanned to his chest and believe him.

Texas Marty's another painter and seems to have more or less moved the great bulk of himself into Janey's room, though she doesn't consider him her boyfriend.

Bobby doesn't exactly know what he plans to do with his growing collection of pebbles. "I'm trying to figure it out. They're the fragments of an idea," he says in his preoccupied way. "You know how it is. I'm simply laying out my materials."

This strikes a chord; "That's how I feel," I blurt, and my sadness rushes in like a tide. "I'm like all these pieces and I don't know what the whole is supposed to be . . ." I flick a round black stone towards a pile of its friends.

Bobby, squatting in front of me, stops trawling. A shout goes up from the table as Jimmy lays down a winning hand and throws himself back against the cushions.

"You've got a cool cat in Jimmy, maybe that's enough for you for now," Bobby says, looking up at me. "What do you reckon?" I try to smile as Jimmy holds up a fistful of drachmas and says, "Baby, we're rich!"

"There you go," Bobby says. "Seriously, Erica. You're a kid. You're lucky that Mum left you enough not to worry for a while."

It's hard to make him understand what I mean, only that I feel like something amorphous, a lump of clay that's been taken from dank storage but must find its own shape in the sun. I tell him about Mum always saying that the world was my oyster and panicking because inside an oyster would be a terrible place to be. I knew, particularly while she lay dying, that there were things she wanted for me, choices I could make that were different from her own, but as she never found the words it was hard to give any sort of shape to them.

"I spent all that time while she was in bed. That might have been the time to talk about what I should do with my life, or at least to be honest about her own."

"Well, look at all this." Bobby gestures to Jimmy and beyond to the sky and the sea. "It's not so bad, is it, doll?"

The sun is beating down on the terrace, the unbroken blue of the sky is at odds with my restlessness. Across the ravine I can hear the children in the playground of the Down School chanting their alpha-beta.

I lower my voice because I don't want Jimmy to overhear. He and Marty have started a new game. Double or quits. "You're right, Bobby, maybe it's enough to live somewhere beautiful with someone who is talented. But yesterday, talking to Marianne, and knowing what we do of Axel's behavior, well, I don't know. And now Charmian's to be exposed as an adulteress by George! Did I tell you that?"

Bobby starts to laugh. "Those two women don't make being a muse look at all amusing, do they?" And I give him an exasperated kick.

"Anyway, Charmian's a man-eater, you can see it in her eyes," he says, returning my pretend kick with a pinch.

I rub my arm. Bobby's pinches are always less playful than perhaps he intends. I skitter on, eyes smarting.

"I know you don't like me talking about all this, but it makes me scared that we didn't really know Mum, and sometimes I can't help getting this wobbly feeling, do you know what I mean?"

He grimaces and shakes his head. I start to wish I could find the brakes.

"It's like that half-fledged starling we once brought home from Kensington Gardens. Do you remember?" He sighs, still shaking his head. "You and just about everyone else on this island, you're all flying." I gesture to the easels, the boxes of paints, the jars of brushes. "I don't even write anything much anymore. I've no idea what I should do or if I'll ever be any good, and sometimes I just wish Mum was here . . ."

My eyes start to sting. "And the starling was always going to die because, for all the worms and whatnot we found, and the teat pipette, only its mother could teach it to fly."

Bobby is silent. I watch the shadows return to his face and regret spoiling our day. Eventually he stands up and growls at me, "I don't know why you worry. We're all going up in a giant mushroom cloud anyway," and lumbers inside for a beer.

I head down to Johnny Lulu's for more beer because I happen to know Jimmy drank the last one. It's the least I can do after sniveling like that. Besides, it's my turn to cook and Charmian's friend Creon has promised me a salami. I'm getting good at ferreting out the island's secret stashes of treats, especially since Jimmy's been so inspired and it's so often my turn to sort out a meal.

An old grapevine tumbles over a wall to the street, its leaves young and tender, just begging to be wrapped around meat and spices for dolmades, if only I knew how. Axel and Patricia come towards me, hand in hand, and I take the butcher's alley, find a shadow and flatten myself to the wall. Patricia's hair is wet and drips onto the front of her shirt. A tabby cat winds around my shins and I am glad to have an excuse to duck down and stroke it while keeping them in sight.

Patricia is tiny, with a powerful walk. She gesticulates with her free hand, the wet parts of her shirt cling and she isn't wearing a bra. Axel cleaves so close to her you wouldn't get a fishing line between them. They look lively together, their conversation urgent.

Patricia stops him just short of the alley. He turns and gathers her hair into a wet bunch.

"This is where we part company," she says and he looks at her for what feels to me an excruciatingly long time. He does not relinquish her hair. She is large-eyed as a child.

He winds the rope of hair around his hand as he speaks. "You have no idea how my little wife is torturing me . . ." I strain to hear what he's saying. "Tonight she cooks *fårikål*. Her big black cauldron of mutton and cabbage has been simmering all day on the charcoal. She knows it's my favorite dish. Every Norwegian man is beckoned by the sorcery in that vapor but tonight I shall hold my nose."

He laughs like it's a joke and lets her hair fall. Patricia remains serious, her eyes ever more shimmery. Axel is blond and spry, a man with the looks of a spoiled boy. His collar is neat and his hair springs from a firm side parting, the sort that a nanny would make with a metal comb.

Patricia is gulping back tears. "I'll say it again until you hear me, Axel. You cannot leave your baby son because you've met me. You can't break your life into pieces." The tabby cat is pulling at the salami in my basket but I can't shoo it away without drawing attention to myself.

Axel is shaking his head. "But neither can I stay drowning in her passivity," he says, and he puts a finger to Patricia's lips. "I will leave them knowing I'm the biggest bastard that ever walked the earth. But leave I shall." His voice starts to crack and then he's got her hair again and he starts kissing her without giving a monkey's who sees him do it. The tabby cat lashes out as I retrieve my basket and scamper away, cursing and licking blood from the back of my hand, running to Charmian as fast as a child in need of a plaster to its mother.

ELEVEN

Charmian and George's house stands solid as a judge where five sets of narrow lanes and steps convene at the town well. As usual there's a huddle of women in the cobbled square, a parliament dressed all in black, quenching things other than thirst since the well offers only brackish water. Bougainvillea bursts from a pot in the most passionate of pinks beside the front door. I fly through the salon to the cool green of the kitchen where Zoe is rolling out pastry, Booli beside her, brown and naked but for his pants.

"Is Charmian here?" I'm panting and Zoe eyes me with alarm. She points to the ladder but makes a cutting motion at her throat. Booli sees her do it and chuckles. I ignore her and tear around to the side door, gallop up the stone steps and through to the hall where Max is slumped. He thumps his tail on the rug while I listen for the sound of the typewriter but hear only tiny bells and pattering feet as a string of donkeys goes by in the street. I leave

Max to his longings and climb the narrow wooden steps to the studio.

I run my eyes around the room. No Charmian. Only George slumped at the table with an unlit briar pipe drooping from his mouth. I see the words "FUCK VIRGINIA WOOLF" in bold capitals pinned among the pictures on his corkboard, balls of screwed-up paper at his feet, a world globe grown dusty on the bookcase beside him. George's fingers have plowed furrows through his hair. He turns and for an instant his tired eyes light up within their heavy square frames. He pats his knee as though expecting me to sit on it and barks with laughter.

The door to the terrace is wide open and, thank goodness, there she is. She is silhouetted against the light, one hand to the terrace wall as she blows smoke out to sea. She turns when she hears him, comes flying through the door with a wail like a cat with its fur on end.

"Erica!"

I rock back a step. Her fury could burn me. A black-and-white photograph shakes in her hand.

I look from her to the picture she is thrusting towards us. It's a stark portrait of a small girl, a Chinese waif with round starving eyes beneath a blunt-cut fringe. She's scrap and bone in a filthy torn dress, like a rag doll that's been flung into the dirt.

"What in Christ's name can you possibly want, Erica?" I jumble my words—Axel, Patricia—my voice shaking. Charmian flings the photograph to George's desk.

"This," she says, stabbing her finger at it, "only this." George buries his head in his hands and, before I've had a chance to pull myself together, she picks up a book from the table and cries, "It doesn't help having you standing there gawping at us!" The book comes flying, pages splaying, and lands with a dusty thump at my feet. She's still yelling as I stagger away, things like: "I'm sick of the way you act around him, when he's got so much bloody work to do." And: "Piss off, and don't come back."

———

I'm almost home but here's Bobby lurching down the steps towards me, two full goatskins of water swinging from the wooden yoke. "I gave up waiting for the beer," he says. It's too late to dry my eyes and he gives me a withering look. "Whatever now?" His T-shirt is dark with sweat from carrying the water.

I shoulder the door to the house, too ashamed to tell him what just happened, though Charmian's roaring is fresh in my ears. I move out of his way to let him pass. The waterskins bump like fat carcasses. I reach into my basket to show him the beer. It received a good shaking-up as I scarpered from Charmian's and explodes when I open it. I confess only to my eavesdropping and what I overheard Axel say to Patricia. I tell him my tears are for poor Marianne.

Bobby grabs the beer and cuffs the side of my head. He takes a swig and grunts before heaving a waterskin above his shoulder.

"Why do you always have to get so wound up about something that's none of your business?" The water thumps into the Qupi. I want to kick him but daren't. Instead I escape to my room and bury myself beneath the bedspread.

Out of the dark they come, the stark raving faces, all screaming at me and distorted as melting wax. First Charmian, her eyes burning absinthe. The book flies from her hand and my father comes looming behind her, rage boiling his face—"Get out! Go away and don't come back!"—and then Bobby led by his uncontrollable fists,

Bobby hurling stones while my mother wears a mask of Pan-Cake and lipstick. A pink powder puff explodes on the carpet. Her hands cover my eyes but behind them Charmian jabs at me with her picture and the little Chinese girl lies broken in rags, eyes luminous with hunger.

After a while I'm nothing but a big baby crying for my mother and that's how Jimmy finds me. Jimmy Jones starts working his magic, pulling away the covers and replacing the nightmare faces with his own, his lips soft and warm with promises. He bounces until the bedsprings are singing and I agree to stop being a misery guts and go with him to the hills to gather flowers for our head-dresses for the party tonight.

———

Our costumes are not fit for the eyes of the port so we climb the back steps and alleys and across to the Tombazi Mansion with me trying not to let Charmian throw a shadow over everything. The moon shines like a dented shilling above the mountains and Jimmy looks more godlike than earthly beneath his garlands of vines and tiny pomegranates but still he has to chivvy me all the way. He keeps his fingers laced through mine as we climb. I shush him because I don't want the others to hear of my banishment. Janey and Edie wear duster coats over their outfits, their eyes huge with false lashes. There's not a chance they'd understand why Charmian matters so much to me. I barely understand it myself.

Bobby leads the way, a makeshift Jason with a bare torso and a pale curly fleece slung over one shoulder. Just before we arrive he pulls me to his chest, calls me "doll" and mumbles that he's sorry he snapped. I sniff back my tears, catch the reek of the fleece's original occupant.

"Tell me I'm not an annoying mosquito," I say and he grunts,

"Only sometimes," and pretends to swat me away. I feel a bit better. I don't think we've hugged since we left London.

The pistachio tree in the courtyard of the painting school is hung with paper lanterns, the path to the door lit by jars of candles. The grey-and-white checkerboard of the grand marbled hall is silky smooth beneath our feet. Some sort of birdman and a black-clad nymph with tulle wings fly past jingling with bells. Someone is bashing away at the piano and Edie and Janey scoot off to find Trudy to present her with her birthday gown.

The room is jumping with shadows and thick with incense. Pushed to the wall is a long table where monastery candles drip into the eye sockets of goat skulls, arranged between plates of food and jugs of wine. Incense burns from nose cavities, red roses bloom along each chalky jaw, mounds of jellies in poisonous reds and greens pulsate and glimmer; there are bowls of little fried squid, trays of tiny dolmades, lamb chops, olives stuffed with anchovies, baskets of bread, and in a great heap at the center a pyramid of honey cakes sprinkled with candied rose petals. Bobby dives in, sloshes wine into our beakers. At the piano, the ex-paratrooper Charlie Heck starts up a new tune.

Out of the shadows springs a near-naked Jean-Claude Maurice in a paisley loincloth, his bare chest and legs streaked with gold paint, waving a fennel staff in his hand.

"Look out, it's Dionysus," Jimmy says.

"More like a rutting old stag," Bobby scoffs and I join in their laughter but in truth I can't pull my eyes from Jean-Claude. Is it true that Charmian had an affair with him? Jean-Claude's gold paint highlights his muscles. He holds the fennel staff between his white teeth as he dances.

Marty—or Orion, as he insists we call him tonight—breaks in with a bellow. The colossal Texan holds up a dagger and shield, his belt studded with stars. Carl and Frank in bedsheet togas run in with torches flaming and Charlie strikes up the "Happy Birthday" tune on the piano as the birthday girl makes her entrance.

You would never guess that Trudy's dress has been made from a faded old awning. From a wide sash the skirt sticks out in stiff pink layers; she sports a large rosette at one shoulder and looks ready to present to the Queen.

We sing to her and while Trudy does a twirl in her debutante gown, her handmaidens stand smirking, shamelessly lit by stolen thunder. They are swathed in nothing more substantial than old fishing nets and glitter. Janey has a modesty slip but Edie has evidently decided to do without. The fishing net gathers and falls in loops and folds; I guess it's more revealing than even she intended. A few silver fish made of cigarette foils glint from the tips of Edie's breasts as someone leaps forward to take a picture with a flashgun.

Bobby is scowling. He catches me looking at him and offers me a squid from his plate. It looks like a glistening Medusa beneath its crispy topknot but I'm hungry since the row with Charmian put me off eating earlier. I bite into it and gulp at my wine while Edie starts to move to the music. A gramophone twangs out rock and roll from the windowsill and Trudy's skirts twirl as Jean-Claude spins her across the floor, though I guess most of us aren't looking at Trudy at all but at Edie who is swaying her arms in the perfumed air and setting the little fish dancing.

Like a man in a trance with his eyes trained upon her, Leonard breaks away from a group in the corner. Bobby's hand tightens around his beaker as, with a few deft dance steps, he comes towards her. Leonard's shirt is open a couple more buttons than usual, but other than that he doesn't appear to have dressed up.

The look on Bobby's face I know of old and my heart starts to thump as his knuckles whiten. I whisper to Jimmy, "I think Bobby's about to blow," and I scoot right up to Leonard whose hand is already on Edie's shoulder. He turns and I guess he's good at reading messages in faces.

He glances at Bobby, nods, and shuffles a step towards me. "Take my hand," he says, and his is a good hand to hold.

We jive a bit and dance the Madison and he leads me across the floor in a gentlemanly way and then everyone's doing the twist because it goes like this and the party spills out to the loggia. We rest our drinks on the carved marble balustrades and thank our lucky stars.

The fat moon gloats in the black glass of the harbor. Soon it will be time for Jimmy to run home and change into something more suitable for fishing. I'm only half listening to him. He and Leonard and Göran are discussing love poetry but my attention has wandered. Marianne stands alone, filling her glass from a jug of wine. She downs first one and then a second glass. I can see her hand shaking as she pours a third.

She and Axel arrived late to the party, he in a full-length djellaba, she in her orange dress with some sort of jewel swinging at her forehead. I wanted to stop dancing and talk to her, I thought she might be able to explain why Charmian had lost her temper with me, but then it seemed that almost immediately she and Axel were having a shoving-each-other sort of a row and everyone was giving them a wide berth. Now she couldn't look lonelier, standing at the balustrade looking out across the gulf.

Leonard hasn't noticed Marianne yet. He's too busy needling Jimmy, asking why he's never written me a poem. "Women! Any woman acquaintance is worth a poem. Think about it: you find a girl, think she is exciting, but can't seem to express yourself properly. The easiest way is to write your feelings down on paper."

A sob sounds from across the arcade and he turns. Like a frightened cat, Marianne's found the only dark space and is crouched with her face in her hands among a stack of easels.

Leonard pulls a handkerchief from his pocket and holds it out to her. He's gentle and kind as he coaxes her from the shadows. He removes the glass from her hand and puts it down and remarkably soon has her tears turn to laughter as he dabs at her face. He takes her hand and as they pass I see that the diadem at her forehead is made out of the shell of a crab and sea glass and wire. He puts his jacket across her shoulders. "Come on, Marianne," he says and bids us all good night.

Thanks to Leonard, Jimmy performs trite poetry to me all the way home and back down to the harbor at Kamini. "Erica, I cherish her, I can't help but stare at her . . ." is about the level of it. It makes me happy enough as we goose each other up and down the twisting steps and through the moonlit alleys. He starts singing the song that had been on the radio but he switches the words so it's: "You'll never find anyone else like me for you," and just then I notice an undarned hole in the elbow of his blue Guernsey sweater and it comes to me like a blessing and a curse that this is likely to be true.

All is quiet at the harbor, not even the soul of a fisherman. We wander up the mole to confirm that Panayiotis's fishing boat hasn't set out without him, but there it is, snug with ropes and nets, bobbing sleepily at its moorings.

Jimmy tells me that as soon as he has money he will buy us our own boat and paint it pea green. "Before we set sail I'd better have another go at mending your sweater then," I say as we wander back to the port. "You're going to need it for winters here." And I think of the sea raging all around and imagine the glow from the charcoal pan in our cave of a bedroom.

We can hear music from the speakers inside Lagoudera. Jimmy says we'll stop for a drink. The bar has recently been opened and we've been only once, put off by the smart weekenders from Athens and the people from yachts who don't seem to mind paying four times normal prices. There's something rowdy going on, by the sound of it, but we're distracted by four bodies lined up at the edge of the harbor. From a distance they might be corpses.

There they lie with the curbstones for pillows, Leonard and Marianne and Axel and Patricia, all in a row, close as sardines. It isn't until we hear Leonard's voice that we realize they are stargazing. Leonard is tracing a constellation with his fingertip. "So small between the stars, so large against the sky," he says. Marianne's crab-shell jewel is gone from her forehead, leaving a dent; her knees are bent so the orange dress falls away from her thighs. She lies sandwiched between Leonard and Axel and though we hurry and try not to stare I can tell that Axel's body veers from his wife and like a plant seeking light to Patricia at his other side.

Across the agora there are drinkers outside Katsikas. Panayiotis and the rest of his crew are there and I shrink when I see Charmian at her table with George and Chuck, Gordon, Patrick and Nancy. This lot wear their winters on the island like some sort of merit badge; they have more signals and in-jokes than the Freemasons, can close in and have someone judged to be a pissant or a bludger and blackballed in the wink of an eye.

Charmian is talking, waving her arms around, and the others are laughing away at whatever their Queen is telling them. I watch her stand to leave, which seems to involve Patrick crawling at her feet and fumbling in her skirts. Before I can stop him, Jimmy is waving and she comes hopping towards us with one sandal on her foot, the other in her hand.

She might be attempting a deck in choppy water. "Come on, Jimmy," I hiss. "She's drunk. Take me home."

"Erica, stop!" Charmian drops the sandal, holds out her arms. "I'm so sorry. A nightcap? Let me explain?"

TWELVE

I go marketing with Charmian as though nothing has happened. It's a fresh morning and I'm light as the skittish breeze that sets the port bunting and flags dancing. Charmian fills her basket with globe artichokes, a vegetable I've only ever seen in paintings, and I offer to run ahead to the butcher to secure some reasonably lean shanks of lamb for us to mince for dolmades. She promised last night to teach me how to make them. She's designated today "a family day" and she told me that I should come and join in, that of course I'm welcome any time they're not working, though I must never again enter the room when they are. Her hat is wide-brimmed, straw, with a faded green ribbon the exact same shade as her eyes. Only the dark shadows beneath them betray something of yesterday's binge.

"Shane and Martin sleep the sleep of hibernating bears when they don't have school, so it would be marvelous, if you're sure you haven't got something better to do with your time."

When she smiles at me I realize I no longer notice the missing tooth.

"I've completely lost track of who's coming for dinner tonight so I'll just have to make enough tucker for the masses," she says, showing me the list she's scribbled on a cigarette carton. She pulls her shirt collar up against the sun and, though her shirt is patched and faded, her glamour persists. Even the knotty old shoelace she uses to tie back her hair seems chic.

She could use an extra pair of hands and mine are available. Jimmy has been out all night dynamiting fish with Panayiotis so I won't be seeing much of him anyway. I take one of her baskets.

"Jimmy says I'm a distraction so I've got all the time in the world."

From beneath the brim of her hat Charmian shakes her head at me and tuts but is sidetracked by a woman who calls out to her in a surprisingly plummy British voice. "Crikey," Charmian says, pointing to her belly. "Again, so soon?"

Charmian's friend Angela is a goddess of fertility with long, flowing hair and turquoise jewelry that matches her eyes. She wedges a baby with white-blond curls across her bump while a second curly-haired scamp emerges from her skirts sucking a thumb.

The house the family are in is falling down around their ears but Angela seems remarkably calm. Charmian calls out to Mikhailis, who might know of somewhere else they can stay. I leave them and head for the butcher, thinking only that it would be preferable if my babies inherited Jimmy's strong curls and not my lanky locks. I dream on: Jimmy's project reaching fruition, his paintings on a gallery wall, his name in the newspapers, a fabulous book. I even allow myself an impassioned dedication.

Apostolis the butcher is clearly an artist too. In his window this morning a new tableau: six tiny flayed lambs propped in a line, their limbs arranged like high-kicking dancers on a stage strewn with rosemary and hibiscus flowers. I feel a pang for Apostolis in his bloodstained apron.

"But goodness, he'll turn everyone vegetarian if he keeps this up," Charmian says, returning to my side.

I have long lost my squeamishness. We both agree that Apostolis's artistic expression is more interesting than the harbor views and colorful little boats that have started popping up on polite easels in the streets.

This island has no use for the prissy. I've watched children feeding flowers to pet lambs and a few days later licking their lips and holding out their bread as fat bubbled and dripped from the paschal pet turning on the spit in the street. Twice a week we hear the slaughterhouse screams. We see blood and entrails sluicing into the sea. The mutton and goats arrive with the market boats; sometimes they break free and run among the café tables on their way through the port: "Oh look! This one has the eyes of Sophia Loren!" We no longer take meat for granted.

We walk back to Charmian's weighed down by baskets. Straight away there's a commotion. Booli's crying, Shane's shrieking, clattering feet on the stairs. We struggle in with enough food and wine to feed the entire foreign colony for a week as Shane flies at us, Booli behind her screaming in Greek.

Booli grips Shane's skirt. He stamps a foot, insists, *"Tha ertho kai ego, tha ertho kai ego,"* as Shane tries to unfasten his fingers.

"Booli wants to come and ruin my day," she cries, attempting to make a break for it, whipping a towel from a heap of laundry on her way. "Rita's uncle from Athens is taking us all on his boat around to St. Nicholas's Bay."

"Is that so?" Charmian says, grabbing her arm before she makes her getaway.

Shane glares from beneath her fringe. "I already told you, Mana. You never listen. I might as well talk to myself."

"*Mazí sas! Mazí sas!*" Booli launches himself at his sister but she steps sideways and he crashes headfirst against the well. Charmian is calm as a practiced nurse. She hacks ice from the icebox and wraps it in a cloth. Booli kicks his legs at her while she holds it to his head. Shane stands over them with her hands on her hips and he looks up at her, his eyes trembling with tears until she sighs and holds out her hand and Charmian runs to find his sandals and hats for them both.

"Well, so much for my family day," she says after they've gone. "Still, if it's the Katsikas uncle I'm thinking of, they'll be roasting a goat on the beach so they'll get their tummies full as googs."

She makes me promise to go to St. Nicholas's Bay as soon as anyone with a boat offers me a ride. "The beach is all smooth pebbles, and so marvelous for swimming," she says and sighs as though such things can only be memories for her now.

I follow her outside to pick vine leaves. Beyond the high courtyard walls the island bells ring: mountain bells from churches and goat bells and the jingling of passing donkeys. The light falls tender green through the leaves of vines that are already beaded by clusters of grapes. An ancient lemon tree is splinted but defiantly bountiful with both blossom and fruit. The scent of ripe plums from a pair of trees is attracting wasps. There are tiny tomatoes on straggly vines and aubergines hanging white and surprising as goose eggs, mint and basil running wild, a rosemary bush so vigorous it has split its wine-barrel container, and stone urns and blue-painted concrete which tumble with bright nasturtiums and herbs and geraniums that smell of attar of roses.

Charmian stands on an upturned bucket and motions for me to hold up my skirt to collect the plums. "Time to grab these before the local urchins come scrambling down the walls. We lost them all the first year we had the house. George sulked for a week," she says, taking a bite from one.

We bring in the plums and she slides a long-player from its sleeve, "Brahms, I hope you don't mind," and takes it to the gramophone. "Might as well be uplifted by tremendous beauty as we work."

Brahms's Fourth swells, and I'm swept along, knowing that I will forever be transported by this piece of music and will always think of her when I hear it. She shows me how to lay out the green vine leaves with their veins facing up. We mince a great slab of mutton and fry and chop onions and herbs. The smell makes my stomach rumble as the mixture cools on the sill while from our fingertips we tumble flour with sheep's butter. "Keep it light, keep it cool," Charmian says. "Use water from the ice tray when you're ready to turn it into dough."

I'm useless with the rolling pin.

"Did Connie never show you how?" she says, ungluing my pastry from the table. "Sorry, that was thoughtless." She bites her lip and gestures for me to hold out my hands for a dusting of flour.

I tell her about Mrs. Dapps who always made our pies and dinners.

"Because she preferred cooking to cleaning."

"Oh dear yes, I remember Muriel Dapps . . ." Charmian retrieves the tea towel she keeps draped over her shoulder and wipes her hands. "She was my char too. She had the most appalling rheumatism. I always felt I should clear up before she came . . ." For a moment I think she might hug me but she turns to the window. "It must have been wretchedly dull for you in gloomy old Bayswater. Mrs. Dapps and you stuck there taking care of your dad. I know he was a difficult sod."

I concentrate extra hard on rolling the pastry. "He was in and out of hospital when we were little. His routines had to be kept the same, day in and day out. She was never off duty, always careful not to set him off. Sometimes it was a relief to go back to school. But after she died, I wasn't going away to school anymore and it was me trapped there walking on eggshells."

"I certainly don't blame you for running away."

I nod, not able to meet her eyes. "The only good thing that happened to me after Mum died was Jimmy and it all came to a head with Dad when he tried to stop me seeing him. And then your book came through the post and, well, here we all are."

I can tell she's pleased when I bring her book into it. We talk a while of Jimmy and I don't imagine she winces several times as I tell her our plans. She's quite outspoken on account of my age but says, "It's not my place to tell you what you should do in the big bad world." And her words bring on a wave of longing so intense that for a moment I think I might cry. She shakes me out of it with a few brisk anecdotes; is good with practical advice. Apparently families like Angela and David's can live on Hydra for five hundred a year. "It all sounds very romantic, very audacious, but do try to have something for yourself. Whatever you want to do, try to get it bloody well done before the babies come along . . ."

I like being taken in hand and I enjoy the flush that flattery brings to her. "But, Charmian, you seem to manage it. Having books published, and children and George and all of this." We talk about the new book she has coming out and she says that goodness she hopes it will be well received because it's the first novel she's written which will have only her own name on the cover.

"When Faber published our collaborative novels no one once asked my opinion about editorial changes or anything like that. I was always too tired to make a fuss"

She lights a cigarette, squints into its smoke. "Did I tell you about

the time we met T. S. Eliot at his office in Russell Square? No?"
I hunger for her stories, even those she's told me before. ". . . So
there he was on his hands and knees, muttering about his Nobel
citation which he swore was somewhere in the papers and manuscripts scattered across the floor." Apparently Eliot liked to write
the dust-jacket copy at Faber. ". . . And there was I with J. Alfred
Prufrock himself, something I had never dared to dream, and do
you know what I was doing? I was worrying about my hair, and
whether I had a speck of soot on my white gloves as I poured the
tea that his secretary brought in. As you might imagine, I was terribly cross with myself afterwards. I don't suppose George was
thinking excessively of his hair pomade or pocket handkerchief as
he talked to our idol."

She thinks that girls of my generation might make a better fist
of fighting the status quo. "Just look at the island women here: it's
the Middle Ages, all cooped up in their houses and servile to their
men. I suppose we should be thankful we're further along than
that."

I think about Mum and the post-office savings she left me. Had
she bought me my freedom by cheating a little bit every week on
her housekeeping? I can almost see the tic beneath her right eye as
Dad checked over her receipts.

"I would still be dependent on Dad if Mum hadn't saved all
that money for me. I'd like to think that being here and all this isn't
squandering it. I've still no idea what she really meant when she
told me to live by my dreams."

Charmian shrugs, hands me a knife and we start on the plums.
Brahms has been replaced by the small hiss of the needle stuck in
a groove.

"When I was your age I dreamt of a silver lamé gown and a white
sports car with red leather upholstery. But I reckon that you're not

as silly as I was. What I can tell you is that Connie was my most encouraging pal when I first mooted throwing everything up in London. I remember she drove me in her little car to Stanfords and she bought me a map of the Greek islands."

I almost leap at her. "The car! You knew about it?"

Charmian flaps her hands at me to be quiet. We can hear people moving about upstairs. "You can't expect me to know what Connie dreamt for you. I remember she was proud of how well you were doing at that posh boarding school. She became rather boastful when you won a prize for something you'd written; maybe there's a clue in that . . . As for the car, it was a nice green convertible that she had for nipping around town. There was nothing mysterious about it to me."

I can't help thinking she's relieved to be interrupted as George staggers in, coughing. A folded letter protrudes from the breast pocket of his shirt. Silently Charmian goes about the routine for his injection while he fidgets, his hand drawn to the pocket.

Martin appears the moment food hits the table. Lunch is the miraculous globe artichokes, their great pulpy leaves dabbed in olive oil and lemon. George doesn't have much of an appetite; he nibbles sesame seeds from the bread, lighting and relighting cigarettes while Martin chats about an octopus at Vlychos that old man Stavros claims can play Nine Men's Morris. Martin plans to borrow a rubber mask and hike over to take a look. Once I reach the choke, he leans over and with surgical precision instructs me in dissecting the heart.

Charmian has not spoken a word to George and he's avoiding her eyes. The silence stretches and trembles like a membrane between them. Martin senses it too and slinks away with a couple of cold chops. Charmian sits drinking her wine as though neither George nor I exist. George never stops fidgeting, rolling small pill shapes from a piece of bread which he lines up on the table, touching the letter, occasionally stealing a sidewards glance at her.

"Who is the girl in the photograph?" I cut in when I can no longer bear it. "I haven't been able to get her face out of my mind. Is she in your book?"

George leans into the broken silence and stares at me. He tears miserably at a fingernail. "I was there when our man took that photograph," he says. "Heartless bastard. Kweilin 1945, thousands fleeing from the Japs straight into famine . . . That little girl was alive while he was focusing but dead when he hit the shutter. He might as well have been holding a Luger in the kid's face. But he was hardened, didn't care. We'd gone through it, mile upon mile of dead and dying rotting by the roadside, and we'd arrived at this place where the troops were foraging on their hands and knees, digging with their teeth through the bare earth for roots. The girl's mother was already being pecked at by the bloody birds . . ."

He rocks back again and throws wine down his throat as though to douse the images his words have conjured. "And now, while the rest of the island siestas, I'll be up in that room tapping away trying to turn a bloody nightmare into a potboiler." Charmian's attention is back in the room. I see her wince when he adds: "But where there's a pot that needs boiling someone has to be bloody doing it."

He helps himself to the contents of my wine glass. "However, it's not that bloody book that's chewing at my guts today, it's my last one." He pulls the letter from his pocket. It might be a death warrant, the way he stares at it. "Notes back from the editor. Last chance to make any changes before they print." He looks at Charmian, and pushes the letter towards her. "They're happy to publish the novel as it is," he says and I can't be certain that he isn't smirking as he scrapes back his chair.

Charmian's cheeks redden. She raises and puts down her knife.

Her voice trembles. "Oh, how I wish Billy Collins had never sent you that five hundred pounds."

She ignores the letter, seizes George's barely touched artichoke and tears away the leaves.

"We'd have sunk without it," George mutters and, pretending to bow to me, stumbles back to work, taking the wine jug and all of the joy of the day with him.

Charmian snatches up the letter, "George is pissed off because he drank too much booze last night," and puts it unread into her pocket. "And he's in a strop because of all the people coming for dinner. He's becoming a very unsociable version of himself." She sweeps crumbs from the table into the cup of her hand. "I keep telling myself it's his illness."

I stand at the sink rinsing plates. "What is the book you were talking about?" I just can't seem to stop poking around in her anguish.

She sighs deeply. "It's a novel called *Closer to the Sun*." Her voice is dull, monotone. "It's a sort of morality tale about rich people on yachts and a bunch of creative bods who arrive on Hydra and the impact they have on the locals."

She's fumbling for a cigarette but I can't let her be. I'm surprised to find myself baiting her. A mosquito after all. "Is it based on something that really happened?"

She lights her cigarette and takes it to the courtyard door. "Oh Erica, why do you have to ask so many questions?" she says and stands smoking and looking out like she's seeking an antidote. Her eyes fall on some jasmine and she buries her face in it, pinches off a sprig and puts it through the buttonhole of her shirt. A bird in a cage on her neighbor's balcony is singing its heart out. Gulls glint in the sky. She's much calmer when she turns back to me.

"Buried within this novel of his is a rather humiliating story based around a version of something that happened here. Something that makes me want to die with regret. The trouble is the publisher has already paid for it and we've no hope of paying him back because every penny of it went on lifesaving treatment in the hospital for George. So there it is. I'll tell you more about it another time, if you insist. But don't you think it's a rather gloomy thing to discuss on this beautiful day?"

I feel guilty for goading her throughout the long silence that follows. I try to make it better by chirping about Axel putting very intimate things about Marianne in his novel. "She seems fine with it, to be honest," I say, partly because I can't imagine myself not being thrilled if Jimmy wrote about me.

At the mention of Marianne, Charmian stubs out her cigarette, and I follow her upstairs to Booli's room, stand in the doorway while she ransacks some baskets for baby clothes. The sight of Booli's old things softens her until she has to use a romper suit to wipe her eyes.

We kneel together to sort through them. "For reasons we don't need to expand on here, I'm dreading an enormous fuss on the island when certain people get their hands on George's novel, and that could be so terribly embarrassing for the kids," she says with the rompers pressed to her cheek. "If we weren't so broke maybe we could spare the time to rewrite it in some way. It's the first time George has put a version of us into something. By which I mean that we're recognizably us but twisted to fit his narrative and that is a tremendous problem for me. And for the children . . ."

I wish I had a way to comfort her. She gets back to the smoothing and folding, gives herself a shake. "He wasn't very well when he wrote it. Tortured, really. But who knows? All that pain and injured manhood on the page. Maybe it's the best thing he's ever written." And she looks up and gives me her saddest smile.

We tie the softly worn baby things into bundles with some ribbons she finds in her workbasket. She fastens a blue bow around a pile of nappies that are so thin they're threadbare in places. I curse myself for being an annoying mosquito, uncertain she really wants me to accompany her to Marianne's.

We have the clothes in two baskets and while we climb Kala Pigadia Charmian talks about her irritation with drifters and I can't help wondering if she's having a dig at me. As though reading my mind she turns and shakes her head.

"I'm talking about all the poste-restante drongos who drop in and move on, people like Charlie who pretends to be an African chief and wears that silly loincloth over his jeans, or that wretched Patricia drifting through Europe, sitting on the curb looking so very appealing with her paints in her lap and causing bloody havoc." The marble slabs are warm beneath our bare feet, worn smooth by the winter rains. "They keep coming," she says. "All with their pocketbooks of names who might be relied on for a meal or a bed in Ibiza, Paris, Venice, Tangier, Corsica or Casablanca. Passed from one to another. Star-rated, can you believe? Charlie wasn't even shame-faced showing me. I was mortified to see that we only merited four bloody stars."

Close to the sweet wells, the foliage becomes richer, the trees big enough to spread shade and share fruit, noisy with birds. The stray cats look less mangy than on other parts of the island. Charmian points out the mayor's walled gardens. The last part of the climb is almost sheer on steps cut straight into the rock. Marianne and Axel's house seems to grow out of the ridge, an eagle's nest carved into the hill from which to look out for pirates. It's hard to imagine how she manages with the baby carriage. Charmian and I are both sweating and out of breath.

Marianne is stirring a pot; the air is fragrant with steam. She seems as delighted by the bundles of clothes as she would be by a Bond Street trousseau. The room is whitewashed; the windows frame the sea. Painted bookcases are orderly with books. Straw mats and knickknacks hang from the walls and the simple furniture and shutters are painted a delicate pale green, the color of new leaves. She's barefoot and pretty in a clean white shirt, the baby at her hip. Charmian holds out her arms, takes him, cradles and croons while Marianne unties her apron and repins her hair.

Charmian lifts the lid of the pot with an appreciative sniff.

"*Fårikål*, Axel's favorite," Marianne says, inviting us to sit at the table, and I wince to remember Axel telling Patricia that he would hold his nose. The tablecloth is edged with lace, at its center a Japanese bowl with floating pink blossom.

The baby gurgles and giggles. Axel Joachim is the chubbiest, sweetest little chap I've ever met, the sort of baby you see in an advert. His eyes are blue and enormous as pansies. His smile could be used to sell anything. Marianne brings us water on a tray with a posy of daisies.

She shows off a mobile that Axel has made from wire and stones. She lays the fat baby on a folded mat beneath it and he goes googly-eyed and kicks his legs around and she lifts his vest to blow raspberries on his tummy and they both explode with giggles. A small white dog is sleeping on a rag cushion beside a wooden rocking crib in which a black cat is curled. Marianne lifts out the cat and begs it not to be jealous.

If I hadn't witnessed what I had with Axel and Patricia, she would have had me fooled with her carefully choreographed happiness. "Baby-bun-cheeks will be content there for a while just cooing at his clever papa's mobile. Will you take a little wine with me? I have a jug right here."

We drink our wine on the terrace where yellow marguerites run crazy between the stones. She has a large ornate rocking chair with a rope that runs through the door of the house and she shows us how clever Axel has tied the other end to the crib.

"I can sit here at night with my glass of wine and look at the stars and just rock, rock, rock our baby to sleep." She is smiling, closing her eyes, as one overcome with ecstasy. Charmian shoots me an anguished look.

We sip our wine. We look down over the harbor, at the colorful boats and the sugar-cube houses spilling up the hills, the windmill at the crest of the cliff, the domes and spires of the many churches, the crosses on the peaks. Marianne scoops up the cat and nuzzles it as though she can't bear not to be cuddling something. She nods towards the house.

"As you can see, Axel's not here. He's once again at the boat-yard. Yet another thing he needs to do for his beloved boat instead of getting on with writing his book."

This time Marianne catches what is passing between Charmian's eyes and mine. "*Pfft*," she says, waving a hand. "That Patricia is leaving the island tomorrow. Going back to the States."

Good riddance! I want to cry but Marianne lowers her eyes and turns to Charmian. "I went to see her at Fidel's place this morning." Her voice is barely more than a whisper. "I don't know why she would choose to live in that stinking tip anyway; everything's falling down, rotting food, Fidel's horrible paintings propped up everywhere you look, and all the island's sickest cats going there to breed. Patricia is covered in fleabites." Marianne lifts a leg as though checking she isn't similarly afflicted. Her tan is uniform and golden, her legs smooth and hairless.

"I didn't see her room; Patricia and Fidel were wild not to let me up there. But I'd come all that way over the rocks with the baby carriage so, anyway . . ." She wrinkles her nose. "The cup she gave me was all caked and cracked around the rim. All the time I was there she did her best not to look at my son. Fidel wouldn't leave us alone, put his dirty finger in the baby's mouth. No matter. I didn't know how brave I'd be face to face so I'd brought a letter and I left it in an envelope on the table. She came running after me, caught up at the windmill. She had my letter, unopened, and when I wouldn't take it back she started to cry. That's when she told me she was leaving. She has an arts scholarship at Chicago to get back for." Marianne buries her face in the cat's fur. Charmian grimaces at me as baby Axel's cries summon his mother indoors with the cat in her arms.

THIRTEEN

The studio dances with shadows as Charmian puts a match to a lamp and leads me to the bookcase. Beside George's dusty globe, a dog-eared paperback lies waiting, tan with black lettering. *The Second Sex* in curly type that makes the S's look like serpents.

"One is not born but is made a woman and it is high time that we break those bonds and learn to soar, to create for ourselves a world of free choices, and though a wide-open vista can be terrifying it is also more thrilling than plodding on along the worn tracks in a man's world." Charmian is lecturing me as she hands me the book but adds with a snort, "Which is, I suppose, all very well if you're de Beauvoir and Sartre and don't have children's feelings to consider."

She's led me up here just for this book. It's vital reading, she says, though I suspect she mostly wanted to get away from George who has started ranting below.

I'm still here, long after the final farewells of the other dinner guests, helping to put a dent in the clearing-up. Shane, Martin and Booli all scarpered to their rooms when the night was still young and not yet slurring, and around two in the morning the others staggered out, with the exception of Jimmy who is still busy baiting George. A brandied disagreement about Kafka escalated to include Dostoevsky, Rilke and Robbe-Grillet. "Pissants!" George was spluttering as Charmian pulled me away.

I recognize the book she's handing me. It's the one she hurled at me before. There's a wobble to her voice as I take it. "If I had an eighteen-year-old daughter I would want her to read this," she says. "Your generation has many more choices than mine. I feel certain that Connie would have wanted her daughter to flourish in a system that doesn't assume that female 'otherness' makes her only of use in service to the real deal that is a bloody man. I'm pretty sure she read it, actually."

The book is dismayingly fat. I'm still waiting to be seduced by Henry Miller within the forbidden green covers of Jimmy's treasured Olympia editions. I'm shamefully only on the first volume and Jimmy is insisting I read all three.

Charmian can sense my resistance and changes tack. "George hates it. He thinks de Beauvoir's a prophet of a change in values that is bogus and can therefore only be destructive. But it seems utopian to me. Shared ideas and history and commitment with the added spice of lovers . . ."

The flame of the lamp dances in her eyes. "Oh dear, too much vino. I don't know why I'm rambling on, and hell it's all very well for Simone and Jean-Paul to let it all hang out and spill the beans with no children left crying."

As though on cue we hear a baby in the street. Someone's banging on the door; the baby's got a good pair of lungs. Charmian snatches up the lamp and we fly down to the hall to find George taking Axel Joachim while Marianne looks up at us, ashen-faced and smeary with mascara. The white blouse she was wearing earlier is now spattered and stained. She speaks in gasping sobs.

"My husband's gone mad. He threw this." She points to her shirt. "It's the dinner I cooked for him."

"Oh Marianne, it can't go on like this," Charmian says, thrusting the lamp at me.

Marianne is shaking. "I told him to leave me alone and be with his American brainbox and that made him go mad." There's blood on her feet. "He found out about the letter I wrote to Patricia and now he's smashing the house up, all the windows, everything. I had to get away. I thought he might hurt the baby. I have to get back before he hurts himself."

Her knees are starting to buckle and Charmian guides her to the couch. George walks back and forth shushing Axel Joachim as his mother struggles to calm down. "It should be simple. A man lives with his wife and together they make a good life for their baby."

Charmian brings a bowl of water with rags and disinfectant, squats at her feet.

"Axel says I think like a farmer," Marianne wails, and fresh tears run down her face as Charmian tweezes splinters of glass from her feet.

Jimmy takes my arm, steers me away. "Time to be going," he says.

As we are released into the night Charmian is persuading Marianne to let her make up the divan and silencing her protests that Axel might kill himself. Jimmy puts his arms around me, holds me tight. I rest my head on his chest as we stand catching our breath, in the dark shadows beneath Charmian's bougainvillea.

Max's barking alerts us; a figure is lurching our way. Jimmy holds me tighter when we see it's Axel and he might be an ogre for how we shrink against the wall as he hammers his fists on the door. George stands above him, the lamp swinging, making a monster of his shadow.

George blocks the way. "Go home, Axel. You've terrorized your wife and child enough already tonight. And for God's sake, man, your hands are bleeding."

Axel lunges, tries to barge past, but George shoulders him so hard he half falls and half stumbles down the stone steps. "Go home, you great galah, and put some disinfectant on your cuts and think about your bloody idiocy while you do it. I hope it bloody stings." Upstairs the baby is awake and crying again.

I met Dinos for the first time that night. Charmian had told me about him while we made the dolmades. In fact it was Saint Constantinos's name day and the dinner was in his honor. Constantinos: Dinos. Handsome, she said. The scion of a sponge-merchant family, he brings a bag of good Aegina clay and takes it to his kiln high up on Episkopi and barely comes down to the port all summer. She says his pots are good and that she likes him very much.

As well as Dinos, who was indeed handsome, Patrick and Nancy, Chuck and Gordon, a playwright called Kenneth, his wife Janis and sleepy child, pregnant Angela and her husband David, who was some sort of aristocrat but looked like a bum, a Californian couple called Demetri and Carolyn, a bumptious New Zealander called Bim who was writing a novel, and Robyn his pallid wife. There was plenty of wine, Jimmy and I made to feel like honorary members of the true foreign colony when we declared that we intended to stay on. "Oh, I don't like that word 'colony,'" Charmian said. "But I don't know what else to call it."

"Ah, when you've lived on Hydra you can't live anywhere else . . ." Kenneth said.

"Yeah. Including Hydra," George and he chorused. George had
left his bad mood upstairs with his typewriter. He was loquacious,
spoke more than anyone.

I find I can write very little about any of it in my notebook. Any
pleasures of the evening have been blotched by Marianne's tears.
The morning comes too soon, poisoned by my hangover. Maybe
it's true, what Charmian says about me so easily accepting the role
of drudge, serving the talents of others. I am Cinderella-ed in soot
from the charcoal range, ragged from lugging stuff up and down
the steps. The lavatory is stinking because no one else has bought the
right chemical, no one but me ever seems to remember to refill the
slosh buckets or deal with the malodorous bin. It's overflowing as
usual. We're almost out of kerosene, the Buta needs changing over.
Jimmy is going out fishing again tonight and needs to sleep in.

I stomp upstairs and, though I know he'll give me hell for it,
throw open the door to Bobby's room with a great rattle and immediately regret it. The shutters are closed but there's no mistaking
Janey and Edie on the bed platform. They are naked, facing each
other even in sleep, entwined. Bobby is alone on a narrow mattress
by the window, his hands folded behind his head, staring at the
ceiling. Canvases are propped along the walls; there's the stench of
unwashed clothes, stale smoke, turpentine. Bobby turns to look at
me from the bare ticking. Says nothing as I back away.

The ice is already sweating at the foot of the steps. I tie our bit
of sacking and rope it into position. The wet hessian is unpleasant
on my back and I haul it up the hill with every cock on the island
crowing, every builder's hammer hammering and the cicadas singing only ugly songs, like they're frying in hot fat.

Walking bent over makes it easier to climb the steps but my
mouth is filling with acid drool. I spin around, willing myself not

to vomit, and look for the cure beyond the jagged orange geometry of roof and wall, but the vastness of the sea's glitter hurts my eyes and the bruise-colored folds of the mainland look like they're made out of lumps of my brother's old plasticine. I think of him looking at me from the mattress, his eyes without light. I reshoulder the ice. The weight of his misery almost makes me buckle.

Of course, Edie and Janey have now joined the ranks of those who must be left to sleep. Beauty sleep, I think, with the tide of bitter water rising once more. On this island of painters, how come not a single person ever asks me to sit for them? Edie and Janey are in constant demand up at the art school, earning a few drachmas, sometimes posing late into the night. Disrobing and lying around comes naturally as breathing to the pair of them. I swallow hard, tell myself I only care that they still do their share of the tasks. The church bells are too loud, discordant, like children banging wooden spoons on saucepans; the ice a clammy cold burden.

There's no sign of Bobby or the girls when I get back. Jimmy has lit the Primus and is waiting for the coffee to boil. He's absently walking up and down in his shorts and yellow T-shirt, biting into an apple and reading Charmian's Simone de Beauvoir book. He puts the book down when he sees me, holds the apple between his strong teeth and unropes me from the ice. He soaks some pieces of sponge and leads me outside to the shadiest part of the terrace. "Poor baby," he says as he lowers me to the mats. He presses the icy water to my hot face, shushes me.

"Bobby's OK," he says. "Give him time. At least there's plenty of that here."

He fetches hot coffee sweetened with NouNou and peels me some oranges. We talk about Marianne; it feels vital that I hear him condemn Axel, and he duly agrees, but says he's read Axel's book about the Sahara and it's quite possible the man is a genius.

"She'll be all right, pretty woman like that," he says, and winks and taps his nose as though he knows something I don't.

All this kindness just makes it worse to think about Bobby upstairs, so miserable alone on that mattress, and no mother to run to. Jimmy takes my head into his lap and strokes the hair from my temples.

Sad thoughts wash over me. I think of the first time I saw Marianne, her white shawl and baby, a radiant Madonna with her dashing husband at the tiller, the red-and-white boat. I replay my visit to her house with Charmian. Marianne on her hands and knees, making the stones and wires of Axel's mobile spin and bob, "Clever papa," the rope that he'd tied between her rocking chair and the cradle, a bowl of radishes that lay waiting, each one carved into a rose. I see her bleeding feet, her ruined blouse, Axel kissing Patricia. For once Jimmy is content to sit still. I open my eyes and look up at him. The sun is filtered through the almond tree and his eyes glint as gold as my mother's eighteen-carat wedding ring. "Tell me you'll never be cruel," I say and he sits there and rakes back my hair until I fall asleep.

I am cured by my sleep beneath the old almond tree and the sweet slices of melon that Jimmy brings when I wake. The songs of the cicadas seem romantic once again. The promise of the afternoon, just the two of us on the beach at Plakes, is restorative, as is aspirin. It's as though the morning has broken anew as we pack our bathing suits and towels into my basket.

The ferry is due in half an hour. Jimmy is expecting a letter from a friend of a friend of a literary agent and if he's lucky a check from his mother. I still live in hope of some word from my father.

"You'll have to write to him, to ask permission to marry me," I say, as we smooch to the radio.

"I'd better find out what sort of a dowry he's offering first."

Jimmy tickles my ear and I push away the thought that Mum's post-office savings won't last forever as Brenda Lee sings of sweet nothin's.

The blazing bougainvillea, the whitewash, the noonday sun. It's too much for our eyes. I've filched Edie's Jackie Kennedy sunglasses; Jimmy looks like Jean-Paul Belmondo in his Wayfarers.

We arrive at Katsikas hand in hand, order sardines. "Good morning, dewy youths," Charmian says with a throaty chuckle and I feel bad that I let Jimmy talk me out of *The Second Sex*. Instead he's given me his collection of Sartre's stories. "He's the better writer." *Intimacy* has a vampish woman on the cover but at least it's pleasingly slim.

She picks up my book and turns to the first story.

Leonard smiles when he sees it.

"I suppose you read it in the original French," Jimmy says, and I see a brief flare in his eyes that might be envy as Leonard inclines his head in affirmation and strikes a match for his cigarette. Though not boastful, Leonard gives off an unmistakable air of a man who has always been there before you. He possesses that old-soul thing of wisdom more ancient than his body and his face. He also has beautiful Lena beside him. She takes the cigarette from his lips, puts it between her own. Yesterday Lena was a painter from Sweden, fresh from the ferry; today they seem acquainted well enough for her to be wearing his amber *komboloi* as a bracelet.

Charmian unsuccessfully stifles a snort as she reads out loud from the Sartre. "A woman doesn't have a right to spoil her life for some impotent," and puts her hand to her mouth as George hoves into view. She closes the covers, regains her composure. "These are terribly good. I remember this title story 'Intimacy' especially. Some of what I was so incoherently saying last night about choices and freedom is debated marvelously well in this story. Do read it, Erica."

"Well, that was some bloody evening," George is saying as he comes from the cigarette shop. Overnight he seems to have gained in stature. He's a good head taller than anyone else and walks like a gunslinger, a cigarette pasted to his underhung lip. Charmian calls to Nikos Katsikas to bring him a drink.

"I don't know what would have happened if you hadn't been there, George," she says. She lowers her voice to include only me and Jimmy, widens her eyes. "We had quite a scene after you left. Axel turned up and wanted to fight George. And once George had seen him off I almost had to tie Marianne down to stop her running after him. I dread to think what that maniac's capable of doing when he's in one of his rages. Patricia's left the island, thank Christ, but to think Marianne could've married Sam Barclay and sailed the world on that splendid boat of his."

Patricia has left the island. That is good news. I look around me, at the tables and their chattering groups, a hundred dramas unfolding. I love this time of day with everyone here, the chink of coffee cups and sudden bursts of laughter, the familiar cats, even the donkeys seem to gossip amid the traffic of working men, trundling carts, the stalls of fish and pyramids of fruit, the women with their baskets. There's lightness, hope, good humor, beneath the noonday sun, a frisky air of anticipation at who or what might drift ashore. There are so many more awnings now than when we first arrived. Dark blue ones, and stripes, and beneath them tables stretching all the way to the ferry dock where any of our wildest dreams might disembark.

Panayiotis has brought his pretty young wife with him to drink cold orangeade and Charmian trots over to ask after her mother's health while Jimmy engages Panayiotis in an excitable conversation about catching a shark which involves more miming than words. Panayiotis's wife has her white headscarf crossed at the chin in the traditional Greek way, but her eyes are as carefully painted as any teenage girl. She laughs behind her hands as Jimmy gets carried away doing his shark impression.

A plump woman in a voluminous blue shirtwaister is being led across the harbor on a sagging donkey with blue reins. She holds a blue parasol at a haughty angle, but her steed lets her down with a dump right in front of us and her donkey-boy has to go back with his shovel. George is struggling not to laugh. "Good to have you back, Katerina," he calls and she waves to him before clapping her hands at the boy to hurry.

"Everything blue in her house, every pot, jug, even the linen, all blue against the evil eye," he says and hacks away coughing and laughing telling us a story. Apparently Marc Chagall had the cheek to fill two pages of her visitors' book. "She was incensed, ripped them out and threw them on the fire, didn't have a clue who he was because she only had eyes for Princess bloody Margaret and assumed the doodling little foreigner was a lackey from the boat Her Royal Highness sailed in on."

All around me people are chattering, as though every trouble has faded and disappeared with the moon. George's sunny good mood is barely dulled by the sight of a near-naked Jean-Claude Maurice. Jean-Claude has sensibly chosen a spot three coffeehouses along. He has his feet on the checkered plastic tablecloth and his gaze flicks quick as a lizard's tongue from Trudy, who wears a crown of yellow marguerites in her red hair, to a German girl blancmanging out of a playsuit towards him from a yacht.

George picks up my Sartre stories, grunts and turns to Leonard. "I take it that popinjay over there has bored you shitless with his pointless bloody tales of hanging around at Les Deux Magots with the author. I try not to let it affect my reading of his texts," he says and Leonard splutters into his coffee. George plays around, maligning Jean-Claude until his own laughter is overtaken by coughing and his handkerchief.

Leonard shoots a glance at Jean-Claude and returns to the book of stories that everyone but me appears to have read.

"The thing about Sartre is that he's never lost his mind. He represents a wonderful Talmudic sense of human possibility, but I know he's never going to say, 'And then the room turned to gold.' He'll say, 'The room turned to shit.'" He leans across to offer a bang to George's back, continues: "But the room sometimes does turn to gold and, unless you mention that, your philosophy is incomplete." He looks at me from beneath his sixpenny cap and when I don't respond gives me an awkward smile and returns to Lena's conversation with Göran, despite it being in Swedish.

Charmian watches George stuff away his handkerchief and pours him a glass of water. George waves it away and lights a cigarette. Sofia brings the sardines and the cats follow every forkful with orphan eyes.

For once George has an appetite and he picks at Jimmy's ambitions to be a writer in much the same way as he takes to the fish on his plate.

Jimmy says, "Let me show you some pages," and his eyes are as hungry as the cats'.

Charmian smiles at him, as one might at a child who charmingly believes in fairies. "So many of the young people who come here to write and paint end up frittering their talent away. That is, if they have any talent to fritter."

Jimmy hardens his jaw. "I have talent," he says. "And I get more work done here than I ever did in London."

"Well, if you're going to wrestle with the muses on their home turf you'd better be good and don't be surprised if you come away with a bloody nose," George says, and a look passes between him and Charmian that speaks of a thousand old bruises.

The stage is emptying as people trail off to the post office or back to their houses or to the rocks, to seek inspiration or love or to swim.

Jimmy and I buy bread, wine and peaches and a pat of goat's cheese. The sun is beating and we detour to the pharmacy for sun cream. Inside Rafalias's the blue glass bottles are ranged on carved wooden cabinets, beneath a Venetian ceiling. A plaster bust of Hippocrates demands silence. We see Marianne and Axel stride past the door in matching blue-striped shirts, the sun in their hair and the little white dog trotting behind. Marianne laughs at something Axel says, and buries her cheek in his shoulder. Axel is carrying a window frame, his hands wrapped in bandages. In several places the pale-green painted wood is broken and splintered, jags of glass wink from old putty. Marianne clutches a wrecked chair beneath her arm. We walk behind them through the lanes to Francisco's workroom. They don't stop talking all the way.

FOURTEEN

The Vespers are ringing. The island grows mellow in the evening sun. Though I usually go barefoot, I'm wearing sandals and, instead of my shorts, the Capris that I've recently had Archonda take in so they fit like a second skin. I've washed and rinsed my hair with well water and my skin is glossy with olive oil. I've given more thought than usual to my clothes. My Aertex shirt I washed and ironed especially and I've helped myself to Edie's shell-pink lipstick. It isn't without shame that the prospect of finally meeting mad Axel Jensen thrills me.

I climb to the top road, up the twisting steps that rise between ever more tumbledown houses, some lots marked only by rubble and boulders clad in vines, occasionally a brave bread oven or a chimney left standing where nature reigns. Crumbling stone walls host fig trees and passion fruit, sudden clear vistas to the sea, wild squashes and capers, a family of kittens. The low sun burnishes every tuft and seed head softest gold and releases the scent of night jasmine. From above, a donkey is playing its violin of a face at me and I clamber up the loose wall to its tether and scratch all the places it tells me are itching.

It's Marianne I'm visiting, not him—at least that's what I keep telling myself. Marianne mentioned a woman who might sell me some leaves for a tea to cure Bobby's depression and I've spent all day making a little dancing Dutchman for baby Axel. It's electrifying to think of big Axel's eyes on me; there was something about the way he held Patricia when he kissed her that I haven't been able to get out of my head. Her long hair falling, her body fluid in his arms, as though she were fainting and dissolving with desire. I will have to try not to touch him. I might get a shock.

I hope baby Axel Joachim will like the dancing Dutchman. I cut it from card and Bobby let me use his paints for a red, green and black harlequin's costume. I jointed him with knots and threads, and put a bead on the end of the cord that makes him jig, like Mum used to do for us. Bobby only grunted when I showed him but I think it's pretty good.

I can hear voices from the terrace while I'm still climbing the path through the trees and almost turn back due to shyness, but the little white dog shoots out of the gate barking and giving me away.

Lamps have been brought outside, insects buzz in the haze, the sun has left a sky streaked with purple welts. Marianne sits motionless in her rocking chair, the others positioned like hand-maidens or nurses, Charmian talking, Nancy stroking Marianne's hand. Patrick Greer is stooped over administering wine.

A woman in an emerald silk tunic comes shushing the dog with baby Axel Joachim in her arms. "Hi, you! I've seen you before," she says, rocking the baby to and fro while he pulls at her necklace. "You and your English crowd. But why do you never come and have fun at the marine club?" The baby is tugging a chunk of her carved jade pendant to his mouth and I recognize her as Magda, the Czech woman who charged Jimmy a fortune for two beers at Lagoudera. Magda's perfume is strong enough to be heady. She is chatting about all the famous people who have sailed in to dance at the bar. "Henry Fonda, Princess Margaret, Melina Mercouri . . ."

Patrick Greer lurches over with the bottle. He's wagging his schoolmaster's finger at Magda to interrupt. "It's that Babis Mores taking pictures of all the starlets for the society columns. Oh dear Jesus, that's what they come here for; I'm telling you, it's obscene. Babis's camera. To be is to be seen. And now your damned night-club and its loudspeakers are destroying this place."

"Oh never mind," I say, hiding the baby's present behind my back. "Maybe I'd better return tomorrow."

Magda snatches the glass that Patrick is offering to me. If it weren't for the baby I think she might throw it at him.

"This island needs tourism and I need to feed my son," she says, jiggling the baby who whinges louder as she untangles his fingers from her necklace.

Charmian gives Marianne's arm a small shake. "I think the little man needs his bed," she says, but Marianne gives no indication of having heard her. She's flopped into the rocker as though she's been flung there.

Magda is glaring at Patrick and such irritated jiggling is not working on the baby, who has left a dark trail on her emerald silk breast. I reach to take him. His cheeks are reddened with spit and he is gnawing at his fist.

Charmian sweeps a lamp from the table. "Poor little blighter. Teething and hungry and tired all at the same time." She motions for me to follow her inside. "Let's see what we can do. I don't think Marianne's in any fit state."

The room bears few scars of recent battle. A ring of fresh vine leaves wreathes the water jar. Yards of lace catch the breeze at the missing window. Charmian's lantern makes water pitchers of flowers dance across the walls and we see that the bookshelves are now almost empty of books, an arrangement of broken pottery and icons lies behind a brushwood broom, a guitar that had been hanging at the foot of the stairs is gone. The moon is a ghostly face through the lace veils of the empty window frame. Charmian lights the stove and sets a pan of water to boil.

I don't seem to be any better than Magda at comforting poor Axel Joachim. Charmian takes him and almost immediately his crying subsides and he lays his head to her bosom. She looks so soft in the lamplight with the baby in her arms. Some sort of lovely music is playing in her head that makes her sway her hips as she finds the bottle and the teat and drops them in the water.

She's dancing with the baby and fixing his milk, shaking a drop onto her wrist which sets him clamoring, and at the same time talking to me. "It's all been terribly emotional for poor Marianne. Lots of tears as he sailed away, though she's the one who told him to bugger off. Now she seems to be in some sort of a trance."

I follow her upstairs. "Seriously. Axel's upped and left her?"

"Yes, of course. He pushed her until she had no choice, really. It was pretty awful at the dock, the baby screaming blue bloody murder and Marianne falling to her knees, every inch of her begging the bastard to stay while all the time she was yelling at him to go. He was keen to get the wind in his sails, I'll tell you that. This way he can always say it was she who sent him away. She says he may sail back to Oslo."

Soft glimmers in the gloom. Fleeces on the boards, hangings around the bed, a washstand of elaborate wrought iron with a shining white china bowl; through an archway, a large worktable is scattered with papers.

"I see he took his typewriter," Charmian says.

She sweeps aside bolts of embroideries from around the high bed—a grand Russian affair of carved black wood and brass curlicues—dampens a sponge at the washstand, finds a fresh nappy and pins. I hold up a candle while she cleans and changes the baby who is humming softly as he sucks at the warm goat's milk.

"I'm guessing she'll want to sleep with this little fatty tonight." Charmian sighs as she settles the baby into a nest at the center of the bed. "Just look how she makes everything beautiful. All these lace pillows. And such terribly pretty flowers on the nightstand."

The night has grown deeper and the temperature has dropped. Nancy and Magda come inside to chop tomatoes for sauce. Only the bellowing of a donkey and distant goat bells disturb the silence.

Marianne remains on the terrace, looking out to space with a woven blanket pulled across her shoulders, singing breathily to herself in Norwegian. Patrick Greer is refilling her glass. The wine glows like rubies in the lamplight.

"Hi there, pretty little girl," she says, slurring, patting the wall beside her. "Have you come here to taunt me with your youth and beauty and unbroken heart?"

"Sorry, no. I came to ask you about the woman who makes the tea . . . but it seems like the wrong time." I'm as red as the wine, I can feel the blood. Patrick Greer is rude enough to snort. He passes me a glass of the Kokineli and I gulp at it. Charmian joins us with a new bottle and the corkscrew, tells Marianne her baby is settled.

Marianne seems to be having trouble focusing and it only strikes me later that she's been given a pill. She's repeating over and over that she was the one who told him to go.

"Oh what will I do if he does something reckless all alone out at sea?"

Charmian motions for me to shift along and takes my place beside her. She pulls Marianne close to soothe her, reminds her that Axel's a fine sailor and far too ambitious to risk drowning himself. Magda cuts in with the news that Nancy's ready to serve up.

"You have to let this one go, he's too bonkers. There'll be no shortage of blokes who will happily take his place, you know that."

Marianne closes her eyes and we all fall silent before she leaps to her feet with a cry.

"There is only him, that's the thing. Him and his golden voice. Just as my grandmother predicted. Momo said my man would have a golden voice and that's Axel Jensen."

Magda shakes her head, mouths, "Here we go again," and stomps inside to help Nancy.

Marianne is unsteady and not making much sense. She holds out her hand to Charmian. "Come with me, help me write him a letter. I love my husband. There's nothing I can do about it. If it goes in the mail on tomorrow's steamer, he'll get it as soon as he checks in to Athens."

I'm left with Patrick Greer who refills my glass before I can make an excuse to leave.

"She really is quite a woman—but you'll have noticed that for yourself," he says, watching them go.

"Marianne?" I say. "Because she wants to put up with whatever rotten thing her husband does?"

Patrick snorts. "Ha, no. I was talking about Charm. Here she is, a ministering angel, while her own husband and kids are God knows where . . . scrounging dinner from one of the neighbors, no doubt." His eyes shine black with malice as he leans towards me, his lips winking wet and pink as a mollusk from within the weedy beard.

"You know things ain't great at home for her right now? Everyone's waiting for George's book; it's making her paranoid.

And with Jean-Claude back here sniffing around. Well, you could say it's leading to an interesting atmosphere."

The greasy, defeated smell of him makes my stomach clench. "I really don't know what you're talking about."

He's got his hand on my knee. "It's nasty of George, really, to take his revenge in this way, by so publicly humiliating her." Though I'm desperate to get away and know I'll feel soiled, I find myself keening towards him.

"So?"

Patrick squeezes my thigh as Magda appears with a stack of willow-pattern plates which she scatters around the table. She clinks her glass to mine.

"I will make special prices for you if you and your beautiful English friends will come to Lagoudera during Yacht Week. We need a few more young bohemians to mix it up a bit."

Patrick scowls at her and bends to light his pipe.

The stem makes an unpleasantly juicy sound. "George is a victim of his own jealousy. I've read the manuscript and he's ruined a perfectly good novel by including a totally gratuitous sex scene. It's only there to humiliate Charm and Jean-Claude."

"Oh, do stop going on about it," Magda snaps. "It's no one's business but theirs."

"Excuse me, but it's George who makes it everyone's business by writing so luridly about his wife," Patrick scoffs. "A self-proclaimed once-a-year man sticking the knife in because that's all he's got left that he can stick in."

"Ugh, you're drunk," Magda says, but Patrick is back to wagging his finger.

"He's never believed his luck would hold, having a woman like that. She's too red-blooded to lead the life of a nun, and he knows it."

Magda gives him a shove that almost topples him. "Oh you are enjoying it, aren't you? Is it because Charm went with Jean-Claude when you made it so obvious she could have picked you?"

Patrick glares at her. "I make no secret of my admiration for the woman," he says.

Charmian reappears with the cutlery. In the Sartre story we'd all read, Lulu, the wife who chose to stay with her impotent husband, was, rather conveniently, medically unable to enjoy sex. I can't bear the thought that Charmian's marriage to George might be doomed. They're the closest thing I have to a family. I love them all: their banter and moods and tears and wild laughter, all of it, every chaotic bit of it.

Patrick and Magda are still sniping at each other as Marianne strides across the terrace, the cat at her heels. She kneels down with an envelope in her hand and starts filling it with yellow flowers from between the stones. "There we are," she says to the cat. "He'll see the daisies from our own little terrace when he reads my letter." She looks up and nods when I pass on my way out, laying my present beside her. "It's just a little nothing I made for Axel Joachim," I say and leave them all to it with a lump in my throat and a babyish need to cry.

FIFTEEN

Jimmy pokes me in the ribs as I pay for our tickets at the ferry picket. "Looks like somebody's scarpering," he says. The gangplank is down, people are swarming with cameras and beach bags and spearguns and masks, boys jostling and touting for business. I'm amused to see Martin running with the other harbor rats, charming the day-trippers who, for a few drachmas, might want directions to the best swimming spots or tavernas. Jimmy nudges me again and points.

Jean-Claude is shuffling to the front of the embarkation line, naked to the waist and strung with bags, a bulging portfolio, a large rolled-up canvas under one arm. A steward is pushing his ticket back at him, beckoning for others to pass. There's an explosion of shouting in Greek and French until Jean-Claude, still cursing, wrestles his scarlet rag of a shirt from a bag and puts it on.

Trudy ambles by in a floppy blue sun hat with a handkerchief pressed to her mouth. Her red hair hangs in a plait over one shoulder, fuzzy and thick as a bellpull. We chat over the picket while

Jimmy comes strolling back from Costas's ice-cream cart in a clean linen shirt with his precious typewriter in one hand and two cones in the other.

"Ahhhh, but you're a lucky girl . . ." Trudy says, giving me a pinch. "And I don't mean the cornets, honey." I ask about Jean-Claude but she bats his name away.

"He's heading for Berlin, as far as I know, meeting his dealer," she says, with a dismissive shrug. Her face has a greenish tinge and she says she's been feeling bad ever since she got out of bed and that the meatballs at Stephanos's taverna must have been off. Among the confusion of people, the men have come with a consignment of evil-smelling black sponges which they are piling at the dockside.

Jimmy hands me the ice cream, wipes a drip from the case of his precious typewriter. "All the way to Athens to get this baby fixed," he says.

"Ah yes, but a night in a hotel," Trudy sighs.

"And a hot bath," I say, giving myself the biggest hug at the prospect.

There's a hold-up in front of us. Two of the stewards are helping a one-legged man up the ramp. The man is old and wears his patched fisherman's trousers with the empty leg dangling in a knot that swings as he spins around and spits at the port so savagely he makes me jump. Two old women dressed in black start to wail. The *Nereida* lets out a series of impatient bellows and everyone shouts to make themselves heard.

"You wouldn't believe the list of things we're to bring back," I tell Trudy. "Contraceptives for everyone, and nail varnish and Pond's Cold Cream and *Paris Match*. And we have to go and start up Bobby's car, which is a bit of a nuisance. I don't know why he doesn't just let the battery run flat."

I am looking forward to a night at the Lyria, however. It's worth the extra money, Charmian said, for the big old bath down the hall on the second floor. "An ocean of hot water," she sighed, her eyes shining their greenest envy. She told me to buy the best cake of soap I could afford, to make the most of it, so that's top of my list, and I long to find some embroideries like Marianne's to hang around my marital bed. I take a lick of my dripping ice cream.

"Will you go to the record store?" Trudy says. "If they've got it will you get the Ray Charles LP and I'll pay you back? And three tubes of burnt umber and two of sienna if you're going that way." She scribbles a list of an astonishing number of items and shoots off saying that the smell of the drying sponges is making her think she might well throw up.

The *Nereida*'s horn is deafening. We stand on the sundeck, watching the island recede and trying to spot our house among the tiers of white cubes. The ferry dips and breasts and as we lean over the rail I have to cling on to my hat as I watch the waves dash spume against the hull.

Demetri Gassoumis is on board, his Rolleiflex slung around his neck, and New Zealand Bim has a notebook protruding from the pocket of his safari jacket. He points to Demetri's camera. "We're going in for a few days to do a magazine story about the meat market at Piraeus," he says, but it turns out they don't actually have a commission. The quay is not yet out of sight; Robyn and Carolyn are still waving as they turn their attention to a pair of Dutch girls, helping to steady them as they stow their backpacks.

Downstairs Demetri buys lottery tickets for the Dutch girls as well as himself when the man comes around with his tray. The four of them settle at a bench, Bim lowering his sunglasses and leaning over his knee to narrow his focus on the prettier of the two.

I am relieved that Jimmy doesn't want to sit with them; both

Bim and Demetri have a way of looking at me as though they can see through my clothes. I am sad for Robyn and Carolyn who always seem to stay at home while their husbands carouse at the port. I wonder if it's because Demetri is half-Greek that Carolyn is prepared to live like an island woman, but that doesn't explain Robyn. In my secret heart I hope they are lesbians and wild about each other.

Jimmy ducks down the iron stairs and I follow him into the saloon where Jean-Claude is untying his bags.

"Look. We'll be able to ask him about Charmian. Find out what he knows about George's novel," Jimmy says.

"Don't you jolly well dare!"

Jean-Claude settles himself in his seat, one leg swinging over its arm. His shirt has remained unbuttoned, his tan testifies to the months he's spent working on it, his chest hair glints gold and curly as a poodle. He has stowed his luggage with the exception of the canvas. He pulls at its bindings. His faded jeans are so tight he must've put them on wet; at some point he's burst the fly which is held together with two straining safety pins.

"The paint is still mouillé," he tells us, unrolling the canvas and angling it to the porthole light. "*Sleeping Aphrodite*."

The paint is dauby but this sleeping goddess is unmistakably Trudy. She lies on rumpled white sheets by a window, her nipples shiny and orange as kumquats.

He smiles at it, and licks his lips as one might at a well-remembered meal. "*Si belle*, yes? Your American friend. It is one of my best. I will be sad to sell it."

He lays it flat on a seat and reaches around his feet for his knapsack. "*Vous voulez partager?*" A bag of oranges. He takes the largest for himself, stabs a hole in the peel and releases the juice by poking his thumb around in its flesh. No doubt Jean-Claude believes he's being sensuous as he lifts it and suckles the juice, all the time gazing up at me through his tawny lashes.

"Stop it, Jacques!" Squirming, I blurt out the name Charmian gave him in her book.

Jimmy almost bursts. "Jacques! Sleeps on a goatskin rug and lives on raw eggs."

"*C'est vrai*. These things I do," Jean-Claude says, licking his fingers. "I eat my eggs from a cup; my goatskin is rolled up over there, if you look. And, yes, I'ave read Charmian's book." He pauses to yawn and twiddle his earring. "I don't know why she wants me to look *ridicule* but she's free to choose what she writes about. *Pooft*. To be free, it is all there is." He scrabbles again in his bag and extracts a paperback. He doesn't open it immediately. Instead he gazes towards the porthole and smiles to himself. "It's years since I 'elp Charmian out, but I don't forget."

He flicks through the pages of his book for his place, and raises slow eyelids, his eyes yellow as a goat's. He has a powerful smell, which I can't help thinking emanates from his jeans. "You know I like to 'elp out where I can. You know what I'm talking about, yes?"

I gulp and nod and gesture towards his heap of luggage. "Is this it? Have you had enough of Hydra?" I want confirmation that this serpent is to be gone, and especially before George's troublesome novel arrives.

Jean-Claude nods. "It's the 'usband who makes problems. Sets Police Chief Manolis on to me, report to the station for this and that. *Pooft*, no island is so special that it's worth putting up with George Johnston . . ." He stops for a moment to pick something from between his bright porcelain teeth.

"Last night, he was so drunk I feared for my life. Came to read me what he's written about me and his wife. *Tant pis*, except with George I can never be sure I won't be physically attacked and *that* gets expensive at the dentist." Jean-Claude leans back, scratches lazily at his chest. "I tell you one thing. I won't be 'elping 'er out again," he says.

"I'll be 'elping you out tonight at the Lyria, my girl," Jimmy snorts in my ear and Jean-Claude rolls his eyes and returns to his book.

———

Oh, the deep joy of a bath! I take Charmian's advice and splurge on a cake of ivory soap that smells of almonds, and a new elephant's-ear sponge that is smooth and slippery as silk when it's wet. I'm enjoying it so much that I almost don't want Jimmy to get in with me; at least, that's true until he starts soaping my back.

The mirror at the basin is misted over, the hot-water tap chugs, the soap gives a creamy lather.

After our day in the city we feel grimier than at any time on the island. It really hit us when we got off the ferry: the smell of the streets, the thundering lorries. For a moment it was like arriving on an alien planet and I was quite dizzied by the fumes and the speed and the noise and the honking. So many buses, dirty yellow and dirty blue, and builders' dust and cement mixers, and people stopping to sell you things, stalls and baskets. It was lovely to have Jimmy there, holding my elbow, guiding me through the traffic and the gritty streets. He is my gypsy-haired gentleman. He bought me a ring from a stall, just silver but with a pretty Greek key pattern. He says it's only until he sells his book and can buy me a proper one.

———

I return to the island with Jimmy's ring on my finger, yards of fine embroidered linen, some antique brass bowls, my first proper bikini, a red silk kimono that I intend to wear as a dress. Jimmy pretends to stagger under the weight of the parcels he's saddled with.

As well as his newly mended typewriter and our market finds, we have everyone's books and records and newspapers, paints, canvases, typewriter ribbons, guitar strings, lotions, potions, johnnies, a wheel of Athens bread.

They're all here at Katsikas, waiting for treasure. Jimmy moves among them like a merchant prince. Trudy lurks in the shadow of the wall, still a little green to my eyes, and without, as it turns out, the cash to pay us back for her LP and oil paints. Jimmy chucks Bobby his keys, fills him in on the state of his car. ". . . Eventually Erica managed to flag down a lorry driver with jump leads," he says. Bobby looks a little more cheerful today; he's changed his clothes, had a shave. Edie is sitting across his knees in a wide-brimmed hat so he has to push her to one side while I describe how the lorry driver became grumpy when we got to the car park and Jimmy was there. I want to tell him that, after all this time sitting in the shade of a bitter orange tree in Piraeus, Mum's little green Morris has started to smell once again of her scent. Bobby grins and thanks me, calls to Andonis to bring us retsina.

There's been a postal strike in Athens for the last few days and a whoop goes up when the mail sacks are carted by. There's the chatter of hasty arrangements in several languages, coins clattering across tables, chairs scraping as notes are wedged under cups.

Marianne remains drinking orangeade at Charmian's table, the pram pushed against the store.

"Don't worry," Charmian is saying. "George will check if there's a letter for you." Marianne chews her lip. There's a line between her eyes that's not just from squinting at the sun. Her shirt is the twin of the one Axel was wearing yesterday in Athens, a fine blue line running through the linen.

Marianne lays a hand on my arm. "The clown puppet you made for the baby has made us both happy," she says.

Charmian smiles up at me. "How was the trip?"

"Oh, I meant to say: Jean-Claude was on the ferry and he's not coming back here."

I blurt this out, wild with panic at so immediately having to face Marianne. I try not to look at her. I don't want to be the messenger. Don't want to say: "Look here, I saw Axel . . ."

I babble about how frustrating it was with all the shopping we had to do. "We never did make it up the Parthenon," I say.

Even though Jimmy and I had split up for a while to save time, there were still too many errands to run. Jimmy took his type-writer to the mender's in Pouliandros Street while I queued at the American Express office with my traveler's checks. As time ticked by, our trip to the seat of the gods was looking increasingly unlikely.

The American Express building was stifling, panelled with dark wood. People shuffled along; in front of me two men in shorts and ragged espadrilles were so stinky with old sweat I had to turn my head away to breathe. I was struck by our mass, the backpacks and bedrolls, and by how many of the men needed a shave.

There were blinds to keep out the heat, apart from a top win-dow where they were torn and shafts of sunlight fell to the floor in front of the tellers' desk. When he turned around, his Nordic hair flashed almost silver in the brightness of the beam. It took me a moment to believe it was him. Axel wore his fine-striped linen shirt untucked and was stuffing banknotes into the back pocket of his sailor pants. In his hand was a letter. His smile cut a dimple in his cheek and I followed his gaze to where she waited with their bags. So, not in Chicago after all, but standing not even ten yards away from me, with hair newly washed and shiny as treacle. I edged closer. Patricia's dress was penitent black silk and almost to her ankles, a row of jet buttons down the front.

She was pointing to the letter. Axel looked surprised to find it in his hand. She dumped the bags and stood on tiptoe to peer over his shoulder as he opened it. Yellow daisies came spilling as he shook out the folded sheets. He brushed them from his shirtsleeve and I watched as he tore up the unread pages and threw the pieces into a corner. He snatched up their bags and grew impatient with Patricia, attempting to pull her behind him, but she resisted and stooped down to the fallen flowers. She chose two or three and pressed them between the pages of her sketchbook before following him into the street.

I am glad to be shaken from thinking about this by George who returns to our table with his letters.

"Nothing for me then?" Marianne says and George shakes his head and Charmian pats her hand.

There's nothing for me either and I wonder if this is it, if my father really meant it when he disowned me.

Leonard's received something bulky from Canada and draws up a chair to read, leaning back with his feet to the wall and his sixpenny cap cocked to the sun. Nikos brings a jug of retsina as all around me everyone settles down to bulletins from the outside world. Jimmy has an encouraging letter about his first few chapters from a friend in England and, with much relief, a small check from his mother.

Charmian curses, pushes a bill across to George. "Last warning from Foyles before they close our account, darling."

George is using his pocketknife to slit open an envelope. Our Majesty on the stamp. Charmian notices the letterhead of William Collins Publishers. She stops talking as he scans the letter and refolds it. It's hard to tell if it's pain or pleasure that makes him close his eyes.

"Well?" Charmian says as she shakes out a cigarette.

His hand tremors a little as he lights a match. "Looks like Billy might be going all guns blazing on *Closer to the Sun*," he says as she leans to the flame. "He's getting that Kenneth Farnhill who does all the Agatha Christies to design the cover and they're using puffs from Muriel Spark and J. B. Priestley for an advert."

Leonard is back with us, still chuckling to himself over the contents of his letter. "What's up?" he says when he notices the look on Charmian's face.

"Oh, George is rather pleased with himself," she says, with a martyr's smile. "Looks like Collins think they have a bestseller with his new novel."

Leonard narrows his eyes as he looks at her, dangles his *komboloi* behind his chair. Click, click, click; the amber beads drop.

"The thing is, I so terribly want to be pleased for him—for us, really—after all these years of keeping that pot boiling he deserves a success; but there's a character who too closely resembles me in this damn book and I'm wondering if I should reserve myself a place in the loony bin in time for publication."

George groans the deep groan of a man returning to battle in heavy armor.

"My God, woman," he says. "Give me some credit for having an imagination. *Closer to the Sun* is not only about you and bloody Nature Boy, you know . . ."

Leonard comes between them, with the delicate authority of one attempting to unite Khrushchev and Eisenhower.

"If you can make something that is beautiful out of something you've experienced, I think that everybody concerned is happy about it," he says.

Charmian shakes her head at both of them. "But what about Zelda and Scott Fitzgerald? You can't say it worked out all that bloody well for her that he used their experiences, can you?"

"Yes, well, she wanted to . . . I guess she had ambitions as a writer, but I don't know . . ." Leonard's words peter out as he catches the look on Charmian's face. It's as though he's only that moment remembered that she too is a writer.

"But would you do it?" Marianne says, springing to life. "Would you use the woman you loved in your work?"

Leonard scrapes at his sandpaper jaw, back and forth, back and forth, while he feasts his eyes on her face. "I don't think I take anything that anybody could use anyway, another way . . ."

They smile at each other before Marianne lowers her eyes and attempts a more sympathetic expression for Charmian. "I know how you feel. I'm glad I shan't be in Oslo when the film of Axel's novel is on," she says, unable to completely stanch her sunny smile. "I know it feels bad to be in the pages of a book, but imagine the fuss when this teenage actress who is supposed to be me is lying naked in the pine forest with everything showing."

Leonard gives her an enormous grin. I can see him imagining the scene, appreciating it. "When it comes down to it, all subjects are just an allegory, a metaphor for human experience," he says.

Baby Axel Joachim is stirring; Marianne leans across to jiggle the pram, sees me watching. "Would you like to take him?"

I sit with the baby on my lap and she gives me his bottle of water. The baby plays with the teat but is more interested in wrapping his fingers around my ponytail and staring into my eyes. His eyes are as blue as the ocean, as blue as the sky. I'm trying not to think about Axel standing with Marianne's yellow flowers scattered around his feet because for all I know the baby can see the pictures in my mind. I glance across at Charmian who is nodding at something Leonard is reading out from his sister's letter. She stops and catches my eye for a moment and I feel my mouth almost contort with the effort of not becoming the bearer of bad news.

There was a small café in the street off Syntagma Square, opposite the American Express office, on the way to the art shop. It was where I'd agreed to meet Jimmy, at one of the tables beneath the dark blue awnings.

The gods we'd made no time for must have been having fun with us from their temple on the hill. Patricia was there, leafing through her sketchbook, and I was surprised to see Jimmy's hand on her waist, before Axel came out of the café's door, shaking water from his hands.

He stopped when he saw me.

"Hydra?" he said and his face paled.

He spoke rapid Greek to the waiter, turned to Patricia. "Now I've got the cash, you're the one who is going to have to make up her mind . . ." He was drumming his fingers on the table and his eyes were darting and bright as minnows.

"There's my Karmann Ghia at Piraeus. But you'll have to drive it because I don't have a license right now and it's a long way to Troy. Maybe there's somewhere you'd like to sail to instead? Kos? Mykonos?" He threw back his glass of water, almost buzzing with desire to be somewhere else.

Patricia explained that they were looking for somewhere quieter than Hydra where Axel could write his novel and she could paint. Axel took his coffee like a shot. The scars on the back of his hand were minutely raised and pale as silverfish. He made no mention of Marianne or the baby.

I'm trying not to think about it. I take Marianne's baby inside with me to the grocery store; I like his babbling, am lost in a daydream that this bundle of warm sweetness is mine and Jimmy's.

Charmian is beside me, checking the price on a tin of corned beef. Of course she's picked up on all the looks I've been giving her outside. "Go on, what is it you're not saying?" she says and I tell her about Axel and Patricia.

Outside Leonard is standing with his towel over his shoulder, Marianne smiling up at him, shaking her head. "It would be so nice, but . . ."

Charmian gives her a shove. "Go on, Marianne, a swim will do you the world of good. I'll take this little fellow home with me and you can pick him up later. I could do with the distraction, to be honest." She takes Axel Joachim from me, holds him in the air and nuzzles his fat belly through his vest. "And I promise not to eat him all up . . ."

She turns to me once they've gone. "Now, what were you saying about Jean-Claude Maurice?"

SIXTEEN

The days grow so hot I don't know where my skin finishes and the air begins. By lunchtime there's only one place to be and that's in the sea. Jimmy carries the basket packed with our towels and books and a picnic of feta, fresh bread from the baker, and tomatoes as big and knobbly as my fist.

A cruise ship is moored at the mouth of the harbor. Its passengers disgorge in a flotilla of rowing boats and, with not enough to interest them at the port, now swarm over the rocks above the cave at Spilia.

Jimmy and I pause beneath the fig tree at the turn. Maybe there's fun to be had? I follow his gaze, check all the bikinis, like none as much as my own. My new two-piece is stitched from pale blue-and-white-striped seersucker. I wear it with my dress buttoned over because, unlike the Edies and Janeys of this world, I'm not willing to risk a fine. Police Chief Manolis patrols the waterfront with a new vigor since so many beautiful young women are flouting the public-decency rules of the island.

Music floats up to us from a transistor radio; the sea ripples with bright rubber hats, flippers, snorkels, mermaids on the rock; and a pair of young gods in matching red swim shorts have roped inflatable beds to the iron steps and lie golden and bobbing side by side. Toddlers squirm beneath their mothers' sun-creaming hands, two beach balls are in play, Lena is at the lip of the cave with the other Swedes and has daringly removed her top to sunbathe.

Jimmy and I have been talking about Bobby. My brother has gone off on another long hike by himself, heading out straight after his chores with his backpack.

"He's looking better for it, whatever it is he does while he's away," Jimmy says as we continue along the clifftop path. The heat is hazy, the rocks beaten bronze and rust and iron by strong light, faceted, run through with scraggly olive and pine, clumps of thyme and balls of acid-yellow euphorbia. Most of the wildflowers are brown with seed, only the occasional bright stab of a poppy flares and, as we turn a corner, below us a miraculous swath of yellow meets the lapis-blue sea.

We decide to head for the beach in front of the old olive mill, which is never too crowded, and wander on through the lanes to the supermarket at Four Corners for a bottle of retsina.

I can't wait to cool off in the pebbly shallows, while around every corner the sun-dazzled white walls offer enchantment, splashed with hibiscus bright as blood, or overhung by cascades of baby-blue plumbago and clashing pink and purple bougainvillea, narrow passageways leading us back to the sea. We stand high on the crest of the harbor, the fishing boats rock at their moorings, nets have been stretched out to dry on the shoreline. A gang of tabby cats are sleeping in the shade of a grove of cypress trees with a donkey snoring beside them, a white cockerel and his hens scratching about.

The Taverna Mavromatis stands square and boldly painted in rusty red and ocher with strong yellow awnings and tables with checkered cloths. Theodorakis plays through a small loudspeaker. Manolis Mavromatis cooks the best lobster on the island and his wife makes sweet cakes with candied prickly pears. Panayiotis and a couple of the older fishermen are playing *tavli* at a table outside, but it isn't them that my eye is drawn to.

Marianne is laughing with Axel Joachim on her lap. Leonard is with them, making airplane noises, loop-de-looping a teaspoon towards the baby's mouth. The sun pours through a gap in the awning and pools at their feet. Leonard wears his old tennis shoes without laces and one of her dainty feet rests beneath its freed tongue.

Panayiotis calls to Jimmy with his sunbaked growl. Marianne blows a shy kiss as we approach. She is plainly dressed in faded fisherman's trousers and a man's shirt but still manages to look as fresh as a new day's gardenia. Axel Joachim is pulling a disgusted face at whatever is on the spoon and Marianne calls to Manolis not to take this as a comment on his cooking.

"He's tasting things for the first time, look he has two little teeth," she says, opening his mouth with her finger to show us.

Leonard is waving to the baby, pulling a monkey grin.

"Look how he waves back!" Marianne cries as Axel Joachim raises his chubby hand. "I think my son is a genius."

There's an almost empty bottle of wine on the table, a flush to her cheeks, and as we go on our way it's with music in our ears.

———

The next day is cooler and after our siesta I must leave Jimmy working in our room, his typewriter set up beside the door for the breeze. He returns to his writing slender and brown and naked as a reed. I dance about for a while, trying to distract him. I swirl within our new embroideries, doing my best Salome or at least attempting to interest him in working out how to fix them from the rafters above our bed. Red and blue flowers, birds, look at those millions of stitches . . .

He springs and I let him wrestle me. We tussle and play and it isn't long before the bedsprings are singing their immodest song. After that I promise to give him the peace he needs. I make him a sandwich before I set off to consult Charmian.

I am so pleased with my flea-market find, and tell myself my mum wouldn't mind me splurging out, just this once, on something so fine. The old lady at the stall in Monastiraki didn't speak much English but I gathered they were from a bride's trousseau, every stitch from her own fingers while she sat on her stoop, maybe more than a century ago. There are red peacocks, blue-and-red-striped jugs, a repetition of tiny knots of red thread that make flowers and vines.

There's a blue boat in every corner. "And look, a dolphin for luck," Charmian says, running her eye across the needlework. "She must have been waiting for her sailor boy for a very long time . . ."

Charmian tells me about the old families on Kalymnos, about wedding festivities that would go on until not another morsel could be eaten nor another drop drunk, at which point the bride and groom were locked for three days in their new house. "To fuck," she said, as though I might not understand. "On the third morning the families would gather, very solemnly, at the door of the house and wait for the boy to emerge with the blooded sheet . . ."

My flea-market sheets are without stains, uniformly aged to the color of palest sherry.

It's chaos; the whole family here. Shane's had her way with the music and "Alley Oop" plays on the gramophone. Charmian is doing about eight things at once, a ragged tea towel at her shoulder, and a wildcat's prowl as she chops and tidies. Zoe is filling the iron with charcoal embers, lettuce leaves crisp in an enamel pail. Shane and Martin peel potatoes at the table, bickering in English and Greek about one of them having to give up a room, about Shane's appalling taste in music.

George looks up from the lamp he's fixing to tell me about his friends who are coming with their children from Athens and, Martin hopes, some new comic books. "Charlie Sriber's me old cobber, used to sub my copy in Melbourne. They let us bunk at their place in the Metz when we need to be in Athens and we have them here in return. It's all fireworks and dancing on the island this weekend . . ." He touches the wire with his pliers and the lamp sparks and fizzles, making us all jump; Charmian begs him not to electrocute everyone.

There's always a festival of some sort, the bells are constantly ringing, but this weekend is a big one in honor of Admiral Miaoulis, whose statue guards the harbor mouth to the east, a ship's wheel in his hand and a dagger at the ready in his cummerbund. Martin knows all the facts, every detail of the skirmishes with the Turks, the revenge our great hero took against the Sultan's fleet for the massacre of Chios . . . The boy's a walking encyclopedia and his parents couldn't be prouder, though Charmian shoots George a furious look each time he calls him "Professor."

"It brings out the worst sort of nationalism in the people who come for the fireworks and parties," George grumbles and Martin starts begging him for gunpowder so he can make his own fire-crackers this year.

Someone Charmian refers to, with a grimace, as "Big Grace" will be arriving too. "Big Grace has designs on my hubby. Isn't that right, darling?" she says, planting a kiss on George's cheek while he growls at her. A whole cask of wine stands beside the sink, its spigot dripping into a jug. Charmian has a devilish gleam; her skirt swishes around while she teases him. "Big Grace took very good care of my husband while he was recovering after the hospital in Athens. Very good. All his favorite delicacies—isn't that right, darling? Dressed crab and teeny-tiny portions of veal tartare . . ."

George rocks back in his chair, watching her perform.

"Any titbit to tempt him with his poor invalid appetite. A perfect Manhattan shaken on ice on the balcony looking across all of Athens to the Hill of the Muses, really nothing was too much trouble for her."

He starts laughing and coughing and lunges for her, grabbing her by the waist as she tries to skip past.

"Oh, do cut it out, Cliftie. You're getting yourself worked up again; not every relationship with a woman has to be about sex, as you very well know." He pulls her to his knee for a growly kiss that sends Martin and Shane running from the room making gagging noises.

Little Booli is grasping my hand and leading me up the ladder to show me his new den beneath the couch. We run in and out of the rooms playing hide-and-seek and Booli bursts with helpless giggles and gives himself away every time.

I help Charmian to make up the beds and couches for the guests. She tucks and straightens, takes snips of lavender she's brought from the courtyard to lay on the pillows. She tells me Big Grace is under the impression that it's constant rowing with his wife that's made George ill. "She is determined to rescue him, you'll see if you meet her," she says. The sheets, though thin and darned, smell of new ironing, of charcoal and steam and best intentions.

"Oh, it's all such a bloody bother when I could be getting on with my book, but we owe them an invitation and better they come now while there's still water in the cistern." She stands from the bed, easing her hands to the small of her back.

"You can't imagine the fuss of having people stay when we're dry, which often happens in high season when we have to pay for every drop to be delivered by Elias, plus it's a terrible chore having to flush through the privy with sea-water. Water becomes terrifically hard work and so pricey; I feel I must warn you, Erica." She's stuffing a few things away in drawers, straightening the rug. "Though, when at last the rains come, the sound of the water filling the cistern will call to you and you'll want to dance starkers through the streets."

She surveys the room and cocks an ear. A ting and a burst of clatter from George's typewriter, another ting and then a pause and the sound of paper being wrenched from the carriage with a roar of her name. "Soundtrack to my life," she says with a pantomime curtsy and smile.

Shane calls to us from the courtyard. "Look, Dissy has found Penny," she cries, pointing at the tortoises who are bashing shell to shell, as if locked in mortal combat. The heavy breathing and orgiastic grunts sound all too human as the old boy scrabbles in a frenzy of lust on top of his smaller mate. Booli is horrified, runs at them: "Óchi, óchi, óchi," pulls Odysseus off and banishes him to the furthest corner, behind the privy.

We run around with a tennis ball. Shane is the champion in every possible sequence of bouncing the ball against the wall or the well, and clapping and turning and touching the ground, and Booli is good at fetch. It's a relief, sometimes, to mess around with the kids.

Charmian comes out with a basket on her arm. She says it's her last chance for freedom before the guests arrive. "Anyone fancy a walk?" The others shirk. "If you like we can go to Marianne's with your embroideries. She has a good sewing machine and she'll know about fixings," she says, and offers to wait while I grab them.

Booli skips off to the port to see if Martin has found some live bait for his fishing rod. He's only four but he has the run of the island, a golden-haired princeling welcome at any table, wonderful really. Charmian smiles as she watches him go. We talk about Bayswater, about being cooped up in a flat and all the trees we weren't allowed to climb in Kensington Gardens and the dirty gutters and constantly coughing because of the beastly yellow smog.

The golden hour lights our way up the lane of the roses and on towards the graveyard where wild raspberries grow. "I think your mother would've loved this island," Charmian says and tells me of an afternoon they shared in Mum's open-topped car with a swim in the Thames and deviled eggs in a tea shop in Cookham. She shakes her head when I ask her: "Really, she never mentioned a lover?"

The graveyard has a glorious view to the sea; you can almost imagine yourself happy to die knowing you'll rest with this vista among the pines and the flowers. We stand beside the grave of a young sponge diver, an anchor, an iron boot and the round window of a diving bell set into his headstone. I haven't entered a graveyard since we buried Mum in a corner of Kensal Green Cemetery so shaded it was dank. Charmian reaches for my hand. I tell her how I long for my mother to come back and haunt me. "I suppose that everyone feels like that when they miss somebody," I say and wipe my eyes with the back of my wrist.

"Do you feel ghosts, Charmian?"

"Oh yes," she replies, and she sighs long and hard. "I have ghosts, not all of them dead."

"What do you mean?" She opens her mouth to say something, stops. I feel her change tack.

"It's a strange thing when you miss someone who is there," she says, and she looks down at the sponge diver's grave as sadly as if he were her own son. "There but not there. Right before you all the time. Like George, by which I mean the George I married, with his tremendous verve and unbroken spirit."

She tells me it can't have escaped my notice that things are not right between them, says how awful she feels for the children having to witness their fights. "I should have put my foot down about that wretched novel of his."

"You know I shan't read it," I say, making a cutting motion at my throat and giving her my Girl Guide's honour which at least makes her laugh. "But if it's embarrassing for you, why has he done it?"

"To understand George, you have to know something of his childhood in Australia: a fragile boy, bookish, rather artistic in temperament, the opposite of his beefy brother Jack. His father was a brute with the razor strop. Savage beatings and never for something naughty he'd done, that was the thing, but just in case there was some misdemeanor that he wasn't admitting to. Can you imagine what that does to a sensitive little boy?

"The saddest thing is he's become like his old man, now his leaping time is behind him. It's buried so deep in him there's nothing he can do. He suspects me and imagines all sorts of bullshit things, and he thinks he should punish me." She manages a rueful smile. "You know, just in case.

"*Closer to the Sun* is a difficult one. There's often a green-eyed nymphomaniac stirring up the troops in George's books . . ." Again the rueful smile. "But this is the first time he's written from within his own skin. An Aussie writer, a former war correspondent, a wife and a family on a Greek island. No doubt people are going to read it as though it were the truth—memoir, if you like, and not some twisted product of his poor tortured imagination."

I've been silent but can't help myself. "Hang on, what about Jean-Claude?" I daren't look at her once the words are out.

"Really, Erica, you're just as bad as the rest of the mongrels." She stamps her foot. "And, if you must know, Jean-Claude Maurice does not merit the literary attention that is lavished upon him."

She changes the subject as we cut across the top of the gully. "I've been mulling over what you told me the other day at the store and I think you really have to pluck up the courage to tell Marianne that Axel's with Patricia." I know she's right but still it feels like a punishment. "It would be a kind thing to do, if you can bear it. The poor girl's under the impression that he's alone on his boat, thinking how to save his marriage."

I follow her into Marianne's, my stomach queasy. A small breeze ruffles the lace at the broken window. Stems of pink rambler roses have been arranged in a pewter jug on the table. Someone has been attempting to sketch her on a sheet of paper that lies with a stub of pencil beside it. It's a good likeness, catches the Sphinx-like smile, the modest lowered lashes against the bloom of her cheek.

We call to her from the foot of the stairs and she appears above us in a white dress, like a sun-bleached angel. The dress might once have been a peasant girl's petticoat but Marianne is wearing it with a belt of plaited leather. We pass a sleeping Axel Joachim as we tiptoe outside.

Marianne moves dreamily, clearing some beakers and an earthenware jug from the table. I can't seem to speak without crushing my r's. She has a peach-colored shawl, despite the heat, which she keeps wound around her face.

She ends my agony by resting her hands on my shoulders to silence me. Above the peach silk her eyes are sharp with tears.

She drops her hands and I feel dismissed as she turns from me to Charmian. "So, I guess he picked Patricia up from where she was waiting on Poros as soon as he left here." Her voice is shaking. "I suppose it was all arranged. Maybe he thought it would cause me less humiliation if I didn't see them leave together as a couple."

Charmian's eyes flare with dislike. "Who does he think he is, to parcel out pain like that? He's nothing but a moral coward. A child-man like Axel can never be a good father for your son."

Marianne speaks through the scarf, her face turned away from us. "He is crazy about Patricia. There's nothing I can do about the bones in his nose. He thinks only of her."

"I know how forgiving you can be, but not this time, Marianne," Charmian says. "And what's all this with the shawl? I can't really make out half of what you're saying . . ."

Charmian reaches a couple of times to pull it aside and eventually Marianne gives way and unwinds it to reveal skin that looks sore and red around her mouth and chin. "Oh, what is to be done?" she says, giggling and burying her head in her hands.

"Has something been biting you?" Charmian asks with a wicked arch of her brow.

"It's not what you think." Marianne is still trying to conceal her hot face. Tiny blue sparks dance in her eyes. She squeaks through her fingers, "I am allergic to the face cream Magda got for me."

"Marianne!" Charmian says. "I really do think you might tell our Canadian friend to buy some new razor blades."

SEVENTEEN

The harbor is jostling with yachts. The port is so crowded you might think the whole of Athens has come to the island for the festival. The artists are hopeful, displaying their paintings along the wall of the Lagoudera Marine Club; the sponge sellers arrange their wares in tiers and pyramids at the dock and have more success than the painters. Every taverna is open, the coffee shops and bars along the waterfront are bustling, the grand stone houses high above the port throw open their shutters and old Vasilis the knife grinder wheels his stone through the lanes.

At home I sit chin to knees in the deep window nook and watch Jimmy as he hammers nails into the rafters for my hangings and for some netting against the mosquitoes. I don't have a bite on my body thanks to the superior bait that lies sprawled beside me every night. He balances, naked and effortless, with one foot on the bedpost, reaches for the furthest beam with a mouthful of nails. His calf muscles flex, and I watch the shifting contours of his bum which is as burnt-honey tanned as the rest of him. No wonder the mosquitoes thirst for his body. I see the way other girls look at him, grown-up women too. I'd like to build a moat around him and fill it with crocodiles. I hug my knees tighter, say what I've been meaning to say for the last few nights. "We could always convert to Greek Orthodox and get married on the island."

Jimmy swivels to check I'm not joking, retrieves the nails from his mouth.

"There can't be any wedding at all until I've sold my book," he says, and I pull a pout and look out of the window to where the breeze has whipped up a whirl of fallen wisteria blossom.

He springs down, the boards barely register his landing, and he tups me under the chin to make me look at him. His eyes are the color of brown-bottle sea glass when you hold it up to the sun, amber flecked with gold.

"I'm afraid it would be the final straw. My mother wouldn't send another penny." And he flutters his dark lashes in a Mummy's poppet sort of a way though really he hates to talk about his mother sending money.

"But I quite fancy a full-immersion baptism," I say and he chuckles, his fingers starting on my buttons.

"The priests will enjoy it, that's for sure," he says with a lecherous grin. "They insist on full nakedness, you know . . ." I've given up wearing bras and he feigns surprise as he pulls open my shirt.

"Ah, yes. I reckon we could drum up some support from that bishop at Profitis Elias, 'Come, come, my child. That's right now, shed your sins . . .'" and because Jimmy's got the gift of mimicry and a rubber face to go with it I can't help but laugh.

The original plan had been to get out of town along the clifftop to Vlychos. There's a good and wide shingle beach there, turquoise waters, some scrubby pines for shade, enough to accommodate the whole crowd now we're so outnumbered by the grand Hydriot

families and their Athenian scions. There are brass bands and children's processions. The bells will keep tolling until Vespers when
the great Admiral's heart is due to be processed through the streets
in its gold casket.

Greek and Hydriot flags honor him from the corners of houses,
water taxis putt-putt by, low in the water with families and pic-
nics heading for the less-inhabited coves. We see Bim and Demetri
waving from Manos's boat, hanging off the side and posing like
film stars in their white shirts and dark glasses. Madam Pouri's
donkey-boy passes in a blue cap, his beasts laden with hampers
and blue parasols and blue beads and silver bells that jingle on their
reins.

At the point where the road peters out to a dirt track and the
land dips away to the sea, we find Cato. Many times I have been
drawn to this place at the crest of this gentle gully. The slopes are
terraced, there are grazing sheep, stripes of golden barley, in the dip
a shepherd's hut among a grove of olive trees, the only building for
as far as the eye can see. There's a low crumbling wall to sit on and
I can blur the blue triangle of sea between the rocky mountain and
the rusty hill and no one ever passes or interrupts me.

At first we think the cries are a hawk circling overhead but it's
hard to be certain. Cockerels are crowing and a donkey is making
a racket. Dionysus, the rubbish collector, rarely makes it to this
part of the island and we follow the faint mewling to where the
stench is almost overwhelming. There's a fetid heap of old cans and
rotting cabbage, bursting bags, fermenting melons, eggshells. Flies
frenzy around half a rib cage and Jimmy pulls his T-shirt to cover
his mouth, cocks his ear and dives for a sack.

"Oh good God," he says as he sets it on the ground, and we
see something squirming inside. I drop to my knees to pull at the
rope. The cat's mouth is a piteous pink triangle. Its sparse black

coat is bare in patches and the poor thing is unable to open its eyes because they are glued together with gunk.

Jimmy is kicking up a red and glittering sandstorm. "What sort of a bastard does this to a cat?"

He unscrews our canteen. The cat's tongue is lapping at the water and I'm astonished that it manages to purr. Jimmy wets the corner of his handkerchief to bathe its eyes but has to stop when it mewls and tries to crawl away because we aren't sure if they are crusts or scabs.

There isn't a vet on the island, as far as we know. Jimmy makes him a nest of his T-shirt and we head back to port with "Cato" in our basket.

Charmian knows what needs to be done. She's in her kitchen, stirring something that smells delicious and garlicky over the charcoal, her face shiny from the heat. The table is laid, a bunch of wild honeysuckle we picked on our way back from Marianne's in a jug at the center. Zoe is folding napkins and there's chatter and glasses and children's laughter from the courtyard. Max runs in and out with his tongue lolling and his tail wagging, more pleased about the guests than his mistress appears to be. She's pulling the tea towel from her shoulder to wipe her face, and I notice that an uncharacteristic attempt at eye makeup has smudged, making her look more tired and worried than ever. The last thing she needs is a mangy cat.

She lifts little Cato out of the basket and holds him, wriggling to the window. His coat is matted with sores but already I can see the fine creature he will become.

"Everyone who comes here ends up with a cat," she says. "It looks like this young man has found you—if the tragic mite survives, that is." She sends Jimmy off, tells him to run to Rafalias's pharmacy for a small-sized hypodermic and iodine tincture.

"His best chance is to give him a course of George's streptomycin. You'll have to inject a tiny dose for the next few days. Don't worry, I'll show you how." She's checking behind his ears. "And you'll need benzoate to deal with these fleas too." She folds up a blanket on the bench and from her cooking pot spoons out a lump of meat and blows on it before feeding it to him in tiny pieces.

"He's a nice cat," she says. "Though the Greeks say a black cat is unlucky in the morning."

A man is standing in the doorway watching her. He is small and wiry with a reedy voice: "I've been sent in for a refill." His face is ruddy enough to clash with his sandy hair, and he's waving an empty jug in his hand. From behind him I hear a woman, American, a boomer. "Hey, Charlie, find out how much longer Charmian intends to be with the food. Tell her we're all getting too sloshed out here."

"It's thirsty work keeping up with George. I'd do well to remember his reputation at the press club," the man says, and as Charmian reaches to take the jug from him he grasps her by the waist and spins her around, stops when he notices me, "Crikey, sorry, I'm Charlie . . ." and lets her go.

"Erica's a talented young writer but she's yet to show me a word she's written," Charmian tells him—rather cruelly, I think. I start to object but they're not listening to me. Charles's eyes are fixed on Charmian and his fingers are flexed as though he still has her in his grip.

———

Cato needs drops put in his eyes and ears. Now his eyes are unglued he gazes up at us from a box at the foot of our bed, as lovestruck as Titania waking from her dream. We stand there soppy as new parents over a crib.

Though it's hard to tear ourselves away, we leave him with a mashed sardine and catch the tail end of the candle bearers solemnly intoning as they wind through the lanes from the monastery with the Admiral's heart in its casket.

We foreigners gather at the tables in front of Katsikas and across the alley at Tassos. Many splendid yachts have been shoehorned into the harbor and there are uniformed stewards and tables on decks laid with silver service and napery.

Marianne and Leonard arrive with the baby in his pram. Demetri and Carolyn look on a little anxiously as their toddler enthusiastically lifts out baby Axel and totters around with him in her arms like a doll.

Behind the waterfront a small fire is being lit and, as the brushwood is set crackling, Charmian grasps Shane's hands and mine and leads us towards it.

"This one's very much for the women," she's saying. "You see how they've all brought their May Day wreaths from their doors? Ours fell to pieces or was plundered, as usual, or we would have brought it and cast it to the flames."

The women start dancing around the fire, singing and throwing their dried flowers to the pyre. They have coins sewn on to their bodices and ribbons wound through their hair. Children are wetting their hair from a bucket and jumping through the flames and the women spin around faster, holding hands, while the men in their waistcoats slap out time with their palms and boots.

Back at the table, Big Grace is helping George to a refill. "Saint John's fire: it's a final bugger off to winter and disease," he tells her. "Oh, brother. I should bloody jump through it myself," he says.

Grace lays her beringed hand over his. "I'd advise you to do no such thing, my dear. You've played with quite enough fire for one lifetime . . ." She looks pointedly at Charmian coming back out of breath and laughing, gripping Boo's hand and shouting to Shane to take off her skirt in case it catches alight.

The town crier is ringing his bell and everyone starts for the mouth of the harbor to watch the re-enactment. There's cannon fire, a megaphone, and Lefteris the baker in patriotic attire with flaming torch is being rowed out to a wooden boat that's been stuffed to the gunnels with petrol and gunpowder. When Lefteris throws the torch he has to dive into the sea to escape the blast.

The streets become wild with firecrackers, everyone has stories of boys losing fingers and eyes; and men old enough to know better, with every cell of their bodies fizzing with arson, light fuses and run, and the high walls ring with explosions, every one of them making me shriek. Jimmy pulls me into Grafos's taverna where platters of fried squid and stuffed peppers are already being served to smartly dressed Greek families but there isn't a table for us.

Outside, beneath the ficus trees, Charmian is in the center of a group. "Hey, what's all this I'm hearing about George's drugs being plundered?" Big Grace is demanding to know.

Charmian stops laughing. "I knew I shouldn't have told you," she says. "I couldn't think how else to get some antibiotics into the poor little blighter." The way Grace looks at us, we might have been mangy cats ourselves, though her general expression tends to bad smell, except when she's talking to George about violence and war in the Old Testament.

"Bloody wasting my medicine . . ." George growls at us.

"Oh, darling, they found the poor thing suffocating in a bag on a rubbish heap."

"That's a terrible thing to do. To just throw a cat away like it's any old household rubbish," Ruth Sriber says. "But I swear the cat population doubles every time we come here."

Chuck and Gordon turn their chairs from the adjoining table where they've made claim to a recently arrived Beat professor of poetry, an Italian American with the wide troubled smile of a clown.

"*Yia sou*, Gregory, it's good to see you here again," Charmian says as he jumps up to greet her. "We didn't get a chance to say goodbye last year. The last I saw of you was just after sunrise, at Palamidas boatyard, and I called out but you seemed to be in some sort of a deep trance . . ."

I overhear George moan to Grace: "As usual my wife's got more faggots around her feet than Joan of bloody Arc."

"Oh my God, but they never stop breeding." Gordon is still on about the cats. "Do you remember that time Jean-Claude Maurice couldn't stand the sight of all the starving pussies any longer and he went to the pharmacy and got sleeping pills which he mashed up in food . . ."

At the mention of Jean-Claude's name George stops talking and the air starts to crackle around him.

Chuck hasn't noticed and takes up the story. "And then, because I happened to turn up to look at his paintings—"

Gordon interrupts. "To look at his *paintings*, you say?"

"Mmmmm hmmmm. Obviously that divine body was on display too," Chuck replies, fluttering his hands to denote perfection. "Anyway, there were all these cats and kittens lying about and Jean-Claude was scooping them up with tears running down his face while he did it. Said he didn't know if they were dead or sleeping. When he had filled the sack I went with him to the cliff. He put in two big rocks and by the way he was carrying on I thought he might hurl himself off after them."

"Bloody should have done." George can't seem to help himself and Big Grace asks in an urgent and audible whisper, "What is the situation with the Frenchman this year? I take it he's not here?"

"Nature Boy has been and gone, thank Christ . . ." George replies.

Charmian hasn't yet caught on to the change in the weather. She's too busy leaning down to hear whatever it is this Gregory is telling her.

George points a prosecuting finger straight at his wife. "Yes, Nature Boy's departed but look at her now. Like a fucking great praying mantis . . ."

I almost choke on a mouthful of wine as Big Grace joins in. "She's barely spoken to me since I got here. I've been wondering if I've offended her somehow, but I guess it's always been men who turn her on, and not women like me." She throws a suffering glance Charmian's way.

I can't let her get away with it. "I'm not a man," I say. "And she always has plenty of time for me, and for my mother before me."

Charmian seems to have caught the tailwind and snaps to attention.

"Oh yes, my wife likes playing mother to little Ricky here," George announces, swaying and clearing his throat. Charmian flinches. He raises the volume. "Yeah, well there's a bloody special reason for that, isn't there, Charm?"

Charmian has lost the color from her face, apart from her eyes which are astonishingly green. She reaches to steady herself on the back of Gregory Corso's chair.

"Don't you dare, George," she hisses.

Again he clears his throat and she lurches to silence him, her hand raised to slap his face. Big Grace springs from her seat. Maybe I imagine that she snarls.

Charmian lets her hand fall and turns on her heel.

"Yeah, off she goes like Lady bloody Macbeth . . ." George jeers as she flees with a napkin pressed to her face.

"Don't worry, darling. Little Ricky of Bayswater is the only one letting a cat out of a bag today," he hollers after her.

EIGHTEEN

There's something of the exclusive club about the writers' community and we're a little nervous the first time we arrive at Chuck and Gordon's. I'm all dressed up in one of the petticoats that Magda has started to sell behind Lagoudera, the bodice patterned with dye made from beetroots and onions and ruffled with lace she's dipped in a tub of Indian tea. Jimmy wears his one and only tie loosely knotted, his best poem in the pocket of his trousers.

The rooms of Gordon Merrick's house are like something from a magazine, with perfectly placed rugs and paintings and exotic *objets* he and Chuck have collected on their travels. Through an archway lies a tantalizing glimpse of warm polished boards and a lamp beside a velvet-canopied daybed, rose-colored cushions, an entire glowing wall of leather-bound books. We barely linger, lured on by the scent of roasting lamb and rosemary, and in the courtyard Chuck trots over in his colorful shirt, demanding I twirl because he knows Magda made my dress.

Jimmy checks his pocket, yet again, for the dog-eared copy of *Ambit* with his dystopian poem on page eleven.

"I can't possibly read in front of Gregory Corso," he says, like he is some sort of mouse who's been granted an audience with the king. According to him the clown-faced American is famous and has hung out with Jack Kerouac and William Burroughs, and almost caused a riot with the Beats in Paris. We're each of us shy for our own reasons. I am so much younger than anyone else here.

Chuck's chestnut beard is neatly trimmed to a point and he dances around us with a jug of fresh mint julep, swooping us to Gordon who stands by the grill in his Maxim's de Paris apron, spatula in hand. Jimmy asks if he's read much of Corso's work and the way Gordon inclines his head makes me realize that he must be slightly deaf. He smells of exotic oils, cocks his hand to his ear and moves closer to Jimmy. He has zero interest in me.

I'm relieved to see Charmian and George standing together. She's in a fresh cotton blouse with blue and yellow dots, and he's his usual bushfire of gossip and gasping and coughing.

His arm is around her waist and Charmian rests her head on his shoulder while he takes center stage. There's Göran, a brooding poet called Klaus, the playwright Ken and Janis with their sweet child, Leonard and Marianne. There are lanterns hanging from the trees. The widow Polymnia moves among us with bite-sized pastries of cheese and spinach and cocktail sausages on sticks.

"Ah, Polymnia is like a mother to the boys," Charmian says, watching the widow, whose pinafore hangs from the vast dado of her bosom. I can see how Chuck might be described as a boy, being so small and lively, but not Gordon who looks semi-embalmed.

Polymnia is clucking around Greg Corso, serving him from a

bowl of aubergine dip. I like the look of Corso; there's mischief in that worn, torn, old, young face. Charmian says that he'd been on the streets as a kid and spent his youth in Clinton State Prison. "It's a tremendously upsetting story," she says. "But it was in prison that he found Shelley and that's when he started to write . . ."

"Quite typical Chuck and Gordon behavior, I reckon, to suck up to the famous beatnik and invite only the published writers of the island," George says, speaking perfectly audibly from the side of his mouth.

"Oh *pfft*, George. It is good of them to invite us, that's all," Marianne replies, and adds with a giggle, "After all, what is it you think I have published?"

"You qualify because of Axel," George says. "Any news, by the way?" And when Marianne shakes her head Leonard mutters darkly under his breath.

George waves his glass around, indicating everyone.

"Seems a bit rough to exclude Paddy Greer, poor sod, but please don't think I'm so bloody rude that I criticize our hosts, in fact I'm very much in favor." He raises the glass in salute to Chuck and Gordon. "This way we're shot of the bloody decadents for a night," he says and downs his drink to fuel his oncoming tirade.

"Oh George, please . . ." Charmian says, as he starts to gather pace.

"They come to me sticking one hand out for a favor and with the other they're thumbing their noses because they think I write commercial shit. Meanwhile, the Russkies aren't taking too kindly to being lied to by a president over the bloody U-2, we could be on the brink of atomic war, but does any of that ever enter their pleasure-seeking little noggins as they hop like bloody fleas from bed to bed?"

Leonard narrows his eyes at him through the smoke of a newly lit cigarette. I'm still angry with George for his cruelty to Charmian the other night. For once I find my tongue. "Why does it have to be a crime for a young person to spend some time, if they can afford to do so, just living somewhere peaceful for a while? Who are we hurting? I can't say either of my parents made being in the rat race seem that appealing. And do you really think it would make a jot of difference if I joined a march to ban the bomb? I don't see what harm I'm doing just dreaming a while or why I make you so angry . . ."

George couldn't look more taken aback if Gordon's cat had suddenly spoken. He starts cursing and letting go at me with a great torrent about how he's pouring with sweat over the keys of his typewriter while everyone else is siesta-ing and playing around. His ranting is muddled in with stuff about the American spy plane, so anyone might think it was all my fault that guy has been caught red-handed by the Russians.

Charmian raises her voice above his, "George, I really think you might lay off for one night . . ." but still he rages until Leonard leaps in and by force of pure charisma makes him stop.

"If we assume the role of melancholy too enthusiastically, we lose a great deal of life . . ." he starts while George growls, "There won't be any life if there's an atomic war." Leonard bows his head and continues, "Yes, there are things to protest against and things to hate but there are a vast range of things to enjoy," and he looks up and lets a warm smile settle on Marianne, "beginning with our bodies and ending with ideas . . . If we refuse those or if we disdain them, then we are just as guilty as those who live complacently."

George's entire face is harrumphing. "Tell me that still feels like the truth once you've tried to write your novel through the crazy season," and he grumbles on until, at last, Marianne distracts him by reaching up to plant a kiss on his cheek.

"What a grumpy old moose you are tonight, George," she says as he lurches off for a refill and Charmian accompanies Greg Corso on Kyria Polymnia's tour of Gordon's house.

"Little dumpling is with my neighbor's daughter," Marianne says when I ask and for a moment she looks downcast and reaches for Leonard's hand. "I haven't left him before but sometimes I want to be free to join in."

George returns and immediately starts mocking Gordon's novels whilst simultaneously recommending Leonard read one.

"I learned everything I know about queer sex from his manuscripts," he says. "You know *The Strumpet Wind* was on the *New York Times* bestseller list for sixteen weeks? I'm sure Gordy's told you that himself by now . . . Sixteen damn weeks!"

The wine flows. Chuck brings out the gramophone and plays Bizet's *The Pearl Fishers* while we eat at the petal-strewn table. The lamb is melting; Gordon claims he's been turning and basting it for five hours, though I hear Charmian snort and say to George, "We all know it's old Polymnia does the cooking."

Greg Corso is sitting in a high carved chair at the head of the table, his face one broad smile, like a pixie-emperor on his throne. To his right Charmian, both of them talking so intently they barely find a moment to eat. From across the table I hear them quoting Keats and they match each other drink for drink. He's telling her about a dream he's had where he's a prisoner in Red China and has to stack a jar containing an atom bomb on a shelf or die on the end of a bayonet. "So I stacked it and got caught in my infamous action by a million flashbulbs . . . What can it mean?"

Leonard seems as enthralled by the poet as Jimmy, though

unlike Jimmy he isn't awed into silence. He keeps leaning across Marianne to ask about the scene, about protest and performance, bop and cut-ups, about this poet they all find so impossibly interesting called Allen Ginsberg.

Charmian is following their conversation, and several times they speak over her when she tries to join in.

"It's all very well, but where are the women's voices?" she manages when, as luck would have it, both men simultaneously need to draw breath. "Why are there no female Beat poets?"

"There are female Beats," Corso says with a fist to the table. "The trouble is their families have had them all locked up in institutions where they give them electric shocks."

Later I wonder if he isn't a bit of a show-off as he starts to riff about running on the Beat platform for President. Leonard plays along and they list all the people who'd vote him in: the Beats, the jazz musicians, the pot smokers, the Italians, delivery boys and girls, poets, painters, dancers, photographers, architects, students, professors.

"Even though I've had two felonies I'd be voted in," Corso continues. "America is essentially a Dadaistic country. Could you imagine anything more Dada than me as President?"

George catches the end of their skit. "So what you going to do about bloody Russia when you're in command?" he growls.

"I'd go to Khrushchev with a stick of marijuana and together we'd lie down and listen to Bach as though we were dead to the world," Corso replies.

After dinner Chuck ushers us to the top terrace where we sink among low cushions. There's a small stage that he's constructed, swathed with tasseled red silk rugs. There are sticky honey cakes and proper pastry forks and Polymnia brings a tray of coffee served in delicate blue Sèvres cups and a bottle of French cognac. Corso reaches for the bottle, uncorks it and drinks deeply straight from its neck.

Leonard bets Jimmy he can't do a handstand while maintaining the lotus position. Corso takes up the challenge but even with Charmian holding his knees he tumbles into the cushions. Before everything gets too rowdy Chuck leaps on to the stage and claps his hands. A kerosene lamp with a gooseneck stand lights the glow of pride as he speaks of the studio that wants to make a film of *The Strumpet Wind*.

"So this, my island friends, is to be adieu, for now," he says with a curtsy and holds out a hand for Gordon.

Gordon has discarded his chef's apron. He steps onto the stage, his silk shirt unbuttoned. "And now, because it's my party and I get to show off first, I'm going to be reading to you from something new. The novel's to be called *The Lord Won't Mind*," he says, adding with a smirk: "Great title, huh?"

Gordon turns his profile like one used to being lit. The backdrop is the black sky and stars. He throws back his shoulders and starts to read, and read, and read. An entire chapter goes by as a man who is blessed with a prodigious penis has a pretty boy come to stay.

"Peter's sex leaped and quivered before him, the head as taut and smooth as ripe fruit . . ." Gordon delivers his lines as he might a Shakespearean sonnet.

"He anointed his sex liberally, as always slightly in awe of it . . ." I see Charmian throw George several eye rolls as Gordon's honey-eyed tones continue through pages more of vigorous thrusting and splashing semen.

Beside me Jimmy is thumbing at his poem.

"Don't be nervous, we're among friends," I whisper and he grins at me.

"That's precisely why I am nervous," he says.

Leonard has buried his face in Marianne's hair; her feet have found their way to his lap. Greg Corso appears to have passed out among the cushions, with trailing hand in an attitude of the death of Chatterton. Gordon pauses to take a drink and Charmian and George start to clap, so we all join in and Göran leaps up and announces that he will read his new poem in Swedish.

Göran adopts the position of a great orator, a handwritten page dramatically aloft, but he manages only a few lines before Leonard cuts in with a splutter, "Hey, that's my poem," and Göran bounces back laughing and bows deeply before him.

"I admire it so much I had to translate it into Swedish," he says, reaching down as though to shake Leonard's hand but pulling him to his feet and giving him a push towards the stage. "Now, you."

Leonard shambles, looking reluctant and patting at his empty pockets, perhaps made a little shy by Göran's enthusiasm. He's certainly not born to performance like Gordon, who was once upon a time a matinee idol on Broadway.

Leonard gives a bashful cough before he begins, says he thinks he'd do better to tell a story than read one of his poems. His demeanor is apologetic, but the lamp catches the twinkle in his eye.

"So, I was looking at the back of *True Story* this afternoon. And I saw . . ." He looks at us and gulps. "I saw, about twenty ads for unwanted hair. The hair was a . . ." Marianne starts to giggle and he waits, shrugging and deadpan, for her to stop.

"A lot of people were offering to get rid of hair. They were offering to sandpaper it away. Shave it away. Pull it out. Cut it. Dissolve it with cream. Electrocute it."

Marianne's giggle is infectious; even Gordon, whose bruised ego is in the process of being eased by Chuck's foot massage, snorts. Leonard continues. "I mean, you're very concerned with unwanted babies but nobody cares for unwanted hair."

He lopes on, his face set to doleful, almost pleading. "I think there should be a place for unwanted hair in this society. I think, at the very least, there should be a hair museum. I mean, there should be somewhere, a hair asylum. There should be somewhere where, um, middle-aged ladies' mustaches reign . . ." His scenarios become ever more ridiculous as he breaks into a gallop. Eventually he leaves the stage, but seems unable, even then, to pull up, muttering, "College beards abandoned for careers. I mean, a man should be able to go into one of these hair asylums and, you know, review his whole life," until George silences him by shambling onto the stage.

George unfolds some pages and holds them to the light, clears his throat. "I was thinking I'd read to you from the book I'm currently writing, but it's about thousands of Chinese refugees starving to death, fleeing the Japanese, so it doesn't seem quite the thing for this happy occasion." He has brought his glass of brandy to the stage and raises it to Gordon. "Keep on keeping on, Gordon, and congratulations on the film. I hope it makes you lots of dough," he says, and we all cheer, apart from the guest of honor who is still passed out among the cushions.

"Damn, I was hoping he'd read his bomb poem," Jimmy grumbles, as Corso's snoring grows louder.

George is giving his glasses a quick polish with his handkerchief. He looks like someone's uncle about to tell a dirty joke. "So I'll read to you from the galley proofs of *Closer to the Sun* instead. It's set among a group of cosmopolitan misfits on an Aegean island not unlike this one . . . but, I hasten to add, any similarities to living people end there."

I hear a sharp intake of breath from Charmian. I daren't look at her. It seems we all sit up a bit straighter as George adjusts his specs. Marianne whispers, "Please, not this."

George is enjoying the tension, he almost swaggers as he begins: "Poseidon's Playground. The element of surprise was in fact that the newcomer was not nearly as young as expected . . ."

It takes a few sentences before we can breathe. George has chosen a scene about a suave but aging theater designer named Janáček who arrives on the island. Janáček has "the teeth of a dentrifrice advertisement and a cared-for complexion." Impervious to panic, this Janáček is cared for and fussed over by the younger Kettering, who wears a garishly striped Mykonos shirt and who George, with a little devil perched on his shoulder, is busy describing as a diminutive man with a chestnut-colored spade beard "who fluttered around Janáček's feet like a hummingbird."

It's hard to tell if Chuck and Gordon fail to see themselves; they manage well if they do, unlike the rest of us.

Thank goodness Charmian's got something she wants to read. She's swaying a little as she stands on Chuck's platform but her voice is steady and clear. She has only a couple of typed pages and she holds them so close to the lamp that her face has an almost ghostly luminosity.

"I wrote it, quite suddenly, this afternoon," she says. "It's about a visit to the family of a sponge diver, a proud man with neither work nor money because it's been declared that he has the evil eye. I've no idea what it's to turn into yet, but here goes . . ."

It's incredibly vivid, the short passage she reads. I can see it all. The diver's wife, Irini, with an entire set of stainless-steel teeth that glitter when she speaks, "as if the silver *ikon* above the bedpost was making a pronouncement." The hungry and sick children piled up on the bed shelf like grubs.

Jimmy's poem is about the rats in the sewers beneath the Houses of Parliament. When it comes to his turn to read, we are all so drunk he might be P. B. Shelley.

NINETEEN

It has rained overnight and the marble streets around the port are gleaming, the air fresh with the scent of quenched white flowers. I walk with Jimmy and Bobby. We link arms and for once Bobby doesn't shake me off, as though a sprinkling of rain has freshened him up too. The light has returned to his eyes and the shadows receded. He doesn't silence me when I find myself remembering a song about a fair young maiden and the blue, blue sea that Mum used to sing to us and he even joins in with the chorus.

We've left the others sleeping, didn't try to rouse them, though Bobby's done Edie the kindness of leaving a jug of water beside her head. Such messy slumberers. There were ants crawling around the rims of sticky glasses and lumps of sweating cheese among the fallen, some of whom were daubed in paint.

The pharmacy has become like a magical sweetshop to many of our friends on the island.

"I think count me in next time," Jimmy is saying. He got back late from fishing to find them dancing to Trudy's records on the terrace and he says everyone looked phantasmagorical in the moonlight, like they were underwater and dissolving.

"And Leonard was saying the other night that he can work for twenty-four hours straight on the Benzadryl." Jimmy is enthusiastic about pills. I am always too scared.

Bobby hops over to where Elias waits in the shade behind the marketplace with his bulging goatskins of water. Bobby fills our cans and shoulders them cheerfully, as though they are empty instead of full. He doesn't even moan about Elias's ratcheting up of the price of the water for foreigners and flips a spare coin to skinny Stomasis, the candlemaker's son.

The sun has chased away the last of the rain as we thread our way through strings of waiting donkeys, with nothing much before us but a boat ride to the western end of the island where the Swedes have set up camp at Bisti Bay.

We buy the last four loaves of bread at the bakery and Bobby bumps smack into Charmian as she comes with her tin of meat and potatoes, calling hasty *Kalimera*s and looking with disbelief at the empty bread shelf behind Kyria Anastasia.

"Here, take this," Bobby says. "No, no. I insist."

Kyria Anastasia checks that the name tag is stuck fast to Charmian's tin and slides it alongside the other dinners that are slow-cooking over the embers. I have failed to take advantage of the bakehouse oven, and vow to become better at this sort of thing once Jimmy and I are settled.

"It's only a loaf of bread," Bobby is saying, as Charmian kisses him on both flaming cheeks.

"Well, I'm glad of it, so thank you," she says. "George has been in bed with a fever but I'm hoping he'll manage a little gruel today."

I hold out my hand to relieve her of one of her baskets. "Oh, poor George. I hope it's not serious? Will you let me know if there's anything I can do?"

Charmian flaps me away. "Goodness, Erica, you are kind. But it's his own fault. I think he hit the grog rather hard the other night at Chuck and Gordon's, don't you?"

"We all did, and that's the truth," Jimmy says, adding with a snort, "Oh, but Gordon's novel!"

We walk down the lane together, milking our memories for every last drop.

Charmian quotes with gusto: "'His sex swelled and rose heavily before him. He had to step back to give it room . . .'"

I beg her to stop. My sides have only just given up hurting.

"Oh man," Jimmy says, "do you think he and Chuck seriously failed to see themselves in George's thing?"

"It's as well to know that George can be exceedingly cruel," Charmian says, and returns to Bobby before I've had a chance to tell her how much I enjoyed the passage that she read.

We weren't expecting all the marrieds with their children to be part of our group. The Goschens have come down from the hills with their brood; the curly-haired girls have their baby brother toddling between them and Angela is wearing one of David's nightshirts to cover her bump. Demetri and Bim are outside Tassos with Police Chief Manolis who is tapping a finger at a sheaf of documents on the table. Carolyn and Demetri's pretty young housemaid, Angelika, waits at the mole with their baby while Demetri, slumped back in his chair and laconically bored, interprets between the policeman and Bim.

"Oh, it's probably the usual business with visas," Charmian says. "They can make it such a bother, especially if they think you're not behaving yourself," and I guess by the look that she throws him she knows something of Bim's ways after dark.

Demetri slopes over to ask her if she can find the time to take a climb through Kamini to view a ruin with him and Carolyn. "I know you'll tell us straight if you think it'd be mad to attempt to rebuild it," he says and it amuses me that this grown man with Greek blood in his veins, an American family and the beginnings of a paunch, appears to need the approval of our island Queen as much as the rest of us.

Charmian beams, "Oooh, *kaloriziko*! Have you fallen in love?" and starts looking around for a drink with which to toast but stalls when she sees Leonard ambling towards us, strung with bulging bags, two sacks of laundry, and Axel Joachim asleep, head lolling against his shoulder.

"Well, well," Charmian says. "Our Canadian friend has been left holding the baby. Quite literally."

She calls out to him. "My goodness, whatever is that you're using for nappies?" And Leonard looks down as though surprised to find a baby in loosening wrappings and joins her laughter, shushing himself, trying not to wake him, then shushing and patting and doing a jig.

Charmian scoops up her basket. "Will you excuse me, I think I must help him out."

Charlie Heck is waving at us from the mole as Manos's boat hoves into view around the headland. Charlie has wide-eyed and fresh-from-the-ferry Francine beside him and Jimmy can't seem to help an impressed whistle as we gather our things.

Francine is a dancer from Paris, almost as young as me. "He tells them he's an African prince," I snap and as I turn to mask my bad temper I catch sight of Charmian and Leonard and the gentle choreography as he decants the sleeping baby into her arms.

"Hey, where's Marianne?" I ask but everyone's rushing for the boat: Jimmy and Bobby hefting the water cans, Robyn and Bim swinging a basket between them, children scattering.

"Marianne's in Athens with Axel," Angela tells me as she scoots by, calling to the Gassoumises' pretty maid.

"Angeliki! Angeliki! Please hold Mariora's hand. Look, the boat is docking."

We sit around Manos at the tiller with our backs to the rail. Bim and Demetri have rushed to the prow where it's quieter and they can stretch out on the mats. Charlie Heck has brought a large bag of pumpkin seeds which we split between our teeth. We are all laughing and being showered with rogue spray, whooping at the prismic flash of flying fish from a sea so bright they are like shards of its own dazzle.

Charlie holds on to Francine like she might fly overboard, and despite the noisy putt-putt of the engine I catch enough of what he's telling her to know it's the usual routine: "Nearly blew my own brains out in Korea, matter of fact . . ." and on through his wanderings. "But this island is right for me. You know, Hydra is the only place I've rented a house where I haven't been given bother about my race." Francine shrieks as the boat hits the bow wave of the incoming ferry.

I'm thrown closer to Bobby who puts an arm out to steady me. He's talking to Jimmy about Edie. "You know, I feel so much better since I worked out that I can't keep her for myself," he's saying as again the boat thumps down and we are showered with spray. "It's as Dinos said, something of a relief not to be constantly watching her."

I wait until Manos steers a less bumpy path. "Dinos? The sponge-factory guy I met at George and Charmian's?"

Bobby has pulled off his T-shirt and is rubbing the water from his hair. His eyes are as blue as airmail paper. "Yes, that's my man. He's pretty cool, actually; lets me use his kiln up at Episkopi. Tell you the truth, doll, I've been unburdening myself to him like he's some sort of head doctor."

I'm astonished to think that Bobby has talked to anyone, let alone that now he's discussing it with me. I've become so accustomed to his gruff pronouncements and brooding silences. He continues talking as we drift in the lee of the sleeping man of Dokos island.

"Thing is, I met Edie right after Mum died and I've been clinging to her ever since. It's not fair on the chick," he's saying and I look across at Jimmy and catch him enjoying the sight of Francine as she stands to grip the rail, very pert in pink checked shorts and a tiny fluttering handkerchief of a top, and wish that he'd go blind.

Manos steers the boat closer to the island. The smells of wild thyme and diesel and the rhythmic thumping become so soporific we all fall into a lull.

Now we are beyond Palamidas, the shoulders of the island grow sparse. We pass the sheer cliff where the old people used to go to die—sometimes, Manos says, in a basket which was rolled off the edge, sometimes by leaping. "They'd say to their family, why waste a good basket?"

Soon a landscape that includes the occasional olive tree or pine gives way to nothing but bold muscular rocks. It's hypnotic watching the striations and marblings pass us by, dusty bronze and dusty grey and ironstone where sudden great rivers of malachite green and butcher's red flow. We pass pirates' caves, one with an old hermit who guards its entrance, and Manos tells us the story of the pink chapel in a bay where red wine is used to mix the whitewash in remembrance of an ancient wrecking of a wine boat, when all the souls along with the barrels of wine were miraculously washed ashore.

You can't help but gasp when you see Bisti Bay for the first time. It's a perfect horseshoe with steep pine forests rising up around a jewel box of pebbles. The water flashes blue as a million king-fishers. When you look down into it from the boat it's rippling with gold. The clearest water in the whole of Greece. Closer to the beach, the reflections of pine trees stipple it with scarab-green iridescence.

We are met by Lena who comes splashing and cheering, wear-ing little more than plaited seaweed that hangs in tendrils from her waist. "Hey, hey, ahoy there!" A white shell flies on a cord between her brown breasts as she throws up her arms to catch the rope.

The others come scootling from the trees when they hear her shout. It's like being greeted by a particularly golden gang of sav-ages as they wade towards us to help carry the supplies ashore. The boys have all grown beards, Ivar wears nothing but a crown of feathers in his yellow hair, one of the Dutch girls has painted petals around her nipples. Bim's foot barely touches the shore before he's shedding his shorts.

Albin and Ivar have been out spearfishing and their catch of three lugubrious-faced grouper fish are being prepared by Göran, who has paused beneath the pine trees with his knife in the block to scribble in his notebook. He is crouched over, trans-fixed by the fallen fish scales that glitter up at him from among the cross-hatching of pine needles.

A couple of hammocks hang between the trees and the sail-maker has done a good job with the tents which have kept out the overnight rain and are now steaming in shafts of sunlight beneath the pines. Albin shows us around. There's a neat stack of logs for their fire and a pole roped between trees for gymnasium. At the

shore the water barrel and the wine casks are kept cool beneath a
wet mound of towels. Albin reckons they'll stay all summer if they
don't get thrown off.

Some of us swim out with a mask. A seal lives in one of the
caves but he's making himself scarce today. Beneath the trees it
isn't too long before Jimmy and Bobby start competing with the
other men, doing every sort of pull-up, Göran keeping count in
Swedish. No one can match Jimmy, not even Ivar. Demetri and
Charlie go haring back to the water to swim with Francine who
has discarded what tiny clothing she arrived in. Angelika stands in
the shade of a salt tree, with the babies. She's talking earnestly to
Manos. I see her make the sign of the cross across her buttoned-up
blouse as her boss splashes naked into the shallows.

Beneath the pines Angela wears the scowl of an unwilling cap-
tive. She sits on a log, cajoling her smallest girl who is refusing to
join Daddy and her siblings at the beach. It's been like this since the
boat, little Mari-mou wanting only her mother.

Ivar scoots past with Lena in pursuit, shouting, trying to dodge
her through the low branches. She catches him and snatches the
crown from his head and comes laughing and running back with
it. Mariora is pulling her mother's hand; she wants to collect pine
cones. Lena is reaching up to crown Jimmy. I'm glad to see that he's
still wearing his shorts. I wish she wouldn't press herself against
him like that.

This is the first chance I've had to ask Angela about Marianne.
She's been stuck at the front of the boat and buried in sleeping children the whole way over. "So, Marianne's with Axel in Athens . . . ?"

Angela nods. "Patricia's had an accident," she says as Jimmy
bounds over with a watermelon in one hand and a cleaver in the
other like they're a scepter and chalice, the feather crown askew.
He squats and places the melon at his feet.

"I've no idea why Marianne has to go running to Axel, but there it is. She got a telegram from him begging her to come because Patricia is in hospital," Angela is saying as Jimmy brings down the blade and splits the melon.

He drops the cleaver. "What? Has something happened to Pat?"

"She had a crash in Axel's car. It's very serious," Angela says, though the child is rearing and making it difficult. "They say all her bones are broken and her lungs are bleeding."

The color is leaching from Jimmy's face. "Oh God, no. Poor Pat. Is she going to be OK?"

Angela shrugs. "Police Chief Manolis has heard talk of a prosecution. Everyone wants to know if the poor lamb will pull through, but all the news is bound up in yards of red tape to do with Marianne's name being on the car's papers because Axel was banned from driving, and the Norwegian consulate is involved—a big mess, so of course Axel can't cope at all and Marianne has flown in like the angel she is. No one seems to know if Patricia will live or die," she manages before the little girl pulls her away.

"Oh, good God. Poor Pat," Jimmy says again, and it's unnerving to witness his shoulders heaving as he grips his feather-crowned head in his hands.

Lena is crouching on a mat showing the two Dutch girls how to whittle a flute and, though Robyn wants to join them, Bim has dragged her off like some sort of caveman and is currently butchering her in one of the tents; at least that's how it sounds to the rest of us.

Albin starts fiddling with the radio but the tinny noise does little to drown it out so we all start singing.

There's a game of ball, the Scandinavians against the rest of the world, that involves many dunkings—especially, it seems, of Francine. We're all ravenous by the time Göran has finished with the grouper fish he's been sousing with lemon and herbs, olive oil, salt and pepper. The fire is lit on the beach, the chunks of fish cooked on spears in the flames and eaten on Anastasia's good bread with pickled cucumbers. We drink chalky-white ouzo with water and Ivar plays some Woody Guthrie songs on his guitar.

The sound of the boat breaks a silence that descended on the camp with the amber hour as we sat in a circle and Lena played her flute to the owls.

Manos hurries us aboard. A squall has come in and the sea has grown choppy. We all lie on the mats at the front and ride it like a rodeo and fall against each other, grabbing for the rail and clinging as the waves slap the boat and cover us in blankets of foam.

Amethyst clouds gather across the horizon and Francine cavorts at the prow, attempting to keep Charlie's billowing shirt gathered around her. I silently congratulate myself that I haven't allowed such aphrodisiac nakedness to ruin a perfect day, though I've been tortured by her splashing through the shallows with Jimmy.

Manos doesn't want to take the boat around to the port so we pile out at Kamini fishing harbor. Charlie is in a great hurry to walk Francine back to her guesthouse. The rest of us linger while Angelika herds the children and carries the babies up the hill. There's music at the taverna, the golden glow of lamps through its windows, its yellow awnings flapping, summoning us inside.

TWENTY

"Her thumb had to be amputated, gangrene had set in," Marianne is saying as Charmian leans against the counter beside her smoking a cigarette and I bounce Axel Joachim on my knees, singing: "This is the way the lady rides, trit-trot, trit-trot, trit-trot, trit-trot . . ."

Marianne has been back from Athens a week but this is the first we've seen of her and Charmian is lapping up the details. Marianne looks surprisingly cheerful as she stands over the chopping board preparing a sandwich while a faded fisherman's smock that skims the top of her golden thighs looks like something from *Queen* magazine or *Vogue*.

She turns to us and raises a thumb. "Of course, it is her right hand: the thumb she uses for painting," she says. She holds an imaginary paintbrush and I can't be certain she isn't smirking as she mimes making tiny and precise pointillist dots on her canvas of air.

"Higgledy-ho, higgledy-hi, and . . ." Axel Joachim squeals as I down him into the ditch.

"Sshhh, sshhh, not so noisy please, Erica," Marianne pleads, pointing to the ceiling. "Leonard says he doesn't mind if the baby cries but I think he can work better if we don't make too much distraction, huh?"

Charmian tuts and reaches to take the baby from me, nestles him to her hip. I'm shocked about the gangrene. Marianne says Patricia's lucky she lost only the one thumb.

The cat lies asleep on the table, curled around the I Ching which has been left open and facedown beside a page of neatly drawn hexagrams. I lift a glass jar to smell a posy of violets that is tied with a green ribbon.

"Leonard has been so kind but he's lost enough writing time helping with Barnet while I've been away," Marianne says.

Charmian snorts and gives the baby a squeeze. "Oh, I see, we're Barnet now, are we?" and she hands him a discarded crust to chew on.

"I must say he did tremendously well, despite running out of nappies and having to resort to some rather fine-looking Norwegian damask," Charmian says. "Has he confessed that he raided the chest?"

"Ah yes, Mama's wedding gifts to Axel and me. Silver sauce boats and salmon platters, monogrammed napkins; whatever was she thinking?" Marianne says, flattening the slices of bread with a rolling pin. She lifts a pat of butter from the cool-water depths of its earthenware jar. "I need to tempt him. He's been working on his novel in twenty-four-hour shifts since I got back. I'm worried that he doesn't eat," and fills the buttered bread with slices of salted beef, tomatoes and cornichons.

"That might be because of the pills he's getting from the pharmacy," I pipe up, longing to sound knowledgeable and join in.

She gives me a worried glance, nips some rosettes of new leaves from a pot of basil. "Whatever it takes to get this book into the hands of a publisher. He says he needs to be purged of the words before he can relax." She scatters the basil over the sandwich.

"I know the feeling," Charmian says.

Marianne adds a sprinkling of crushed pink peppercorns. "Axel's the same. In agony! Raving about getting his novel to Capellen the whole time he's sitting there at Patricia's bedside. It was the same when I had my operation. He's got his typewriter across his knees, banging away at it like a crazy man, and he forgets to drip the disinfectant over the bandages. Not eating. Really, I had no choice but to help out," she says, taking a chunk of ice from the box and, ignoring Charmian's sarcastic snort, hacking some pieces and plinking them into a jug.

"Ah, where would these male writers be without their ministering angels?" Charmian says.

Marianne settles an unmistakably longing glance at the stairs. "Maybe my mother is right and I should be searching for a bourgeois man in the suburbs of Oslo, but this is what's familiar to me." She starts tidying her hair and excuses herself to take the sandwich and iced lemon tea up to Leonard.

Charmian sighs and huffs. "She's so happy to serve, so content to sit at the poet's feet when she should be at the table." She settles the baby to play on his mat. "Really, Erica, I could despair of our sex," she says, lighting a cigarette. "Christ, but sometimes I think who am I to talk? It's so tiring, all the kicking and screaming and demanding George do his share, arguing all the bloody time." She takes a hungry drag on the cigarette. "I sit on that step by his writing table, urging him on, and often I'm thinking ugly thoughts because my own work can only get done in the margins of his. I'm sorry, darling, I'm ranting. Maybe I'm jealous and wish that the simple pleasures of domestic harmony were enough for me too."

She smokes some more. She isn't finished. "I suppose what I'm trying to say to you, Erica, is that you should be very cautious of pinning all your dreams to a bloke, however talented and marvelous he may be."

I'm glad she can't see inside my head. I'm lost in a daydream where it's me taking a sandwich to Jimmy in an ordered house not unlike this one, with pretty pots and herbs with sunlit leaves on the windowsill. It's Cato on the table and our baby who lies kicking his legs and gurgling on the mat. I snap myself back.

"I hope Patricia won't be crippled," I say.

I think of that day in Athens, of Patricia bending to Marianne's flowers discarded on the floor, graceful and slim as a stem. Marianne is convinced that she was driving that fast because she'd had a row with Axel. It was dawn, around the corner a fruit seller on his way to market with donkey cart, the wrong side of the road. The car was barely damaged when, swerving to avoid him, she crashed into the bridge. Patricia was less lucky. She had been flung over the bonnet and on to the rocky bed of a dry river below, breaking her hips and collarbone, her rib cage, puncturing a lung. Her face was a mess, her teeth smashed, her top lip torn clean away, infection had taken that precious painting thumb; it was a miracle she survived.

Charmian is wreathed in irritable smoke. "What I want to know is why Marianne went there at all. Was it simply because Axel needed her to sign the papers to do with the car? Or was she hoping for something else? What I don't believe is this Florence Nightingale bullshit. Do you really think that she's been there a week to help Axel with the nursing? What, of her rival? And how must poor Patricia have felt every time she swam into consciousness to find Marianne dabbing at her wounds? He has plenty of friends in Athens, Else and Per to name but two, he could have called on any of them for such things . . ."

She stops talking as Marianne returns. Marianne pours us some wine, puts out a plate of feta and olives. She clears away the I Ching from the table but keeps it open at the page to show us hexagram 19.

"This is Leonard's. It's very clear. He must put in the hours now if there's to be a fruitful harvest. Spring doesn't last forever, the work needs to be done before there is a reversal in the eighth month."

Charmian smiles indulgently at her until, blushing, she realises she's lost us and changes the subject.

She gives Charmian an impish grin. "Anyway, never mind about Leonard and me, what is it I hear about you and Corso?"

"I have no idea what you are talking about," Charmian says.

"Birds have beaks to sing with, you know." Marianne becomes a little sprite when she teases, so pretty it might hurt your eyes.

Charmian chuckles. "Marianne, really! He was only here a few days. I went for one midnight dip. You're as bad as the rest of them!"

TWENTY-ONE

The port throbs with tourists and the street cats grow fat. The cicadas are busy breaking a hundred hearts with their songs. We pull our mattresses out to the terrace and sleep beneath the stars, wake with the sun and Cato sleeking in from a night's hunting to pat at my face with an imperious paw. We pick over platters of fish at taverna tables, or drift from courtyard to courtyard with our records and poems, or take bottles of beer and eat bread and meatballs beneath the tumbling vines of the outdoor cinema in Economou Street that shows Greek films with English subtitles.

We have all become leaner, our legs muscled from the steps, Bobby's and Jimmy's shoulders almost amphibian from swimming. Sometimes we take a bag of peaches and a flask of coffee to the cave and grab a dip before the port is fully awake, other times we swim late at night and lie naked between the moon and the tide on the still-warm rocks.

Jimmy works best in the relatively cooler hours of the evening

and we go out late to the starlight bar Xenomania high up on
the cliffs above the windmill where they play old-fashioned jazz
records and an arrangement of low tables and cushioned benches
favors comfortable slouching.

Jimmy and I wait a moment outside to catch our breath. There's
silver laughter, swooping familiar voices. We drift and yet always
run into the same people, as though the foreign colony moves with
a force as mysterious as the murmuration of starlings. The mountain sheers up behind Xenomania black as the sky. It looks less
like a bar and more a lit stage in a dark auditorium, two shadowed
trees at the entrance its proscenium arch. George's words reach us
rapid as gunfire, a splatter-attack of laughter and coughing, and
Charmian's jangled: "Darling, please, stop there. Let's not be dis-
agreeable on your birthday!"

We go straight away to wish him many happy returns. I could
kick myself for not making a card. Only yesterday I helped Booli
and Shane with the wrapping of a wind chime.

He's on growling bad form, despite Nancy Greer, décolletage
jellying from cabbage-green ruffles, handing him the last slice from
a cherry cake she's baked especially for him.

He stuffs his mouth with the cake, speaks in a rain of crumbs
and coughing. "Yeah well, forty-bloody-eight and what have I got
to bloody show for it? Up to my arsehole in debt, oh brother, yes.
Look at me here, the great success. Marooned on this rock without
the fare out, chained to the bloody typewriter by all the people
who depend on me, like some old donkey to the millstone." He
is set to go on but Charmian stops him by throwing her cigarette
packet at his head.

"Oh do stop feeling so sorry for yourself, George," she snaps.
"Though if we're to tarry with so many sorrows let's at least get
another bottle to drown them in." She has a locked sort of smile

that comes with a great blinking-back of tears. George's eyes are narrowing as he dabs at his mouth and she flinches as he takes a breath, the menace so palpable that Jimmy springs between them.

"Man, it seems to me you've got plenty of good stuff going on."

George grabs Jimmy by the arm, thrusts his ravaged old face at him. "This is what it looks like, Writer Boy. You sure you want this, eh?"

Patrick Greer is slumped at the far end of the table, birthday-cake crumbs in his beard. George is as drunk as I've ever seen him. He shoves Jimmy towards Patrick with school-bully force.

"Buy this Irishman a drink and he'll give you some bloody good advice about trying to live by the pen on this godforsaken rock."

Patrick obediently waves a sheaf of papers in his hands, "Rejection slips, all of them," and adds with a melodramatic burr, "I keep digging away but where are my nine rows of beans? I should just throw in the shovel and go back to teaching." He's still slurring away as we retreat, using Trudy, who comes in a chattering group with Demetri, as an excuse to escape.

Demetri is rattling off something in excitable Greek to the cook, Alexeos. Carolyn and Robyn nod as though they understand every word. Bim bounds over to George, inciting another stinging attack, this time of some pages Bim has recently given him to read.

"You spend more time with your hands in girls' panties than you do with them at your typewriter and it bloody well shows," George says, and Charmian begs him to stop being such an oaf. Luckily Robyn is out of earshot and doesn't hear this assessment of her husband's ability, but now she's coming back, trailing Demetri and Carolyn from the kitchen where they've been inspecting the remains of Alexeos's catch.

Robyn looks especially prissy tonight, her myopic helplessness magnified by the librarian glasses. Bim has enough vim and vigor for both of them, though even he is deflated by George. Luckily, Alexeos is on their tail with two jugs of wine and keen that we should all try the spider crab.

Trudy throws her hands to her mouth. Her formerly lustrous red hair hasn't seen a hairbrush in months. She's flopped down beside me, fanning her face with the menu. "What I'd give for a bottle of Coca-Cola and no rotten mosquitoes," she says and she looks so washed out it's hard to remember the Titian beauty of the spring-time who skipped across the rocks pursued by a cloven-hoofed Jean-Claude Maurice.

Behind me Bim is pumping Charmian for news of Patricia. She tells him Patricia is waiting to be flown home to the States to be put back together. "Whereas Axel's Karmann Ghia needs only a new bumper . . ." she says while Trudy goes on about the island's culinary deprivations, unzipping her shorts and complaining that the olive oil is making her fat.

". . . Meanwhile Marianne's had a letter from Axel, a cruel and heartless letter. He makes it very clear that he will be following Patricia to the hospital in Chicago. Says he'll wait a lifetime for her."

I turn away from Trudy, catch Bim leaning towards Charmian with his elbow to his knee. He uses the heft of his shoulder to block George who keeps trying to interrupt.

"Does Axel know that Leonard's moved right in on his wife? I mean, those tennis sneakers were under Axel's desk almost before he'd hoisted a sail," Bim says.

"It's true that I don't hear much chattering of the keys coming from Leonard's own digs when I walk past these days. But Axel doesn't have the capacity to either wonder or care. He's moved on. That's what's so hurtful. All he can say to Marianne is that . . ."

here Charmian stops to take a swig from the wine that Bim pours, screws up her eyes and says in an approximation of Axel's accented voice ". . . my heart bleeds for you, my little wife; I feel for you and suffer with you and the thought of little Axel growing up without me gnaws at me."

She takes another gulp and resumes in her own husky tones. "Shalom, shalom for Leonard, or who knows what sort of state the poor girl would be in. And it's hard yakka up there because the little mite has some sort of gastric thing going on and she's stuck when the genius of the house wishes to down tools for the night and head out for action. Still, he does seem to have cheered her up and he's very tender with the boy."

George isn't having Bim's body language exclude him from a toast. "To Marianne and Leonard!" he roars and pushes him aside to clink his glass to Charmian's.

"Good on our Viking girl that she has hooked the Canadian. Just in the nick of time," he says, throwing back the wine, and through the smoke of a newly lit cigarette blooms a sudden boyish grin, the sort that his grumpy old face is still sometimes transformed by. "Oh brother, she must be one hell of a fuck."

Bim rallies; how easily all is forgiven when there's mockery in play.

"Well, she'll be sucking not fucking . . ."

Robyn gapes at him, her nose greasy from sliding her glasses up it. "Bim, what a thing to say. How would you know?"

"I've read a few pages of his novel, and of course his poetry. Promising stuff . . . but it's fellatio all the way." Bim is enjoying himself, Patrick Greer also: the turn the conversation has taken promises delicious pickings.

"She'd better be good at it down on her knees!" Patrick says, with his mollusk of a mouth wet and shining.

George laughs and says it's hard to think of many poems that celebrate "the art of the gobby" and everyone tries to come up with something. Catullus? Joyce, surely?

Charmian waits until they've run out of steam to trump them. "Of course there's Shelley," she says and she starts to recite: "'Soft, my dearest angel, stay/Oh! You suck my soul away/Suck on, suck on, I glow, I glow!/Tides of maddening passion roll/And streams of rapture drown my soul.'"

I know she's drunk but I'm disappointed when she gears the conversation back to Marianne. I wish I'd stayed at home rather than wasting good money up here at Xenomania.

"Anyway, I'm sure Marianne is perfectly proficient in all the feminine arts," she's saying with a saucy grin. The words dart poisonous, at odds with the beauty of our surroundings, the gentle strains of a saxophone, "Petite Fleur."

Charmian settles her naughty eyes on Robyn. "But what an art it is to live in service to a man. Maybe it's the greatest creative art, and should be accorded respect, like the geishas in Japan—"

"Maybe you could take lessons from her, Charm," George interrupts, still bellowing with laughter over something Bim is saying in his other ear and going one better. "Yeah, I bet she bangs like a dunny door in a gale."

"Be quiet a moment, all of you, I mean it. Stop sniggering. What do we know of the flower and willow world?"

"Polishing Axel's shit until it shines is hardly the same thing," George says.

"Well, you might say that Marianne has been so beautifully trained by Axel in the arts that facilitate good writing, Leonard is getting a ready-made muse. Lucky him, that's what I thought when I was up there today. She was on her knees, as it happens . . ."

I don't need this. The sourness is curdling the night.

"I saw them this morning on the beach at Kamini with the baby. They seemed very happy," I say.

"So, Marianne was on her knees . . . ?" Bim is jockeying her on, like a rider into a fence.

Charmian relishes keeping them waiting. How cruel they all look, how ghoulish by lamplight. I think about Marianne with Leonard on the beach, splashing together into the sea. They took it in turns to swim and spin the baby around in a blue rubber ring. On the beach they lay face to face with the baby between them, a tangle of limbs and endearments. I watched Leonard kiss each little piggy to make the baby squeal.

Charmian pours herself another glass of wine and asks George to light her a smoke from his own before continuing.

"I came in from the terrace; they didn't see me at first. The room was cool, shuttered but for the one window where she knelt at his feet, the polished floor shining around her." Charmian's storytelling voice is low and warm. The others fall silent. "There were fresh flowers, a jug of wine and two glasses beside her. The air was still and sweet with the scent of the flowers—something else too, monastery incense perhaps. Leonard was among the cushions on the couch strumming his guitar, the baby sleepily sucking on a bottle of milk tucked beside him, and there she was kneeling in that pool of light, holding up a plate on which she'd arranged wafers of salami sliced so thin they were almost transparent, overlapping and spread out like a Japanese flower. That's when I thought of the geishas. But it was beautiful, the way she looked at him, the offering; enough that I felt very much an intruder at a private sacrament. He was picking out a tune, a lullaby for the baby; rather lovely, actually."

Charmian takes a drink. If she thinks that will draw the sting from the evening she's mistaken. George has been harrumphing the entire time she's been speaking. Now it's his turn.

"She'll drive him away, just like she has Axel. Eventually a man with more than half a noggin wants to be stimulated in the head as well as the bed and the stomach. Axel's had her parroting all that Ouspensky and Gurdjieff stuff for years, but I'm not sure Leonard finds it any more convincing than the rest of us. But what else can she do? As the only man here who's ever met a geisha, I can tell you they have many accomplishments. Calligraphy, conversation, music. I'm not aware I've ever seen Marianne getting her mouth around the shakuhachi."

Even Nancy joins in. "It's not like she doesn't try, sweetheart that she is. Do you remember when she took up pottery? Bowls in every shade of excrement. I remember Axel found it all very amusing, despite that he was the one having to eat from the dolloping things."

Patrick Greer can't resist. "And then there was poetry all last summer while she mooned about with the baby in her belly. Luckily none of us was ever asked to read it, though I won't deny that she did look pretty sitting chewing her pencil."

The plates of fried spider crabs arrive which gives everyone something else to pick at.

Trudy is the only person other than George not eating. "You oldsters are all so nasty about each other," she says. "That's why Jean-Claude scarpered; he said he couldn't stand another minute living among vipers, and the more time I spend listening to you tearing Marianne apart, the more I think I can see his point."

No one pays her any attention. Patrick is rambling. "Of course, our dear Charm was quite a thing when she was big with child . . . Mmmmm, I remember her down there on the rocks with her swimsuit straining. So ripened was she, I could think only of melons. Honeydews, watermelon, the juiciest of fruits hanging heavy on the vine."

"Oh goodness, Patrick dear, have you been taking writing classes with Gordon?" Charmian says.

Trudy is not to be deterred. George is as alert to Jean-Claude's name as one might be to a lover's footstep on the stair. Trudy addresses him over our heads as we scrabble like a flock of gulls over the tin tray that Alexeos has placed between us.

"Whatever it is you've written about him in your book is what drove him away. He started packing straight after you came round and showed him those pages."

George nods and smiles but says nothing. Trudy almost shouts at him.

"Gee, even you won't tell me what it's all about and you wrote it. I guess I'll just have to wait, like everyone else, until I can read it for myself. I've already written to my London aunt to get a copy sent from Dillons. Not long now . . ."

George looks at her and grins. Trudy blinks her innocent eyes back at him. Charmian lifts her hand like she wants to slap her but has to settle instead for reaching for a cigarette.

Patrick Greer strikes her a light. He's having quite the night and now we are on to his favorite subject.

"You see, George, this is just the start. I told you not to do it to your wife; people will read it as the truth and you know it."

"Thank you, Patrick," Charmian says, blowing out the match, while Trudy stares at her with widening eyes behind which the pennies are dropping.

"Ah, my wife. She can only tell the truth, curse her, so why shouldn't I for once?" George bangs the table, making Trudy jump, and waves his glass at Charmian. "Just look at her there, preening with her wampum belt of male scalps. Does she look like she cares? I'd have to be a bloody fool to ask where she's been when she comes in at night so alive. I'm too bloody scared to ask who she's been with or what she's been doing. It's her honesty that scares the bloody pants off me."

Charmian stubs out her cigarette, throws back her wine. "I'm sorry, everyone. I can't do this tonight."

"It's my bloody birthday. Where do you think you're off to?" George says.

"For a swim," she replies, gathering her things.

"But, Charm, you've had far too much grog." Nancy is begging her to sit down.

"Alone," Charmian says, with a final glare at George.

"Here's rue for you," George barks at her, shaking his fist as she flees down the path. "Plenty of it. Go drown yourself!"

TWENTY-TWO

The best time for a night swim at the rocks is when the moon is full. I'll never forget my first phosphorescence: Jimmy coming up the ladder, streaming with stars, one caught on an eyelash still blinking away as he reached and pulled me in, our limbs moon-silvered, our fingers trailing through constellations.

This night the sea has no use for such frippery, the moon but a toenail clipping over Dokos island, the water obsidian-dark in the deep plunging shelf where we swim.

Though I scamper as fast as my flip-flops will allow down the craggy track from Xenomania, I can't catch her. A wind has come in from the east. The waves slap at the rocks. Past the fig tree at the turn, I follow a trail of her discarded clothing down the steps and find her already at the lip of the cave. The waves battering the rocks silence my shout. Her hands reach skywards and with one spring she's free, flying, arced, and gone to the seething water twenty feet below.

She surfaces, gasping, just clear of the jutting finger of rocks

that ruptures the dark skin of the sea. I watch her break through
the waves with her powerful crawl and turn on her back, a floating
crucifix with her face to the stars, and I feel like an idiot for pursu-
ing her but Nancy said, *For Christ's sake, somebody go.*

It's too late to skulk away, she's already swimming back. I call
out to let her know it's me gathering up her limp and patched clothing. I put her things at the top of the ladder and sit in the hollows
where the Hottentots grow. She floats on the heft of the waves for
a while. When she powers back to the rocks she lets one throw her
halfway up the ladder, exhilarated and whooping.

"Isn't it marvelous being able to wash away the taint of an evening like that!" she calls as she steps into her skirt. She comes but-
toning her shirt, shaking water from her hair.

"A swim at night is never a mistake. How lucky for us it's always
available. Just a hop from bad temper and here it is, this mysterious
other dimension that buoys you up until you can slip through and
accept the night's mood. I feel marvelously new again." She's con-
vincingly cheerful as she sits down beside me in the hollow with
her hair dripping.

"Oh, Erica, there really was no need to panic. I've been doing
this my whole life. I grew up on Bombo Bay, a mile-long beach
I had all to myself. Can you imagine? Every night I lay naked,
star-baking on the rocks, believing I would turn silver if I stayed
out long enough. I rather fancied myself going back to school with
an astral tan." She pulls up the hem of her skirt to use it to give her
hair a rub.

I'm keen to shift the blame for my intrusion. "Nancy thought
it wasn't safe because of the booze. She told me to come," I say,
and she smiles at me and reaches for her basket, takes out a bottle.
"Talking of booze . . ."

It's French brandy. "It was supposed to be for George's birthday but he doesn't deserve it." She pulls out the cork with her teeth and takes a swig, offers it to me. Her eyes are dark and glassy as the sea.

I tell her I don't know how she tolerates George's drunken rages and she shuffles closer, uses my shoulder as a pillow and puts her arms around my waist until, unexpectedly, I'm taking the full damp weight of her.

"It wasn't always like this, you know. When George and I were first married and I was expecting Martin, he came to Bombo Bay and slept under the stars with me every night. He said he didn't mind if our baby was born silver. He was up for anything then, the cleverest man in the world and the wittiest. Unbroken . . ." She sighs the first in a series of long smoke-and-brandy sighs. The fumes on her breath mean I could be just about anyone. At some point I think she even gets my name wrong, calls me "Jennifer," but I pretend not to notice. Much of what she's saying she's told me before.

"Those were some of our happiest times, in the garden of my mother's house writing that first novel, bashing away with our typewriters on our knees. The great published writer and me, his keen apprentice. Oh, I was tremendously in awe of how easy he made it seem and we were magnificently in love. Our first collaboration and we won a big prize for it, it seemed we were really flying . . ."

"I suppose that's what Jimmy was trying to point out to him up there: all those books he's had published, living in the sun; it's the dream, isn't it? It's what the rest of us all aspire to," I say.

"Darling, please believe it's his illness that makes him so cantankerous. It's what I have to believe myself." She reaches for the bottle. "His jealousy will be the death of him," she says, and she shivers. "And of me."

She pats our stone and concrete cradle. "Even this. The very ground I sit on. These rocks. That sea. Those mountains behind us. He's jealous that I love this island with a passion I might once have had for him. He was the golden boy, remember; adoration is his oxygen. It's hard to believe he's the same man I married. I still swoon to think of him in Melbourne, striding in, the way his shirtsleeves were rolled, the cigarette stuck to that sexy underhung lip, the great hero war reporter returned to the newsroom from the Orient and there wasn't a girl in the whole *Argus* building wasn't checking herself in her compact."

She takes another alarmingly thirsty slug, hugs her knees through her skirt.

"I'm so sorry you have to see us at our worst," she says. "Over the years we've both done things that have tainted the clear spring at our source. And now we're so stony broke this island has become like a prison to him. In some ways to me too, though you'd have to bash me from it with a hammer to get me to leave. So, here I am, stuck like a limpet to a bad-tempered booze artist who excuses his impotence spouting some convenient mumbo-jumbo theory about how ejaculation takes away from creativity. And me only thirty-six years old, for Christ's sake!"

She looks at me and chuckles. "Thirty-six: I know that sounds ancient to a girl like you, and maybe it's a disgusting thought that people of my age do have sex; at least judging by your face it is."

I object but she silences me. "It has a role to play for the elderly too, you know, even if only as liniment for our poor aching souls. We always fought, George and I, even in the more glorious, romantic days, but the difference was that we had bed every night to nurse all the wounds we'd inflicted on each other. The George you see now resents my good health, wants every scar to be Promethean. Every happy sigh makes him imagine such terrible things about me. His spirit is shriveled to nothing but suspicious hard bone."

She's crying steadily while she talks. I uselessly pat her. She scrunches her skirt up to her eyes and blows her nose in its hem, takes yet another large pull on the brandy and, though her hands are shaking, manages to put a match to a cigarette.

"Maybe I should walk you home?" I'm alarmed at how rapidly the bottle's emptying. "Where are your sandals?"

"I was always barefoot. I think if I have one campaigning bone in my body it's for the freedom not to wear shoes. Growing up on the beach, I don't think I even owned a pair. I've always needed something to curl my toes around and I've found it here."

"I feel the same way . . ." I start to say.

"Everything comes at a cost. There are snakes in every paradise, and here always there's this antagonism around the foreign colony that grows out of boredom, like a sore tooth that one must prod with one's tongue. There is only one waterfront; scenes like tonight's are the sole form of entertainment and, believe me, it gets wearing. I could have slapped your silly American friend for bringing up Jean-Claude and George's wretched novel. It really wasn't the night for it."

I reach for the bottle, take a burning swig and hand it back. "Oh, everybody's talking about the book, I'm afraid. They're all going to read it as soon as it's published. It's Patrick stirs them up. Is he in love with you or something?"

She shakes her head. "As far as George is concerned, everyone I've ever smiled at is in love with me. It used to give him pleasure— you know, if I dressed à la mode and he could present me like his prize filly at the Savoy or the Press Club—but not now. It's the tyranny in his lungs makes him resent my vigorous good health. I walk in the hills, I swim here at night, all of these things make him angry."

I grab the moment. "Isn't it rather masochistic of him to have written about your love affair with Jean-Claude Maurice?"

"Love affair?" Charmian snorts. She curls herself into the rock and holds out her arm, ushers me in, cradling the bottle between us. "Shall I tell you something about that?" I nod and take up my position beneath her wing, snug as a little girl waiting for her bedtime story.

"I curse the way it happened. The stupid self-fulfilling prophecy of it all. Now we're stuck with it; George's medical treatment doesn't come cheap so we couldn't pay back the publisher even if we wanted to. George can rattle off plotlines, that's his speciality; he could so easily have replaced the Jean-Claude thread of his novel with something less troublesome, but Big Grace was there, buoying him up, and he refused to change a word when he was given the chance.

"Meanwhile he's lumbered with five mouths to feed while we pray for remission, and another two novels on the go, neither quite what he came to a Greek island to write but write them he must if we're to have soup in the pot and a fire to boil it with. He can't seem to break the habit of having me there to prompt and temper, even when it's only his name on the book. He bashes out the words but he finds it hard to get beneath the skin, to present the things his characters don't say as well as the things they do. He can give you the look and the smell, the taste and the sound of an experience, usually an exotic experience because he collects exotic experiences like luggage labels, but he can't or won't tell you how it feels. Emotional reactions, nuance, atmosphere: you know, the stuff that goes on between the lines.

"It was the year before last he started writing *Closer to the Sun*. His weight had dropped to the bone; we didn't know then that it was TB and curable. I was helping any way I could but it was a nightmare, the baby with measles, and Shane and Martin being kept off school.

"I told him he was free to help himself to any snippets I'd jotted in my journal, which I knew would be useful as it was the first time he was setting a novel on Hydra. I had my own book to write, I wasn't paying him as much attention as he was used to, maybe he found it callous that I could lose myself in the faraway world of my own novel and push away thoughts of his impending death . . .

"The summer whirled on without him and his accusations grew crazier by the day. Something happened, I don't know what, maybe he caught me coming back from a moonlight swim and jealously assumed Jean-Claude had been with me. I'm sorry to say it ended up with his hands around my neck."

Charmian crosses her hands at her throat and stifles a sob.

"But before you think too badly of him, that's not what George does. It was our worst of times. The savagery of his night sweats meant we'd stopped sleeping together. Still, I'd never felt in danger of my life around him before and I lashed out with my tongue, as though all the kindness had been wrung out of me. He stopped choking me and stared at his hands as though someone else's had been sewn there in place of his own.

"My rage was uncoiling. I spat at him about his impotence, I mocked his self-pity, thanked him coldly for the way he robbed me of the time to do my own work. He went on about my decadence around that 'pissant.' The more he shouted over me the more venomous my words, until I said that yes, I had often been stirred by the sight of that muscled young body. At last he heard me. He urged me to go on, blocking the exit. In the past, as I told you, our rows always ended in bed—you know how it is. But since the TB we can't rid ourselves of fury that way.

"Instead, he marched me to the table, rolled a new sheet of paper into the machine and told me to write out this fantasy of making love to Jean-Claude.

"I did it. I imagined a seduction and was spurred on by my rage as I wrote Jean-Claude as Dionysus, gleaming, bronzed and almost naked." She starts to laugh and buries her head in her arms.

"I wrote myself in, like a sex-crazed maenad following him up the lava-hot rocks. My furious fingers flew over the keys. The crescent moons of his buttocks beneath the wisp of paisley loincloth, the smell of the sun bottled in the abandoned windmill he led me to, the soft powdery hay that I lay in while he asked if I'd like him to make love to me. I think I even had a butterfly opening and closing its wings. And on and on it goes. It was done out of cruelty, all of it. But now it's in George's book, word for word, and everyone will know that it is me and Jean-Claude. It comes down to a choice between my dignity and food in the bellies of my children. No, really. We live hand to mouth. George threatens to sell the house but where would we go? I'll simply have to weather the jeering and rotten fruit when the blasted book comes out, I suppose."

She shudders and stares across the black gulf to the sleeping mainland, its charcoal burners a scattering of garnets before the distant dreams of its mountains.

Only Cato is waiting up for me when I stagger home, exhausted from half carrying, half cajoling Charmian back to her house. He winds himself around my legs while I light the lamp and fumble in the icebox for something that might please him. I go through to the terrace expecting to find Jimmy sleeping but he isn't there and I wonder if someone has offered him a chance to go fishing. The others are all in a mound at the far end. Cato follows me. Just the five bodies tonight, sprawled across the mats. I can see by the flare of her hair that it's Trudy who lies in Bobby's arms, a little apart from Edie, Janey and Marty.

I curl up alone on the mattress that Jimmy and I have positioned, for reasonable modesty, behind the almond trees. I have a

single candle in a jar, enough to read by. I think that a few pages
of *Peel Me a Lotus* will be a comfort after all she has told me but
find in its pages an existential angst that I hadn't noticed before.
I read Charmian's words and this passage, again and again, while
through the branches Jimmy's absence echoes beneath the sky.

"My face is cold turned up to the cold stars. Inexorable and orderly
they move across heaven, star beyond star, nebula beyond nebula,
universe beyond universe, wheeling through a loneliness that is
inconceivable. Almost I can feel this planet wheeling too, spinning
through its own sphere of loneliness with the deliberation of a process endlessly repeated, a tiny speck of astral dust whirling on into
the incomprehensibility of eternity. How queer to cling to the speck
of dust, whirling on and on, perhaps at this moment even upside
down. There's no comfort in the stars. Only darkness beyond
darkness, mystery beyond mystery, loneliness beyond loneliness."

TWENTY-THREE

Axel has returned with the hot breath of the meltemi. Not one of us has caught sight of him yet, not even Marianne, but it's rumored he's holed up at Fidel's house; at least that's what Dionysus the dustman told Charmian this morning.

The scorching winds lick at the already sweltering island. Sun flares from every white wall, our ears buzz with insects, the cicadas sizzle incessantly, everything stinging and biting and not even the jasmines can sweeten the stench of the litter-strewn streets. Our hair has grown tangled and our eyes sore from grit. Shutters bang, things get broken. Gusts whip away our covers and sweep spiteful dust into our dreams. Tempers fray in the hair-dryer heat, the harbor is whisked to a frothing custard-colored scum and our cistern has run dry. Bobby seems to spend half his life queuing at the wells where Elias the waterman has positioned a dozen crones to monopolize the town supply which he brings down by donkey and distributes door to door at an inflated price. Each day we haul buckets of seawater up the steps to slosh through the privy and I have to be up extra early every morning for the scrum at the ice-factory doors.

The ferry hasn't made it through the churning gulf for the last three days but still we gather—"like bloody paupers waiting for alms on Maundy Thursday," George grumbles—but the air makes us so listless, what is there to do other than huddle around these few tables and peck at each other?

George and Charmian are drinking cold beer at their usual spot beside the grocery door. Patrick Greer brings a fresh scandal to the table with the swagger of a gundog with a duck hanging from its mouth. Last Saturday a German girl was raped by three sailors outside the slaughterhouse toilets but Police Chief Manolis has talked her out of pressing charges.

Charmian points at Leonard sloping towards us along the agora.

"Look, no Marianne. I hope this means that Axel's turned up and she's busy giving him his marching orders," she says as he approaches, flicking his *komboloi* back and forth between finger and thumb.

Leonard stoops to kiss her on both cheeks. "Christ, you look crapulous," George says, and it's true he's not at his best. Last night the wind snuck in through a window and whipped away the only carbons of his novel and his face hangs heavy with loss. Bim calls him to join a feverish debate about marital fidelity and, with *Kalimera*s all round, he scrapes up a chair and Demetri shouts to Nikos to bring this *filos* a *sketo* and a Metaxa. As well as no Marianne, there's no sign of Robyn or Carolyn. It's often this way. I squeeze Jimmy's hand under the table.

The foreign colony has fallen into two distinct camps. There is the ancient court of George and Charmian and then there's Bim, who gathers new people around him like a debauched Regency prince. Demetri is usually to be found at his side, slyly clicking away at girls with the Rolleiflex he keeps propped on the table.

Leonard's an increasingly rare sight these days, his work ethic more resistant to loafing than most. He's noticeably thinner than earlier in the summer, almost jumpy, distracted, his body stooped as though he's stuck in the typing position.

I'm melting on the cobbles in the hinterland between the two camps, next to Trudy, her face puffy from crying. The pale blue shirt she so often wears appears to have shrunk. She hasn't been able to do up all of the buttons and her breasts look bulging and marbled in the cruel light.

Leonard and Bim are laughing at something Demetri is saying. I swivel from Trudy to catch the tail end of their ribaldry, and with one turn of my head replace tragedy with comedy.

Demetri has removed his sunglasses. He might still be wearing them, so dark are the shadows beneath his heavy brow.

"So, Bim, how old are you?"

"Twenty-seven last birthday."

"And Leonard, you?"

"Twenty-five."

Demetri uses the glasses to point at his friends. "Well, I've got a year on Bim and three on you."

"Time's running out for you, old boy," Bim snickers. "Do you think these chicks at Lagoudera are going to let some old man of thirty stick his hand up their skirts?"

Demetri replaces his glasses and leans back in his chair. He speaks with a groan, his hands resting over his stomach.

"Here's what I think. It's exhausting! Every night I have to fuck Carolyn. I can come crawling home, drunk and longing for sleep, but there she is in the bed beside me and fuck her I do! I tell you, this compulsion is so tiring." He looks into his lap and shakes his head. "I can't wait to be older and for the rampant beast to be tamed."

Leonard looks across at him and laughs. He takes a pencil from his pocket and scribbles a few words on a corner of the paper tablecloth, tears it off and pockets it.

The lack of mail is making us stagnant. A four-day-old *Athens Daily* is still being passed around, starving eyes scan the horizon for boats, there's some desultory talk about the literature of maroonings.

Jimmy and Göran are bickering about Thoreau and *Walden*, which of course I've never read, and Charmian chips in: "I believe it was Robert Louis Stevenson who wrote that it was somehow unmanly that he should live and write in such solitude. Do you think he meant that it was feminizing to be doing so without a slave?"

George grins at her. "Every Prospero needs his Caliban, darling."

Even if the ferry does make it through today and there's mail, there'll be nothing for me. The light burns my eyes, my legs are itchy with fleabites. The first anniversary of our mother's death has passed without word from our father; Bobby's birthday too, my letters all unanswered. A gust of wind brings with it a sulphurous taint, a clatter and a yowl. The bell of the monastery tolls inconsolably. The burning speck of dust whirls on while the conversation is batted to and fro, largely over my head, until at last Jimmy catches my eye and smiles at me and I have a sudden urge to throw my arms around him and hang on to him for dear life.

Sofia brings out a few plates of greasy cheese pies and fried green peppers, cucumbers, bread and oil. Edie and Janey float by in dresses they've made from old silk and lace from the flea market. Demetri calls them over, toying with the strap of his camera.

"Hey! We need to fix a date for you chicks to come to my studio," he says as they flutter towards him. How easily Edie settles herself on Leonard's knee, Janey on Bim's. How complicit the smiles of the men.

Bobby is talking to me, tugging my ponytail to get my attention.

"So will you do it? Will you find a moment when no one else is about to ask Charmian if there's anyone can help fix this in Athens?" He's gripping Trudy's hand, speaking into my ear.

"Carolyn said she thinks there's a doctor in Monastiraki who sorted Charmian out last year." And he touches his nose at me in a way that suggests some knowledge that he's party to and I don't need.

He turns and kisses Trudy's brow, tells her he'll do whatever he can to help her, sell the car if she needs the dough, and she cries softly and says, "You'd do that for me? Oh, Bobby."

I don't tell Charmian that Jean-Claude is most likely the father when I go to her later on Trudy's behalf. I don't need to.

"My goodness, four missed periods and the silly creature does nothing? What was she thinking of? All one has to do is stand next to Jean-Claude when he sneezes to fall pregnant," she says with a bitter laugh as she leafs through her red address book. She scribbles a name and some details on a scrap of paper, drops it in my basket and ushers me away because George is already shouting for her.

I trudge back along the waterfront, a leaden-heeled messenger with my casket of doom. Rotten melons bob in the harbor like skulls. Boats jostle, bashing fender to fender, heave at their moorings; the fishing caiques creak with boredom while the yachts are affronted by scum and detritus that drifts from the slaughterhouse rubbish chute. The cats gather snarling around a rat that has been washed onto the cobbles; gulls fight in a pool of fish guts. The café awnings flap and complain. Stranded tourists wander listlessly among the tables, getting in everyone's way. Quite a number of my crowd haven't moved all day and are still haranguing each other outside Katsikas. I can't face Trudy yet. Charmian was insistent I should warn her that she may have left things too late. It was silly to think that praying might deal with it, or believing she could rely on someone like Jean-Claude to pull out. This last bit she said looking at me like I was the one who was pregnant, and so sternly I blushed.

All my chores are already done for the day, my many dealings with insects. I've sent whole regiments of ants marching in an outside direction, found the weevils hiding in the lentil jar and thrown the whole lot down the privy, filled the wasp traps with honey, and picked fleas from Cato which I took a vengeful pleasure in watching drown in a glass of water.

Jimmy has already gone back to work. I have left him some bread and cheese and, weighed down by a jug of sweet *foulis*, a note to say I'll see him at the cinema later.

I've a couple more hours to keep myself scarce. The wind makes me too restless for a siesta. There's nowhere safe to swim on a day like this, unless you hike across the island through the sickening heat to Limnioniza, and even then you can't be sure that Boreas won't find a way to stir things up. I think vaguely of the notebook in my bag, of finding some shade to write in and the energy to do so.

I wander up the alley and past Apostolis the butcher's latest display, rather meager as befits a marooning. A lone bullock's head on a slippery bed of gore has been crowned with a twisted arrangement of tripe that when I squint looks like a turban. Through the door Apostolis thanks a customer, wiping his hands on his streaked apron, taking a handful of coins. The customer fills the doorway and I see it's Axel, a bloodstained bag and a look that says he might not wait to cook whatever is inside before eating it. His eyes are cold and dead as two stones, his face patchy with parched-looking tufts of straggly yellow beard, skin scorched and scabby across the bridge of his nose, his shirt torn from one shoulder like he's been in a brawl. He gives me a furious scowl before striding off.

I turn on my heel. It feels urgent I let Marianne know that Axel's presence on the island is now a fact. The meltemi works itself up into one of its hot gritty tantrums as I climb.

I find her tangled in sheets, attempting to unpeg her washing from the line, but the wind has other ideas. She's more like a girl than a woman, high-stepping and laughing with her hair blowing around. She whirls, chasing errant T-shirts and vests. I untangle Leonard's khaki shirt from a thornbush and hand it to her.

Marianne gleams in the sun, makes light, shrugs when I mention what I heard about Leonard's carbon copies blowing away.

"*Pfft.* It is not too much trouble for me to type the whole thing out for him when he's ready to send it off," she says. "I told him already I have a certificate for typing so he doesn't need to be so stressed." She doesn't seem to mind about anything too much. Still laughing, she conquers the last of the billowing sheets and stuffs them into a big basket where the baby is rocking back and forth, clapping his hands at the dancing sails and his mother with her gold hair flying.

"I just saw Axel," I say reluctantly, not wanting to pierce the bubble of happiness all around them. "He was coming out of Apostolis's. He looked awfully ill."

She stoops for the baby and the basket and looks up at me with a sad smile. "I know, he's already been here," she says and I follow her inside to where Leonard's guitar now hangs from the nail at the foot of the ladder, and on up the steps. She puts the baby on a rug and

parts the bed curtains, pulls out the tortured remains of her diaphanous orange dress. Someone's really gone for it with the scissors.
Some pieces are only streamers and she looks almost gay with them
fluttering from her fingers, her pretty smile at odds with her words.

"It's the only dress I ever felt beautiful wearing."

She holds up a finger to silence my questions. "Yes, I know
Axel's back and I know he's lost his mind," she says. "I must forget
all about him but that's not so easy to do."

She bends down and scoops up the baby and laughs as he covers
her bare shoulder in slobbery kisses while I struggle to follow what
she's saying as we clatter downstairs—something about making a
charm to help Leonard. "Maybe you should do one for your Jimmy
too, I'll show you how."

There are herbs, sprigs of lavender, some numbers written out
on a grid. She pulls out a chair. "From tonight the planet Mercury
will be in retrograde and it can be very bad for creative people. Oh,
I can see by your face you think I'm ding-a-ling in the bowl," she
says, tapping her head. "But I always did this for Axel and I know
your Jimmy will appreciate the gesture, even if he doesn't believe."

Her cheeks are round, pinchable as the baby's; her eyes set at an
adorably mischievous slant. I pick up the pen and obediently copy
out the grid and the numbers on a new sheet of paper. She pours us
both a glass of tea and shows me how to draw the seal of Mercury,
talks more of her atmospheric fears for Leonard's novel than she
does of Axel losing his mind.

"He needs to get it written before he burns himself out. He's
desperate to stay on here, so it's Benzedrine to stay awake and
phenobarb to sleep." She shakes her head. "Not healthy. And it's
not just because he needs the dollars. The I Ching is quite clear that
in the eighth month the reversal will kick in and that could be any
time now."

She gives the baby some strings of beads to play with and brings out her workbasket. I hope to become lovelier by osmosis as I watch her slow and graceful movements. She cuts two pieces of purple fabric from an old shirt and together we sew the herbs inside, with the magic numbers and symbols: lavender for expression, sage to protect, lemon balm to soothe and, because she tells me to, an eyelash for love. As an afterthought she writes out the title of Leonard's novel, *Beauty at Close Quarters*, and slips it inside before tightening the cord and stitching it shut.

There isn't time for much more. I have to fly. I have Jimmy's charm hanging from a cord around my neck. I've almost forgotten about the cinema, I've been so absorbed in this witchcraft.

"It's *Boy on a Dolphin* tonight, you should come." How thoughtless I feel as soon as the words leave my mouth. Of course, she isn't free. But where is Leonard? How come he's not here writing his book?

"Leonard has gone to Fidel's house to see Axel," she says with a shiver. "I haven't a clue what he'll say to him . . ." She widens her eyes. "I only know that he's taken him a new steel razor blade," and just for a moment a vision of Axel's throat hovers before me. She laughs, dispels it, "Leonard told me his mother believes a good shave will sort out any problem," and grasps my hand and pulls me towards the baby. "Look, Erica, look at him! My little caterpillar just managed to move himself all that way across the floor."

———

It's rowdy at the film. Beneath its ceiling of tumbling vines the courtyard is crowded with extra rows of chairs, and men who swig beer and cheer as Sophia Loren emerges from the sea in a pleasingly wet and clinging yellow dress. She is poor, hence the tiny scraps of ragged clothing, and lives at the windmill above the rocks where every crag and cannon and step and stoop is familiar to us. The locals erupt to their feet whenever they spot themselves in the crowd sequences. Yiorgis, the limping boatman, who despite his simple mind makes himself indispensable with ropes on the quay, appears several times to the greatest cheers of all. A shutter is thrown open in the middle of the screen. A roar goes up. Maria leans out from her window, shouts, "Alexi! Come inside at once!" as Sophia swims along the ocean bed in her rag of wet dress. The reeds and the fishes embrace her, a mermaid is singing.

"If the boy whom the gods have enchanted should arise from the sea, and the wish of my heart could be granted, I would wish that you loved only me."

Back at the windmill Sophia's bad-boy lover throws her roughly to the bed. Bats flit across the screen as her breasts heave with temper and desire, but now here's Bobby interrupting, bursting through the door from the street. "Quick, quick. He's been beaten up." He's yanking me to my feet. "You have to leave right now if you want to go with him." There's a chorus of shushing and someone throws a chicken bone at his head.

"Who, what?"

"Jimmy."

"Go where?"

"Away from here. Now!"

Bobby hauls me down the street and along the waterfront. He's making no sense. Something about an old friend of George's with a boat who's willing to take Jimmy across the channel to Metochi.

I force Bobby to a standstill, wrench myself free. My voice is shaking. "What? Where is Jimmy going? I don't know what you're talking about."

And though he grabs my shoulders and looks me straight in the eyes, still what he's saying won't come together.

I hear: "Spiratoula . . ."

"Who?"

"The wife of Panayiotis . . ."

I hear: "The sailmaker's loft."

He's dragging me so forcefully my legs keep running despite my screaming desire to stop.

"Quicker, Erica. Come faster. He has to cast off. There may be a worse duffing on the way for him. Panayiotis's uncle is coming from the Three Brothers Tavern." Again I wrench myself free, we're both panting. The words still haven't come together but I hear my voice howling. "No!"

Later, much later, I lie listening to the tomcats on the prowl. There's low rumbling, growls, an explosion of snarls and a lady cat's ear-piercing cry that signals anything but pleasure. The pill Bobby has given me is taking effect; the agonized screams slide away. I lie on my bed between Edie and Janey while they stroke my arms and my back and I drift towards dreamlessness.

TWENTY-FOUR

Didy Cameron arrives on the island like a breath of cool fresh air with the passing of the meltemi. She is an elegant woman, fortyish, dark-haired and deeply tanned with observant eyes that burn as blue as the center of a flame.

My first encounter with her is at Charmian's. She strides in, after one sharp knock and a musical "cooo-eeee." She's tall, dressed in a safari skirt suit with a string of bright pearls at her collar and a chunky gold bracelet hung with charms that clink as she shakes our hands. She comes bearing books, says: "But don't worry, I'm only half-Greek so there's no need to fear my gifts."

Her smile is so huge her gums show above her teeth, and this and her liveliness lend her an air of eccentricity that is slightly at odds with the smartness of her clothing.

The books are her friend Elizabeth Jane Howard's new saga *The Sea Change*. She hands one to Charmian, tells her it's signed, and then a second—"Goodness, how many copies of her novel do we need?" Charmian says—but Didy tells her that this one is personally inscribed to Martin, and explains that it was the author recommended Didy come to Hydra to buy a house, instead of following her mother's roots to a grand manse on Chios.

"Jane is right, of course. Once I'd cooled down I had to concede it would be foolhardy for me to attempt to renovate a big house with so many children and a husband working in Africa for months at a time," Didy says.

Charmian tells me that this Jane spent a summer writing her book on the island and by the way she only glances at the inscription I guess she hadn't liked her very much. Though it's still early, she pours us all a glass of retsina, and Didy doesn't bat an eyelid.

They clink glasses, "Here's to you and your family," Charmian says and opens Martin's copy, reads what the author has written to her son. When she looks up, her eyes are much softer. She gulps at her wine and calls up the hatch for Martin to come down.

Didy chats on. "Oh yes, she's had rave reviews," she's saying as Martin arrives crashing and blinking, a copy of *Tristram Shandy* held inches from his nose.

"Jane has told everyone just how fearsomely intelligent you are," she says, grinning at him. "Which as you might imagine is not so nice for my Petey, who is around your age, and is now too intimidated to come with me to meet you."

Charmian gazes at gawky young Aristotle while Didy shows him the sections of the book in which he appears as the boy "Julius." From the parts she reads out we all recognize this wise child with as wily a grip on the island's ways and economics as he has an insightful understanding of the Greek myths and the heavens. Charmian is taking more pleasure in all of this than Martin, who stands first on one leg and then the other, his streaky blond mop falling but failing to conceal his discomfort. As Didy turns another page he manages to interrupt.

"Did the cat get back to England? Do you know? It was a black kitten. I found her a basket to hide it in, one with a fastening over the top . . ."

Didy claps her hands. "Katsikas! Of course." Her charm bracelet tinkles. "He's a lovely cat. I'd forgotten that she smuggled him from here. He's very spoiled these days, quite the little prince. Jane roasts him duck gizzards and he has her leopard-skin coat for a bed."

Charmian beams at her. "Oh, how lovely for all of us that Jane gave us such a good review. Welcome to Hydra, Didy!"

Didy turns out to be just what I need too. I'm rather glad Charmian has so bossily dispatched me to walk her back through the port to Spiti Heidsieck. Charmian wanted to drop tools, was really quite crestfallen not to show Didy around herself, but impossible, of course, with George at the crucial final chapter of his book. "Two men, a jeep and a hundred thousand corpses. I'd far rather come with you," she said.

Didy has a lively interest in everyone and everything. She speaks Greek to the shopkeepers, and even Kyria Anastasia at the bakery is charmed. She exclaims over the organ-pipe beauty of the beeswax candles at Stomasis's, the intense smell of honey in the streets. She gets me laughing for what feels like the first time in weeks. She exclaims over the glowing pink marble beneath our feet, and at every corner and wall and courtyard and doorway she talks of the geometry of light and shadow, of how Hydra is surely the birthplace of cubism, of the Raoul Dufy boats and the shameless blue sea. She can understand why artists are drawn here, she says, and I'm seeing it all as though through her eyes and falling in love all over again. I take her via the sponge factory and Fotis is there and demonstrates the superior water-retaining qualities of the local sponges over those from the Arabian fields and how silky the elephant ears are, five of which she buys, without even quibbling, one each for herself and her children.

Though dark-skinned, she looks impossibly English, with her purposeful brogues and good tailoring. I can imagine her riding to hounds and being fearfully brave. Her new baskets are full. She's almost emptied the shelves of tins at Katsikas and Martin's promised to track down Manos to introduce him as Didy will need a boatman to run her back to Kamini. She steers me to a shaded table outside Tassos.

"It's too hot to keep marching about. Let's have a nice cold drink and while we wait you can tell me what a young girl like you is doing running wild in a place like this," she says and her bright eyes flicker with interest. "My Annabel says she won't leave the house, she's in such a funk at being dragged here by me instead of being allowed a season in London, so I'm rather hoping you might help me to winkle her out and into the direction of some fun." There's not a condescending note to her tune and I fill her in on the basics: my mother's death and the mysterious car she left Bobby and the post-office savings for me and my dreams. Didy asks me quite practical questions like how long I think I can make the money last, and when I shrug gets me to do the maths there and then and scribbles a few figures on the paper tablecloth.

She orders a coffee for herself and an orangeade for me, asks for cake. "And, my dear, do you have a beau?" she says, once it's all dealt with. I swallow hard. It's too squalid to have to tell her about Jimmy and it's still too raw.

"No, not anymore," I say with a forced shrug.

There's been not a word from Jimmy Jones since the night he ran past me wailing "Sorry, sorry" and leapt for the boat. I'm trying to get over it, really I am. Edie and Janey have been helpful in this respect, not saving me from a single detail of Jimmy's many island adventures. One morning I caught a glimpse of what had been done to Spiratoula's face, not simply the bruises but the light that had been washed from it, and yet still I can't seem to stop the craving. The sudden ownership of a typewriter is a bittersweet souvenir. I bash so hard the keys cut holes in the paper, the carriage jams, the ribbon slips, my words fail me.

"Oh, my tears could fill the cistern," I say, attempting to quell my bitterness and longing, but everything starts going blurry, especially when she calls me a poor lamb and says how horrid that my first love should turn out to be such a rotter.

"Concentrate on the things you didn't like about him," Didy says and looks around for Tassos to bring us more drinks, like she has all the time in the world for me and my broken heart.

"This is the only known antidote. You need only one thing at the beginning," she says, with the efficiency of one offering advice on getting over hiccups or removing stubborn stains. "One thing to focus on. Something physical," she insists, lifting the cake to her mouth and waiting for me to come up with my own medicine. "It'll help with the if onlys, I promise."

It's not hard to summon Jimmy to my mind's eye. He flickers there constantly, reel upon reel. His soulful gaze; his elastic mirth, tumbling and diving, leaping and bounding; the chatter of the typewriter; the raking of his hands through his hair. I see his white teeth as he sings to me over a fistful of drachmas, misappropriating the words, "There'll never be anyone else for you but me," and remember feeling the curse of it then, and now it seems to be coming to pass because since he's been gone I've woken up beside Tomas, and Marty and handsome Angelos from the naval school, and that sort of thing has never felt right with anyone but Jimmy Jones.

Didy looks on expectantly, head cocked to one side. I see Jimmy's face turned towards me on the pillow: sooty curls and lashes, lips swollen by sleep, his thumb in the nook of his collarbone.

Didy's eyes are an electrifying blue against her mahogany tan. I turn back to Jimmy on the pillow beside me, and now I find myself zooming in as he wakes. His armpit is inches from my nose as he stretches and yawns. He smells spicy, familiar—it's not that. I wince as it comes into focus. The hair that sprouts from his pits is not dark like his head, but weedy and yellowish, like something from under a stone, crusty with sweat, repulsive. I start to laugh and Didy clinks her glass to mine when I manage to find the words.

"To Jimmy's revolting yellow armpits!" she says.

She tells me about her children who are all sulking about being dragged away to Greece on another of her whims, apart from her youngest, Fiona, who is excited to ride the donkeys and who, Didy hopes, will make friends with little Jason Johnston. "There he is now," I say as Booli sprints past with Max nipping at his heels. We watch as he bounds aboard a peppermint-green caique and settles on deck, a little man with a job to do, picking tiddlers from the nets and plopping them into his bucket. Didy crosses her fingers. "I do hope Fiona will be jolly enough for him," she says.

The monastery clock clangs the half hour, tables are filling up, here and across the alley outside Katsikas. Donkeys file past, the more cash-strapped or lovelorn of my friends sit smoking or gnawing at their nails while they wait for the ferry, Costas wheels his ice-cream cart into position. Bim and Demetri saunter by like hunters scenting fresh meat aboard the approaching *Nereida*.

Didy wants everyone's stories. I point out Edie and Janey, who have made themselves new bikinis out of Jimmy's favorite yellow T-shirt and breezily flout Police Chief Manolis's rules, wearing little else as they loll at a table where Marty and Charlie Heck are arm-wrestling. Across the way the Swedes are all talking over each other. The word "Wittgenstein" keeps jumping out. Lena downs a shot of raki and snatches up a book and reads a passage out loud. Axel Jensen breaks from his conversation with Leonard to give her a slow handclap. A little tribe of Goschens are shrieking as David wheels them along in a market cart, tumbling together all naked and brown and haloed with curls. Only Göran is hunched over his notebook, oblivious to all but the heavens as he writes.

Some boisterous Greek kids climb a mast and leap into the harbor; men unload vegetables from caiques onto straw mats spread along the quay. The cats sprawl on the warm rocks with eyes to the mole and an incoming fishing boat.

"But who is the ravishing creature with the legs and the baby?" Didy says as Marianne maneuvers her pram into position by the grocery door. Her fisherman's smock is only just long enough as she bends to her son. She joins Leonard and Axel who are laughing and talking. Leonard pulls out a chair for her but still has his ear cocked to whatever Axel is saying.

Axel's rucksack is at his feet so I guess he's about to set sail again. This has been his first return to the island since Leonard's gift to him of a poem about a man who burned the house he loved and sailed away in a boat of scorched and mutilated wings. This poem and Leonard's visit with a razor blade were, apparently, all it took to transform the quivering wreck I saw at the butcher's to this freshly shaved and free man. If Axel feels ashamed, he wears it lightly.

Didy gasps like it's some sort of thriller, especially when I get to the part about Patricia's accident. We both try not to stare at Axel, who is still too busy talking to pay attention to Marianne or his son. It's Leonard who calls to Nikos to bring her juice, Leonard who pulls a funny face at the baby.

"What a very civilized and kind young man," Didy says. I agree with a sigh as I watch him and Marianne twine their fingers beneath the table. The sun breaks through the awning to find her, all lightness to his shadow in her white smock. "Oh, Marianne's living the dream," I could almost wail it. She glows in Leonard's gaze, her eyes sparkle, her hair shines palest gold against her honey skin. She laughs a lot, and easily. He's brought out the girl within the saintly and martyred Madonna.

Sometimes the girl is wild. It's like she stores it all up for the evenings she gets a babysitter and joins us at Xenomania or down on the port. She and Leonard never stop touching; little things: his hands cup her heels when she's worn out from dancing, his fingertips leaf through her hair, he plants kisses on her brow, the tip of her nose. His reverence borders on the religious when he's looking at her. At Lagoudera she whirls across the floor and he watches with a great grin on his face like he's found his own salvation in her happiness. Her face gives him more pleasure than any face he's seen before, he says. He told me once that he sits in the moonlight and watches her sleep.

"Axel wants nothing but for Patricia to be patched up and returned to him. He's agreed to give Marianne the house in exchange for a divorce," I say, pleased that our island dramas interest Didy enough to want to know more.

TWENTY-FIVE

Didy and I meet again at ouzo hour, when a milkiness hazes the horizon. I've come straight from the beach beneath the ruined *castello*. The sea spangles silver, mauve and tangerine as swimmers take their evening plunges from the rocks at Avlaki and Spilia. Whoops fill the air as a clattering of kids race donkeys through the port, scattering cats and pigeons and Captain Yiannis's carefully constructed pyramid of oranges, some of which roll into the sea. The cats seem to have multiplied overnight. Didy is surrounded by the most pitiful crew: torn ears, missing eyes, scabrous maws mewling with whiskers adroop, the very experts at sniffing out a soft heart. She sits with her legs graciously crossed. "A ladies' salon" is what she called it, and as I join them I feel clumsy and salt-crusted in my swimsuit and patched shorts.

Didy looks immaculate, despite many difficulties with pumping the water and the recalcitrant seep-away up at Spiti Heidsieck, and beside her is an equally neat young woman with a satin hair band who I guess to be the daughter from her first marriage.

"Annabel Asquith," the girl confirms in her bored English voice as she holds out her hand. Tassos provides forks with the cakes—"how delightfully bourgeois," says Charmian, who has made an effort with coral lipstick and her hair pinned beneath her widest-brimmed hat. Her left wrist is cuffed by a bracelet as chunky as Didy's, but where Didy's is gold and tinkling with charms, hers is heavy bronze.

"It's part of a Tibetan prayer wheel that was given with great ceremony to my dashing husband, by the Dalai Lama himself," she says when Didy asks. She says that she hopes their friend Jane hasn't only gossiped about their poverty and rows.

"Sixty-four countries, wars, famine; he stomached the lot and told the world about it. By the time he married me he had double, treble the readership of any other correspondent in the whole of Australia," she says, turning the Tibetan symbols around her wrist. She wants Didy to know the unbroken George: "He met Nehru, Churchill, Mao and walked beneath a black umbrella with Gandhi by the River Ganges."

Annabel retreats behind dark glasses while Charmian boasts and, having shaken my hand, calls me "cutie" as one might a child.

I'm glad I've got my big, fat book with me. I've finally got around to the Simone de Beauvoir and I see both older women smile as I lay Charmian's copy of *The Second Sex* on the table.

"Since Jimmy's been gone I've had more time," I say and to Charmian: "Now I wish I'd hit him over the head with it. I should have read it when you first lent it to me." It's dog-eared and tatty, I've been carrying it around for so long.

Charmian picks it up and opens it. "Let's see what the library angel has to offer," she says and stabs her finger at the open page. "I'm not much into prophecy but I often find de Beauvoir comes up with the goods." She starts to read aloud where her finger points:

"'No one is more arrogant towards women, more aggressive and more disdainful, than a man anxious about his own virility . . .'" falters and snaps the book shut, hides behind her hands. "Oh what a sook I am," she says and dabs at her eyes. "So tremendously silly to blub. Whatever must you think of me?"

Didy shoos Annabel to track down her siblings, requests more ouzo, including one for me, which is reassuring as I'm not sure if she meant me to buzz away too. Oh God, what with me and now Charmian, Didy will think we're all ready for the nuthouse with all this crying.

"I should be celebrating: George has at long last finished his torturous novel and it leaves me free, maybe even to do a little of my own writing, but unlike de Beauvoir my freedom comes at a price," Charmian says, sniffing and snatching the new ouzo from Tassos's tray and downing it before it touches the table.

Didy orders her another. Not the best idea, in my opinion.

"I'd be fibbing if I told you Jane hasn't mentioned something of your difficulties. It's what makes her such a good storyteller, she can't stop herself . . ." Didy is saying while Charmian blots her eyes and blows her nose.

"Sometimes I think it would be easier if I didn't have such strong urges," Charmian says, adding with a darting smile, "To write, I mean . . ." Her hand shoots to the side of her mouth with the missing tooth.

"I don't know how you manage any of it," Didy says. "But give in to your urges because your books are marvelous."

Charmian reaches for a cigarette. "It would be so much more restful, and much better for George, if I were to surrender to living more 'Greekly,' as I've come to think of it, like Marianne, or Carolyn or Robyn or any one of these lovely young women who are happy to serve their brilliant menfolk. I envy their basking in reflected glories, the blind eyes they turn when the genius strays, in a way that I never could with George." She empties her glass and points to the book on the table. "I think Simone de Beauvoir is interesting on women like Marianne and the rest of them. Doesn't she say that the freest women in all Ancient Greece were the *hetaeras*? They may have been courtesans but it was the lower-ranking *dicteriads* and *auletrides* who took the brunt of the fucking while the *hetaeras*' independence, culture and spirit made them near equals."

I gesture to Tassos, a silent plea not to bring her more ouzo.

"Actually, Marianne was thoroughly miserable when I saw her earlier today," I say, as soon as she pauses to light her cigarette.

"Well, it can't be very pleasant the way Axel refuses to bond with the boy . . ."

I shake my head. For once it's not Axel.

"Oh, I do hope she'll be joining us. Jane spoke so warmly of her, said what a marvelous cook she is," Didy says while Charmian smokes and waits for me to tell her what happened.

———

There was no more putting off getting water and I'd trailed Bobby to the wells through the hottest part of the day. My time with my brother has become precious now it is no longer infinite. While I'm glad Trudy's at last over all the hideous complications of her operation, it means he's abandoning me. I was trying not to whine. "But why? Why do you have to go all the way to America?" I already knew why. Making Trudy well has been his project. Turns out he has a gift for nursing after all. "The night she nearly died from that fever I made a pact with the universe to never leave her," he tells me. Her family doctor is in Boston, so that's where they are going. But what about me? All he can do is shrug. I want to grab what I can before he disappears. "You're always saying that family is an outdated concept. Does that mean we'll never see each other again?" I wailed as we waited at the well, wringing what I could from him.

I went on alone through the dung and the dust to return a couple of gramophone records to Marianne. I could hear the sound of Leonard's typing from the upstairs window, but apart from sudden bursts of cicadas, and those clattering keys, all was silent. There was a peculiarly melancholy atmosphere inside the house, the shutters were closed and the smell of trapped incense was almost sickly.

I noticed the baby was sleeping beneath a net in his cot and the little white dog lay slumped at the foot of the stairs with his chin on crossed paws. Leonard's sixpenny cap was hanging with his guitar from the nail. An Egyptian vase lay in two jagged pieces on the stone floor in a pool of water, among scattered stems of mountain yarrow. On the table, a sheet of paper with something in Norwegian scrawled across it, many crossings-out and an angular script; the crusts that had been cut from a sandwich; an empty glass; a full ashtray; a knife. I crouched down to put the gramophone records away and found her curled into the space between the shelves and the cabinet. She was bleached out from crying. She put her finger to her lips, asked me not to make a sound.

———

"Sshhhh," Charmian says. "Here comes Marianne, now."

She doesn't look like she has a care in the world. She's changed into her striped skirt, walks with a swing she only has when she's free of the baby. She stops at the corner to chat to Magda. I see them both laugh. At the table beside us an airline crew has settled with some bottles of cold beer. The women wear false eyelashes and pearly lipstick, tightly fitted dresses that look incongruous at the waterfront. The pilots have placed their peaked caps on the table and I watch as they swivel around to check her out. She feels their eyes, turns, notices the familiar insignia and smiles. "Oh, you're Scandinavian Airlines," she says. "What brings you to Hydra?"

Didy and Charmian take one look at Marianne chatting away and dismiss my story as nothing more than a lovers' tiff. They're elbow deep in Martin's education. "Jane says he's most certainly Oxbridge material. Is the Greek system going to be enough for a boy as bright as him?" Didy is saying.

"It's another of those things I'm trying not to think about," Charmian replies. "We need George's new novel to hit the jackpot, and I say that despite its subject matter . . ." and, of course, Didy asks what she means and I doubt it'll be long before the water-works get going again.

I turn back to Marianne. One of the stewardesses has a hand on her arm. "So you know him? You know Axel?"

Marianne's face is contorting. Naughtiness flashes as she catches my eye. "You might say that, yes."

The second stewardess looks triumphant. "There you are, Nita. I said you'd find lover boy on Hydra."

The one called Nita sniffs. "Well, he's a very strange guy. Just disappeared in the morning, leaving me with his suitcase and not a clue what he expected me to do with it."

Marianne nods. "Typical Axel," she says, chewing down on her lip. "My husband really is crazy."

Nita throws a pair of mortified hands to her face. "Oh, I'm sorry," she gasps. "Nothing happened. Really. He was very drunk and stayed up all night telling me the most gruesome stories about what the Nazis did to his father. I think he really needed to talk about it."

Marianne nods sympathetically. "Axel's father owns a sausage factory in Trondheim," she says. "I don't think he's ever met a Nazi in his life."

What a relief it is to hear her laugh and such a contrast to earlier when she talked about wanting to die.

I think it was only because she thought I might disturb the baby or Leonard that she allowed me to coax her out of her miserable cubbyhole. I settled her in her rocking chair on the terrace where she made herself tiny, knees drawn to her chin. She spoke through her fingers. "The pain is too much for me. I can't go through all this again."

"Is the baby all right?" I was starting to panic.

"The baby would be better off with my mother in Oslo. What use is a miserable drag like me in a place like this?"

Through fresh tears she told me that Leonard had been out on the mountain all night, waiting for the sunrise at Profitis Elias. "I thought he was with Axel, but when Axel showed up to say good-bye he told me he hadn't been with him at all. 'Ooops,' Axel said, 'looks like I've stepped in the salad,' and it turns out Leonard saw in the dawn with that Francine. I can feel it all happening again. Everybody wants to steal my man. I don't know what to do. Maybe lock him in and swallow the key," she said, while above us the symphony of keys and carriage return was reaching a triumphant crescendo.

There's no trace of tears now and she has the aircrew enchanted. I've never seen her flirt like this before. "Wow, you fly an empty plane all the way back to Oslo?" she says, and sunlight flares her eyes.

TWENTY-SIX

Sunshine stalks us. It binds us to the rocks, casts us in bronze. It sharpens shadows, blazes the mountains, strikes the white walls so they almost blind us. We slake our thirst with retsina and beer, live on fruit and salad and bread. The thought of cooked food makes everyone feverish. We take long siestas among the fir trees with our many new friends and bob around in the merciful blue sea making plans for sundown and nightfall. We hop like fleas from bed to bed. Those with houses the least number of steps up from the port find their beds get hopped in the most.

Even the most disciplined among us have given up pretending to work. The revolutionary poems stay half-written, paintbrushes stiffen in jars of congealing spirit, my notebook grows vague and filled with doodles. The moon rises like yeast from its bowl in the mountains. Beneath us the rocks remain warm from the sun. The breeze is laced with pine and mountain herb and suggestion and as I settle deeper into my crevice the crushed leaves of rockrose are sticky with the smell of churches.

These rocks and the sea belong to us once the tourists have finished with the sun and gone back to their yachts and hotels. We're all of us complicit in this freedom and there's nothing to fear; even wicked Police Chief Manolis seems to have been defeated by the sheer numbers. The music is almost deafening some nights from Lagoudera where girls in bikinis dance outside in the street.

Leonard sent off the manuscript of his novel on the same day that Marianne dispatched the baby to Norway. He says it's the only copy in the world that's now winging its way on a prayer to his publisher in Canada. It appears he can think about little else but burning boats and drowned mail. He scans the horizon from his favored rock, threading his *komboloi* beads back and forth through his fingers with a look of such anguish I can only suppose it was the I Ching told him not to make a copy before sending it.

It seems like Marianne has been hiding away since getting back here from Athens without her baby. Now she and Charmian climb out of the water and stand drying off, taking turns to rub a towel through their hair.

"They allowed me to walk right onto the plane with him," Marianne's saying as I stand at the edge and pull off my dress, look around and decide nobody will care if I step out of my pants.

"It was an empty flight, just Nita and Suzie and three men in suits. I almost stayed; it would have been the easiest thing in the world to have just buckled myself in . . ."

I can feel Leonard watching me. I turn and catch him at it. He doesn't look away. I glance at Marianne; she's noticed him looking. Something starts hatching inside me.

The sea slaps the warm rocks, but only gently. I plop myself in and flip onto my back and let the waves bob me while I wonder at this thing that seems to come fully fledged with the power to wreak havoc. I squint up at them all ranged on the ledge with the moon

and the mountains behind them. I swim back to the ladder. Little
Booli crawls across the slippery wet rocks. The seawater makes his
underpants droop like a nappy. Charmian's swimsuit does her no
favors and is so worn out it's becoming transparent. Marianne is
a silver sylph in a new yellow bikini. She's asking Charmian about
a recipe for curry and hurriedly hands me her damp towel so that
I can cover up.

"He says he wants spicy," she's saying, and I'm trying hard not
to condemn her but can't help feeling shocked that she can be this
relaxed when she's just packed off her baby with virtual strangers.
It's been the talk of the island, the way that it happened. It came
out of nowhere, a sudden blazing blast of temper.

It was Francine lit the fuse. I spotted her over Marianne's shoulder the day she was busy gossiping about Axel to the air hostesses.
I thought to myself, Oh, *merde*, here comes trouble as Francine
mooched over with yellow flowers in her hair and an open book in
her hands, which turned out, unfortunately, to be Leonard's poetry
collection.

Apparently too engrossed to look up, she pulled out a chair and
read on. Didy leaned across and admired the sprigs of mountain
yarrow that were woven through her hair and Marianne's conversation with the air hostess about Axel's suitcase came to a screech-
ing halt. "Oh, just throw it in the harbor," she said, as Francine
touched the flowers and laughed.

"Wow. I've been up on the mountain all night. I had no idea . . ."

Francine ducked her head to free her ponytail of its band, leaned
to shake out her hair, letting her halter top fall open along her slim
and supple back. Some dry twigs had become tangled in her hair,
she had to twist and snake, so there was plenty of time to admire
the curve of her spine and to notice the fresh grazes at its bony
peaks.

And that was it. Quick as flash paper. All arranged. The baby would take the empty return flight via Paris and on to Oslo in the care of the aircrew. Though a little astonished by the suddenness of Marianne's request, Nita and Suzie seemed happy to help, and Johan, the senior pilot, gave it his blessing, though wasn't paying much attention as Francine was still doing the Medusa with her hair.

"I shall send a telegram to my mama in Oslo to expect him," Marianne said and there was a jut to her chin when Charmian leaned over and asked her, "Darling, really? Are you sure?"

Pomegranates split their sides, spill rubies to the steps; the air is musky with hot figs. I sleep every night on the terrace, curled around whoever has fallen beside me. I have burned the letter I finally received from Jimmy Jones. Back to law school he trots with his tail between his legs, a year behind his peers and somehow that's my fault for leading him astray. My tears have been ill spent.

An American friend of Leonard's called Doc Sheldon arrives for a holiday on the island at the same time as little lumps of Lebanese hashish start to sweeten the air of our late-night courtyard gatherings. The first time I tried it I thought I might die laughing. I was with Marianne, running, holding hands, downhill all the way from her house to the port, crazy as schoolgirls. By the end we couldn't brake if we wanted to and Marianne was whooping, "See, it's like flying!" and we had to grab hold of Marty and Leonard to stop ourselves falling.

Leonard and Marianne walk hand in hand like a honeymoon couple. The rest of us can't help feeling jealous, especially since news got around that Leonard has come into an inheritance of 1,500 dollars from his granny and has decided straight away that he'll buy a house with it. He thinks he's found the right one: three stories and a large terrace with old lemon trees that sits solid in the saddle between the port and Kamini. It has a good vibe, apparently, and he and Marianne hope little by little to do it up. The I Ching is very much in favor of this purchase. Charmian has given it her blessing too, with the promise of an ironwork flowery bed. George twists him a wry grin. "Maybe now you're a property owner you'll have to stop whining about Canadian government grants," he says, downing a brandy.

Leonard and Marianne take trips to Piraeus and come back laden with oriental rugs, fine old linen and an antique gilded mirror wrapped in blankets that will hang in his hall. They are rich in love and rich in books which they bring tied in bundles, new records too, and a gang of us follow them from the boat and up the streaming hill through a rainstorm with their parcels and baskets strung between us. We arrive at Marianne's out of breath and soaked to the skin. She hands out towels and while we shed our wet clothing stays outside on the terrace and sings encouraging words to the marijuana seedlings that have started to thrive among her tomato plants.

We dry off and she pours us all wine, arranges bunches of grapes on a large copper plate. We settle around a low Turkish table. Through the shutters the summer downpour hammers and steams and I have to resist an urge to run outside naked and dance in it. I look around at us all reclining among the cushions in our wrappings of towels. We're as gilded and gleaming as ancients at the symposium. The grapes are pale as polished jade and everyone is smiling, shining from the rain. Göran reads aloud from a book that is lying there, Cavafy's *Ithaka*. Lena peels him a grape. Marty pulls me close, and I settle, grateful to have this happy giant's chest for my pillow.

Marianne rolls a joint while Leonard slides the record from its sleeve and, with the care demanded of a sacrament, places it on the turntable. The loudspeaker crackles as he stoops to blow a speck of dust from the needle before lifting it to the groove. He takes the joint from Marianne and settles himself beside her on the goatskin rug. Mahalia Jackson sings gospels while Marianne curls herself around him and they lie very still.

———

There's a day when the whole quay smells curiously of ouzo and the talk turns to departures. At the waterfront the oak wine casks are being hosed down with salt water. A priest stands beside the wine boat sprinkling holy water and intoning prayers for its return filled with a good vintage by Saint Demetrios Day. Each empty barrel sports a festive bung of bay leaves that flutter farewell as the bell tolls. The circles shrink around the café tables.

"Bloody decadents, the lot of them," George says as the students start to slope away with their bedrolls and rucksacks.

The grand houses are being shuttered, easels disappear from the streets, Maria's tourist shop opens only one hour each day and sometimes the ferry brings nobody at all. The painted wooden caiques outnumber the yachts in the harbor, the port returns to the business of caulking hulls and mending nets. The quay is piled with netted mountains of sponges from Benghazi and, though the crop is meager, not a soul has been lost. The cannons have been fired from the roofs of the captains' houses and from the workshops comes the sound of men working on engines, the fresh resinous smell of newly planed planking. The mountains sigh with relief and birds gather on the wires of the awnings to sing of Africa. There are tearful farewells. I cry me several rivers when Bobby leaves with Trudy, but Charmian mops me up at her table, reminds me of the unhappy boy he had been when he arrived. I hang on her words. Perhaps by taking such good care of Trudy, she says, Bobby has managed to put the ghost of his failure to nurse our mother to rest.

George is in a despicable mood—no surprises there; he has been for days. He sits coughing and bellyaching in his own smoky cloud of brandy and funk. Didy is attempting to chivvy him while at the same time deal with the kids, his three as well as her younger two, all talking at once and slurping on strawberry milkshakes.

Leonard and Marianne share a dish of tiny prawns. Marianne doesn't mind the cats snaking around her legs, not even the manky, one-eyed ginger who jumps on her lap. The intense adoration is making Leonard sneeze so he moves away a little, and wipes his fingers before opening his newspaper.

Today's ferry has delivered to Bim a fresh rejection letter, this for the third draft of his novel. "Look at this," he says, licking his finger and rubbing at the signature. "They couldn't even be bothered to sign it. It's printed on."

Leonard looks up, but only briefly. Something in the *Herald Tribune* is making him frown. He's scribbling some words in his notebook. Marianne picks up Bim's cup and turns it three times on a saucer. She tells him she sees a dollar sign in his coffee grounds and Robyn sighs and agrees to send off for a new supply of paper and carbons so he can have another stab at it. Bim's bloodshot eyes betray the decaying spirit behind his handsome brow. He makes a perfect victim for George who shifts over to have a pick while he's still fresh from the blow of the publisher's rejection.

"Look, I don't mean to be some old-bastard Chronos here but take it from me, mate, sitting around on this rock and drinking too much does little for the syntax and only blunts the wits. Maybe it's time you asked yourself what it is you have to say that's so bloody important?"

Bim tries to defend himself but George talks over him and ends with theatrical despair, motioning to his children who are attempting to get the cats to fight for sardine tails.

"With these three and a voracious wife to provide for, I'm no longer free but civilization is going to hell in a handcart and you young writers need to get your hands dirty and tell the world about it. Go to Cuba, Korea, Hungary, Ethiopia . . . You know, I covered over sixty countries before getting myself manacled to this rock. What's the bloody matter with your generation? We're being brought to the brink of atomic annihilation and all you want to do is moon about sucking on lotus? Why are you not more angry?"

Leonard looks up, startled.

"There are lots of things that anger me," he says, tapping out a cigarette and narrowing his eyes at George as he lights it. "But let us not destroy ourselves with hostility, let us not become paranoiac. If there are things to fight against, let's do it in health and in sanity. I don't want to become a mad poet, I want to become a healthy man who can face the things that are around me." He smiles at Marianne before returning to whatever has been preoccupying him in the newspaper. Eichmann's thin, surprisingly ordinary face stares back at him from the page.

"Very well put," Bim says, but George swipes the grin from his face by pointing to the publisher's rejection slip on the table in front of him. "Proof of the pudding, mate."

George has said his piece and is now waving to an old friend who is saluting him from the deck of a large wooden caique. It's *The Twelve Apostles*, a former sponge boat, and it's been moved from its mooring at the western mole to a slot right in front of us.

Captain Andreas gives George a thumbs-up. Martin pulls at his father's sleeve.

"You know, I suddenly have a very good idea," George turns a roguish smile on Didy. Martin has his fingers crossed under the table. It's slightly uncomfortable because we both know that whatever George is about to suggest has not only just occurred to him at all. He points to the harbor. *The Twelve Apostles* gleams with new paint: pink and lemon yellow with a blue strake at the waterline. Captain Andreas has waxed his whiskers and looks rather like a walrus beneath his blue cap. He is sitting on deck at a marble table playing dominoes.

"If you want the kids to see some of the classical sights, you should let me set you up a charter with my old friend over there, an excellent sailor and a top bloke. I've loaned him a little to get kitted out now sponge is truly over. Mercedes engine, comfy bunks," George is saying, Didy nodding away.

"What a very kind thing to do."

"She might not look as sleek as some tourist boats, but she'll give you a smoother sail on these seas and he could make you a beaut little trip to Mykonos." He ruffles Martin's hair. "And I don't mind sparing the Professor here, should you need an interpreter."

"Oh, but that's a wonderful idea, all of it!" Didy says, clapping her hands, all gums and teeth and rattling bracelet. "Do you think Charmian would allow me to borrow him?"

Pete and Martin are bumping their fists together. Shane's eyes blaze. "And you too of course, Shaney!" Didy says, and little Fiona pipes up, pointing to Booli, "Please not him as well, Mummy, he's so horrid," and Didy has to tell her off for being rude.

I don't think Charmian's noticed us at all, she's so intent on something the American painter is saying as they come from the alley and the light is against her. I think his name's Chip or Chick;

he's only been on the island a few days and Charmian has been helping him to find a house and settle in. Chip is almost as tall as George; she has to tip her face up to his to talk to him. From our vantage point, the light that momentarily blinds them only highlights their folly. They are too close, even I can see that. His hand is on her waist, her lips almost brush his ear. Too late, she springs away, puts a decent distance between them.

Shane scrapes back her chair and turns to her father. "Why don't you have them both killed, Daddy?"

George sets his mouth to a snarl and staggers to his feet.

Didy gasps. "Really, George, you all need to get away from here." She puts a hand on his arm to detain him. "I want you and Charmian to think seriously about my offer. Some decent medical care and a stint in the Cotswolds will do you all the power of good."

TWENTY-SEVEN

The sun is setting as we scramble from the sea. On the beach Göran and Lena pile up armfuls of brushwood brought down from the hills and here comes Marty, hefty and blond, with Edie and Janey bearing gifts of a wicker-covered *galloni*, a box of cakes from Eleni's and a watermelon as big as a baby. It's Leonard's birthday, his twenty-sixth, and over a month since he sent off his manuscript. He sits on the smooth shingle at the edge of the water, hunched over his guitar. Marianne says that there's still not been a word from his publisher, though the I Ching remains nothing but encouraging. The furrows from his nose to his mouth run deep as a ventriloquist's dummy, make him look old for his age. He growls some words to the ocean as he strums.

I'm shivering a little, I've been in the water so long, and Charmian gives me a rub and slips her cardigan over my shoulders. We've both been watching Leonard, trying to catch what it is he's singing. He turns, still strumming, as Marianne comes to him wrapped in her white towel. He smiles and changes key, picks out

some notes. His fingers pluck a melody right out of the air. She has
a taper from the fire, and she brings him a Greek cigarette, keeps
her hand cupped around the flame.

The Twelve Apostles is anchored at the tip of Shark Bay and
beyond it the familiar chain of islands—the sleeping whale, the
pyramid, the squatting toad—and a sky the fuzzy mauve of sugar
paper. Captain Andreas has fixed up a hoist and Shane and Martin
are showing off to the other kids, swinging out into the water from
the top of the mast. George is watching them, smiling and pulling his jumper around his skinny frame. His cough has been so
bad it's a wonder he's had the breath to make it all the way to the
beach. Didy's had her donkey-boy bring down a couple of chairs
from Spiti Heidsieck and sits beside him in her hacking jacket and
pearls. She talks about England while he smokes and admires his
fine healthy children.

Demetri and Bim have lighting the fire under control; they
don't need old George to tell them to get down on their knees and
blow. They've already hauled sacks of splintery wood from the
mill and hefted large stones into a ring for Marianne's cooking
pot. Carolyn and Robyn scatter woven rugs and cushions, Göran
strums Leonard's guitar, Charlie Heck has scored two racks of
chops which he lays on a bed of rosemary branches. A truce has
broken out between Charmian and George and she settles herself
at his feet. I surreptitiously sniff at the wool of her cardigan, and
we watch as the dry brushwood crackles and releases swarms of
cinders to the night.

Our Vespers is the fire and the shore and Leonard's guitar, the
children's laughter across the waves. The stones retain warmth from
the sun; the last few days have been blazing. "The Little Summer
of Saint Demetrios" is what the locals call it. Charmian turns her
face to the first sprinkling of stars and, in a dreamy counterpoint to

our surroundings, starts to recite Keats on autumn. George stops tearing at his nails as he listens and his worn, addled face shifts to one of devotion. She talks, her voice low and warm, of mellow mornings with dew-dampened grass underfoot and English church spires rising from the mist, of suet puddings and bramble jelly, of wet dogs and Wellington boots.

"My darling, brave Cliftie," he says, her wistfulness not lost to him. He puts his lips to the top of her head. "All this will still be here for us when we return."

Leonard retrieves his guitar and Charlie Heck sings of union men at the factory gates, of freight trains and of riding an old paint through the prairie. Lena weaves in some silver notes with her flute. Demetri taps time on the back of a box. The children have all been settled for the night on Captain Andreas's deck and we catch brief snatches of their voices from the bobbing silhouette of the boat. When Marianne sighs and says, "I wish this summer would last forever," she speaks for us all.

I think she has added an extra ingredient to her grandmother's recipe for meatballs. Her pot plants cropped well. Leonard gives thanks to Demeter for this munificence and Marianne giggles, "Well, it is a special occasion," and we fall silent as Leonard starts to sing his first song of the night.

I'm suffused in a haze, blissful. I float on a rug between Edie and Janey and let them baby me. The sea shushes the shore and the moon shimmers in a spectral halo a mile wide. Fire licks night to a swirling vortex of leaping flame and ironstone shadow, whirling cinders, moon-silvered waves, stars. I am cosseted within this dreamy circle, like a sleepy, milk-fed child listening to the grown-ups chatting beside the fire.

There's a melancholic note setting in as talk turns once again to autumn.

"I hate having to accept that we've lost our spirit," Charmian is saying. "And that we might never find it, nor indeed find our way back." But Didy's not having it, telling her to simply buck up. "A change is as good as a rest and if you're to be in England you couldn't wish for a more fairy-tale setting than Charity Farm. You'll see."

I've been party to much hand-wringing by Charmian, and tears, at the house by the well since Didy made them her offer of swapping houses for a year. A farmhouse in a picturesque Cotswolds village "nothing younger than Jacobean," an excellent grammar school a bus ride away, proper medical care, an easy train to London and the coffers of Fleet Street—of course it makes sense.

"A bloody life raft," George called it while they to-ed and fro-ed and she paced and wept and then one morning Billy Collins tipped the scales with an enthusiastic letter about a party for George's novel.

For me her departure is whatever is the opposite of a life raft. It leaves me adrift. I can't imagine life on the island without her any more than I can will a dream. I'm scared that I'll wither and die without the nourishment of those hectic meals at her table, the quick-fire banter and intrigue, the sudden tears and laughter, the family jokes and dramas, the wise counsel. I'll even miss George's teasing. I sniffle into the sleeve of her cardigan and am assailed by its smoky cinnamon scent. A wave washes over me, big as grief and so strong I almost beg her to take me with them, but I know she'd recoil if faced with the depth of my hunger.

Didy is well aware that Charmian's resolve could spring back at any moment. She handles her with care, soothes her with reason.

"Quite apart from George's condition, it's the perfect moment to see what can be done about Martin's schooling," she's saying. "He's sure to get every scholarship going . . ."

"I know, I know."

I sit cross-legged with my head on Edie's shoulder, my eyes blurry with sorrow as I watch them through the flames. Charmian surprises George with a peck on the cheek as she reaches for the bottle. "As long as my husband doesn't get so lionized by his newspaper chums that his head won't fit through the farmhouse door," she says, topping up Didy's drink and her own.

George waves his empty beaker. "If you think I like going back there cap in bloody hand, you must be crazy, woman."

She hands him the bottle and rolls her eyes at Didy. "And Billy Collins has tremendous plans to have him hobnobbing with all the right sort of literary types, isn't that so, darling? I just hope he doesn't have to spend too many nights in town while I wait at home with the children in my pinny . . ."

Didy has been on the island long enough to sense dangerous currents. She taps her beaker to Charmian's. "But, my dear, isn't your own novel coming out in England this autumn too?"

"Oh that," Charmian says. "My publisher calls it 'a sprightly little tale.' I'm not holding my breath. No, what we have to do is everything we can to ensure *Closer to the Sun* is the tremendous smash Billy Collins believes it will be. Our future depends on it and George jolly well deserves a bestseller."

The talk of bestsellers and departures has caught Leonard's attention. Montreal is calling to him. "I guess I'll have to renew my neurotic affiliations at some point," he says, swallowing the ache in his voice. A flare from the fire catches his unease in dark shadows and furrows. Marianne hugs her knees to her chest, rests her chin. His eyes are softened by love every time he looks at her. She can join him, she knows that. She pulls her knees tighter, looks into the embers. It's as though he's forgotten the existence of her child.

She can't hide her unhappiness when Didy presses her on how

much longer she'll stay. "I have to get Axel's car back to Scandinavia before the year's out because I sure don't have the cash to pay import tax on it," she says.

Didy looks like she would horsewhip him if he were present. "Can't he even manage that for himself? Thank the Lord he's in Athens and not here tonight."

"Axel's banned from driving. He never does anything a little bit. The police were amazed he could still walk a straight line," Marianne says and Leonard frowns and moves away to crouch closer to the fire. "Besides, if I don't get his silly car back to Oslo to sell it I don't know where we find the money for our divorce," she says, as Leonard squats poking the flames with a long stick. "And of course, there's Axel Joachim. I don't want him to forget that he has a mama," she adds. Leonard broods and smokes. Bim crouches down beside him, accepts a toke on the joint.

"My wife's deserting me because she's got herself a nice little earner in London," Bim is saying. "But I'm not budging from here until my novel is damned well accepted by a publisher." He turns to call to Didy over his shoulder. "So you'll have me for the foreseeable." And Didy shakes her bracelet: "Marvelous!" Though I can't say she looks overjoyed at this prospect and neither am I.

Robyn's job is at *Reader's Digest* and she's excited about it but Bim is talking over her. "I mean, why would any right-minded woman choose to stay here and be a moat around my tower?" he says, standing unsteadily to pass the spliff to Demetri.

"You talk such rot," Robyn says, and tells him to shush.

"Or, come to that, why stick around and be a tap on my barrel?" Bim says, swaying and plonking himself down beside her, pointing to his lap. "Or a muffler on my horn?"

I look across at Charmian and we both grimace. Bim won't be shushed.

He has his hand on Robyn's belly. "My wife won't stick around if I don't give her a baby. So tell me, Leonard, how do I make that work if I want to be true to the words that roar away inside me demanding to be free?"

"Oh, brother," George says, throwing back his drink. "Where to bloody begin."

Leonard turns his back to the fire and looks across at Marianne. Her eyes are downcast and she's made herself tiny around her knees. Firelight catches her shins, the apples of her cheeks, glints in her hair. He rubs his palm back and forth along his stubble, before answering Bim.

"When there are meals on the table, order in the upkeep of the house and harmony, it's the perfect moment to start some serious work." He speaks like an incantation, serious and considered, and returns to Marianne's side. "When there is food on the table, when the candles are lit, when you wash the dishes together, and put the child to bed together. That is order, that is spiritual order, there is no other."

It feels true and right and heartfelt when he says it. Marianne looks up at him and they both smile.

She lowers her eyes again. Everyone falls silent. The night holds its breath. In a while Leonard, almost casually, tells Marianne that he'll come with her in the car to Oslo. I glance across as he settles his guitar against his knee and again picks out the bittersweet melody I heard at the shore. All the time he's playing he can't tear his eyes from her face, and no wonder. She is radiant with the smile of a saint given leave of execution. The fire dances in her eyes, he plays his guitar. So why do I feel sad?

The purchase of Leonard's house delays their departure. They finally move in while the workmen are still digging out the floor, and although it's noisy and chaotic everything looks fresh with new whitewash, all the shutters fixed and painted chalky grey, and a beeswax, linseed and elbow-grease gleam brought to the old wooden boards. Mules cart furniture from Axel's house: the wicker rocking chair, the carved Russian bed, some rugs, pots and pans. They have a table and chairs from George and Charmian, who also keeps her promise of the flowery iron bed which they paint midnight blue and pile with cushions beneath the lemon trees on the terrace.

The island empties; most of the tavernas close. In the evenings we start to gather inside, our chairs pulled together around Sofia's charcoal brazier at the back of the store. The circle is tightening. Edie and Janey will leave soon to take up a lease on a shop in Carnaby Street that Janey's uncle has arranged, Göran can't wait much longer to be reunited with his girlfriend in Stockholm, the gaggle of Goschens have recently departed for the birth of their new baby, the Greers are on their way to Beirut.

I stay. I brood and dream. I have no offers and no reason to be anywhere but here. There has been no letter from my father. I have no home to return to. An orphan's tears are at one with this stark and moody landscape of rock and sea and weather. I tell myself my loneliness is romantic, heroic even. The mountains hold me. I gather saffron in their foothills and dye all my clothes yellow. I dream of my mother and wake with the weight of her absence on my chest. She's given me time to miss her as well as time to dream. When her money runs out I'll have to find my way back to a bedsit and a job, but until then there's Cato to think of and I can hardly leave him to starve on the streets.

The clear days are beautiful. I thank her for every one of them. The hills are blanketed with cyclamens, crocuses, tiny green lilies; it's sunny enough to swim, and at night to sit on the terrace and read a book by moonlight. When it rains I write in my notebook with the music of water cascading from the hills to the cistern.

———

Leonard and Marianne cling on, one more day, another week, and in the end Charmian and George leave before they do. The island conspires to make their departure as painful as possible by offering up a white-and-blue morning as dazzling as the Greek flag.

We gather at Katsikas to wave them off, hangovers from last night's shindig abated by medicinal *tsipouro* and a special cake made from vintage grape mush that Andonis brings with the muddy sweet coffee. Charmian sits at her usual table in a traveling suit of black gabardine so formal and stiff it might do for a funeral. Her eyes are ringed with shadows and filmy with booze. George leaves her to her final farewells, says there's something he needs to sort out with their tickets at the Hellenic office.

"I'm so terribly sorry we haven't cleared the account," Charmian's saying to Nikos Katsikas who only beams and pours her another brandy for the voyage.

"Philoxenia, it's a Greek thing. You must not apologize. You are our friends. Mr. George will pay us when you return. This way we know that you will have to come back."

Marianne arrives with Leonard. She's been up since the seven o'clock bells, painting some pots for the terrace with a design of blue and ochre flowers inspired by her dear Momo's dinner service. According to her, the morning was too fine to miss, and she doesn't look remotely tired, she has a gift for that, despite that we've all been carousing at Douskos Taverna until dawn. She and Leonard put the rest of us to shame. They've already been swimming and there is paint in her fringe and on her hands, an adorable blue smudge on her cheek. Leonard's hair is speckled all over with whitewash. Charmian thanks him for last night's songs. "We couldn't have wished for a better send-off," she says and bursts into tears.

Now that Marianne's moved in with Leonard, Axel's on the island more often, finishing his novel and awaiting the reappearance of Patricia. This morning his arrival is preceded by the little white dog which chases pigeons at the waterfront and comes unapologetically wagging its tail when he whistles to it.

Bim lounges beside Leonard as Axel bends to kiss Marianne's cheek.

"You guys, this is civilization; what's the point of alternatives if you're not free to leave or take them, eh?" Bim says as Axel scoops up the squirming dog and places it in Marianne's arms, and joins in her laughter as it licks her face. "Robyn just doesn't dig it. I mean, it's a burden to the imagination to have to build a fence to ward off the excitement and titillation of other choices . . ." He looks across at me as he says this, making me squirm.

Charmian catches him at it, gives him a sharp "tsk" and he winks at her and says, "Tsk? Really? You?"

Charmian gathers herself, and I think how sad it is that her last morning should be tainted by bickering with Bim. Leonard saves the day, says he'll tell her right away what he thinks. He leans across and takes her hand, steadies her with his eyes. For a moment it's as though there is no one else present and he speaks to her as slowly and seriously as a priest offering benediction.

"To really turn your back on all the other possibilities and all the other experiences of love, of passion, ecstasy, and to determine to find it within one embrace is a high and righteous notion—only compatible with the strangest kind of will and most gifted individuals."

She tries hard not to laugh but her shoulders start to shake as he goes on. "Oh, Leonard," she silences him, wiping her eyes. "I do think everyone makes rather too much of these things. When it comes down to it it's all about having the same sauce for goose and gander."

The *Nereida* appears around the headland. It feels ludicrous to be crying the way I am; it's not my place to be the chief mourner.

"Oh, why is George taking so long?" Charmian cries as we straggle in her wake to the ferry dock. Zoe is waiting with the luggage and Booli who is wailing and burying himself in her bosom. Shane is crying too, trying to snap some final Polaroids of her friends, and Martin's crouching on the ground with his face in Max's ruff. I wish they'd miss the boat, change their minds, anything, but find I can't stand another moment of this painful departure and offer to scoot to the Hellenic office to find George.

The door is open. He is stooping over his suitcase, removing some books. He plonks them on the counter. Two neat stacks in bright orange dust jackets.

Wheezing and hustling. "Arrived from the printers just in time. It's my latest. The whole thing's set here on the island so I'm thinking you might sell them and we'll split fifty-fifty."

"George, the ferry's about to dock." I'm pulling on his arm as Yiorgis attempts to push the books back across the desk at him.

"Look, I'm sailing for England, I can't bloody take them with me anyway."

I heft up his case. "Come on!" I say. "If you really insist on leaving."

"Quick, hand me that pen. I'll sign one to you, Ricky."

It takes mighty willpower to refuse him. My promise to
Charmian hangs in the air. He picks up a copy. Yiorgis hands him
a Biro.

"No, thank you, we haven't got time," I say, grabbing his suitcase. I look at the books. Fifteen shillings a copy. "I'll come back
and buy them all," I say as I fly out of the door.

"You opening a bookstore, Ricky?" George gruffs and I carry
on as fast as I can with his heavy suitcase banging my shins and
him coughing to keep up.

The port shines pink as a shell in the midday sun. The painted
boats creak at their moorings as the ferry draws in; the harbor is
scattered with opals.

She stands in a sea of well-wishers, her handkerchief pressed to
her eyes. The children board first. I take my turn to hug her. "Oh,
I do hate to think of you left alone. Do take good care of yourself, Erica," she says. "And don't let anyone take advantage of your
sweet nature."

I can barely let her go. "Please don't leave me!" I want to cry
but strangle the words. She hugs me for the longest time. "Keep
writing," she says, but it's not enough.

"Good luck!"

"Bon voyage!"

"*Ha det bra! Ha det moro!* Have fun! Enjoy!"

"*Kalo taxidi!*"

Leonard has been helping George with the luggage. He grasps
Charmian by the waist at the foot of the gangplank. "Remember
me for my silences," he says, kissing her, and she laughs: "Between
you and my husband I don't think I ever got a word in."

Dinos has come down from Episkopi and, though I've barely
seen him all summer, he stands with me, offers me his good, broad
shoulder to cry on.

The family press together on the sundeck, waving. Didy calls up that they must each throw a drachma to the sea, for luck. The ferry deafens everyone with its horn. "Do it! It means that you will return to the island," she shouts and as the boat pulls away Charmian leans over the rail and sends a handful of coins glittering to the harbor.

TWENTY-EIGHT

I met Charmian again, quite by chance, the following spring. My heart almost burst from my chest as she stepped from the bus, and I cried out, "*Kalimera!*"

In place of the battered straw I'd become so accustomed to on Hydra was a man's trilby, and beneath it her eyes slanting and dark with makeup. She came towards me, self-consciously stroking the nap of a long suede coat the color of milky coffee. "So deliciously impractical. I have no idea what George was thinking," she said, as though we'd last spoken only the other day.

People swarmed from the entrance of Paddington Station and had to step around us as we embraced. "You look younger," I said, though it wasn't true, despite that she'd had her teeth fixed.

"Well, Erica, you look *older*! Really quite grown up. Is that a permanent wave? Crikey, this is a pleasurable surprise!" She was a bluster of apologies, for leaving lipstick which she dabbed at with a handkerchief and also for her failure to get in touch. "I got your letter and I've been meaning to invite you to the farm; it sounds like you've been having a horrid time . . ." For all her makeup and chic clothing, London light betrayed her. Without her tan she was more drawn than ever, hollowed and harried, fiddling with the clasp of her handbag and chewing her lip.

"Ah well, I know you've been busy," I said, keeping my voice light. I didn't want to scare her away. I'd had a long island winter to think about things and could see that my hunger overwhelmed her, that already there wasn't enough Charmian to go around.

"But now, here you are! So, darling, tell me: how long has it been since you left Greece?"

She was delving into the bag which hung open like a jaw from the crook of her arm.

"It was February," I said as she pulled out her cigarettes. "A lifetime ago." A matter of a few weeks and already the island felt about as real to me as a lovely dream. A fantasia. "I left on the day the almond trees came into flower."

She took my arm and drew me aside to make way for a woman with a pram. "It's so sudden, isn't it, so airy and pink. And such a glorious portent of spring." She glanced at the sky above the buildings, which managed to be both glaring and grey, scowled and told me that she couldn't wait to go back. "I think it's fair to say that the house swap has been a disaster," she said. "Now we're praying for a miracle to get us back to Hydra. George has been given the old 'we'll call you next week' up and down Fleet Street, which as you might imagine has given him quite a knock, especially when it's from the mouths of those he helped on their way up the ladder." She rummaged for her lighter. "But enough of my woes—tell me about you. I take it by now you've found somewhere more salubrious to live?"

She shook out a cigarette and stuck it between her lips. "You'll be pleased to know that I no longer have a cockroach problem,"

I said, the thought of the secret night scutterings still making me shudder. "In fact, in a way, it's all thanks to your friend Greg Corso . . ."

"Why, is he an expert on insect extermination?"

I could feel myself blush, a giggle in my throat. "I've moved in with my boyfriend!" I managed to splutter. "And it's because I told him I knew Corso that he took me on. I mean, there were many applicants with much better qualifications, but he's big on the Beats so that swung it for me."

She looked at me and snorted. "You applied for a *job* as a live-in girlfriend?"

I'd forgotten about her brows, the green of her eyes. Goodness, I'd missed talking to her.

"No, I got the job as his assistant!" I said. "He runs a small press from his front room in Pimlico, mainly poetry. Six quid a week, and living in since it turns out we can't keep our hands off each other . . ." I couldn't seem to do anything about my silly laughter while I told her about my gallant knight in rumpled corduroy. What a fool I must have seemed. Her cigarette remained unlit. The way she searched my eyes was making my words ever more mangled, flooding me with desire to confide in her but too ashamed to admit that I'd run out of choices, that I didn't have a penny to my name.

"Oh, but you're still just a girl . . ." she said, with a troubled frown that brought with it a memory of her kitchen in Hydra, my hands held out for a dusting of flour, Brahms. The music, the way it soared, brought the tears to our eyes when she made me promise her that no man would ever clip my wings.

But that was Hydra, not London. "Oh gosh, and I was sorry to hear about your father, about the breakdown," she was saying. She pressed me to take her handkerchief, brushed a finger within an inch of my cheek and snatched her hand away.

I took the proffered hankie, blotted my eyes. "Someone had to be here. And you know, Bobby wasn't about to come dashing home from Boston, so there was only me, and by the time I got back from Greece the bailiffs had taken every stick, even the picture frames, and he was catatonic . . ." I let it all tumble out and fell into her arms.

The island swam up to meet me. It was spread out beneath the rosy glow of my final morning, high up in Episkopi, a cacophony of goat bells and Cato curled around my feet while Dinos threw open the shutters and called me over. I sat up and gathered myself in the sheet. Dinos stood silhouetted in the square of light. I came to him, surprised at how natural it felt to have him pull me close, to rest my head upon his shoulder. The island managed to make each departure more painful than the last and for me it excelled. Dinos was smiling like he'd produced a rabbit from his hat: the almond trees had bloomed overnight and it looked like the hills had been draped with pink lace.

I was mortified to see that I had left a trail of snot and tears on Charmian's suede coat. "Really, don't worry," she said. "I'm just glad to have run into you, to know you're OK." She indicated the station. "Are you catching a train?"

I smiled and shook my head. Fortune had presented the perfect moment for this meeting. "I'm on my way to picket British Transport HQ," I said, raising a zealous fist.

"Good for you," she said.

"We're protesting about that Family Planning Association poster being banned from the Tube stations," I said, well aware of the good light this was throwing on me.

Ah, yes. She had seen it on the news.

"Fancy giving in to religious nutcases, and besides, what sort of a God is it that wants to foist unwanted babies on to women?" I continued and she gave me the look I'd been craving, the look that said I was a true daughter, if only of the revolution.

My heart was skipping like a schoolgirl with a crush. I'd have given anything to detain her. I pulled at her sleeve. "It's outside their headquarters, not far from here. Why don't you come?"

She glanced at her watch. I laid out my wares, piling one shiny thing after another. "You haven't told me yet about the children. And we can talk about Hydra. You missed a big drama with Axel when Patricia finally showed up. He had that air hostess on a stopover, really bad timing . . . And did you hear that Magda was carted off to prison because her ex-husband scarpered without paying taxes? . . . And Greg Corso came back for a while and drank himself so stupid he fell in the harbor . . ."

I kept going until she was shaking her head at me, telling me I was incorrigible. "I'm supposed to be on the ten o'clock train to cook lunch in Stanton but I think, for this, George can spare me," she said, taking my arm as we crossed the road. We were both sighing for Hydra, for the spring flowers that were blooming without us and for the gossip of the port, as the No. 27 to Baker Street pulled into the stop.

"Though, I must say, it's very peaceful at Charity Farm. The entire village is golden stone, like it's been carved out of cheese, and I've become quite the lady of the manor, albeit one who rolls up her sleeves and helps with the lambing . . ." She was acting the part of jolly countrywoman, telling me amusing stories about the local characters, a fox that she kept hidden from the local hunt in the woodshed, an orphan lamb that she fed with a bottle, Didy's fat Labrador. We settled at the front of the bus. I already knew that her eyes would be sad, I could tell from the false chipper tone of her voice. "I have a lovely big study all to myself with a view across the valley, great drifts of daffodils . . ." she was saying as I paid the conductor.

She was more up to date than me on Hydra's dramas. She'd recently received "a marvelously gossipy" letter from Didy. She told me that Marianne was making plans to go back. "Everyone's agog, waiting for the next installment. You know, which house she will choose to make her home: Axel's or Leonard's?"

I thought of Marianne's sweet smile, the devotion in Leonard's eyes, his lighting of the Shabbat candles in her honor, his compact brown body and warm hands, his lovely house, Hydra. "Cohen is crazy about her. It seems like a fairy tale, the way it's all worked out." I couldn't help sighing.

"If it's a fairy tale, it's a dark one and I'm not sure she's quite out of the woods yet," Charmian said. "She and the baby are stuck in Oslo waiting for her divorce, but our Canadian pal has buggered off to Cuba, so if she comes it'll be alone in the hope that he'll join her and go down on bended knee. One thing I know about Leonard is that he'll never make a promise he can't keep so thin chance, I'd say."

I was thinking of the house, of the room at the top freshly painted for the baby, burning with envy despite what Charmian was saying.

"Sam Barclay's been keeping up his own lovelorn correspondence with Marianne. He reckons she still holds a flame for Axel. She told him that her best option might be to try to make it work with the father of her child. Silly girl, she does rather cling on where there's not a shred of hope, doesn't she?" Charmian arched a brow at me. "You know she always suspected you of having it off with Leonard?"

"No, nothing, nothing ever happened," I spluttered, as the blood rushed to my face. "Really! Nothing at all."

"Oh, always so much intrigue on Hydra. How I miss it! You'd think all these months away would leave space for writing, but I've never felt less inspired in my life." She craned to the window, to look down on the grey, greasy streets and pedestrians, the businessmen all hurrying to somewhere they didn't want to be.

"The only writing I seem to get done is letters about the children's schools. It's exasperating, truly. They've been lumped in with dimwits because no one thought to warn us about the eleven-plus, which, of course, the Greek system did not prepare them for. So I write like some wretched Cyrano de Bergerac for George to put his big manly signature to, and that's the thing I really resent, that a letter from a father is taken more seriously . . ."

"Outrageous." I was glad enough the subject had changed, and told her how I'd been refused a bank loan because I couldn't produce a husband or a father to sign for me. I hadn't been asking for a fortune. Just enough to pay key money on another filthy room. She held out an arm and, when I rested my head, stroked my hair, told me how good it was that I'd stopped mooning around, that I was fired up and ready to join the fight.

My boyfriend's sister Nina waited at the railings, all busy and bossy with her leaflets. She worked for the Family Planning Association and had rung me earlier that morning to nag me into coming. I was impatient with introductions, would rather have shoved Nina under a bus than have Charmian suspect my presence here was anything other than activist zeal. We were each handed a placard on a wooden stick, END THE BAN in block letters, and I steered her well away from Nina, to where a baby-faced copper swooped and offered a light for her cigarette. We didn't shout, but stood against the railings in a group of a hundred or so, men as well as women, looking cross and holding up our banners while the newspapermen took our photographs. Charmian's smart coat was not out of place; many of the women around us sported full mink.

We stamped our feet and talked about women's rights to contraception, and the irony isn't lost on me today that, though I didn't yet know it, the cells of my son were already busy dividing inside me.

"Only when the scientists come up with that pill they keep promising will women's liberation be a possibility," I remember Charmian saying.

Once the photographs had been taken, she and I crossed to the Star and Garter to use the loo. It was still early and the ladies' saloon was empty. We settled in a crimson plush nook and she shook out a Capstan Full Strength.

"Don't even think about paying," I said, when she suggested that since the wind had been chill a tot of cognac might be medicinal.

"Better just the one, though. George will be working himself into a frenzy imagining what I'm up to if I don't get on the next train," she said, and I noticed her hand shook as she lit the cigarette. "And I really don't want him to get ill again. He's had pneumonia for most of the winter, poor bugger."

The brandies were small; I should have got doubles. "Talking of George's fevered imagination," I said, overcome with an urge to mock him in revenge for so soon snatching her away, "has the dreaded novel been a success? Was he the toast of the town?"

More than anything I wanted her to know of my most glorious action, to lay down with a flourish what I'd done with all those copies he had left on the island to defame her. But she was wincing and swallowing her brandy. Miserable that I'd even mentioned it.

"I don't know which upsets me more, if people read it or if they don't. It's humiliating for me if they do and humiliating for George if they don't." She looked to the bottom of her empty glass with a sad shrug and called to the barman for another. "The only thing I dread about *Closer to the Sun* is our children coming across it."

"Well, if it's any comfort, I kept my promise. I haven't read a word of it," I said, almost bursting with the effort of not blurting out what I'd done with his books.

She snorted. "But, Erica, why should I give a fig if you read it, or not?"

I don't think she noticed how lonely that made me feel, how it stung. I reached for my glass but it was mysteriously empty and she was still talking. I remembered my elation at the rocks, how I whooped as I sent them flying, one after the other, flaming orange against the sky, and watched until, sodden and swollen, they were carried away by the waves. I'd done it for her.

The barman brought us new drinks, doubles. "It was the worst thing George could have done, bullying me, accusing me, making me write in a fury like that. Afterwards, I started to notice that I was feeling almost indignant each time I ran into Jean-Claude with one of his willing muses. It was as though this incredibly romantic thing that George had forced me to write had really happened between us. When we finally got to it, it was nothing like I'd written it. There was no seduction in the bottled sunshine of a windmill, no bed of sweet-scented hay, no butterfly to open its bright wings. It was humiliating, but you know what? I kept going back with my jug of retsina. His squalid room always smelled of the pee he left too long in his pot . . ."

She laughed and pulled a dejected face. "And the bastard never once even pretended he wanted to paint me," she said, adopting an enraging poor-little-me pout. I thought of telling her that back in Boston Trudy had been told she would never have children, as a result of her botched abortion in Athens. She stubbed out her cigarette. "Oh come on, Erica, stop looking at me like that. I'd already been beaten for the crime, I thought I might as well have the fun of committing it," she said.

She looked at her watch, shook it as though it might be lying to her. "Christ, I really must get to the train."

The combination of brandy and her rush to be gone fed my fury. "And was George right about Greg Corso as well? All that stuff about letting a cat out of a bag," I said. "It's always puzzled me. It was the day I found Cato. Corso was there. Look at you! You're blushing!"

"Oh, Erica, you're so nosy. You know what? I used to watch you watching everyone on Hydra and think to myself: there sits a writer. I hope you're still keeping your journals . . ."

I nodded, though it wasn't true. "So, Corso?" I persisted, enjoying the flush his name was bringing to her cheeks.

She chuckled to herself, avoiding my eyes. "You remember that night at Chuck and Gordon's?" and I nodded to encourage her.

"After Kyria Polymnia had finished showing us around, I ran into him coming out of the cloakroom. He swept me close, looked me deep in the eyes and took my hand. 'I came for you,' he said and when he let go there was something sticky all over my palm." She bit her lip, pulled her hair across her face.

I squealed. "Ugh! What did you do?"

"I'm ashamed to say I let him kiss me," she squeaked from behind her hands.

"You know, I always thought George was being paranoid. I didn't believe a word anyone said about you," I said, feeling a clot for the tears that were stinging my eyes.

"Oh, do stop it, Erica. You should know by now what my views on monogamy are. As I say, anything goes, as long as the sauce is the same for the goose as it is for the gander. Tell me, where is the law that ties me to my husband, when it was he who broke those bonds long ago?" She was swaying across the table at me, glass in hand. I reached out to steady it. We might have been on the waterfront. "In fact, it was your mother caught them sneaking in. Patricia Simeone was her name. His secretary. How original was that?" She had forgotten all about her train, was starting to slur, calling for a refill and telling me about my mother, about Connie nursing her through the worst, with kindness and by confiscating her sleeping pills. She told me that each night my mother came upstairs and doled a pill out to her with a cup of hot milk.

"It was as well she did or I might easily have taken the lot. I felt like my head might burst cooped up in that Bayswater apartment with my broken heart and two babies. Our doctor friend Joe Leitz was helpful for a while but George became jealous and made me stop seeing him . . . It didn't help that Joe L. was so damned attractive . . ." She stopped with a small sigh and I leapt, gripped her by the shoulders like she might make a run for it.

"Joel?"

She looked me in the eyes and nodded. "Yes, Joe L. Your mother's friend, and for a brief time my doctor."

"The friend who secretly bought her a car?" I said, just to be sure, and Charmian nodded again, told me he'd bought it so that Connie might drive herself to their love nest. I downed my brandy like it might souse my anger. I demanded to know why she hadn't told me when I asked before. Why she'd insisted on lying to me about everything.

"Erica, please understand," she pleaded. "I struggled not to tell you all those times you asked me on Hydra, but you know . . ." she reached for my hand, held it to her cheek ". . . she was my friend." I wanted to snatch my hand back but it turned out I couldn't.

"But she was my mother," I whimpered, as she carried on.

"She used to come to me in my dreams . . . I wanted so badly to protect you . . ." She was trying to explain. "You were wide-eyed like something that had suddenly hatched, so terribly vulnerable and surrounded by savages. I kept an eye on you, tried not to lecture you too often, as though the boys you slept with were any of my business . . ."

"Oh stop it!" I interrupted with a sniffle and we both managed a rueful laugh.

She gave me her handkerchief. "There I was nagging you about contraception and what you should read, a hundred things to do with lentils. I didn't want you to think that I was trying to take Connie's place. You had so much to deal with, quite apart from her eternal absence. Bobby's moods, that awful boy you were so smitten with. It was never the right time to tell you that your mother wasn't a saint. But look at you now! I can see you're stronger and that you have a right to know how she managed her life."

I nodded to the bartender: big ones please. Visions of my mother were pooling behind my eyes. She was kneeling at my father's feet, scrubbing congealed casserole from the floor. She was shielding me from the man I'd seen in the mirror. We were running at night along a gnarly path through woods. Her hands were shaking as she presented my father with her accounts, a twisted seam in her stocking, sherry on her breath.

My mother reasserts herself, stands from the floor. She drives her secret car, meets her good doctor in the woods.

"It was our mate Peter Finch she was really out to get that night," Charmian was saying. "It was Finchy brought Joe L. to cocktails, and boom. 'Joe L.' to distinguish him from Finchy's other friend who was 'Joe O.,' a playwright."

I plagued her for details. "So this was the 'chance' you believed she still had when you wrote to her?" I said and she nodded.

"Why didn't she take it? Why did she stay with our father if she loved this other man?"

Again Charmian tried to make sense of her watch. "Connie believed, with some justification I think, that your dad would have had her declared an unfit mother by the courts if she ran off. She couldn't bear the thought of giving you up."

We were out of time. "I'm sorry to leave you so rattled but I think my last direct train's on the hour. I must go," she said, as we rose unsteadily to our feet. "I'll tell you everything I remember when you come to the farm."

By the time we went our separate ways it had started to drizzle. I returned, with my head in a spin, to Nina and her banners and Charmian to her train. "To give up a child is a pain that not many women can endure," she said as we parted. That has stuck with me, agonizing to think of now.

That was the last time I ever saw her. I watched the lovely suede coat become speckled with rain. I regret that I never did visit her at Charity Farm, but I had other things on my mind—not least, the beginnings of my son and an uncertain marriage to his father.

TWENTY-NINE

I t took me ten years to return to the island. I came alone, my son with his father, our first trial separation, the beginning of our end. I boarded the ferry at Piraeus, armed with a bundle of notebooks, longing for Hydra's big shoulders and wishing for the moon.

In the taxi from the airport, a Leonard Cohen song came on the radio. "Bird on the Wire." I took it as a blessing, wondered if by any chance he'd be there despite the military junta, if his midnight choirs of fishermen would still be wending their way in three-part harmony through the lanes. I knew from something I'd read in the newspaper that in his way he had failed to be true to Marianne but perhaps she would still be there waiting.

I'd lost touch with everyone, moving around as much as I did, didn't have a clue if anyone I knew would be around. I had mentally prepared myself for the absence of George and Charmian as they'd finally said goodbye to Hydra and been back in Australia for five or six years by then. He got his bestseller, his television series, his important literary awards. The thought that another family would be living in the house by the well was so disturbing I drank several shots of ouzo on the crossing to steady my guts. The last I heard from Charmian, she told me she was writing a weekly newspaper essay that had a wide readership and an impossible mailbag. After that we lost touch. I hadn't wanted to add to its weight.

There were military police on the ferry, the only sign that Greece was now ruled by the Colonels, but they took their coffees at the bar, lolling and smiling with the tourists.

The *Nereida* was crowded with memories: Jimmy, my brother, Trudy, Jean-Claude Maurice, jostling one after the other through my ouzo-clouded mind. I fell into a stupor, a welcome relief after many nights of sleepless warfare with my husband, woke with the bells of Poros, someone shouting dockside. I climbed to the top deck where the diesel fumes were as strong as I remembered.

The month was July and I was glad of my sunglasses, could feel the sting of sun and salt on my bare arms. I was growing ever more exhilarated, and fearful, my stomach lurching as the island's first rocky shoulder swept into view. I clung to the rail, suspended between the dazzle of sea and unbroken blue sky. The boat turned and there it was! Hey presto, the sudden flourish, conjured from bare rock by the gods and lit by the sun. A theater for dreamers. The trick worked every time. The white houses, the crescent harbor: it took a moment to believe it was real. My heart lifted and I wished for wings so that I might fly the rest of the way.

I went soaring for the mountains of bold stone, for the town they held in their lap. My eighteen-year-old self was still there, and I let my eyes trace her footsteps through the pines to the monastery and on, climbing to the peak of Mount Eros, with the cold sweat of night on her skin and Charmian's deafening silence. I drifted over the hills, silver with olive groves heading for the groove between the rocks of her favorite valley, looked for the grand house of the artist Ghikas to get my bearings and found in its place a burnt-out wreck. What on earth had happened? Apart from Ghikas's blackened arches, all was as I remembered. Spires, cupolas, windmills, the beautiful ruins, sun and sea spangling the grey stone of formal mansions with gold coins, the best seats in the house. I could see people in the wings, at the naval school and on the rocks at Spilia, splashing and diving, bright caiques, cannons lined up along the walls. I watched a boy leap from the lip of the cave and longed for my son.

I bounded down the steps with my holdall as the port drew close, impatient to leap ashore. The fishing boats waited at the mole, flags were flying at the quay, blue and white pennants looping the harbor front, café tables, awnings, bells clamoring, donkeys, men with wooden carts. I drank it in, almost drowned in it.

I wanted to be the first to set foot on the island, as I had ten years before, but two military policemen held me back, told me to start a line. One of them took out a clipboard and asked me for my name, which spoiled the moment.

I made it down the gangplank on shaking legs, almost sick with stage fright. New dramas were unfolding around me in several languages: family reunions, groups of backpackers greeting one another; one particular boy kissing his girl brought on a wave of nostalgia and loneliness so powerful I almost cried out. The policemen were taking everyone's names, the donkey-boys jostling, the smell of donkey shit, the flagstones beneath my feet not gleaming as pink as I remembered. A gang of blond ragamuffins came flying past, a boy pursued by two little girls and a younger tot, all brandishing wooden swords. They were shouting and clanking, strung around with battle dress made from flattened tin cans. The blondest boy, who looked only a little older than my son, swerved and crashed against the picket fence to get away from the others. One of the policemen spun around to admonish him but he was a fleet-footed sprite and was off, brown limbs flying. The other children had run out of steam, their armor clanking, the smallest boy calling his name. "Axel! Stop! Wait for us! Axel!"

I kept my eyes fixed on the child in his glinting carapace. He doubled back through the marketplace and, panting, joined a queue for ice cream halfway along the waterfront. I was out of breath. The taste of the creamy *foulis* flavor that Costas used to make came to my mouth but, instead of Costas's wooden handcart, the ice cream was from a humming freezer plugged into what had been the chandler's and now sold cigarettes and fading postcards.

The boy had his back to me, peering with one of the girls through the misted glass top. I dropped my bag, found my breath. He turned around when I said his name, and beneath the blond mop he had an anxious little face, but he was beautifully, luminously, unmistakably, her son.

"You were just the most darling baby, the last time I saw you," I said while his eyes remained solemn and loaded with suspicion. "Axel? Marianne's son?" He nodded, left me with the top of his head to look at. I told him who I was, opened my purse. "Here, let me treat you."

Still he didn't look up or smile. "You can buy us ice lollies if you like, lady, but I don't know you from a donkey," he said and the girl jabbed him with her sword and told him not to be rude and yes please. She was an appealing child with freckles and wise grey eyes. She pointed across the alleyway, at the chattering groups beneath the caramel awnings of Tassos Kafeneo.

"His mum's over there. They've been arguing all morning about whether to have a church service for their old friend who died." She lowered her lashes and stuck out her bottom lip.

"Oh dear, how sad. Was it someone from Hydra?" I asked.

She nodded. "He used to live here but he didn't believe in God." Her lip started to quiver. "I'm sad too because he was funny but I was only little when they went away."

"Liar," Axel said. "I'm older than you and I don't remember him one bit."

I crushed a drachma into each of their hands, leaving them bickering, and went where the girl pointed, towards Marianne who was huddled with two other women, surrounded by cats. She wore a sundress with a print of pineapples, a matching scarf in her hair.

I called out her name. The other women turned around to see who had shouted; there was wine on the table. Her sunglasses were large; she was smoking a Greek cigarette.

She lowered the sunglasses; there were bags beneath her eyes.

"Remember? Summer 1960?" I had to prompt her with my name.

"Sweet, pretty Erica from London?" At last she smiled. She scrambled to her feet to hug me and we swayed in each other's arms. Her perfume was strong—like something from a head shop, I thought. Not a smell I associated with her. We sat facing each other, clasping hands, but didn't find words, beyond sighing, as we tried to read each other's story.

"I didn't even think to write, what with Leonard becoming so famous. I thought you moved to New York?" I said.

She shrugged and smiled. "*Pfft.* I've been living here, there and everywhere but it's summer now, and nowhere feels as much like home as Hydra."

She introduced Lily and Olivia, the mothers of Axel's ragamuffin friends. Lily was Russian and wore long earrings. Olivia was younger, in a hippie dress and many bangles.

"I didn't expect there would even be a foreign colony, what with all this," I said, eyeing a pair of uniformed officers who were patrolling the port with guns in their belts.

"Oh, it's not so bad," Marianne shrugged. "At least the ferries run on time and the rubbish is cleared from the streets. It's different on an island; everyone has to get on and it hasn't stopped the tourists from coming."

"Yeah, but it's a drag to have to keep reporting to the police station," Olivia said, bangles rattling as she slid her arm around the back of Marianne's chair. Marianne leaned forward and poured me a glass of wine. Lily swallowed the remains of hers, said it was her turn to round up the kids and feed them. Two young men joined us, pulled up chairs. Bill had a beard and twinkling eyes and Jean-Marc an unlit roll-up stuck to his lip that waggled when he talked.

"Baby, it's so hot. Let's go swim," Olivia said, as the men ordered beers and set up a backgammon board. She put her feet on the chair that Lily had vacated and sat jingling and fanning herself while Marianne and I talked. When I glanced down I saw that Marianne had a matching string of silver bells around one of her own ankles. I told her about my son. Marianne clapped her hands, delighted for me that I had a child, asked me about his father. Olivia said she'd like to give me a healing. I looked past her to the mole, to the familiar business of the port, the men and the barge bringing goods from Ermioni, the donkeys uncomplaining, couples strolling towards Kamini arm in arm, and back to Marianne's dear, kind face.

"My heart lifted as soon as all this came into view, I dreamt about it so often. I've been dreaming about coming back here since the day I left. If it wasn't for my boy in London, I think I'd never leave again."

Marianne shrugged, gave me a sad sort of a smile. "It was better when you were here before. It's not like that now. We were inno-cent children. The drugs hadn't started screwing with everyone's minds . . ." The policemen were passing again; she glanced across at them and grinned. "But hey, we still have plenty of fun. The dif-ference these guys make is we've hidden all the dope and we tend not to party in public. Oh, and do not even think about swimming nude like you used to, Erica."

Olivia said she'd seen a young German get punched in the face for it at Spilia. "Even in this heat we can only be naked in the pri-vacy of our own homes—right, Marianne?" she said, coiling her arm around her friend's neck.

Olivia was either very drunk or very stoned. She hooked down the strap of Marianne's sundress to work her thumbs into her shoulder while Marianne asked me what had gone wrong with my husband. I gave her the short version. I'd fallen pregnant and mar-ried my boss. He was talented. The balance of power was skewed out of my favor from the start. "I think it's taken me ten years to discover that I'm not the gardenia-and-little-sandwich-on-my-man's-desk sort of a person," I said, rather clumsily, because I hated talking about myself and wanted to steer the conversation back to her and Leonard.

She wriggled herself free of Olivia, adjusted her strap. "Oh, Erica. What times we had. It was such a summer, like a roller coaster, but you know, Leonard hypnotized me. As you know, I'd have done anything for him . . ."

"Yeah, baby, you've turned more blind eyes than there are in a peacock's fan," Olivia said but Marianne was still talking.

"It's all got a bit messed up since I lost our little baby and we've both grown battle-weary. But tell me, do you reckon he was happy with me then? Sometimes I think I only imagined it."

Olivia groaned, put her hands to her ears. "Hush, my little

Nordic troll, I don't think I can stand another long soliloquy about Leonard." She grabbed her basket, said she'd meet us at the beach.

"You were so beautiful together, and everything around you was golden," I said, to make Marianne smile, and because it was true. "I was so jealous. I used to think of all the candles he lit for you, the way he looked at you, how tender he was with little Axel. When I left Hydra I thought about you often, the way you lived your life. It's what I dreamt of for myself."

Olivia turned back to me, making gagging noises. "Whatever you do, don't get her started about the damn song," she said and she affectionately booped the end of Marianne's nose while Marianne flapped her hands at her to be off.

Of course I knew which song she meant. I'd listened to it many times, but Leonard was nothing if not enigmatic. "Well, it does seem kind of sour at the end . . ." I started to say.

Marianne silenced me, still flapping a hand. "I don't think it's even about me, really. He'd been playing it for years and it was called 'Come on, Marianne,' which gives the song a different meaning if you listen to the words, but some other act already had a record with that name so he changed it. *Pfft*," she said. "'Bird on the Wire' is the best one he wrote for me because it is more honest." I noticed tears in her eyes. "*Pfft*," she said again, as though they were meaningless. "Leonard doesn't want to have babies with me, so there it is."

I shook my head. "Oh, Marianne, I'm sorry."

She fought her tears, attempted a smile. "It's OK. Seeing you like this has made me remember how sweet it used to be. Too bad. He's found himself a nice Jewish mare now . . ." She checked herself, apologized for sounding bitter. "The last time he was here he gave me such a bad shock."

She was pulling a small gold key that she wore around her neck back and forth along its chain while she spoke. A present from Leonard. The key to his heart, she told me with a sniff.

"What sort of shock?" I prompted.

"He'd already had that woman in our house, but hey, who was I to complain about that? But that day it was like looking into the face of a ghost," she said. "I've seen him wrecked many times over the years, exhausted, empty, hallucinating. It was all of that but he's never scared me before. When he walked off the boat I looked into his eyes and they were dead as the fish in that crate over there," she said, and threw her hands to her mouth. "Forgive me going on. We all got a bit tipsy this morning because of the terrible news. It's George who is dead, poor soul," and the tears that had been wobbling spilled from her eyes.

"George Johnston?" It was absurd; surely he'd be along at any moment. I looked across the alley to Katsikas, longing for ten years to have fallen away, expecting him to be there, throwing down a brandy and roaring with laughter at his own story, making a toast, a check in the mail more potent than anything he could get at the pharmacy, his eyes tender with love. Calling her "Cliftie." Chinking his glass to hers.

But Marianne was nodding and dabbing her eyes. "The TB finally did for him," she said. "We've been here since Lily got the call. I suppose it's only right we got drunk in his memory."

I thought of his swagger, his gunslinger's grin. "Oh God. Poor Charmian. Has anyone spoken to her?"

Marianne blanched. Held up her hands. "Hey. You mean, you don't know?" Her mouth fell open.

I shook my head. "What?"

She picked up the bottle and refilled my glass. "Drink," she said.

"Oh God, what?"

Again she gestured for me to drink. I took a gulp.

"Charmian's dead," she said. "She killed herself last summer."

———

There was the hotel, the front desk, checking in, rickety stairs to my room. I had a glass of water in my hands. The room was sweltering. I could smell my own sweat. I cranked open the shutters to the balcony, threw myself onto the bed and let the great torrent of disbelief wash over me.

I tried to picture it, forced myself to make it real. Charmian, menopausal, lonely and despairing, George's hatred too much to bear. Drunk, naturally. A bottle on the table, the glass in her hand half-empty. I could imagine her laughing bleakly while she wrote out the Keats. They were George's sleeping pills, Marianne told me. A full prescription and the doctor said she had ceased without pain on the stroke of midnight, just as she promised him she would in her suicide note.

I unpacked my holdall, placed a picture of my son beside my bed, stared at it for I don't know how long. I was thinking about the last time I'd seen her, calling her back to me on the pavement outside the Star and Garter and the rain that was starting to fall. Not many women could endure the pain of losing a child, she told me as we stood, drunk and unsteady, about to embrace for the final time. Did she imagine the same wasn't true the other way around? It was hard to believe she'd inflict such unendurable pain upon her children. I went down the hall to splash my face with water, overcome with sudden rage and a need to escape.

There were throngs of tourists; the shops selling jewelry, sandals, sponges; the smell of frying fish too much for my stomach. My feet found their own way to Voulgaris Street and up the steps towards my old house, drawn on by a horrified fascination at just how painful I could make this. I was out of breath as I rounded the final twist, and there it was, with its windows shuttered and barred, the tips of almond trees just visible above the terrace wall. My heart was pounding. It seemed impossible that I had once run up and down these steps several times a day. I turned and looked across the familiar view, vandalized now by crisscrossing lines of wires scrawling all the way from the port, jumping out at me like graffiti. I sat down and put my face in my hands. There was cat shit all the way up the steps. I could hear buzzing flies and noticed the crucified remains of a rat among the roots of a fig tree, discarded cans in the dusty oleander bushes.

I remembered now. It was Marianne walked me back to the hotel, dealt with Sofia on the front desk, saw me to my room, poured me the water. She sat me down, like a dumbfounded child, on the edge of the bed while she knelt and unlaced my plimsolls. She told me Charmian's suicide had been on the eve of publication of George's new novel. Once again he had shamed her but this time he'd lain the blame for his oncoming death from tuberculosis on the stress of loving her.

"It got very ugly between them here at the end; it seems like none of the marriages can survive Hydra," Marianne said. "To tell you the truth, the whole island couldn't wait to see the back of the Johnstons. George was a skeleton, Charmian told anyone who would listen that he wouldn't fuck her anymore, for a long time she was madly in love with my friend Tony. They were drunk all the time, there were public fights, Leonard and Demetri used to have to carry George home." She showed me a scar, a small crescent above her top lip. "This is from when he threw a bowl of yogurt at Charmian and a shard bounced up and cut my face.

"They stayed too long," she said and I sat there numbly while she told me what she knew of the children. Martin wrote for a newspaper in Sydney. Can you believe Shane's married? Jason was living in the countryside with his cousins. That a light as bright as Charmian could snuff itself out seemed impossible. Marianne left me crying, said she'd see me on the beach. As soon as she was gone I started to laugh. It seemed like the bleakest cosmic joke that I should hear of Charmian's death as a sort of postscript to George's, and on the day I finally made it back to the island of my dreams.

I was a fool to think of returning. The sun was beating and I needed water but, slave to an impulse a decade out of date, I kept climbing. The steps wound on, past ruins with rickety scaffolding, drilling and hammering, strings of donkeys loaded with pallets of bricks; thirst turning the spit in my mouth to paste.

I kept going, beyond the gorge to the top road where the ruins of Ghikas's house crowned the hill, blackened arches like Gothic aqueducts across choppy charred timbers and collapsed floors. The path was peppered with black grains; burnt shutters still lay among the broken-down terracing and scorched scrub.

I walked straight past, like it would be bad luck to linger. I remembered with a shiver Leonard telling me that he had cursed the place.

There was nobody about; far below me the sea was as blue as enamel, the sun low enough in the sky to turn the bare boulders bronze. It lit the barley stubble of my valley, made gold dust of the air. Donkeys threw long shadows among the scrub of its far terraces and the cockerels called as I settled on my familiar ridge. A muleteer came clattering, all hooves, dust and proud machismo, whiskers and waistcoat. A pair of curly-horned rams roped, one either side of his saddle, were bellowing, sheepdog yipping and mule trumpeting in protest. Once the hullaballoo faded, the silence came on all the greater for the violence of its interruption. I watched tiny jeweled beetles in the dust at my feet. I let myself weep about the end of my marriage, and I gulped the scented air.

I was empty of tears when I saw him at the prow of the hill. He was strolling with his dog; his easy amble and strong shoulders made me recognize him several strides before he ground to a halt and pulled off his cap.

I jumped up. He couldn't have looked more astonished. "Is that really you?"

"Oh no, not you as well. Marianne didn't recognize me either," I said as we fell into one another's arms, laughing.

"Ten years!" I was still trying to take it in. At first I thought I'd only imagined it. It felt like I'd willed him since I'd only that moment been thinking about him, wondering if he still came in the summers with his bag of Aegina clay.

I had replayed so many times my last night on the island, it had taken on the shifting quality of a dream. It had been a breathtaking hike to Dinos's house. I'd never climbed to the top of Mount Episkopi before and was surprised by the valley where gorse and scrub gave way to almond and olive groves and barley fields and pine forests with their hidden orchestras of goat bells. I carried Cato in a basket all the way. The house was so high up you could see the sea on both sides of the island.

Dinos was Bobby's friend. I barely knew him but he never for a moment made me feel shy. He gave me a tour, stopping at the kiln shed to show me what Bobby had been working on. Small figures sprawled among marble-sized stones, some in attitudes of relaxation, chins resting in their hands, or facedown; others with wings and exultant expressions. Inspired by something Charmian said to Bobby, Dinos told me, about people being either Daedalus or Icarus.

I took Cato from his basket, told him he'd be happy up here.

Dinos and I didn't stop talking, not that night nor for a minute the next morning and all the way down through the blossoming almonds to the ferry dock when I left for England. He gave me a bowl he'd made for me, and it makes me sad that I have no idea what became of it.

Now here he was again. Dinos, standing right in front of me with his knapsack and his dog, a decade gone by and not looking like he'd aged a day. He was grinning and offering me water from his flask. I almost had to pinch myself to check I wasn't dreaming. He told me that Cato still reigned at Episkopi. He offered me his hand when I said that I would like to come and see him. There was magic to this spot; I always did feel the pull of it but never more so than at this moment. In the very place I'd first found him, my little black cat was returning the luck.

THIRTY

I change. I am the same. I change. I am the same. I change. I am the same. Leonard painted it in gold around the mirror in his hall. I can't imagine it isn't still there.

There was a night he nearly had me mesmerized. I was almost giddy when we'd finished dancing and he spun me around to face myself in that mirror. My head whirls a little and my eyes swim with memories. He had to keep his hands on my shoulders to stop me squirming away but all I could see, as he held me in front of it, were the candle's twin flames reflecting in his khaki-green eyes—anything but look at myself. He was pretty stoned, the whites of his eyes were pink, he was standing so close I could hear him swallow. His hand slipped from my shoulder to my collarbone, slipped again and I let it. His breath was growing hot on my neck, and the guilty thrill that had hatched inside me at the rocks was taking powerful flight by the time Marianne came in a gust of air and broke the spell. She had her lamp and a bundle of firewood and for several weeks refused to speak or even look at me. He changed, he remained the same. The words he painted around his mirror were honest and true.

They apply to me too. I carry my old age like a cloak, am glad of the steps that keep me almost as spry as the girl who lives within its inconvenient folds. I put my fist to the sky in defiance as I'm hit in the face by a spattering of rain. The sea looks flat as hammered iron. It will take more than a few raindrops to stop me swimming later if I fancy it. I think about the beans that I have simmering with a ham hock at home, about my son and the little ones coming for Christmas, about our cozy house with its store of winter wood. Thinking of my son and grandchildren fills me with spirit more powerful than grief or any other ache the years wish to throw at me.

The rain on my face has a salt tang. I stop at a gap between houses and watch as the sun breaks through a tear in the clouds and falls on the sea. I climb on. I can't seem to shake thinking about Leonard and Marianne now both of them are dead.

I saw less and less of Marianne over the years. She got married to her boss in Oslo, and acquired stepdaughters and a Buddhist guru. When she died I wondered if her husband felt sidelined when the letter that Leonard wrote to her as she lay dying was shared with the world.

Charmian was right about Marianne's blind optimism; she clung on long after hope had slunk away. Leonard left her waiting for years.

She was still hanging on at his house the first summer I came here with my son. Axel Joachim was only a couple of years older than my boy so I hoped they'd be friends. I remember I had been to Hamleys, had bought a boxed game of Risk especially. I chivvied my son all the way down from Dinos's house, telling him all I could remember of this bright older boy. I mentioned fishing, masks and snorkels, donkey races, flying kites. Axel Joachim had been to boarding school in England so there wouldn't be a language problem. I was sure they'd have fun.

Leonard's house was unchanged: the writing around the mirror in the hall, the table with its treasures and cracked monastery bell, the white walls and woven rugs. A gang of Scandinavian students were making breakfast in the kitchen, a boy in his trunks and two slender girls with sunburnt noses and shoulders. Victoria was the one who spoke the best English. She apologized about the mess everywhere, explained that Marianne wasn't home. She poured coffee and spooned several sugars into a mug.

"I was here the summer Marianne and Leonard met," I said. I caught myself in the mirror, a smile twitching my lips. "It doesn't feel so long ago."

The others milled about, slurping cereal. They were playing one of Leonard's old Chuck Berry records, and their languid choreography gave me a sharp pang for the freedom I'd tasted over a decade before. Victoria was telling me that Marianne hadn't been around much for the last few days. She seemed irritated and, thrusting the coffee cup into the reluctant hands of my son, insisted he go upstairs and tell that lazy oaf Axel Joachim to get out of bed if he wanted breakfast.

After what happened next I had to stifle my disapproval whenever I ran into Marianne, but it always lurked and rumbled, dark and unstated, as though the meeting of our sons that summer had poisoned any chance we'd be friends. It was hanging there between us the last time I saw her, which was many years later, on a gusty October day. We bumped into each other at the post office and paused to sit outside the Pirate Bar, drinking hot chocolate, both of us shocked with the news of Martin Johnston's death. Shane's suicide, three years after Charmian's, had been incomprehensible, and now Martin had done it too, though he'd taken a little longer and used alcohol as his poison. We walked together up the lane to Australia House and stood at the well in disbelieving silence.

A last few blossoms clung to Charmian's bougainvillea which had flourished and cracked its pot. Someone had planted an anchor in concrete beside the front door. An American woman owned the house now, I knew that, and yet I couldn't quite bring the curtain down on the Johnstons. I hoped they might haunt their house forever. If I could only stop crying and concentrate hard enough they'd be here in full flow, Martin squinting up at me from his microscope, Shane's skirts twirling, George pulling Charmian to his lap. All I had to do was walk through that door and make myself useful. I remembered how badly I had wanted to belong, how I'd tap-danced and sung my way through every audition for a role in her family.

"Dead, and all by their own hands," Marianne was saying and I told her how years before, in London, my mother had suspected Charmian might kill herself and had confiscated her sleeping pills.

"Shane and now Martin, it's too much. I think the children paid the price for our freedom, really I do," Marianne said as we started walking back through the lanes. I thought about the relatively boring safety of my own childhood and the sacrifice my mother made to provide it. I had met her lover, the good doctor Joe Leitz, by then. His club had dim lighting, strong whiskey macs, low-slung leather furniture. I made up my face and hair to look like her, made him clutch at his heart when I entered the room. His pass was gallant and, mortifyingly, exactly what I had hoped for.

Marianne was talking about Axel Joachim. "You remember, he was such a sensitive child, so intelligent; maybe I should have given him a more stable upbringing." Her voice was quiet and miserable. She reached for my hand. "You know, since his relapse last year, the doctors say he will never live a normal life."

There were rumors. I had hoped with all my heart they weren't true. I didn't want her to think people had been talking behind her back.

Her shoulders had become hunched with the years, her breathing wheezy. She retreated inside her shawl. "He was desperately unhappy at every school I sent him to. After Summerhill, New York and then Switzerland, he couldn't fit in anywhere, so when he was fifteen I let his father take him traveling to India. I should never have let him go. I mean, his father was almost a stranger to him. I wasn't there to protect him when crazy, idiot Axel gave him LSD . . ."

"Oh, Marianne, I'm sorry . . ."

"And now our special boy has been in one clinic or another for most of his life. I think every parent should know about this, Erica," she said and her eyes were pleading. "You should write this for the newspaper. For some fragile souls just one trip can turn out to be a cul-de-sac in hell."

I thought of Axel Joachim, the day I left my son at her house, wondered if he hadn't already been on the path. The girl Victoria had been rather bossy and, having dispatched my son with the coffee, told me it was best if I went away and fetched him around sundown, when there was a chance Marianne might be back.

I left a copy of *The Female Eunuch* I'd brought as a present for Marianne. I've no idea if she read it because I managed to avoid her for the rest of that summer.

Marianne still hadn't returned when Dinos and I came back for my son. Victoria seemed a little dazed and I think it was only the sight of us standing there reminded her there were kids in the house.

"You know, I didn't come to Greece to be Marianne's babysitter. It's like she has some sort of tunnel vision. She doesn't see her son, or even his need for food. Her sights are set only on this French photographer she chases on his merry cha-cha around the island."

I found my son with Axel Joachim in his den on the top floor. The air was thick with dope, the shutters unopened, the box of Risk still in its cellophane. There was music blaring from a radio, screaming guitars, overflowing ashtrays. Axel Joachim sat cross-legged and skinny on his bed, wearing only his underpants and a string of glass beads. A single icon of Saint Thaddaeus was hanging at an angle off the wall. Axel Joachim had a fat spliff between his fingers, his shaved head thrown back from the rigors of air guitar, and was having such a ball he hadn't noticed that my darling boy had passed out on the floor.

For years after that Dinos and I had a back-and-forth time of it. My heart ached more acutely each time I went away, but my son belonged both with me and with his father in London. I joined a housing association in Notting Hill, sharpened my pen and my wits with jobs at *Spare Rib* and *Time Out*. At home I placed a gardenia and a little sandwich on a desk where I blackened pages of my own, and another decade passed with the island and Dinos existing mainly in my dreams.

These days, when I'm alone at the crest of my valley, I don't often cry. It's still as inviting of introspection as the first time I sat down, there's no vista more peaceful, but it's not a place for tears anymore. Halfway down the far hill a tumbledown shack with chickens and netting is the only addition; breezes still ripple the silver lake of olive trees in its hollow. The sun has come streaming from the clouds and I can smell the good earth and feel its warmth on my face.

I despair of every tear I cried for Jimmy Jones, at my younger self's blind desperation, and then I chuckle to think how scary he must have found my attempts to steer him down the aisle. But in

1960, which in reality was almost half a decade before the sixties began, how was a rudderless, motherless girl to know lust from love—or, as Marianne once remarked, love from service?

Marianne may have been a poor role model but for a while Charmian really had been the mother I needed. I remember she came looking for me the night after Jimmy Jones fled, when I thought the whole island might dissolve in my tears.

I was winded with misery and shock. Dusk was descending. She had brought whiskey and figs and sat down beside me, hugging her legs through her skirt. My eyes were puffy and sore. Her concern was balm more soothing than the pills Bobby had been making me swallow.

When I asked her how she knew where to find me, she unscrewed the top of the whiskey and took a gulp before answering. "It's very strange, isn't it? It's almost as though there's some sort of thread that pulls at me. I wish I could explain it," and she took another swallow, and gave me a troubled and troubling smile.

I told her my intention was to follow Jimmy back to London and demand a showdown and she hooted with derision. I sniffed and sniveled while she painted a picture for me of my life as Jimmy's wife, told me it was a blessing I'd seen his true colors.

"Think how your mother was tied to that kitchen in Bayswater. Darling, I know she dreamt of something less earthbound than housemaid's knee for you . . ."

The last of the sun bled into the sea; the purple twilight was balmy. "Before George became ill we used to walk together up here in the gloaming. We used to sit right here with a bottle of wine and plan the next day's writing . . ." She gave me a broken smile. "I wish I could feel again the enchantment, everything golden, thistle-down and barley, stone and dust, the life we'd made . . ." and she sighed as though all her dreams had already been dreamt.

She shook herself out of it, gathered me closer, kissed the top of my head. "Darling, don't waste your tears on that very ordinary boy," she said, and the combination of the whiskey on her breath and her warm scent made me forget that I was completely alone. She rocked me in her arms while one by one the stars lit the sky.

I used to think it was one-way, my hunger for Charmian. Once Bobby had put it into my head that I was an annoying mosquito, I watched myself carefully. I tried not to be greedy but she gave herself generously. She caught me when Jimmy threw me away, steered me through bad times with Bobby, came back from Piraeus with a white leather-bound notebook and insisted I write every day. She fed me Brahms and crab sandwiches while she nagged about contraception, and took me so often under her wing. Wrung-out, hungover, tired or just hungry, there was always a haven at the house by the well.

She's with me still in the tea towel I keep draped at my shoulder, the shoelace I use to tie back my hair; she's with me in the food that I cook and on every page that I have fought to blacken.

A few years after Martin's death a friend of Dinos's in Australia sent a news clipping that made me feel so peculiar I had to lie down halfway through reading it. *Jennifer.* Did I only imagine she'd called me that name on occasions? I still can't be sure but I do think I picked up on something.

The face on the page told the story. The dark-haired woman with striking bone structure and generous mouth was almost a dead ringer for her mother. Her name was Suzanne Chick and she had written a book. She was the same age as me.

The daughter's eyes were familiarly up-tipped and soulful, my own too blurred by tears to read on. Charmian's face leapt at me,

ashen with terror. We were outside Johnny Lulu's and she sprang
at George who was rearing away and holding up his hands like she
might strike him.

Jennifer was the name of the cat that he had threatened to let
out of the bag, I'm certain of that now. It was the day I found Cato,
the festival; he'd been drinking all day. She was flirting with Corso
who was making her giggle and Big Grace was sniping that his wife
only had time for men. Not so, I had started to say . . . and *bang*,
the public performance. George with pointing finger, playing to the
crowd: "Ah, but there's a special reason she has so much time for
little Ricky here—isn't that right, Charm?"

My heart was breaking as I read on. The daughter had been told
her mother died giving birth to her. In a fundamental way, perhaps
she had. Charmian had called her Jennifer. She was relinquished,
along with her name, at three weeks old. The matron's beloved
brother and his wife were without children. Charmian was nine-
teen and unmarried, with nowhere to turn to but the hospital's
charity. She was unusually beautiful and vigorously healthy; she
spoke with a cultivated voice. She didn't stand a chance.

"This one is special," the matron said, placing the baby girl, all
dressed up pretty in lace, in her sister-in-law's arms. I imagine there
was little opportunity for Charmian to change her mind. With her
firstborn spirited away, losing things came to define her. It wasn't
such a leap that she allowed George to steal the oxygen in the writing room, or that she let her own life spin so out of control that she
lost her grip. No woman can endure the pain of losing a child.

I look across my valley to the sea and it strikes me that I've
ended up living the life she dreamt of for herself.

It was at Charmian's table that Dinos and I first met; I can't
help but see a twinkle in her eye: Bim having to shift along so that I
would be next to him, the way she made sure Dinos knew I'd made

the dolmades. Thank you! Thank you! I shout it out like the proper crazy old island woman I've become. And thank you for writing the book that led me here, despite the howls of despair that I now see in its pages. For all the times I've sat here crying for my losses, I have never felt anything close to the bite of the loneliness that she suffered so unendurably. I can no more imagine relinquishing a child than I can my own grip on this speck of whirling astral dust. No wonder she couldn't find comfort in the stars and let go.

I keep her with me, like a wise imaginary friend, her voice my oracle. I let time slip. It's good to dream.

They're so vivid, the players of that first summer; here in every phase of the moon as though an eighteen-year-old me is forever appearing beneath a gauzy overlay of the present. I change. I am the same.

Not long after Marianne died, Bobby sent me a magazine from the States, along with a fancy invitation to his and Trudy's golden-wedding bash in Boston. I turned to the article. The headline was predictable, SO LONG, MARIANNE, and the pictures of Hydra 1960. I tried to remember the face of the photographer who kept popping over from Athens. Jim was his name, an old newspaper buddy of George's; they'd been through some scrapes together, in fact George had once saved his life in Tibet, we'd heard the stories many times . . .

Trudy had marked an arrow to what was unmistakably the back of my head, my ponytail glossy as I lean into a circle where Leonard plays guitar. Charmian's beside him, so close she looks like she's his woman, a halo of light caught in her hair. Behind them the moon is full as a silver balloon caught in the branches of the old pine tree at Douskos Taverna. Leonard handles the guitar like it's part of his body, sits cross-legged on the wall with his back to the white-painted trunk. Charmian's hair is freshly washed and she's wearing a Norwegian jumper of claret wool patterned with white that Marianne has donated to help with the chill of England.

We've all made a pact to put our thoughts about tomorrow's departure on hold, to squeeze every last drop of pleasure from the evening. There have been speeches, many toasts; it has the air of a wedding. Tomorrow George and Charmian leave the island for a while but tonight we are full of spaghetti and Stavros Douskos keeps the jugs of retsina coming.

Leonard's playing "Red River Valley"; we all join in like we always do but it's Charmian's bright eyes and sweet smile we'll be missing after tomorrow. Axel sits at Leonard's feet hugging his knees, looking up at him like a disciple. He requests "Don't Fence Me In" but bungles the words and is rescued by Charlie Heck's fine baritone and the rest of us join in with the choruses. Marianne catches Axel's eye and shakes her head and he leans across and says something in Norwegian that makes her smile and pretend to slap his face.

Everyone's beaming. Leonard retunes the guitar. He's become a little more studied and serious, adjusts his position. We recognize the opening strum of one of his songs. Only George and Didy keep talking, which strikes me as rude given that it was George who suggested he play some of his own stuff.

Leonard's been making up verses to this one all summer and Charmian looks blissful with her head on his shoulder while he sings.

He launches into a new verse; there's kissing and marriage and all the women who have known him at dawn, and Charmian turns to gaze up at him.

"You know, I was never in love with you, Leonard," she says and he doesn't break rhythm to reply, "No, me neither," and they both laugh.

ACKNOWLEDGMENTS

Thank you Lola Bubbosh for sharing a hunch and so much more. This book would not have been written without your enthusiasm and support.

I am eternally grateful to Charmian Clift for opening my eyes to Hydra with the memoir *Peel Me a Lotus* and to her Estate and Jane Novak for allowing me to quote from its pages. Thank you Nadia Wheatley for confronting the myths and slanders with such an excellent biography and for bringing the essays into collected editions and to my attention. As I write, Charmian Clift's books are out of print and I thank in advance any publisher with the taste and resources to reissue them.

Serendipity has been my friend throughout the writing of this book and it has been a privilege and a joy to spend time with Jason Johnston. Thank you to him especially for the tortoises and for the word "crapulous" but most of all for being so gracious about this book.

It has been invaluable to have access to the complete set of James Burke's photographs of Hydra 1960 and I am grateful to Charles Merullo and Bob Ahern of Getty Images New York for facilitating the contact sheets.

Thank you to Leonard Cohen and the Leonard Cohen Estate for the words spoken in this book © Leonard Cohen, used by permission of The Wylie Agency LLC, and to Ira B. Nadel, Jeff Berger, Helle Vaagland, Rob O'Connor, Ray Connolly, Bård Oses, Sandra Djwa, Malka Marom, Jed Adams and Donald Brittain for recording those words. Thank you Robert Kory.

Annabel Merullo has been a constant source of encouragement and inspiration, as has Rosie Boycott who I must also thank for sharing a Gregory Corso story that I have recast in these pages. Nicola Marchant has gone beyond the call of duty, special thanks to her and to Jaz Rowland. Thank you Kathy Lette for boundless enthusiasm as well as a smattering of extra bloodys and mates and crikeys and for introducing me to Thomas Keneally who generously shared his memories of Charmian Clift and George Johnston.

For stories of Hydra *efcharistó* to Michael Pelikanos, Manos Loudaros, Natasha Heidsieck, Katyuli Lloyd, Bill Pownall, Phainie Xydis, George Xydis, Gay Angelis, Vangelis Rafalias, Myrto Liatis, Dimitrios Papacharalampous, Linus Tunstrom, Alice Arkell, Fiona Cameron, Kip Asquith, Mariora Goschen, Sula Goschen and Victoria Lund. I gained insight to the later years from Sam Barclay's letters to Marianne Ihlen together with essays by various contributors collected by Helle V. Goldman in the book *When We Were Almost Young*. Of George Johnston's novels I am particularly indebted to *Closer to the Sun* and *Clean Straw for Nothing* and also to his biographer Gary Kinnane.

Online I am grateful to Allan Showalter of the now defunct but brilliant *Cohencentric* and to Jarkko Arjatsalo of the excellent

Leonard Cohen Files. The website *Hydra Once Upon A Time*, run by Yianni and Micky Papapetros, has been inspiring. Kari Hesthamar's interviews with Marianne Ihlen and Leonard Cohen, which I first heard broadcast on the BBC, have been invaluable, as has Kari's biography, *So Long, Marianne*. I am grateful to ABC Radio for preserving the *Verbatim* interviews with Charmian Clift and George Johnston and to the National Library of Australia in Canberra where their papers are held. An essay by Tanya Dalziell and Paul Genoni led me to the archive of Redmond ("Bim") Wallis held at the Alexander Turnbull Library, Wellington, New Zealand and I recommend their excellent book *Half the Perfect World* to anyone who wishes to read more about the community on Hydra. I am grateful to Susan A. Perine for her translation from Norwegian of Axel Jensen's *Joachim* published in 1964 and held at the Columbia University Archives and to Princeton University Library for papers and photographs from the Gordon Merrick collection. Thank you Jana Krekic for translations from Swedish of works by Goran Tunstrom. I have drawn on the letters of Gregory Corso from the fascinating *An Accidental Autobiography*, edited by Bill Morgan and constantly checked in with Sylvie Simmons's outstanding biography of Leonard Cohen, *I'm Your Man*.

Readers of early drafts have all made invaluable contributions. Thank you Cressida Connolly, Damian Barr, Charlie Gilmour, Esther Samson, Sarah Lee and John Sutherland. Romany Gilmour has played a good Marianne while I've been writing this book, thank you to her for all the well-timed tea and beans on toast and also to Janina Pedan, Olinka, Gabriel, Joe and Barbounia Gilmour.

I am grateful to Sofka Zinovieff for saving me from Greek language blunders. Thank you to Anna Stein, Betsy Gleick and the whole Algonquin team. Clare Conville, Darren Biabowe Barnes, Kate Burton, Paul Loasby, Chris Salmon, Alexandra Pringle,

A Theater for Dreamers

A Gardenia and a Sandwich
An Essay by Polly Samson

Questions for Discussion

A GARDENIA AND A SANDWICH
An Essay by Polly Samson

There's a fresh gardenia in a small stone jar on my work-table. It sweetens the whole room. They are tricky plants, gardenias—hard to please and reluctant to bloom—and cutting this single flower, moon-white and waxy, and then stealing it away upstairs felt a tad selfish.

The plant has been there on the kitchen windowsill for us all to enjoy, shedding yellow leaves and limp, half-formed buds this entire lockdown year. Google what's up with it and you'll find a dizzying list of complaints: too wet, too dry, too cold, too much feeding, too little spritzing, not hard-enough praying, etc. etc. I have been longing for it to bloom.

The motif of the fresh gardenia and its partner, the sand-wich, runs through my novel. The image was planted there by the Canadian singer-songwriter Leonard Cohen, when he spoke of his beloved Marianne and how she catered to his needs and cre-ated domestic harmony: "There would be a gardenia on my desk perfuming the whole room. And there would be a little sandwich at noon. Sweetness, sweetness everywhere." She's the Marianne he immortalized in his haunting song "So Long, Marianne." The fabled muse. What writer wouldn't wish for such service and care?

In a fever of creativity he wrote two novels, several collections of poetry, and his first songs while they were lovers. They lived in a whitewashed house on the Greek island of Hydra, where there was no electricity and everyone was young and beautiful by candlelight. They met there in 1960, when the island was home to a thriving international community of bickering, bed-hopping, boozing bohemians, and they meet again as characters in my novel, which is based around known events.

The king and queen of the community were the married writers Charmian Clift and George Johnston. They were sociable and their marriage was dramatic. They had bought a house on Hydra in the fifties and managed to scrape by for a decade writing novels. Leonard Cohen later described them as an inspiration, and also noted that "they drank more than other people, they wrote more, they got sick more, they got well more, they cursed more, they blessed more, and they helped a great deal more."

There's a photograph of Charmian Clift taped to my wall with a Post-it that reads: "You know, Leonard, I was never in love with you." Leonard replies: "No, me neither." She's soulfully beautiful beneath her straw brim, cigarette and glass in hand, an old shirt with a buttonhole sprig of jasmine, gazing away from the port, preoccupied. The blur of houses rise behind her like the steps of an ancient amphitheater.

I looked at the photo often when I was writing Charmian as a character. It's from a lucky cache of over fifteen hundred images by the photojournalist James Burke, all taken on Hydra in 1960 for a *Life* magazine assignment about the artistic community. You can't look at them without wishing yourself there: to meet these people and know their stories, to feel that sun on your back.

Some of James Burke's photographs are on the internet because Leonard Cohen is in them. In some he's pictured in a group with Marianne riding donkeys to the monastery, in others he's with Charmian and her family swimming at the rocks, or in the Taverna Douskos with his guitar. He sits with his back to the white-painted trunk of a tree, Charmian beside him. Her head is on his shoulder while he plays to an enchanting and enchanted circle of young people.

Before the photographs there had been Hydra itself, an island for dreamers, ten miles long and mountainous, with neither roads nor airport but the clearest water for swimming and streets that smell of white flowers. I visited for the first time in 2014 and stumbled upon Charmian Clift's long-out-of-print memoir of her life there, *Peel Me a Lotus*. She is an extraordinarily captivating writer, perceptive and acidly witty, her voice so intimate I had to know more. And the more I read by and about Charmian Clift and the community, the more certain I became that I would write about her.

Spending time on Hydra was no hardship, and through a serendipitous friendship I even stayed in and wrote part of *A Theater for Dreamers* in the house that had been Charmian and George's. Leonard Cohen had also lodged there, when he first arrived on the island to write his novel. For a while I was hamstrung at the thought of having him in mine, in the way that only a true fan could be.

I made progress at first by identifying everyone in the photographs. As so many were writers—and writers tend to write— the research became labyrinthine. There were biographies and a wealth of published as well as unpublished novels, diaries, and letters. Charmian Clift and George Johnston published fourteen books during their decade in Greece.

There was plenty to read, but a couple of years went by and I still hadn't found the voice to tell their story. Then Marianne died and the letter Leonard wrote her went viral.

Dearest Marianne, I'm just a little behind you, close enough to take your hand. This old body has given up, just as yours has too, and the eviction notice is on its way any day now.

I've never forgotten your love and your beauty. But you know that. I don't have to say any more. Safe travels old friend. See you down the road. Love and gratitude, Leonard.

In November 2016 I returned to Hydra. As I took a coffee at the port, watching the mules being led away with their cargos, the news of Leonard Cohen's death and the American presidential election results hit me at the same time. "At least Leonard's been spared this," said a voice in my head. This was the first time that Erica, my narrator, made herself known. She was giddy with fear and foreboding that a world she had fought to change would be spinning backwards.

Erica Hart comes of age in 1960. She isn't much older than friends of mine, women who are not so very much older than me, and yet who were not able to get a mortgage or a loan or rent a flat without the guarantor signature of a husband or a father. She, like my friends, came of age without access to reliable contraception or legal abortion.

The final gardenia and sandwich in the novel are the ones Erica places on a desk of her own. I think many women still find it hard to recognize and cater to their own needs, but maybe it's the best thing of all, to be one's own muse.

Across the pond there are glimmers of hope as a new presidential term begins, and here too it is time for something new. The gardenia is on my desk, and downstairs in the kitchen the bread is new and the butter soft.

QUESTIONS FOR DISCUSSION

1. This is a novel set in the bliss of summer on a gorgeous Greek island. What does the author do to transport you to this place? How does the setting make you feel?

2. Most of the action occurs in 1960, a free-spirited time where the characters drink freely, make art, and move in and out of relationships with one another. How does the spirit of Hydra enhance the depiction of that year?

3. Despite the idyllic setting, the characters are not immune to the insecurities, upsets, and disruptions of life. What can we learn from this novel about human nature? How are these lessons emphasized by the setting?

4. The artists on Hydra have all inherited from their parents the anxiety of living through a global war. Erica also inherits a small

fortune from her mother that gives her the chance to escape her father. How do different kinds of inheritances affect the actions and psyches of these characters? What have you inherited from the generations before you?

5. *A Theater for Dreamers* has been described as a coming-of-age novel. In what ways does Erica change? Is it only the younger characters who grow and develop, or does this happen for the older ones too?

6. Before leaving for Hydra, Erica says, "Mainly I dreamt of dreaming." Her dreams of Charmian, Hydra, and her future with Jimmy Jones do not line up with the reality she finds. Have you found it productive to spend time in daydreams, even if reality turns out quite differently?

7. Erica is a teenager amid a circle of adults. In what ways is Erica different from the adults? In what ways is she the same? How does her perspective as an outsider inform the story?

8. Erica certainly misses her mother, but Charmian points out that you can miss someone even if they are still around—for example, the version of George she married who does not exist anymore. What parts of George does Charmian miss? Have you ever experienced grief for someone still living?

9. Erica barely understands why Charmian means so much to her. Her infatuation seems to be equal parts crush and longing for maternal affection. Do you think Charmian handles her position as a role model well? Can she be expected to? In what different ways does Charmian shape Erica's character?

10. Several characters in the novel are fictionalized versions of real people, including Leonard Cohen himself. Do you think you would read the novel differently if you hadn't already heard of them?

11. The epigraph for this book is Marianne Ihlen's quote: "I'm living. Life is my art." Yet, the characters desire publication and other kinds of recognition: they will be known for their art, not their lives. How does that contradiction sit with you? Do the lives of the unpublished writers in this story have any less value?

12. This novel is set against a social background of supposed growing freedom for women, and gender is often a battleground for the characters. How do gender relations play out in the story? How does male desire inform and affect female behavior and creativity?

13. Leonard tells George that life's enjoyments begin with our bodies and end with ideas. However, for the women in this novel, bodily enjoyment can mean unwanted pregnancies, which have life-altering consequences. When Charmian and Erica meet again at a protest for access to contraceptive advice, Charmian says that until there's a birth control pill there will be no women's liberation. With our modern hindsight, do you agree with her? How might the courses of these women's lives have been altered by reliable contraception?

14. Despite the importance of the setting, the characters remain separate from the Hydra islanders. Why might this be? How does it affect your interpretation of the bohemian circle?

15. Erica finds herself surprised to have found a home in Hydra. Through what events does her sense of home and family develop? What places in your life have given you a surprising sense of home? What does it feel like to feel at home in a place you once thought was made for people older or more important than you?

16. If you were to base a piece of art on real-life figures, who would you consider choosing?

© Harry Borden

POLLY SAMSON is a writer of fiction and a lyricist. She has worked as a journalist and in publishing, including two years as a columnist for the *Sunday Times*. Samson was made a fellow of the Royal Society of Literature in 2018. Her first novel, *Out of the Picture*, was shortlisted for the Author's Club Award, and many of her stories, including those from her first collection, *Lying in Bed*, and her second collection, *Perfect Lives*, have been read on BBC Radio 4. Her 2015 novel, *The Kindness*, was named a Book of the Year by both the *Times* and the *Observer*. She has written introductions for Daphne du Maurier's collection *The Doll* and for Charmian Clift's two travel memoirs, *Peel Me a Lotus* and *Mermaid Singing*. She has written lyrics for four number-one albums, including Pink Floyd's *The Division Bell* and David Gilmour's *On an Island*.